Dedication

To my lovely wife Nahid. They say tha successful man there is a woman urging hi saying fails to say is that there was a cattle picture ~smile~.) For thirty plus years, Ms. Nahid has not wavered in her encouragement for me to realize my goals and dreams, in spite of the many challenges life has put in our path. She has been a loyal wife and good mother to our wonderful daughters and grandmother to our precious grandchildren. I dedicate this debut novel of the Wargs Trilogy to Ms. Nahid. H&Ks x 1,000

Wargs
Curse of Misty Hollow

D. Allen Rutherford

Wargs: Curse of Misty Hollow

ISBN: 978-1-4834-3302-8 (sc)
ISBN: 978-1-4834-3301-1 (e)

Library of Congress Control Number: 2015909297

Lulu Publishing Services 2nd Edition date: 07/10/2016

Chapter 1

By mid-day, the sun had melted away the mist which, normally shrouded Misty Hollow most days from the late afternoon, through the night, into the morning hours. Ranger Holmes slowed his truck as he crested the narrow pass that led into Misty Hollow, to admire the picturesque view of the isolated valley below. For the past five years, Misty Hollow has been part of his assigned patrol area. A ranger for the U.S. Forest Service, Adam Holmes normally looked forward to his monthly visits to Misty Hollow where he checked the condition of the roads, fire trails, and watering holes, maintained by the forest service. He particularly enjoyed stopping into the village of Graymere to visit with Dr. Bertram, have lunch at the Wolf's Lair, and occasionally talk with Simon Jarvis who ran the mercantile.

The service road that ringed the valley was still damp from the late spring rain from the day before, making it easy for Ranger Holmes to spot any fresh animal tracks. He would drive slowly along the road with his window down, scanning the edge of the road and ditches for signs of wildlife, stopping to inspect the fire trails and watering holes along the way. As he was nearing Lupine Rock, he caught a glimpse of what appeared to be an animal carcass on one side of the road, across the drainage ditch. He slowed to a stop, stepped out of the truck and scanned the area to make sure he was not walking up on a fresh predator kill. Satisfied that there were no hungry, feeding, bears, wolves,

1

or mountain lions nearby, he hopped across the ditch to investigate.

Making his way up the slippery slope on the far side of the drainage ditch, Ranger Holmes saw that it was, in fact, an animal lying on the ground, but couldn't make out what it was. From where he stood, he could see it was an animal with course fur and at first, thought it was a bear, but the color of the fur was not that of a black bear which inhabited the region. Cautiously, he crept forward to examine the carcass. "Shit!" he said aloud to himself as he got his first clear look at the animal. "This sucker is huge! But, what on earth…" He paused and nervously scanned the area. Slowly, he circled around the carcass, moving closer, trying to figure out what it was. It appeared to be canine, most likely a wolf, but it was much larger than any wolf he had ever seen. It had to be at least fifty percent larger than any gray wolf, weighing at least a hundred and fifty pounds, if not more. Its features were unlike any wolf species he knew of.

Finally, he was close enough to kneel down next to the animal to examine it and discovered that the animal had been shot. The blood pooled near the carcass and the blood trail leading away from it indicated that the animal had recently been killed. He stood and turned to go back to his truck to retrieve his notepad and camera to document the scene when he suddenly became aware of movement in the brush behind him. At first, he couldn't see anything and thought maybe the poachers he presumed to have killed the animal, were still in the area. Then he heard a deep snarling sound coming from different directions. Realizing that the sounds must be pack mates of the dead animal laying at his feet, anxiety quickly gave way to fear. Glancing over his shoulder he saw that his truck was more than thirty yards away. He knew if he tried to make a run for the truck the wolves would be on him before he got across the ditch. He was frozen in his own tracks, no weapon on him, and at least two more of these huge predators now stalking him. He could hear his heart pounding in his chest and he felt flush as his blood pressure spiked. Slowly, he regained his wits and began to step backward, away from the carcass, toward his truck, being careful not to turn his back on wolf creatures stalking him from the brush nearby. When he reached the edge of the ditch he paused, took a deep breath, then turned, bounded across the ditch, and made a mad-dash for his truck. The wolf creatures were quicker than he had imagined and they caught up to him before he got safely inside his truck.

***

It's was Friday, the semester over, and Matt was looking forward to getting out of the office and spending the summer trekking into the wilderness in search of a cryptid that he hoped would turn out to be a new species of wolf.

Matthew Kershaw, known as Matt to his friends, came across as an unassuming sort of fellow, so focused on his work that he paid little attention to the petty routines of others around him. At six-foot tall and slender build, his colleagues considered him moderately handsome, a mix between a nerdy and outdoorsy type. Following the 9/11 attacks, Matt served a tour of duty in Afghanistan as an officer in the U.S. Army. Severely wounded during a mortar attack, Matt received a purple heart and a medical discharge after spending several weeks in the hospital and months in rehab. Returning to college, he obtained his Ph.D. and began teaching at the University of Idaho, where he established somewhat of a reputation among wildlife biologists and cryptozoologists, as an authority on wolves in the wilderness areas of the American Northwest.

Matt was sorting through his maps and packing his research files when the telephone rang. "Hello, Matt Kershaw speaking."

"Matt, this is Harvey. How are you doing, old buddy?"

"I'm doing well. How's it going with you these days?" Matt replied. "How are Carroll and the kids?"

"The family is doing well thanks, and things around the office are the same old boring routines," Harvey said. *"I hope I didn't catch you at a busy time? I know this is the end of the semester and you are busy trying to grade papers and get grades posted."*

3

"Actually, I just finished posting the last of the grades and I'm packing up my stuff from the office trying to get out of here for the summer. I haven't heard from you in quite some time. You must be really busy counting trees, sorting pinecones, stacking acorns and chasing chipmunks."

Harvey laughed. *"Not exactly, but I think sometimes stacking acorns would be a welcome change of pace. Matt, I'm sorry to call you out of the blue like this, but I was hoping to catch you before you left for the summer."*

"No problem. What's up?

"I have a problem on my hands and I was hoping I could persuade you to help me out. I realize that you already have your summer planned out, but I truly need your help on this." Harvey pleaded with Matt.

"I hope you're not going to ask me to dog-sit that ugly mutt of yours again. That little monster crapped all over my cabin." Matt laughed.

"No, nothing like that," Harvey replied. *"One of my forest rangers was attacked and badly mauled by a wolf yesterday. He was patrolling an area in Misty Hollow, the valley where I grew up when the incident occurred."*

"Sorry to hear that. But, what do you need from me?" Matt asked.

"I was hoping I could persuade you to take a couple of weeks out of your schedule and go up to the valley and investigate the incident for me."

"Harvey you know I wouldn't turn you down if you called on me for a favor, but why are you asking *me* to look into this attack? Why don't you call the Idaho Fish and Game Commission? They are the ones who handle this sort of thing."

"Yes, normally that's what I'd do. However, I thought this investigation might serve both our interest."

"How so?" Matt queried.

"For my part, this incident occurred in the small isolated valley where I grew up and there have been other close encounters reported in the area. If I call the Fish & Game, they will send in a hunter to do a controlled removal of the animal

responsible for the attack. Then, when they have the time and the resources, they will do a management study. My concern is that a pack from the neighboring wilderness area is migrating into the valley."

"Again, why are you asking me to do this?" Matt insisted.

"The ranger who was attacked and mauled said the wolves that attacked him were very large and strange looking. His detailed description of the animals he encountered doesn't remotely resemble any known species of wolf any of us recognize. I thought this may be a hot lead you might want to check out while you are doing the survey of the valley for me."

After a brief pause to consider Harvey's request, Matt summarized. "So, what you're asking me to do is drive up to the valley, survey the area and see if there is a possible threat of encroachment from the neighboring wilderness area. If I find the problem child, call Fish and Game to affect a controlled removal. Then submit a summary report with a recommendation for further study and control management, if I deem it warranted."

"That's it in a nutshell. Matt, I hate to ask this of you on such short notice, but I have family and friends in that valley with children who run and play in those woods. The livestock they rely on for their livelihood is threatened. I would feel better about the situation there if someone I knew and trusted were to go in right away and investigate the matter."

Matt and Harvey Langston were roommates at the university when they were working on their undergraduate degrees. After Harvey began working for the forest service, he would call Matt anytime something strange or unexplained came across his desk. So when Harvey called out of the blue asking him to conduct this investigation Matt knew this was important to his old friend and was reluctant to tell him no. Besides, the prospect of following up a hot lead on a cryptid from a reliable source was too tempting to ignore. This could be the possible discovery he has been hoping for.

"When would you like this survey done?" Matt asked.

"As soon as possible," Harvey replied. *"Why don't you stop by the office Monday and I will give you a copy of the report and*

any additional details I can get between now and then," Harvey suggested, assuming that Matt had agreed to do the investigation for him.

"I will need a few days to get things settled around the cabin before I can head up there, but I will see you Monday. We can discuss this a bit more then."

"Ok, see you Monday. Thanks, buddy, I owe you one."

"You already owe me for sitting that ugly mutt of yours during Christmas last year. I'll see you Monday."

Before Matt could finish packing his files and maps, Sarah stepped into his office. "Dr. Kershaw, when do you want me to come to your place to begin house-sitting this summer?"

Sarah Henderson had just graduated with her Master of Science degree and would be starting the Ph.D. program in the fall. During the summer breaks, Sarah house sat for Matt while he was away, trekking through the wilderness. He liked Sarah; she was a young Army Veteran with a strong work ethic. 'You reminded me of a short version of Halle Berry', he would tell her with a chuckle.

"You can come anytime if you have to be out of the dorm. I'll be leaving by next weekend, so before then, I should think."

"Alright, if you don't mind I'll bring a few things from the dorm out to the cabin this afternoon and then I'll go visit my family for a few days. I'll be back a week from tomorrow if that's cool with you."

"Sounds like a plan," Matt said, handing Sarah a key to the house.

Matt resumed packing when Sarah interrupted again. "So, Dr. Kershaw, where are you going this summer? Are you going to be doing anything exciting?"

"Sorry to disappoint, but a last minute request by an old friend just interrupted my plans. It looks like this summer may be a bit mundane. I have to conduct a wolf population survey of a small valley.

"Bummer sounds like your summer may be a bust."

"I'm going to investigate a wolf attack on a forest ranger. While I'm up in that area, I'm going to take the opportunity to scout around a different area of the wilderness looking for evidence of a cryptid wolf species. With any luck, I hope to find something that will make the trip worthwhile."

"Well, researching cryptids sounds interesting. How did you get interested in investigating cryptids?"

"Ever since I was a little boy, my great uncle would tell me tales of Native American folklore. Many of those stories involved some association with animal totems, animal spirits, skin-walkers, waheela, shunka warak'ins and such. Over the years, I developed a belief that the origin of these stories were based on species of animals that once actually lived."

"That sounds cool! But, what makes you think that there's a new species of wolf out there?" Sarah asked.

"I guess you could say it is just a hunch. However, many of the old Native American legends and myths give similar descriptions of animal spirits as those contained in reports of modern day encounters with strange or unusual animals. I believe that there's a thread of fact behind both of this phenomenon that could be explained by an elusive species of wolf that has remained undiscovered deep in the wilderness regions."

"I hope you find one. That would be cool to discover a new species. Well, I will leave you to do your packing. I have to finish moving my stuff out of the dorm. See you this afternoon."

* * *

On Monday, Matt arrived at Harvey's office around mid-morning. He was anxious to get more details of the incident involving the ranger's attack and background on the valley where the attack occurred.

"I thought this might be of interest. I had Janice make a copy of the follow-up report on the incident involving the ranger." Harvey said handing a file to Matt.

Matt flipped through the folder and was somewhat surprised that the report provided a detailed description of unusually large and strange looking wolves. 'Appearing taller at the shoulder than the hips, with a heavy mane over the neck and shoulder area, the animal was estimated to be at least fifty percent larger than an average gray wolf. The head was larger in proportion to the body which was dominated by a shorter snout and beefier jaws. The teeth and fangs appeared to be abnormally large for the size of the jaw and head.' Pictures included in the report depicted graphic evidence of the ranger's wounds and the wounds themselves reinforced the description of the size of the wolves' head and fangs.

After allowing Matt a few minutes to review the report, Harvey proceeded to give Matt some basic background information. "The ranger, Adam Holmes, regularly visits Misty as part of his patrol assignment. The valley is situated in a pocket that extends up into the wilderness area."

"Do you mind if I contact ranger Holmes. I would like to interview him about the valley and maybe gather any additional details of the attack?"

"Ranger Holmes is in the hospital and the doctors plan to keep him there for a few days," Harvey replied.

"In the hospital? I thought he would have been sewn up and sent home by now." Matt queried.

"The wounds were complicated by a crushed bone in his forearm. In addition to treating him for the bite wounds, they had to operate to deal with the crushed bone. Shortly thereafter, it seems he began to exhibit symptoms of some viral infection. They began treatment for rabies but typically, rabies does not cause such severe symptoms so soon after a bite. I called this morning, and Ranger Holmes is in the ICU battling a very high fever and delirium, which the doctors are having difficulty controlling. They are trying to determine if the viral infection is something that resulted from the wolf bite or maybe a viral infection he may have contracted earlier. They are a bit puzzled at this point."

"That is disappointing news. It would be helpful to pick his brain for information regarding the wildlife and habitat within the valley," Matt said.

"I'm sure he would be happy to share any knowledge or information with you. Give him a day or two and then call the hospital to see if he is well enough to have visitors."

"For sure," Matt said before turning their attention to discussing the scope of the investigation plan for Misty Hollow.

* * *

Matt spent the rest of the morning and early afternoon obtaining maps and data related to the valley. Studying the map of the area, Matt noted that Misty Hollow was a pocket of National Forest land nestled deep within the River of no Return Wilderness area. The only way to reach the valley was by a single road that ran several miles through a narrow corridor into the wilderness area before opening up into the valley. Matt thought it odd that the government had established a pocket of National Forest lands so deep within the wilderness area. He was further mystified as to how or why the village of Graymere became established in such an isolated spot. On the topographic map Matt was studying, the village of Graymere appeared as a tiny dot and the name in text so small that Matt had to look at it through a magnifying glass to read it. Matt found it interesting that he was not able to locate Graymere or any reference to the village on the roadmap. The roadmap did not even depict the road leading into the valley. "This is truly odd," Matt thought to himself.

Seeking to learn more about the community, he was surprised that virtually no information was available. Matt couldn't find any population data, no history, or even a directory of the village administrative offices. It was as if the village was just sitting out there, lost in time and space.

* * *

Harvey met Matt at the door of the office as Matt was preparing to leave. "When you get to Graymere go to the '*Wolf's Lair*'; it's a small inn. I arranged for you to stay there while you are working in the valley. A woman named Freya owns the inn. Tell her that Harvey sent you there."

"Ok, thanks. I will call you if anything interesting turns up. Otherwise, I'll see you in a couple of weeks." Matt replied as he shook hands with Harvey on his way out the door.

Chapter 2

Matt spent a few days studying the topographic maps of Misty Hollow and the surrounding wilderness, making a plan for scouting the wilderness area once he concluded the survey of the valley for Harvey. By the time Sarah arrived to take over the house for the summer, Matt was packed and ready to leave. After going over his itinerary and last minute instructions, he was on the road at last.

Matt's first stop on his trip to Misty Hollow was a detour to the hospital to visit the Forest Ranger, Adam Holmes. After reading over the ranger's report several times, Matt was eager to obtain further details from Ranger Holmes of his encounter. Of all the sightings and reports Matt had investigated over the years, this one was a recent encounter involving an experienced and credible witness, who knew the difference from a wolf and Aunt Sally's poodle.

When Matt arrived at the hospital, the nurse instructed him to keep this visit short. "Mr. Holmes is still very weak, and he has just awakened after several days of high fever and delirium." The nurse informed Matt that although the doctors were not certain of the exact nature of the viral infection, they determined that Mr. Holmes was not contagious.

Entering the room, Matt noticed that the ranger appeared gaunt and weak. He was obviously extremely ill. More so than what someone would reasonably expect from an animal bite, even a severe one. "Adam, I'm Matt Kershaw a wildlife biologist from the University of Idaho. I'm on my way up to Misty Hollow to survey the wolf population in that area. Harvey Langston gave me a copy of a report detailing your encounter. If you feel up to it, I was hoping that I might visit with you a few moments about the incident."

The ranger nodded his head slightly and blinked his eyes to indicate an affirmative response to Matt's request. Then he motioned with his head and eyes as he tried to lift his arm indicating for Matt to sit down in the chair next to his bed.

"The nurse tells me that your physical injury was serious but that you also contracted a virus that has taken a toll on you," Matt said with a sense of compassion.

"Yes, I didn't think I was going to be in here for more than a day or two," Adam replied. "I was brought in for a few stitches and a broken arm. They admitted me into the hospital to do surgery on my arm and I don't remember much after that. I'm not sure how long I've been here. What day is it?"

"Today is Saturday; you have been in here for a week."

"Jeez, I must have been out of it," Adam sighed.

"I understand from Harvey that you patrol Misty Hollow frequently. I was hoping you could tell me about the residents of the valley and the wildlife in that area. And, if you are up to it, some details of your encounter with the wolf that attacked you."

"I'm not sure what I can tell you that would be of any help, but I'm happy to answer any questions you have."

Matt began his line of questioning, "Do you go into the valley on a regular basis?"

"I don't go there on a *regular* schedule. Maybe once a month I'll drive the roads, checking the condition of the fire lanes, water holes, food plots, and make note of any wildlife that I observe and where I sighted them."

"From the map, it appears that the village of Graymere is the only settlement in the valley; do you know much about the residents in the valley?"

"Yes, Graymere is a small isolated village. The only road leading into the valley is the Forest Service road. And, as far as I'm aware, the only utility supplied to the valley is telephone service. The valley itself is about seventeen miles long and maybe three miles wide at the widest point. The main road connecting the series of fire trails and service roads crisscrossing the valley intersect at the village of Graymere. Rarely does anyone go into the valley except for maintenance crews to patch the roads or to clear the fire lanes, every few years."

"When you're patrolling the valley, do you often see predators in or around the valley?"

"Not really," Adam paused, "Occasionally I'll see a mule deer, or ram up on the ridge, down in the valley a few squirrels, rabbits, chipmunks, and such. I would say the wildlife population is consistent with other areas that I patrol outside the valley."

Matt probed further. "Have you observed wolves in the valley before the incident the other day?"

Adam stared into the distance for a moment pondering his answer, "I can't say that I've seen a single wolf over the last five-plus years I've been patrolling that area; until the other day when I was attacked that is."

"The day you were bitten; can you tell me what happened?"

"I drove to the valley patrolling the service roads as usual. As I neared one of the watering holes situated just off the side of the road, I scanned the ditch and shoulder of the road for animal tracks. That's when I spotted, what appeared to be, an animal carcass just off the road, across the ditch. I stopped to investigate..." Adam paused to relax his head and catch his breath.

"I'm sorry if this is too tiring for you, I can come back later if you prefer." Matt offered.

"No, I'm ok," responded Adam continuing with his story. "I stopped to investigate and as I approached the animal carcass, it appeared to be a wolf. But, when I got close enough to examine its strange appearance and features, it did not resemble any wolf I had ever seen before. Although the animal appeared to be a wolf, it was maybe fifty percent larger than any wolf I've ever seen and it had an unusual body profile."

"Is this the description you included in your report?" Matt pressed for clarification.

"Yes, it was huge, and when I placed my hand against the animal's front paw, it was larger than my palm with my fingers extended, about the size of a large bear track. I searched the area and found multiple sets of similar tracks. One set I surmised to be that of the dead wolf and the other overlapping tracks I assumed to be of other wolves circling the carcass." Adam paused as if debating in his mind whether to share additional information or not.

Matt looked up from the notepad which he was taking notes. "And?"

"I'm not sure if I should tell you," Adam said hesitantly.

"Tell me what? Is it something not included in your report? If so, I would really like to hear whatever you can to tell me about the incident."

Adam looked at Matt's face trying to judge whether or not to trust him before he continued. "Yes, there is something I didn't put in my report."

"What was it?" Matt inquired with peaked interest.

"I did not include every detail because I was not sure what it was I actually saw. I did not want anyone to think I was nuts," Adam explained.

"I'm interested to hear *anything* you have to tell me. Everything is important to my survey. Please continue."

"What I didn't put in the report was that a short distance away from the carcass I saw another set of tracks from an animal that I didn't recognize. Those tracks were somewhat similar to the other wolf track but huge in comparison. They had strange features…"

"Such as?" Matt pressed for details.

"Well, the tracks indicated a bit longer toe and heel impression – almost like a cross between a wolf paw and human footprint. It's hard to describe, it was like nothing I have ever seen before. I can sketch it for you if you like." Adam offered, gesturing for Matt's notepad and pen.

Matt passed the notepad and his pen to Adam. "Were you able to determine the cause of death of the wolf?" He continued while Adam was sketching.

"The wolf had been shot, apparently running some distance before collapsing and dying from the gunshot wound. It had been dead for only a short time because the carcass wasn't stiff and the blood wasn't completely dried."

"Were you able to take any pictures?"

Adam passed the notepad back to Matt then took a deep breath collecting his thoughts, "I was in the process of examining the dead wolf. When I noticed it was a fresh kill I started to scan the area thinking that poachers might be close by. I was about to go back to my truck to get my camera and notebook to document the scene when suddenly, out of nowhere, I heard a distinctive snarling sound coming from the brush nearby. I guessed that it must have been a wolf pack stalking me. After a few seconds, I slowly and carefully started backing up toward my truck. Just as I was opening the truck door, two of the creatures leaped toward me from the brush across the ditch. I hit one with the truck door, but the other one caught me on my left arm and sunk is teeth in deep. I could feel the teeth tearing the muscle in my arm, and I felt the bone snap, as it tried to pull me to the ground. I had ahold of the steering wheel and was somehow able to wrestle my arm from the wolf's mouth when I kicked it in the throat. Then I managed to climb into my truck and close the door. All of this was in my report." Adam paused to catch his breath.

Matt was sitting on the edge of his seat. "Then what happened?"

"While I was scrambling around trying to get my keys out to start the truck both of the wolves were clawing at the doors and windows on both sides of the truck trying to get at me. Just as I got the truck started I looked up and saw another strange animal leap from the woods, across the ditch, landing in the middle of the road in front of me."

Matt looked up from the sketch of the paw print he was studying. "What kind of *strange* animal?"

"I don't really know, but it was huge; standing upright on its hind legs it appeared to be an oversized version of the wolf creatures I described in my report. By all appearances, it had the appearance of a wolf, but its body mass was almost twice that of a normal gray wolf. I couldn't help but notice the animal's front paws appearing a bit elongated with its toes resembling stubby fingers with thick claws. Its hind feet were huge and a bit elongated more like a foot than a paw. I estimate that it stood about six or seven foot tall. The only way I can describe it is to compare it to what you might expect a large gray wolf to look like if it were standing upright, maybe a bit taller."

"What happened next?" Matt asked, hanging onto every word Adam was saying.

"Well, not much after that, I wanted to get the hell out of there, so I put the truck in gear and stepped on the gas pedal. The animal in front of me dropped to all fours and leaped out of the way. Before I passed out I managed to drive myself to the clinic in Graymere where Dr. Bertram cleaned me up, bandaged me and gave some pain pills then had someone drive me back to the Ranger Station. From there, my supervisor drove me to the hospital."

"The animal you mentioned that leaped in front of your truck, could it have been a bear? They stand on their hind legs like you described."

"I'm sure it was a wolf of some nature, of that I have no doubt, but it was unusually large and the other physical features were distinctive. There is no mistaking what I saw, it was a bright sunny day, the middle of the afternoon, before the mist, and the animal was standing not twenty feet in front of my truck. It was for a brief few seconds, but long enough for me to distinguish that this was no ordinary wolf." Adam was becoming visibly excited describing the animal and events.

"Adam, why did you not put all of these additional details in your report?"

"I was afraid that my boss would think I was crazy. I am very protective of my credibility and I never fudge the data or information in my reports. If it can't be verified, I don't include it."

"I can see you are getting tired and I have just one last thing to ask." Matt got up, leaned over Adam's bed, and spread a map across his lap. "I plotted the location of your encounter on this map based on the information in your report. Can you take a look and see if I've marked the location correctly?"

"I believe that's the correct spot," Adam said pointing at a location on the map. "You will know the exact spot by the distinctive overhanging rock formation up on the ridgeline. The locals call the rock formation 'Lupine Rock'. What a coincidence wouldn't you agree?"

Matt decided that he had pressed Adam enough for the time being. He had gotten a clearer description of the events and of the animals involved. From the details provided by Adam, he believed the animals might truly be the new species he has long been searching for.

"Adam I appreciate your help. I know you're tired and weak from your ordeal and I apologize for coming here without prior notice. The information you provided will be very helpful in conducting my investigation."

"I wrote my phone number on the pad for you. If you have any other questions you can call me."

Matt shook Adam's hand and wished him well before turning to leave the room. Just before Matt walked out the door, Adam called out. Matt paused and turned to hear what he was saying.

"I'm not sure if I should tell you this, and you probably already think I'm crazy…" Adam said with hesitation.

"What is it? Anything you can tell me is helpful. And rest assured I don't think you are crazy."

"Well, when I saw the animal in the road in front of my truck, I couldn't help but feel that there was some intelligence about it." Adam paused a moment to collect his thoughts. "It stood there staring at me with an almost human-like gaze that resembled what you would observe from a human whose angry and squaring

16

off with you ready to fight. It was more than just an aggressive posture you would expect from a wild animal. The look in its eyes was very unusual. Even though it was a very brief encounter, I could distinguish the expression on the animal's face and it keeps popping into my head, almost haunting me. These are no ordinary wolves; there is something evil about those animals, so be careful out there."

"Thank you," Matt responded sincerely before he turned and left the room.

As Matt made the long drive to Misty Hollow, he couldn't stop thinking about the conversation with the Ranger Holmes. He was both encouraged but cautiously concerned about the prospects of identifying a new wolf species. As he drove along, he replayed the conversation with Ranger Holmes, mentally comparing his description of the mystery animal with the descriptions provided in the other reports of encounters and sightings Harvey had given him. If the mystery animals did turn out to be a new species of wolf, and the descriptions were somewhat accurate, this species of wolf could prove to be exceptionally dangerous.

Reflecting on the ranger's narrative of the events related to his encounter, in comparison to details from the other reports he had studied, Matt could not help but recall the stories his great uncle had told him about skin-walkers and wolf-men in Native American folklore. He began to ponder the idea of how these stories may have originated from similar encounters rather than purely myth.

Chapter 3

While making the drive to Misty Hollow, Matt zoned out thinking about his conversation with Ranger Holmes. So much so, that he didn't remember driving the last one hundred and fifty miles. Almost missing his turnoff, he finally regained his senses in time to realize where he was. Checking his map, Matt decided to stop for fuel at a convenience store and gas station not far from the turn off that would take him into Misty Hollow. After fueling his jeep, he went into the store to get something cold to drink and a snack.

"Good afternoon," The clerk greeted Matt with a smile.

"Good afternoon," Matt replied.

"Where are you headed today?" The clerk asked in a friendly tone.

"I'm on my way to Graymere. The turn off is not far from here I believe."

The clerk's demeanor immediately changed from bright and friendly to one of cautious and guarded. "About a mile up the highway, you will see a side road to your right. There are no signs, but you can't miss it, it's the only turn off within the next few miles."

"How far would you say it is to Graymere from here?"

"I take it you've never been there," The clerk stated inquisitively.

"No this is my first time to the valley and never heard of Graymere until recently."

18

"Graymere is another twenty or so miles once you turn off the main highway. Do you mind me asking why you are going, Misty Hollow?"

Matt couldn't help but detect the change in the clerk's tone and demeanor from when he first walked into the store but didn't see any reason not to answer the clerk's question. Besides, Matt was a bit curious as to why the clerk felt the need to ask his business; was it idle chit chat, simple curiosity or something more. He decided to answer and see where the conversation would lead.

"I'm a wildlife biologist with the University of Idaho; I'm going there to survey the wolf population and habitat in Misty Hollow and the surrounding wilderness area. Why do you ask?" Matt was probing to ascertain the source of the clerk's curiosity.

The clerk did not respond. Instead, he remained quiet while scanning the items Matt had placed on the counter.

Matt could sense the clerk wanted to say more but was cautiously reserved in his conversation regarding Graymere. Matt decided not to press the matter, thanked him for the information, and said goodbye as he exited the store.

* * *

Matt found the road into Misty Hollow, to be a single lane, paved, service road that transitioned into a single lane gravel road within a mile or two off the main highway. He thought it somewhat strange there were no signs to identify the valley or even to direct you to Graymere. *If you were not familiar with the area, did not know where you were going, or not able to read a map you might never know that the village of Graymere ever existed.* Matt thought to himself. Once off the main highway, the drive was hauntingly scenic with trees from both sides of the road creating a canopy over the road. The shading made it a cool, comfortable drive on an otherwise hot summer day. Occasionally, a break in the shady coverage would provide a broader view of the countryside as well as the stream flowing parallel to the road. With the windows rolled down, Matt was savoring the freshness of the air and the stillness of the forest as he drove along the road toward Graymere.

Matt noticed that once he drove through the pass leading into the valley, it appeared unseasonably dark for early afternoon. It didn't usually start getting dark until after eight o'clock in the evening that time of the year and it was just a little after three in the afternoon. He surmised that the dim light level was due, at least in part, to the high mountain ridges surrounding the valley casting a shadow over the valley floor as the sun started to dip behind the ridgeline in the afternoon. He also noticed that a misty haze seemed to be forming in the valley though there was no sign of rain. This he attributed to the geography of the valley and the temperature differential of the cooler valley floor versus the warmer ambient temperature higher up where the sun was still shining and creating warmer temperatures. Although he welcomed the cooler temperature, the hazy dim light of the valley created a bit of eerie feeling as he drove deeper into the valley. By the time Matt arrived in Graymere, it was almost four in the afternoon but appeared to be near dusk due to the dim light and misty haze.

The streets of Graymere were of crude cobblestone just wide enough for two autos to pass much like you would expect in residential neighborhoods in the city. More striking was the rustic architecture straight out of the eighteenth century pioneer period. Entering the village from the west, the main street ran for two blocks before intersecting at a large traffic circle branching off to the north and south. Directly in front was, what he took to be the city hall. To the north, the street ran for a couple of blocks then curved back to the northeast, running parallel to a fairly wide stream, past a small water mill of some sort, exiting the village to the northeast. Turning to the south at the traffic circle, the street curved slightly for about three blocks to exit the village to the southeast. On either side of the main street, Matt saw a few buildings such as a jailhouse, a mercantile, the inn Harvey mentioned, trade shops and a medical clinic. Branching off from both sides of the main street were a few smaller streets, more like alleys not wide enough for an automobile, reaching back a block or two, connecting an array small residences behind the main shops. Gas lamps at each corner lighted the streets and wooden plank walkways ran along the store fronts, connecting the shops on each block.

Matt pulled into a small parking area near the inn and got out of his jeep. Looking around, he noted that he didn't see any people as he drove through the village. There were dim lights from the various buildings and he could see movement within the buildings, providing the only signs of life. Otherwise, the village appeared to be deserted. Outside the inn, over the entrance, hung a sign, reminiscent of the type you would see hanging over an old English pub. The sign had the head of a wolf and '*Wolf's Lair*' neatly painted on both sides.

* * *

"Good afternoon," Matt greeted the woman behind the counter.

"Good afternoon," she replied with a bit of an accent that hinted at a mix of French and Native American. "How may I help you?"

"I'm Matthew Kershaw. I was hoping to get a room if you have one available; Harvey Langston told me to stop in and ask for Freya."

"Ah, Dr. Kershaw," The woman said, recognizing the name. "Harvey called and told me to expect you; I'm Freya Fasset," she said. She offered a hint of a smile while brushing the hair from in front of her eyes. "How long will you be staying with us?"

Matt couldn't help but notice the woman's natural beauty; she appeared to wear no makeup, but he found her strikingly beautiful. She was in her early to mid-thirties with black hair flowing over her shoulders and down her back, about five and a half feet tall, lean, petite figure with a hint of Native American skin tone and features accented with beautiful dark brown eyes.

"I'm not sure, to be honest," Matt stammered, distracted by Freya's beauty. "Do you have weekly rates? I plan to be in the area for maybe two weeks and then I hope to spend two or three weeks up into the wilderness area, doing some field research."

"Well, I've prepared a room for you I hope you'll find comfortable. And, you are welcome to stay with us for as long as you like. Will it just be you staying with us or will there be others joining you?"

"Just me, I usually work alone."

Freya laid down her polish cloth and stepped out from behind the counter. Leading Matt across the dining area and through the lounge area, she summarized the amenities. "We don't offer much in the way of internet, or cable TV. The utility companies feel that we don't have a sufficient customer base to justify the expense of running lines into the valley. We rely on electrical power for the essentials since our electricity is somewhat limited by the capacity of the water mill, which drives a small generator. You might've seen it when you drove into the village. We don't get satellite or cellular connection due to the mountains and ridges circling the valley. We have well water fed from underground springs that's cool and refreshing. Our lights are gas as well as our hot water, heating, and cooking. At least we can get the gas company to run a truck up here every couple of weeks to top off our propane tanks."

"Sounds fine, far better than sleeping on the ground in the wilderness, which is where I usually spend my summers. I rarely find accommodations near the remote areas I'm accustomed working in."

Freya motioned toward the staircase. "Let me show you to your room."

"Where do I register?"

Freya paused at the base of the stairs and smile. "We're not much on such formalities around here."

"What are the room rates and where can I buy my meals."

"Harvey has made arrangements to cover your room and board for as long as you are here." She turned and began walking up the stairs. "The accommodations include three meals per day if you like. We serve breakfast at six-thirty each morning, lunch at twelve, and dinner at seven in the evening. If you are going to be out in the field during the day, I can pack a sack lunch for you. Fruit is usually on the tables if you prefer a snack between meals and I keep fresh coffee in the carafes on the counter in the dining room." Freya rattled off as she led Matt to a room upstairs.

Freya opened the door to one of the rooms and ushered Matt inside. Following him into the room, she showed him how to operate the gas lamps and where the linens were stored. She pointed out that the water heater was set up for each room and was an on-demand gas unit so that he could have a hot shower at his leisure.

"Here is the key to your room, make yourself at home, dinner will be served at seven. If there's anything you need, please don't hesitate to ask."

"Thank you Ms. Freya, you have made me feel at home already," Matt said graciously.

"Just Freya," She said with a slight smile as she stepped out and closed the door behind her.

Matt unloaded his jeep and moved his luggage and gear up to his room. As he was making the trips back and forth, he found it odd there was very little activity around the village.

After getting his bags unpacked and his clothes put away, he sat down to relax for a moment and update his field journal, before going down for dinner.

Chapter 4

Matt came down the stairs and entered the main hall where he saw Freya setting the food out on one of the tables in the dining area. "Smells wonderful," Matt said, politely alerting Freya of his presence.

"Ah, just in time for dinner."

"Is there anything that I can help you with?"

"Thank you, but no. I'm almost done, just a couple of things left to bring out."

Looking at the dishes laid out on the table in front of him, Matt's taste buds began to water. It appeared to be a home cooked meal reminiscent of his childhood days enjoying a holiday feast at his grandmother's house.

"I hope you didn't go to all this trouble just for me. This is far more than I expected. I'm a bit simple in my needs and not used to such a feast."

Freya smiled, "No, I often have dinner guests on Sunday evening."

Matt was a bit curious. The meal laid out in front of him would feed several people but since arriving earlier that day, he had not seen any other guest. "How many guests are staying at the inn?"

"Just you, but we do have a few locals who eat with us from time to time. There's fresh coffee, tea, and water here if you would like to help yourself. Have a seat and relax, the others will be arriving shortly." Freya said casually before she disappeared back into the kitchen.

Matt poured himself a cup of coffee and sat at a table, near the window overlooking the front walkway and the street in front of the inn. Peering out the window, he felt a strange sense of nostalgia. Although the setting was reminiscent of a period of history, long before he was born, Matt felt very relaxed and comfortable since he arrived. Freya had received him more like a houseguest rather than a hotel guest, which was a welcome experience. He was soon lost in his thoughts sipping his coffee staring out the window.

"Good evening, I'm Peter Larson."

The sudden presence of a man towering over him startled Matt. Peter stood over him with the general appearance of a lumberjack. Matt recovered quickly and stood to shake the man's hand. "I'm Matthew Kershaw. It's a pleasure to meet you."

Matt had to look up slightly to look Peter in the face who had to be at least six feet, four inches tall. However, he came across as a bit simple, sort of a gentle giant.

"The pleasure is mine I'm sure. What brings you to Graymere, business or pleasure? We don't get many visitors around here." Peter said in a warm and friendly manner.

Matt smiled. "A little of both I guess. I'm officially here on business, but the nature of my work is a source of pleasure and relaxation for me."

Before they could engage in small talk, a woman entered the inn and walked over to join them. She was wearing a type of scarf with a partial veil over her forehead and eyebrow. Matt also noticed that she purposely kept her head lowered in a manner that prevented Matt from seeing her face apart from a shadowy profile.

"Ahh, Keira! Matthew, I would like to introduce Keira Moonjoy. Keira, this is Matthew Kershaw, a guest here at the inn."

"It's a pleasure to make your acquaintance Mr. Kershaw," Keira said, bowing slightly without offering her hand to shake with Matt.

25

"Likewise, Ms. Moonjoy and you may call me Matt if you like." Matt nodded his head in an abbreviated bow without reaching to shake her hand. He noticed that Keira was wearing arm length dress gloves. He thought it odd for the modern era and the summer climate and assumed that maybe she suffered some form of defect or disfigurement she was trying to conceal.

"Keira is our local herbalist and homeopath."

Matt assumed by the way Keira bowed, almost curtsied, that the culture of the village retained old world curtsies and customs.

"Welcome everyone," Freya said as she placed the breadbasket on the table. "Have all of you been introduced to Matthew?"

Peter spoke up. "Keira and I have, but the others just arrived." Turning to the newly arrived dinner guest, Peter began to make the introductions. "Everyone, this is Matthew Kershaw, a guest here at the inn." Standing next to Matthew, he began to introduce the others as they stepped forward as if they were in a formal receiving line. "Matthew this is Dr. Howard Bertram, our town physician."

"Welcome to Graymere Dr. Kershaw, a pleasure to make your acquaintance. Harvey phoned me and told me you were coming. He asked me to offer my assistance to you for whatever you may need," Dr. Bertram said shaking hands with Matt. "This is my wife Allison," he continued turning toward Allison.

"Welcome to Graymere, I hope you have a pleasant stay," Allison said.

Matt bowed to Allison, "It's a pleasure to meet you both." He couldn't help but notice that Dr. Bertram and his wife stood out from the others somehow. They both appeared attractive and intelligent, dressing a bit more modern and their demeanor hinted at a level of sophistication that didn't mesh with the overall atmosphere of Graymere.

"This is Simon Jarvis. He owns the mercantile, operates the switchboard, and serves as the local Post Master."

"Pleased to meet you, Mr. Kershaw, if you need anything during your stay in Graymere come by the store and I'll do my best to accommodate you."

"Thank you, I'm sure you'll see a lot of me," Matt said shaking Simon's hand.

Simon fit the stereotypical personality of a village shopkeeper. Small in stature, he was a bit squirrelly in his physical appearance, accentuated by a bit of a sheepish voice.

"Dinner is served," Freya announced, gesturing everyone to the dinner table.

Dr. Bertram took a seat at the head of the table with Allison on his left. "Please sit next to me," Doctor Bertram said, gesturing for Matt to sit to his right. Freya sat next to Allison and the other guest took their seats around the table in no particular order. "Dr. Kershaw, Harvey tells me you are here to investigate the recent wolf attack on one of his forest rangers."

"Yes, and if time and weather permits, I plan to trek up into the wilderness to survey the wolf population in the region to the north." Before anyone could respond, Matt directed an inquiry to Dr. Bertram, "I understand that you treated Ranger Holmes after he was mauled by the wolf last week?"

"Yes; well I cleaned and dressed his wounds until he could be transported to a hospital. As soon as he arrived at the clinic, we immediately notified Harvey of the incident and he asked that we get Ranger Holmes to the hospital via the ranger station."

"Harvey mentioned that he grew up here. Do you know him well," Matt queried?

"Yes, I know his family and he was the only person in the Forest Service I knew to contact. When I called him, he gave me the name and phone number for Ranger Holmes's supervisor whom we contacted and coordinated with to get Ranger Holmes to their office and on to the hospital."

"Dr. Kershaw, do you conduct these types of investigations often?" Simon asked.

"Actually, I'm a wildlife biologist and I teach full time in the Collage of Natural Resources at the University of Idaho. I also dabble at cryptozoology spending most of my summers in the field, researching cryptids throughout the Pacific Northwest."

"What do you mean by cryptid?" Peter asked.

"A Cryptid is a creature whose existence has been suggested, but has not been discovered or documented within the scientific community; such as, '*Big Foot*' and '*Wendigo*.'"

Doctor Bertram suggested rhetorically, "Doesn't sound like a profession that is very conducive to maintaining a family life?"

Matt chuckled, "No, it's certainly not. However, I enjoy the peace and solitude of the wilderness. I sometimes feel more at home and relaxed sleeping under the stars in the mountains, with the bears, wolves, and other wild animals than I do in my home in the city."

Not looking up to make eye contact with Matt, Keira asked, "Where is your home, Dr. Kershaw?"

"Please call me Matt, no '*Doctor*' please." Matt corrected, "I have a cabin just outside Moscow about three or four hours southwest of here. It's an easy drive into the city and to the university, but it's far enough outside town where I have a bit of quiet and some fresh air."

"Are you originally from that area, and do you have family there?" Peter inquired.

"No, I live alone there; my mother, grandmother and great uncle live near Plummer. From my mother's side of the family, I'm related to the Coeur d'Alene tribe. I don't know much about my father's side of the family. He was a soldier in the Army and died shortly after I was born. After he married my mom, he shipped out to Korea and before we established contact with his family, he died in a training accident. I've never met any of my relatives from his side of the family; they live in Texas, Louisiana, or Mississippi, I'm not sure."

"Were you ever in the military?" Allison asked.

"I was for a short time; I was an officer in the Army and after I was wounded in Afghanistan I received a medical discharge."

"Oh, I'm sorry, but you are alright now, yes?" Allison asked.

"Yes, I'm fine, I was hit in my left side and hip by mortar fragments, which limits my mobility somewhat, but other than that, I'm fine. It's more of an annoyance on a cold damp day rather than any real physical handicap."

Freya interrupted, "Please, let the poor man eat his dinner."

Allison glanced at Freya and nodded in agreement. "I'm sorry Dr. Kershaw; it seems you are being subjected to an inquisition. We don't get many visitors to the valley and it's refreshing to visit with someone new and learn about them and the places they are from." Allison said.

"It's quite alright. To be honest, I rarely have the occasion to sit and visit with others on a casual basis. My social interaction is usually limited to my colleagues at the university and the clerk at the little grocery store where I shop. The former is all academic chatter and the latter about the fruits and veggies."

Everyone enjoyed a bit of a chuckle at Matt's response.

The conversation shifted to small talk related to people and events of the community. They discussed how delicious the fresh vegetables were. Freya mentioned that most of the vegetables were from Declan and Marcie's hydroponic farm. The meat was lamb from Jim and Evelyn Sobel's farm. Eventually, as everyone had finished eating, the conversation came back to inquiries about Matt's assignment and his study of the wolves.

"How long does this type of investigation generally take?" Peter asked.

"It's hard to say. The valley is a fairly large area to cover and I'm not at all familiar with the habitat and terrain. Therefore, I suspect it will take me at least two weeks to collect the data and document observations, and then I'll prepare a report of my findings. Afterward, I plan to trek up into the wilderness area north of the valley and spend three or four weeks surveying the wolf population."

"If it would be of any help to you, I think there may be a couple of residents who could show you around the valley. The two individuals I am thinking of, operate a guide service for outsiders who come to the valley for either big game hunting or hikers who wish to trek up into the wilderness areas. They are well acquainted with the wildlife in the valley and they know their way around the roads and trails not shown on your maps." Dr. Bertram said.

Matt again noticed the others casting gazes at each other as Dr. Bertram spoke.

"It would be a great help if either of them could orient me to the valley."

"Stop by my office tomorrow morning and I'll arrange for you to meet them. My office is just up the street; Freya can direct you there in the morning."

"Thank you, Dr. Bertram, I'm very grateful for your assistance."

"It's my pleasure to help you any way I can." Dr. Bertram said while taking out his pocket watch. "Oh dear, time has passed so quickly, it's after nine and past my bedtime."

Dr. Bertram's pronouncement of the time appeared to be a queue for the others that it was time to depart as everyone began saying their good nights and moving toward the front door of the inn. They all expressed their pleasure to have met Matt and offered their pledge of service during his stay.

"It seems you got stuck with the dishes and clean up," Matt said to Freya as she closed the door behind the last guest out of the inn. As soon as he said it, he realized he was talking as if he were at home with his family rather than a guest at an inn.

"Its fine, Keira helped me clean up and I'll finish doing the dishes in the morning," Freya said with a smile. "Sorry, if we seemed to be a bit nosey, prying into your business."

"No, it's quite alright. There's nothing secret about my work and I rather enjoy discussing it. You might say wildlife biology and ecology are more of a passion rather than a profession and my field work is more of an avocation."

"Well, I'll not keep you up any longer. I'll tidy up and turn in myself."

"Good night and thank you for the hospitality," Matt said.

"Good night Matthew."

Chapter 5

Matt was up early and as he was getting dressed, he caught the smell of fresh coffee brewing. He gathered up his map and notebook, then headed downstairs. He enjoyed the quiet of the early morning as a time to think and plan his day. When he entered the main hall of the inn, he didn't see any signs of life, just the dim light of the gas lamps and the smell of fresh coffee. He poured himself a cup of coffee, sat down at one of the bench tables, and spread out his map and notebook.

Matt was studying his notes and map when he detected the smell of bacon cooking. He surmised that Freya was in the kitchen preparing breakfast.

Freya entered the dining room from the kitchen. "Good morning Matthew; how do you like your eggs cooked?"

"Good morning," Matt replied, looking up at Freya with a bright happy smile. "Over easy, if it's not too much trouble. Otherwise, I'll eat them anyway you cook them."

Freya smiled back at Matt, "Scrambled it is," she said before walking back into the kitchen.

She returned a few minutes later and placed the breakfast dishes on a table next to where Matt was studying his map and notes.

"I'm sorry, I'll put this stuff away," Matt said.

"That's not necessary. You're not disturbing anyone and it's refreshing to see some activity resembling life around here.

Please continue what you are doing," Freya encouraged as she finished setting the table. "Breakfast is served," she announced.

"This reminds me of my childhood when I would stay with my grandmother and great uncle. Every morning my grandmother would cook breakfast for Uncle Charlie and me. That was my favorite meal of the day, except for Thanksgiving and Christmas dinner of course." Matt said, with a wink.

"Please help yourself," Freya told Matt. "There's more than enough, so eat as much as you like. As a matter of fact, I'll feel insulted if you don't eat my cooking. Consider yourself as being at home in your grandma's house."

"Thank you."

"What are you working on this morning?" Freya asked, gesturing toward his maps and notebook.

"I plan to take a couple of days to drive to the valley, to get a firsthand feel of the terrain and wildlife habitat in the area. I've plotted all the locations where wolf and human encounters occurred throughout the last two years. I'm looking for a pattern among the incidents, but from the map and satellite photos, I haven't been able to see anything that stands out. I'm hoping, once I survey the area around these locations, I'll find something that would tie them together. Misty Hollow and the wilderness surrounding the valley is a very large area and I can't cover it all in the time I've allotted for this survey. Therefore, I need to focus my efforts in a specific location where I believe it gives the best chance to identify any wolf activity in the valley."

While having breakfast with Freya, Matt began to take notice that she had an aura of kindness, but at the same time, he detected a sense of sadness or loneliness about her. "Freya, do you manage the inn by yourself or is this a family operation?"

"I own and operate it myself." She replied in a low and solemn tone. "Like you, my father died when I was very young and left the inn to my mother to manage. When the forest service had crews working here, there was a steady flow of people staying here at the inn. Many of the work crews would stop in to eat here on a regular basis. The inn stayed quite busy back then. Now it's primarily my home and I get an occasional visitor as hunters or hikers come through the valley. It's more like a bed-n-breakfast rather than an inn."

"Where is your mom now?"

"She passed away eight years ago."

"Sorry, I didn't mean to pry."

"Oh, no problem. It's just a bit quiet around here when it's just me and the crickets," She said half-heartedly. "That's why I am pleased to have visitors who breathe life into this place."

Changing the subject, Matt placed his knife and fork neatly on his plate and his napkin to the side. "I appreciate the wonderful breakfast. The smell of breakfast cooking this morning brought back fond memories of my childhood."

"You're welcome; it's nice to have someone to cook for who appreciates my talents," Freya said with a big smile and wink. "When you're ready I'll direct you to Dr. Bertram's clinic so he can arrange for you to meet Alex and Frankie."

Matt gathered up his map and notebook and went up to his room. After grabbing his pack and camera, he met Freya downstairs on his way out the front door. Standing on the walkway Freya pointed up and across the street. "The building you see there is Dr. Bertram's place. The clinic is in the front and he and Allison live in the back."

"Thanks," Matt said then turned and walked toward his jeep to put his gear in the back. Scanning the street, he saw a few people a block or so away moving about the town. He thought it odd for normal summer weather, to see a couple of the people wearing hooded pullovers. Not like a winter jacket, but more like a light windbreaker or rain jacket with large hoods covering their heads and shadowing their faces.

Freya called out to Matt. "Oh Matthew, I made you sandwiches to take with you in case you get hungry," she said as she walked out to hand him a packaged lunch. "Remember dinner is served at seven."

After loading his gear into the jeep, Matt turned and walked up the street to Dr. Bertram's clinic. Glancing back, over his shoulder, he noticed Freya standing in the walkway watching with her arms folded across her chest. When Freya saw Matt looking back at her, she promptly turned and disappeared back into the inn.

Arriving on the doorstep of the clinic, Matt was about to knock when the door opened and Dr. Bertram stood in front of him, "welcome, welcome, come on inside."

"Thank you. I appreciate you taking the time out of your day to hook me up with a guide to show me around the valley."

"It's my pleasure. I trust you slept well?"

"Yes I did, thank you. The inn is quite comfortable with a homey quality to it, which makes for a very relaxing atmosphere."

"Freya is a very fine and lovely lady; she goes out of her way to make the guest feel welcome. Come on inside; this is my clinic as you can see." Dr. Bertram began giving Matt a tour of the clinic. "There's not a hospital within eighty miles from here and we lack proper communications for emergencies, so our clinic is the closest emergency medical facility available. We have everything we need for most medical emergencies. A generator out back provides electricity for medical equipment and such."

"In a previous life, the good doctor was a trauma surgeon at a hospital in Spokane," Allison said as she entered the room. "Good morning Dr. Kershaw."

"And my lovely wife is a Registered Nurse," Dr. Bertram responded putting his arm around Allison's shoulder. Together we've been caring for the residents of the valley for more than five years now."

"We have even delivered a lamb or two over the years," Allison joked.

"Sounds as though you are both dedicated to serving the community."

"We do what we can," Dr. Bertram replied. "Well, let's see if we can get you on your way to meet Alex and Frankie," Dr. Bertram turned and led Matt back out the front door and down the walkway. "I've made arrangements for Peter to take you out to meet them. I don't believe you'll find anyone who knows more about the trails, and wildlife in and around the valley than Alex or Frankie."

At the end of the street, they came to a carpentry shop. Dr. Bertram tapped on the door and stepped through to find Peter making a new door. "Good morning Peter," Greeted Dr. Bertram

"Good morning gentlemen," Peter replied.

"Good morning Peter," Matt replied.

"Peter is a master carpenter. He makes lovely hand crafted doors, shutters, windows, as well as very fine cabinets and furniture. Peter can hand craft just about anything you can think of, that can be made from wood."

"You flatter me Doc. Truth is, I'm the village handyman; jack of all trades, master of none, as the saying goes."

"Now you're being modest," Dr. Bertram asserted.

They all chuckled at the jesting between Peter and Dr. Bertram.

"I brought Matthew around so that you could take him out and introduce him to Alex and Frankie."

"Fine, I'm more than happy to take him out that way."

"Very well, I'll leave you and return to the clinic," Dr. Bertram said waving goodbye to the both of them as he exited Peter's shop.

"Do you have your gear loaded and ready to leave?"

"Yes, it's already in the jeep, I'm ready when you are."

Peter untied his shop apron and laid it on the work bench, "Well, let's be on our way then."

As Matt started the vehicle and began backing out of the parking space, Peter directed him to follow the main street out the northwest side of the village. After leaving the village, Matt stopped momentarily to pull out his map to orient himself to their direction of travel and destination. Peter indicated on the map where Alex and Frankie lived.

As they proceeded down the road, Peter gave Matt a bit of background on Alex and Frankie. "Alex and Frankie are brother and sister. Their father descended from a long line of tribal chiefs within the valley. He ran a guide service for many years for wealthy big game hunters who sought trophy bear and elk. All of his business was the word of mouth among rich business owners and industrialist from back east who wanted to take home trophies and tell tall tales of adventures in the wilderness. Mr. Wolfe, Alex and Frankie's father, died a few years ago and Alex continued the guide service for hunters. Frankie caters more to the yuppie crowd, leading hiking and camping adventures into the wilderness."

"So, is Alex a tribal chief and his sister a tribal princess?" Matt inquired.

"Of sorts, you might say. The valley residents associate more with the administrative system of government rather than the old tribal hierarchy. Among the Native American families still living in the valley, Alex and Frankie are still respected as the descendants of the old line of chiefs but there's no formal tribal structure anymore."

The drive out to Alex and Frankie's lodge was just three miles from Graymere. Passing through a stand of virgin trees, they emerged into a small meadow. The lodge, situated in a picturesque setting, the mountains bordering the wilderness area forming a beautiful backdrop as the sun was peeking up over the mountains, and the valley below blanketed with a morning misty haze. The scene was tranquil and serene.

Matt drove up to the lodge and parked near the stairway leading up to the front entrance. Alex and Frankie stood on the front porch waiting to greet their guests. They recognized Peter when he stepped out of Matt's jeep.

"Peter! Good to see you. It's been awhile since the last time you've been out this way," Alex called out, as he made his way down the steps to greet Peter. "And, you must be Dr. Kershaw? Doc called and told me you were coming out to see us this morning. I'm Alexander Wolfe, pleased to meet you, Dr. Kershaw." Meanwhile, Frankie remained on the porch at the top of the stairs.

"Dr. Kershaw is a wildlife biologist from the University of Idaho."

"Please call me Matt," He said. Matt mentally noted Alex's strong firm handshake and he fit Matt's mental image of a tribal chief in both stature and demeanor. Alex stood approximately five feet, ten inches tall with a stout muscular body. Although dressed casually in jeans, shirt, and boots, his overall appearance exhibited a hint of authority and confidence.

"What brings you to Graymere Lodge this fine morning?"

"Doctor Bertram suggested that you or your sister might be willing to help me scout the valley. I'm conducting an investigation of the wolf attack that occurred just over a week ago. Dr. Bertram said you may be willing to help me locate a few areas of interest."

"The doctor is too kind," Alex said, casting a serious gaze at Peter suggesting a hidden meaning in Alex's response.

"I understand the two of you run a guide service, and if this is something you are willing to help me with, I would like to hire you for a couple of days to show me around the valley."

"Unless you are here on a safari to hunt big game or to take a backpacking trek into the wilderness we are not for hire. But, if you want someone to show you around the valley and help you find your way among the roads and trails, we are more than happy to lend a hand." Alex gave a warm, welcome smile to Matt as he motioned them up the stairs toward the entrance of the lodge.

At the top of the steps, they paused for Alex to introduce Frankie. "This is my sister Francine Wolfe."

"Frankie if you please," She said, sneering at Alex. "Pleasure to meet you...?"

"Matthew, Matthew Kershaw." Matt stumbled a bit responding to Frankie extending her hand to shake.

"Well, pleasure to meet you Matthew, Matthew, Kershaw." Frankie jested as she shook his hand with a firm grip.

"Only one Matthew, and please call me Matt."

"Only if you call me Frankie," she replied.

Alex and Peter exchanged sly smiles after observing the exchange between Matt and Frankie.

Matt found Frankie to be a very attractive woman, about five feet, four inches tall. She exhibited Native American ancestry accented by a beautiful skin tone and lovely brown eyes. From the jeans and t-shirt Frankie was wearing, Matt could not help but notice her attractive, and athletic physical appearance. She wore her fine black hair braided into a ponytail reaching down to about the middle of her back. There was a very confident but feminine demeanor about her.

Alex opened the front door for Matt and Peter. "Please come in." Entering the lounge area Alex gestured for Matt and Peter to have a seat.

"Would either of you care for coffee or tea?" Frankie offered.

"Coffee would be nice, thank you," Matt answered. "Black please."

"Same for me please," Peter said.

"Matt, tell us about your work and how we may be of assistance," Alex asked.

Matt began to highlight the general nature of his investigation as Frankie served them coffee. He explained Harvey's concern regarding the number of encounters with wolves over the last several months which prompted Harvey to ask him to conduct an investigation of the attack on the ranger. In addition, Harvey asked him to conduct a survey of the wolf population in the area to assess any possible threat to the residents.

Frankie listened intently to Matt's summation of his assignment before offering her observations on the situation. "We heard about the incident with the forest ranger. We have an occasional lone wolf venture down out of the mountains from the south to kill and feed on a lamb, chicken, or calf. But, this is the first actual wolf attack on a person since before I was born. And, I'm not aware of any encounters with wolves among the locals." As Frankie concluded her observation, she exchanged glances with Alex and Peter for confirmation.

Matt was beginning to get the feeling, that they were holding back something they didn't want him to know about. As Frankie was talking, he reflected on the conversation at the dinner table last evening wherein everyone present appeared to be a bit guarded in their discussion.

"I've plotted the locations of the reported incidents from the last two years on a map and I was hoping that I could get one of you to go with me to identify these points on the ground and orient me to the terrain and habitat in the areas around each point."

"Certainly, we can help you with that," offered Alex. "But, what in particular are you looking for?"

"I'm looking for signs and patterns in the movement of any wolves that might suggest a reason for the increase in encounters over the last couple of years. From the preliminary information Harvey provided me, he believes that the wolf population in the wilderness region is encroaching into the valley." Matt decided to withhold any references to the mystery animal or his quest to identify a new species of wolf.

Matt pulled out his map and spread it out on the table in the middle of the lounge area. Peter and Alex pulled their chairs close as Frankie knelt next to the table to study the map. "These are the points where all of the incidents over the last two years have occurred, according to the reports Harvey gave me. They seem to be more oriented toward the north side of the valley and this is where the Forest ranger was attacked last week." Matt said pointing to a particular point on the map.

Alex began pointing at locations on the map, "Well, as you can see, Misty Hollow is a valley ringed by these mountains and ridges with the entrance to the valley through this narrow pass. You would have come into the valley along this road."

"Yes, I drove up that road yesterday afternoon."

"Are you sure these are the correct locations for the incidents in the reports you mentioned?" Alex asked seeking confirmation from Matt.

"Yes; why do you ask?"

"As Frankie mentioned, and as far as I'm aware, the lone wolves tend to come from the southern boundary of the valley. I don't recall any wolves reported on the north side. Your map doesn't highlight the boundaries but the wilderness boundary begins from the crest of the mountain and ridges around us. Then the area within the valley is mostly national forest lands with the exception of Graymere and the scattered homesteads. The area you indicated on the map borders the north ridge; beyond that is warg territory. From what you described, I suspect wargs may be responsible for the attack on the ranger and the other incidents you mentioned."

"Wargs?" Matt asked.

"Yes; well, that is what we call them anyway. I believe the term '*warg*' or '*varg*' is from Norse mythology and appropriately describes the wolves from the north of the valley."

"I don't understand what you mean," Matt said curiously pressing for a clearer explanation.

"The wolves in the wilderness territory to the north of the valley are unlike any other wolf that I'm aware of…" Alex paused, looking to Peter and Frankie for confirmation, "they are larger and far more aggressive than the gray wolves to the south. If you ask my opinion, they are the epitome of pure evil. We rarely ever see one although we do hear them howl on nights of the full moon."

"Their howls are unlike anything you can imagine; sends chills through your bones," Peter interjected.

Frankie cast a concerned glance at Alex and Peter, "But, no one has seen a warg in years."

Alex glanced back and forth between Frankie and Peter before addressing Matt, "If wargs *are* venturing into the valley and attacking people, then I can understand why Harvey would want you to look into it. Normally, if we spot a gray wolf they bolt and run away, but from what my father and grandfather told us about the wargs, they will deliberately hunt down and attack humans if you venture into their territory. Legend has it, they are seeking revenge for the death of the female alpha mate and her pups that were killed by Frenchmen who first came into the valley in the early 1800's."

"What can you tell me about these wargs?" Matt asked with peaked interest.

"Not much; I've never actually seen one," Alex responded as he looked to Peter to offer any information.

Peter shrugged his shoulders, "Our knowledge of the wargs is passed down from our fathers and grandfathers, who hunted the wargs to near extinction. At some time around the 1920s or 1930s, the wargs began coming down into the valley, attacking, and feeding on the residents. In response, the residents organized hunting parties which tracked and killed every warg they could find. The forest service paid a bounty on them due to the threat to the CCC crews who were working in the valley during that time."

Speaking to Frankie, Alex suggested. "If you'll go with Matt and show him around the valley, I'll take Peter back to town. I have to pick up some supplies and check our mail. If it's OK with Matt, he can drop you back off here at the lodge on his way back into town, when you guys are done."

Everyone seemed to acknowledge Alex's suggestion without a response and Matt gathered up his map and notebook.

"Let me grab my pack and some water then I'll be ready to go," Frankie said to Matt.

"Alex, I appreciate the help. Your input and background knowledge of the area will save me a lot of time."

"We are happy to lend a hand," Alex replied, shaking Matt's hand.

"Peter, I'm ready to leave if you are."

"I'm ready."

Peter wished Matt luck with the investigation and said farewell.

"Ok, I'm ready," Frankie announced as he came back into the lounge.

"Would you prefer to drive since you're familiar with the area and have an idea of where we're going?"

"Sure," Frankie responded.

Matt tossed her the keys as they approached the jeep. Frankie put her pack in the back while Matt situated his map so that he could follow along as Frankie drove.

Frankie leaned over and pointed to a spot on the map. "We are here and I'll take you to this location first."

41

Chapter 6

Driving along the road, Matt was engrossed in tracing the map with his finger trying to identify landmarks and terrain features.

Frankie decided to break the silence. "Did I hear Peter say that you were a wildlife biologist?"

"Yes, I'm a professor at the University of Idaho in Moscow," He replied without breaking his concentration on the map and terrain.

"Is this the type of work you do at the university?"

"No; I generally spend my summers in the field. If I'm not working a project for the university I generally spend my summers conducting research on my own, in the wilderness areas."

Frankie noticed that Matt's answers were short and to the point preferring to focus on the map and terrain features rather than engage in idle conversation.

"Do you specialize in researching wolves or do you study any species of animal?"

"I've done studies on a variety of animals, mostly predatory species. My personal interest is in studying wolves in the Pacific Northwest."

Frankie slowed the jeep as they neared a low water stream crossing and stopped the jeep in the shade of an overhanging tree near the crossing. Without saying anything, she got out of the jeep expecting Matt to follow, walked down to the edge of the stream, and waited for Matt to catch up.

"You will see on your map that the main creek flowing out of the valley is fed by several of these smaller streams. They run throughout the valley, fed by runoff from snow and rain from the surrounding mountains. Many continue to flow even during the summer, fed by a network of underground springs. You will find most of the wildlife concentrated around these springs in the morning and evenings during the summer months."

Frankie pointed out a selection of animal tracks along the bank of the stream. Absent from the array of tracks were any wolf tracks. Matt made his way up one side of the stream for a short distance and then hopped across to the other side before making his way back to the road.

"I don't see any sign of deer or elk."

"As far as I'm aware we don't have much of a population of either deer or elk in the valley itself, except for the eastern end. We catch a glimpse of one occasionally, but relative to the size of the valley, available grazing pastures, and food plots put out by the Forest Service, we see very little sign of either."

"So where do you guys take the hunters for big game hunts?"

"We pack into the wilderness on the south side. We set up a base camp near that small gap in the ridge." Frankie pointed across the valley to a point almost indistinguishable to Matt from their vantage point. "From there we do day trips into the wilderness from the base camp. We pack in on horseback and camp on the other side of the ridge. The trophy elk and deer are plentiful in that area. No one ever ventures up there except for us."

"Is there a bear population in the valley?"

"As far as I'm aware, bear haven't been sighted anywhere in the valley in a number of years. Even from when I was a child, I don't recall seeing one or hearing anyone else talk about seeing a bear in the valley. The only bear I see, are in the area where we guide hunters. On occasion, we have spotted both black bear and grizzly throughout those areas."

"Are there any mountain lions in the region?" Matt continued searching for pieces to the puzzle as he walked back to the jeep.

"You will find signs of them deeper into the wilderness areas, but rarely ever get a glimpse of one."

Back on the road, Matt refocused his attention to following along with his map. They stopped at a couple of locations where the older reports indicated incidents had occurred but they failed to find any evidence of any animal tracks. About noon, they arrived at the location where the attack on Ranger Holmes happened the week before. As they neared Lupine Rock, he asked Frankie to stop the vehicle. He pulled out his GPS in order to confirm his position as a reference point.

"Yes!" Matt said to himself when the GPS connected to a satellite. Noting his exact position in his journal, he began walking up the road examining the roadside and drainage ditch.

Frankie realized that Matt was not going to turn around and come back, so she started coasting along in the jeep, following behind Matt while keeping a close eye on the surrounding tree line.

Suddenly, Matt stopped and examined something alongside the road before he jumped across the ditch and started working his way back and forth.

Frankie stopped the jeep, got out, and walked over to where Matt was studying the ground. "What are you looking at?"

"Wolf tracks…. and boot tracks."

Matt happened to look up and saw Frankie surveying the surrounding area very intently. Taking the queue from her, Matt paused and began looking and listening to the area around him. After a few moments, he continued his examination of the tracks.

"These tracks are several days old. Probably left by the ranger and the wolves he encountered." Matt said while continuing to trace the tracks. He noticed that Frankie appeared to be on high alert scanning the woods on both sides of the road.

Matt followed the boot prints into the edge of the tree line. He didn't go far before he found traces of blood on the ground. "Frankie, take a look at this."

Frankie made her way across the ditch being careful not to step on any tracks. As she reached the spot where Matt was pointing, she noticed that the area was heavily bloodstained.

"But, where is the carcass?" Matt said aloud to himself.

"What?" Frankie asked off hand while continuing to survey the surrounding terrain, alert for anything that might be lurking nearby.

Matt began searching the immediate area, "The ranger said he found a carcass of a wolf that had been shot, lying just off the side of the road. It was while he was examining the carcass, the wolf pack jumped him. From the tracks and the amount of dried blood, this would appear to be where the wolf carcass was laying when the ranger found it. But, where is the carcass?"

"I'm not following you," Frankie said.

"As far as I'm aware, wolves don't drag off their dead, nor do they eat their dead. There's no evidence that a bear or mountain lion ate the carcass. The incident occurred a week ago so the carcass could not have decomposed in that length of time, so, where is the carcass?"

Frankie offered an observation that the carcass was not anywhere in the immediate area. Otherwise, the smell of the decomposing flesh would be pungent and detectable. "It's almost as if someone removed the carcass," Frankie said in a puzzled tone of voice.

"Yes; but who or why?"

Matt began searching a wider area around the spot where he believed the wolf carcass had fallen. He found no evidence of the carcass being drug away by anyone or anything. Satisfied that this was the scene of Ranger Holmes's attack, Matt went back to the jeep to retrieve his camera and measuring stick to begin documenting the sight.

Reaching into his backpack, he found the sandwiches that Freya had packed for him. He took them out and offered one to Frankie. Frankie pulled out the water she had packed and gave one to Matt. While they sat on the hood of his jeep eating their sandwiches, Matt noticed Frankie scanning the surrounding area as if she knew something was out there, watching, waiting.

When he finished his sandwich, Matt grabbed his camera and measuring stick and started taking pictures of the tracks along the roadside.

45

"Why are you taking pictures of a wolf track?"

"So I can study them later to estimate the number and size of the wolves that were in the immediate area."

Matt made his way down the side of the road searching for more tracks when he came upon a very unusual set of tracks that corresponded to the description given to him by the ranger, Adam Holmes. Matt looked in the main ruts of the road to see if he could find tracks from the ranger's truck. Aside from the tracks made by his jeep, he made out two distinctively different set of tracks. He assumed that one set was from the ranger's truck and the other was made by a third vehicle.

Returning to the mystery track, Matt laid his ruler next to the track and began taking pictures.

"Frankie, come check this out."

She walked over and peered over Matt's shoulder.

"What do you make of this?" He asked and studied her face for a reaction.

Frankie glanced down briefly at the track. "I'm not sure I've ever seen a track like that before," she replied casually.

Judging from her reaction, and in spite of her denial, Matt was sure she *had* seen tracks like these before and it obviously made her very anxious. Anyone who is as involved with the outdoors and nature would have been very curious at such an unusual find. Her casual, seemingly disinterested attitude gave Matt cause to be weary of Frankie's intentions.

"Are you sure you haven't seen anything like this before?" Matt pressed for a second response.

After glancing down again, Frankie replied, "No, not that I can recall. She answered. "What animal do you think it is?" Now it was her turn to judge Matt's reaction.

"I'm not sure." Looking up at Frankie, their eyes met for a moment, but in that moment it was evident both of them had a feeling the other was not telling the whole truth.

Matt returned to his jeep and pulled out a kit box. Inside were materials he used to make a plaster cast of the tracks. The tracks were in good condition given there had not been any rain, high winds, or heavy road traffic to erode the tracks. Frankie remained silent as she continued to watch the area, occasionally glancing down to observe what Matt was doing.

Matt began talking aloud to himself, "I'm curious and a bit concerned at this point. The ranger reported finding a dead wolf on the side of the road. Then, while investigating the scene, wolves attacked and mauled him. You Guys tell me it's rare to see a wolf in the valley at all. But now, we find tracks of not just one, but several wolves in association with an unidentified track you say you've never seen before."

Frankie glanced down at Matt then resumed her vigilant watch of the surrounding area.

Matt remained quiet as he waited for the plaster to set. Meanwhile, he continued to take measurements and make notes in his field journal. He examined the area across the ditch for tracks from the point where the ranger indicated that the mystery animal leaped from and landed in the middle of the road. The track impressions and measurements were consistent with the account given by Ranger Holmes.

As Matt worked to make casts of the tracks and record the data in his notebook, he engaged Frankie in casual conversation regarding his methods for collecting and recording data. She asked many questions regarding behavioral characteristics of wolves, to which Matt was eager to share his knowledge. When the sun began to dip below the southwestern ridge, the ambient light started to fade very quickly and a mist began to form. This was the same phenomenon he observed the evening before when driving into Graymere. Looking at his watch it was almost four o'clock.

He decided to begin packing up his gear. "I guess it's a good time to start heading back. Your brother will have his gun out looking for me if I keep you out any later."

She laughed softly, "I'm a big girl and he knows I can take care of myself. But, we should be getting back before dark."

Matt decided to drive back following Frankie's directions so he could better learn his way around the valley. He was thinking about the data he collected earlier when they sighted an animal about fifty yards ahead of them. The animal made one leap from the right side of the road to the center of the road, stood up on its hind legs for a brief second, then leaped to the opposite side before it disappeared into the forest. Matt slammed on the breaks and stopped the jeep. He began scanning ahead hoping to see more of the animal. In the dim light and misty haze, it appeared to be a wolf but one of unusual size and proportions. He and Frankie looked at each other realizing they had both seen the same thing and he detected fear in her eyes. Much different from the expression of surprise or excitement might have expected.

"Are you alright?" He asked Frankie.

"Yes, let's just get out of here!" She snapped with anxiety in her voice.

"I want to check for tracks…"

"NO! GO, GO!"

Matt could tell she was getting agitated as he drove slowly forward, looking out his open window. He was hoping to catch a glimpse of any tracks in the road where the animal leaped.

"Please! GO FASTER," Frankie pleaded.

Matt headed Frankie's plea and sped away not slowing down until they got back to the lodge. When they pulled to a stop in front of the lodge, Matt had not even put the jeep into park before Frankie jumped out and ran up the steps and through the front door. Matt got out, grabbed Frankie's backpack from the back seat, carried it up to the front door of the lodge, and handed it to Alex. Alex stood looking at Matt with a surprised look on his face. Frankie had just run past him without saying a word leaving him to wonder what had happened.

At first, Matt didn't know what to say. Nevertheless, from the look on Alex's face, he knew he had better say something.

"Wow, she's really shaken up," Matt said somewhat calmly.

"No Shit! What happened?" Alex demanded.

"I'm not sure or at least nothing that I can explain."

"How about trying," Alex said in a hostile tone.

"Well, we were driving back when a large animal crossed the road in front of us. At best, it was a brief glimpse through the dim light and haze but it appeared to be an unusually large wolf; maybe one of the wargs you referred to this morning. Frankie

48

suddenly became very agitated and anxious to get away from there. She didn't say anything the rest of the drive back and jumped out of the jeep and ran into the lodge without stopping long enough to get her backpack from the back of the jeep."

"You say you saw a large wolf and that upset her?" Alex asked as if he had an inside scoop on how that would explain Frankie's behavior. "Well, it's getting late and you should be getting back to the inn before dark. I wouldn't want you to lose your way."

"Will Frankie be alright? I'm sorry if I said or did anything to upset her," Matt said apologetically.

"No, she will be fine. Come back in the morning and one of us will go out with you to help you finish your scouting of the valley." Alex said in a hurried and disassociated manner.

✳✳✳

On the drive back to the inn, Matt kept going through the events of the day trying to piece things together. Based on Alex's reference to the wargs, Matt was hopefully optimistic that he may finally have an opportunity to document a new species of wolf. However, almost from the moment he arrived, he felt that something was out of place, he just couldn't quite figure it out. Even when Alex and Peter were volunteering information about the wargs, he still felt that they were withholding information about them.

Chapter 7

It was about half past five when Matt pulled up to the inn. He grabbed his gear and carried everything up to his room. After dropping his gear, he went back downstairs to get a cup of coffee to relax and collect his thoughts. When he reached the bottom of the stairs, he looked up and saw Freya standing by the kitchen door wiping her hands with a dishtowel.

"I thought I heard you come in. How was your first day in the valley?"

Matt was a bit reserved in his response, "Productive."

"Alex stopped by after he dropped off Peter at his shop and said that Frankie was going with you to tour the valley."

"Yes, she was very helpful," Matt responded, not looking up while filling his coffee cup.

Freya could tell Matt was somewhat reserved in his responses to her inquiries and decided not to continue questioning him about his day. "I need to check on the rolls in the oven," she said before walking back into the kitchen.

A short time later, Freya came back into the main hall and saw Matt sitting at a small table sipping his coffee staring out the front window. She walked over to where he was sitting and sat down across from him.

"You look like you are lost in deep thought, is there something troubling you? Did something happen to upset you?"

"No, not really," he replied. Turning to look at Freya, he didn't know what to tell her or even if he should say anything at all about what happened on the road earlier. "I'm just a bit puzzled over some of the information and samples I gathered today."

"Well, I'll leave you to freshen up; if you want to talk we can visit over dinner. I think it will be just the two of us this evening." Freya got up and went back into the kitchen.

Matt finished his coffee and went up to his room to take a shower and change before dinner. While showering, he pondered the events of the day and tried to figure out why Frankie was so frightened by the animal they saw. Although it was a brief glimpse, in dim light, there is no doubt in his mind, what they had seen was an unusual animal. As to what animal it was, he couldn't say for sure. However, it was evident from Frankie's reaction, she recognized it and whatever it was, it definitely scared the crap out of her.

After showering and changing, Matt went back downstairs and sat by the window sipping another cup of coffee. When he heard the kitchen door open and close, he looked up to see Freya setting the table.

"Freya, is there anything I can help you with?"

"No, just a couple more items to bring out and we can sit down for dinner."

Freya disappeared back into the kitchen and reemerged a couple of moments later with the final items for the table.

"Dinner is served," she announced.

"It smells delicious."

"Please have a seat and help yourself."

Freya noticed that Matt was strangely quiet. She decided to remain quiet herself until he was ready to talk about whatever was bothering him. After all, it wasn't her place to pry into his business.

After a short while, Matt broke the ice and spoke up. "Freya, you grew up in Graymere, are you very familiar with the valley outside Graymere?"

"I'm not sure what you are asking."

"Do you get out and about among the homesteads? Do you speak with the people regularly? Things of this nature," Matt explained.

"Well, I guess you could say I do. I rely on the various farmers for my produce and meat. Some of the items I get from them I carry into town, to sell or trade for items we don't grow in the valley. If that answers your question."

"Do you ever hear the people talk about problems with wolves or hear of people being attacked by wolves in the valley?"

Freya hesitated briefly before she answered, "Not that I can remember. Occasionally, someone will mention missing a chicken, goat, or a lamb that they blame on wolves raiding their livestock. I'm not personally aware of anyone ever being attacked by a wolf."

Matt sat quietly again as if in serious thought over some issue. Freya patiently waited for Matt to continue the conversation.

"When you're out in the valley visiting the farms, have you ever seen any animals that you didn't recognize or appeared odd to you?"

Freya pursed her lips and shook her head slightly, "Over the years, I've seen an occasional deer or elk and I regularly see little animals such as rabbit, squirrel, chipmunks, and such. I don't ever recall seeing anything strange or unusual."

Matt again went quiet as he continued eating his dinner. After a few moments, Freya tried to get him to open up. "You appear to be upset over something. I'm not trying to pry, but if it is anything I've said or done, I apologize."

"No, no; nothing like that."

Then, if you don't mind my saying so, there appears to be something troubling you."

Matt looked up and gazed at Freya for a moment. "Ok, here is my dilemma; first, I was asked to come here to investigate a wolf attack on the Forest Ranger. The purpose of the investigation is to determine if the attack an isolated event or a sign that wolves may be encroaching from the wilderness into the valley. Harvey asked me to determine if there is any serious threat to the indigenous population or transient population of hunters and hikers."

"OK, that sounds simple enough," Freya said.

"Yes, but this is what has me confused. Predatory animals are not discriminatory. Once they reach a point of overpopulation and hunger, they act indiscriminately, attacking animals, wild or domesticated, they regard as food. Conversely, they typically go out of their way to avoid encounters with humans. Generally, they will only attack humans if they are cornered and threatened or suffering from the disease. In either case, they are indiscriminate when they attack any human." Matt paused as if collecting his thoughts.

"I don't understand what you're getting at," Freya said.

"Well, curiously, the reports that Harvey gave me, related to human-wolf encounters here in the valley, all involve transients. The reports don't mention a single incident of any valley resident reporting livestock killed and eaten or any sightings of a wolf by valley residents.

When I was talking to Alex and Frankie today, they told me that wolves were not a problem in the valley. Doc tells me that they are two of the most knowledgeable people in the valley regarding the indigenous wildlife. However, the feedback I get from everyone I've talked to since I arrived, contradicts what I would expect to find given the number of reported incidents."

"Hmmm," Freya mused, "I think I see your point."

"From the information I've been given on wildlife in the area, there doesn't seem to be sufficient wild game to support a population of predators within the valley, while there's an abundance of deer and elk outside the valley. It would make more sense that a wolf pack would migrate to areas with sufficient food rather than migrating to an area that would bring them into contact with humans. Granted, there's an abundant source of food animals among the domesticated herds of sheep, goats, and cattle, but from what Frankie says, these herds are not being disturbed at all."

Matt continued, "It's as if wolf packs are coming down out of the mountains to attack transients visiting the valley, while the residents are oblivious to any wolf presence altogether. We know for sure, at least one encounter with wolves has occurred, evidenced by last week's attack on Ranger Holmes. Moreover, my examination of the site where Ranger Holmes was attacked, confirms that a pack was involved rather than a lone wolf. This whole situation doesn't make any sense to me." Up to this point, Matt hadn't mentioned anything about the mystery animal he was investigating, aside from his primary research of the wolf population in the valley. Nor, did he mention the incident of the sighting that had frightened Frankie that afternoon.

Now it was Freya's turn to be silent. After they both finished eating, Freya busied herself with clearing the table. Without thinking about it, he got up from the dinner table and started helping Freya as if he were back at home with his mother and grandmother. When he carried a load of the dishes into the kitchen, Freya looked up at him a bit surprised. "Matthew please, I can take care of this. You're a guest here, not the hired help."

"I don't mind," he responded as he placed the dishes on the counter."

"Please, go have a cup of coffee or a nice cup of tea and relax a bit," Freya insisted.

Matt did as Freya suggested, returning to the dining hall to make a cup of tea before sitting down on the hearth of the large fireplace in the main hall. While sitting there sipping his tea, waiting for Freya to finish up in the kitchen, he began to reflect on the day's events. His thoughts focused on his confusion with what he had found so far; when he suddenly realized that, he was making a fundamental error in scientific investigation. He was trying to make incomplete information fit a preconceived conclusion. It was now evident that this investigation was not going to be as simple as he had imagined and he reminded himself that he must slow down and do it right.

Matt's thoughts shifted to what Alex and Peter told him regarding the wargs. Their description of the mythic warg intrigued him. He noted the similarities to the description given by Ranger Holmes, including the mention of the perceived evil nature of the animal. He was encouraged by the evidence he had collected so far, particularly the casts he made of the unidentified paw prints. Could he finally be close to discovering the new species he believed existed in the wilderness?

* * *

After she finished up in the kitchen, Freya walked through the door into the main hall to join Matt for an after dinner cup of tea. With a hot cup of tea in hand, she walked over to sit on the hearth near Matt. He was so lost daydreaming of the prospects and possibilities of discovering a new species of wolf, he didn't notice Freya enter the room or even making herself a cup of tea.

"A penny for your thoughts," She said.

Matt looked up and smiled at Freya. "Oh sorry, I didn't see you come in. I was just trying to sort out my plans for tomorrow."

"If I'm disturbing you, I can…"

"No, no; please have a seat. I enjoy your company."

Attempting to change the subject, Matt began a casual inquiry of Graymere and its residents. "From what little I've seen of the village and the valley, I've noticed hints of Native American art and culture here and there."

"Yes," Freya began, "in fact, many of the valley residents are predominantly Native American. Our ancestors settled this valley long, long ago, and lived here for many generations before the *white man* first came to the valley. As the story goes, two French fur trappers were preparing to set up camp for the winter when they stumbled upon a '*crazed wolf pack*'. Over the course of two days, the pack attacked the men repeatedly. Eventually, they killed the alpha's mate and wounded the alpha. Relentlessly, the pack pursued the trappers until they found their way into the valley and the safety of the local tribes."

"What about their first encounter with the natives here?"

"At that time, there were three small villages scattered around the valley. They all lived peacefully among one another, helping each other in times of need. A hunting party from one of the villages, in the northern part of the valley, stumbled across the white men, took them in and cared for them, nursing them back to health. These men were not able to figure out where they had come from. After encountering the wolf pack they were chased from their familiar territory and were hopelessly lost by the time they entered the valley." Freya paused to sip her tea.

"So?" Matt prompted her to continue.

"Well, not much more to tell. The winter set in early, before they were well enough to try to make their way back north. By the spring thaw, the men had become integrated into the local community, each took a wife from different villages in the valley and here we are."

"What about later contact from outside the valley?"

"It was not until well after the pioneers started moving west that any other contact from outside the valley occurred and that was not as cordial as the first encounter with the two fur trappers."

"What happened?"

"After the gold rush fever spread among the settlers, up and down the west coast, many of those seeking to strike it rich, found their way into the valley with no patience to establish a friendly relationship with the villages of the valley. Instead, they relied on their guns to take what they wanted. I guess, ultimately they realized there was no gold in the valley and there was nothing else here worth risking their lives. Eventually, civilization began to settle into the rest of Idaho and later contact was more cooperative. It seems fate had ordained that the trappers had imparted some European features among the residents and almost everyone was able to speak French and some English. Ultimately, the outside world viewed Misty Hollow and Graymere as a typical frontier settlement. Due to our remoteness from the rest of civilization and the lack of any tangible resources worth plundering, we have been left relatively unmolested for the last one-hundred plus years."

"What about you and your family? I mean, has your family lived in the valley for a long time?"

Freya smiled, "Oh yes. One of the two Frenchmen who stumbled down out of the mountains was my great, great, great, grandfather. When the prospectors and fur trappers started finding their way into the valley seeking their fortunes, the two Frenchmen established a trading post. They set up the trading post at a location they thought would be the first point of contact for anyone coming into the valley from outside. The village of Graymere evolved from the original trading post. They hoped by making the first contact with outsiders entering the valley, they could serve as a buffer between them and the natives in the valley. They wanted to promote trade with the outsides while minimizing any conflicts between them and valley residents."

"So, how did Graymere evolve economically?" Matt asked.

"At some point, the Federal Government began sending teams of surveyors to map the area, followed by forestry people who cut roads and trails for firebreaks. Then there were other groups who came here to make food plots to help support the wildlife management. The trading post served as a base camp for these teams. Eventually, Graymere grew from the old trading post as the valley residents also came to trade fresh meat and vegetables for hard goods from outside the valley."

"The whole idea of how the valley has remained somewhat isolated from the outside is interesting," Matt said.

Freya decided to change the conversation. "So, what about you Matthew? What's your story?" Freya asked with an inquiring smile and twinkle in her eye.

"Actually, there's not much to tell. You heard most of my life history at dinner last evening."

"Yes, I recall," responded Freya. "If you don't mind me saying so, or asking; here you are at the age of what thirty-eight...."

"Forty; pushing forty-one," Matt interjected.

"OK, forty," Freya continued, "single, studying wolves in the middle of nowhere, and seemingly married to your work, with no social life outside your classroom. What's with that?"

Matt smiled not offended by Freya's interest in his personal life. "Well, when you put it like that, you make me look like a total dork."

Freya laughed, "Well..., not a *total* dork," she laughed. "I guess what I'm getting at is, you seemed to have a strong interest in wolves and you say you feel more at home in the wilderness than with other people."

Matt started to share with Freya that his fascination with wolves began with the tales and legends told to him by his great-uncle and their conversation went on for some time. As Matt talked about his particular interest in the skin-walkers, Freya seemed to pay close attention to his explanation of why he believed these legends had some basis in fact. He explained his belief that there might be an undiscovered species of wolf hiding in the wilderness, which he believed would exhibit such radical physical characteristics that might explain the origins of the legends.

"Oh dear," Freya exclaimed as the grandfather clock chimed eleven o'clock. "Its way past my bedtime and my day starts early every morning."

"Yes indeed," Matt acknowledged. "I'm sorry to have kept you up so late."

"Oh no," Freya countered, "I truly enjoyed our conversation. It's not often that I get to just sit and talk with someone. Besides, I enjoy hearing you talk about the passion you have for your work. I look forward to visiting with you again and hearing more about your work and search for that new species of wolf."

After saying good night, Matt proceeded to his room to go to bed. It didn't take him long to go to sleep after he pushed all of his thoughts and questions about the day out of his mind. He was looking forward to a fresh new day tomorrow and hopes of finding more evidence of the cryptid.

Freya finished turning out the lamps and preparing the coffee pots for the next morning before she went to her room. She couldn't stop thinking about Matthew and their conversation as she was changing into her nightgown and brushing out her hair. She wondered how long he would be staying and the prospects of him ever coming back to Graymere after he completed his work that summer. Freya pulled back her hair and stared into the mirror, she wondered if Matt had noticed anything unusual about her appearance. Generally, the way she wears her hair and clothes most people don't notice anything.

She turned down the lamp to a very low glimmer, turned down the covers, the laid down to go to sleep. But, she was a bit restless, pondering how much Matthew already knew about the valley and what his real purpose was for being there. Was he there to study the wolf population as he said, or was he there to investigate the valley residents? The valley residents were naturally suspicious of outsiders and she was no different in that respect. She decided that time would reveal the truth. For the time being, it was her job to make him feel welcome and maybe he would confide in her.

Chapter 8

Matt woke to the smell of coffee brewing. He wanted to get an early start but he was feeling a bit lazy. After dressing, he headed down for fresh coffee and breakfast. He was pouring a cup of coffee when Freya came out of the kitchen carrying a platter of food for the table. "Good morning," he said.

Looking toward Matt with a bright smile, she responded, "I trust you slept well."

"I did thank you. I fell asleep almost the moment my head hit the pillow."

"Alex called a few minutes ago and said you could head over to the lodge as early as you like. He or Frankie would be ready to head out as soon as you were ready to go."

"Thanks," Matt acknowledged, "I was hoping to get an early start today."

Before Matt sat down at the table, Peter came into the lodge to have breakfast followed closely by Simon. After exchanging morning greetings, they all sat down to have breakfast together.

"Dr. Kershaw, how was your outing yesterday?" Simon asked. "Peter mentioned he took you out to meet Alex and Frankie."

"It was a good day. Frankie seems to know her way around the valley quite well." Matt replied.

"Were you able to find anything helpful to your investigation?" Peter asked.

Matt was beginning to feel that Peter and Simon were probing for information beyond simple curiosity. "Yes, I found a few tracks. I'm hoping that I can complete my initial scouting of the valley today." Matt purposely kept his responses brief and being careful not to elaborate on any details.

When Simon asked, "Did you see any wolves while you were out?" Matt was sure they were fishing for information by asking questions they probably already knew the answers to. He assumed they were probing to find out what he knew or suspected about the 'mysterious' animal he and Frankie sighted the afternoon before.

"No," Matt said in a casual response. "I don't really expect to see any wolves while I'm here. They are a bit elusive and unless I just happened to be in the right place, at the right time, and can observe from far enough away, *I might* be lucky enough to see one. Otherwise, I have to rely on my monitoring equipment and cameras to identify any wolf activity in the area.

Matt caught Peter and Simon casting short gazes at each other. "Have either of you seen a wolf in the valley? Particularly within the last few months?" Matt inquired.

"No," Simon responded.

"I haven't ever seen one myself," Peter said. "But, I've heard them howl from time to time as I mentioned yesterday."

"I've heard them howl on occasion," Simon added.

Freya quietly observed the conversation without offering any input to the discussion.

After finishing his breakfast, Matt thanked Freya for another fine meal and politely excused himself from the table. After retrieving his backpack and gear from his room, Matt left the inn on his way to Alex and Frankie's lodge.

Freya was waiting for him on the front porch with a sack lunch she had prepared for him. "Be careful out there Matthew," she said with caution in her voice. It almost sounded as if she *expected* something bad to happen.

"Not to worry," Matt told her. "I've spent many days and nights in the wilderness on my own and managed to survive."

* * *

As Matt pulled up in front of the Lodge, Alex was waiting for him at the top of the steps, but he didn't see Frankie with him. Matt parked his jeep, got out, and started up the stairs toward Alex.

"Good morning Dr. Kershaw," Alex greeted.

"Good morning Alex, and please call me Matt."

"Will do," Alex agreed and ushered Matt up the steps. "I trust you had a good night's rest and a hot breakfast."

"Yes indeed," replied Matt. "How is Frankie…?"

From behind him, he heard, "Frankie is doing fine thank you. Would you like some coffee before we head out?" She asked.

"I believe I've had my limit of coffee this morning."

"Well I'm ready to go when you are," Frankie said gesturing toward the door.

"Are you coming with us today Alex?" Matt asked.

"No, I have a lot of chores to do around the lodge. I believe you will be in good hands with Frankie." Alex gave a coy wink to Matt.

As they were walking out the front door, Matt noticed that Frankie was carrying a shotgun along with her pack. "Would you like for me to drive again?" She asked.

"If you don't mind, that'd be great."

Matt pulled out his map and spread it out on the hood of the jeep. "This is the area I would like to check out today. If we have time, I would like to visit some of the farms in the area that raise sheep, cattle, horses, or other farm animals. Can you show me on the map where some of these farms are located?"

Frankie studied the map then traced her finger across the points Matt had marked on his map. "We'll take this road along the perimeter of the valley to reach the areas you have marked. When we cross along this part of the valley, we will pass near two farms. The Blackstone homestead is here. They raise sheep along with a few chickens. The other farm is the Crestwood homestead located here. They raise dairy cows."

"Ok, let's do it," Matt said, folding up his map.

Just as he did the day before, Matt was intently studying his map and trying to match landmarks as Frankie drove. At the third stop, Matt was out of the jeep walking the area when he realized Frankie had stood guard at each stop they made. She had not said much since they left the lodge, and he hadn't paid much attention before now. He had been too preoccupied with studying the terrain.

"How long ago did the incident occur at this location?" Frankie asked.

"About eight months ago," Matt answered.

"I don't believe you will find any tracks. It has rained several times since then, including a couple of heavy storms. Any tracks would have been washed away long ago." Frankie said.

"I'm sure you're right."

"Then what are you looking for?"

"Well…," Matt paused, "for one thing, I'm checking to see if there are any fresh tracks and any signs of a traveled trail through this area. Second, I'm trying to identify any terrain characteristics that the different sites have in common."

"What do you mean 'traveled trail'?"

Without pausing from his search of the area Matt explained, "Wolves will mark a territory and will regularly travel a beaten path, the same as bears and mountain lions. Predators, including wolves, patrol the perimeter of their territory, marking it along the way, to ward off other wolves or predators that may be encroaching on their established territory. Typically, you will find a very narrow and faint trail. Along that trail, every few yards, you'll find some marking such as scent, scat or scratch."

"So what does that have to do with these incidents you keep referring to? I'm still not sure I'm following what you're looking for."

"First, let me ask you; have there been any cases of rabies in the valley?"

"Not that I'm aware of," Frankie replied.

Matt paused from his search of the area and walked back to the jeep, where Frankie was standing guard, to explain. "OK, I just told you that wolves almost never attack humans and whenever possible will go out of their way to avoid contact with humans."

"Yes."

"Therefore, in order for the number of incidents to have occurred within a relatively small and isolated area like Misty Hollow, my first suspicion would be a major rabies infection among the wildlife. However, you said there haven't been any reported cases of rabies. And, if there were such an infection, Dr. Bertram would have mentioned it right away when I met him yesterday morning."

"OK," acknowledged Frankie.

Matt continued, "If there are no indications of rabies as the contributing cause of the attacks, we have to consider the attacks might be associated with humans encroaching on the wolves' territory."

"But, we have not been venturing into their territory to the north, and the valley has never been part of their territory. At least as far I know."

"No, but if the wolves are expanding their territory to include the valley, your presence constitutes a threat to them. Nevertheless, for this number of encounters to occur within a relatively short period, within a relatively small area, the wolf population would have to be dense and overcrowded. These are the key things I'm trying to determine."

Frankie listened to Matt's explanation as they loaded up to move to the next area. On their way, they drove near one of the farms that Frankie mentioned that morning. Reaching a point where the forest opened up to a large meadow, Frankie pulled over and stopped.

Frankie got out of the jeep and pointed out across the meadow. "This is the Blackstone homestead," She said waving her hand from left to right indicating the boundaries of the field.

"Can we stop by and visit with the Blackstone's?"

"I don't think that would be a good idea. They are a bit shy of strangers, as most people around the valley are. I'll mention it to Dr. Bertram that you would like to visit with some of the residents and he can pave the way for you to meet them and make the introductions for you."

Matt was taking in the beautiful view of the meadow where he could see a few sheep grazing in the distance. The smell of the fresh air and a gentle breeze was very relaxing to him. It was such a relaxing spot; they decided to have lunch while enjoying the view. He pulled out the sack lunch Freya made and sat on the hood of the jeep to eat as Frankie did the same.

"I love the peace and tranquility of country life, out and away from the city," Matt said aloud.

Frankie didn't respond, she just sat and ate her lunch and listened to Matt describe his love of the wilderness and wildlife. After they finished eating, they moved on to the next location.

Throughout the day, Matt didn't find anything worth noting which would aid him in his investigation. After passing near the Crestwood homestead, they headed back to the lodge. The drive back along the narrow winding road took nearly half an hour during which time, Frankie said very little. Matt could not help but notice that she had a white-knuckle grip on the steering wheel and her eyes riveted to the road ahead as if she was expecting something to jump out in front of her at any moment.

When they arrived back at the lodge, Alex greeted them, "How was your day? Productive I hope."

"Long and dusty," Matt answered. "Other than that, not much to report."

"Would you like to come in for a bit and freshen up?"

"Thanks for the invitation, but I should be getting back to the inn. I need to clean up before Freya serves dinner. She warned me not to be late or I'll go hungry."

"Please feel free to stop by and visit with us anytime. We are usually here, working around the lodge."

"Thanks again for taking the time show me around the valley," Matt said. He said goodnight to Alex and Frankie from the open window of his jeep, then waved goodbye as he drove away.

During the drive back to Graymere, Matt's mind was on what Freya would have cooked for dinner. He thought it strange that he would look forward to getting back to the inn and sitting down for dinner. It was like the anticipation he felt when going to his grandmother's house.

After Matt drove away, Alex turned to Frankie and asked her if she and Matt had encountered any wargs during the day. Frankie summarized the day's activities.

"Has he given you any indication of his knowledge of the wargs, particularly the rogues or the alphas?" Alex inquired.

"No," Frankie paused to collect her thoughts, "I think he is confused at this point. He keeps muttering to himself, something to the effect that the facts don't add up. He wanted to visit the local homesteads but I was able to avoid that today, but he will be out on his own tomorrow and I'm sure he'll make an effort to visit some of the homesteads."

"I'll speak with William to let him know the status. He wants us to try and help Dr. Kershaw along with his investigation, but steer him clear of any contact with the Therians, and to ensure that he is kept clear of any danger from the wargs on the north side."

"I hope William doesn't expect us to babysit Dr. Kershaw for the next two weeks," Frankie said in a disconcerting tone of voice.

"I think he will have the therian betas keep an eye on him during the day. He only wants us to involve ourselves enough to keep him looking in the protected areas as much as possible. He doesn't want to raise any suspicions that would lead him to the Therianthropes or warg alphas."

Chapter 9

Matt arrived at the inn and unloaded his gear. Freya spotted him going up the stairs and informed him that Dr. Bertram and his wife, Allison, would be joining them for dinner that evening.

In his room, Matt pulled out his map and notebook and began reviewing his notes. He had thumbed through the reports so many times the pages had become dog-eared. '*There has to be something that I'm missing, a common denominator, what is it?*' he thought to himself. Then he pulled out the report of the ranger's incident and something clicked, '*Virus infection!*' He began flipping through the other reports searching for any reference to a viral infection among the other incidents, similar to what Ranger Holmes experienced. He couldn't find a single reference to any physical contact aside from the Ranger Homes incident. "Damn!" he said aloud. It was getting close to dinnertime, so he put the reports aside and hurriedly showered and dressed for dinner.

Dr. Bertram and Allison had already arrived and were visiting with Freya when Matt entered the main hall. "Good evening, Dr. Kershaw."

"Good evening Dr. Bertram… Mrs. Bertram," Matt replied with a slight bow of his head to Allison while shaking hands with Dr. Bertram.

"I hope you had a productive day," Freya said to Matt.

With a hint of disappointment, Matt told her, "Yes and no."

Neither Freya nor the doctor pressed for a more detailed response.

Ushering everyone to the dinner table, Freya announced, "Dinner is served and getting cold. Matthew, I hope you like roast leg of lamb?"

Closing his eyes and taking in the aroma of the freshly cooked feast in front of him, Matt commented, "Looks and smells delicious as usual. How do you find time to cook like this, every day?"

Freya laughed. "Our days are not filled with the typical hustle and bustle you are accustomed to in the city. Cooking is my way of staying busy. Besides, I enjoy cooking as long as there's someone around who appreciates my culinary talents." Freya cast a wink and smile toward Allison.

"Coming from a world of fast food and TV dinners, I for one appreciate your talents."

Dr. Bertram inquired from Matt, "I trust that Alex and Frankie were of assistance to you in showing you around the valley?"

"Yes, and I thank you very much for recommending them to me. Frankie has been an excellent guide."

"Have you discovered anything interesting to aid your investigation?" Allison inquired.

"I'm not sure. I found a few unusually large tracks in the area where the ranger was attacked last week, but nothing anywhere else. However, I haven't put out my monitoring equipment yet. The last two days were taken up scouting points of interest and getting acquainted with the area; the flora and fauna you might say."

"What's the next step in your investigation?" Dr. Bertram asked.

"Over the next couple of days or so I'll put out a few motion-activated cameras and some sensors that will help me identify some of the wildlife movement patterns." Before anyone could ask a follow-up question Matt changed the subject of conversation, "Dr. Bertram, have you treated any cases of rabies or encountered any unusual viruses within the last few months?"

Matt's question appeared to catch the doctor off guard and Matt noticed that the doctor exchanging a serious gaze with both Freya and Allison and hesitating before he answered. "No, we haven't had a single case of rabies in the valley since Allison and I came here and started running the clinic."

"How many patients have you treated over the last twelve months, who suffered bites or mauling from wolves?" Matt asked, suggesting that there *had been* attacks within the valley.

Again, Matt's question caught the doctor off guard. "None. Typically, we see patients with a cold or sniffle, an occasional broken bone, or a cut that needs to be sewn up. Rarely, do we deal with what could be considered true trauma cases."

Matt became quiet, considering the doctor's response to his questions.

After a moment or two, Allison spoke up. "Why do you ask," she asked, sharing a momentary gaze with her husband and Freya.

Matt paused before responding, "Just trying to fill in some blanks."

Matt's response to Allison seemed to puzzle her and the doctor, but neither pressed for an explanation.

"Dr. Bertram, Frankie and I passed by the Blackstone and Crestwood homesteads today. I wanted to stop and visit with them, but Frankie suggested that it would be best if you made the introductions. She mentioned the locals are very shy of outsiders."

Dr. Bertram stopped eating, put his fork and knife down on his plate, placed his elbows on the table and folded his hands together in front of his face in a manner indicating that he was taking a very serious posture before answering. "I believe Frankie was correct to recommend this approach. The residents of the valley rarely encounter outsiders and for a stranger, an outsider, to show up on their doorstep unannounced, asking questions, would most certainly be cause for alarm. Not only would you not be welcomed, they certainly wouldn't answer any of your questions. You might get run off with a shotgun." The doctor concluded with a smile and wink before resuming his meal. Matt got a strange feeling that Dr. Bertram's response had a hint of a veiled threat.

"I understand. It's not my intent to create discord. I'm only trying to gather information that would help me with the investigation."

"I'll see what I can do to pave the way for you to visit some of the residents. I'll begin passing the word around the valley that you are here as an invited guest to do some research and not just some stranger poking around the valley. Give me a couple of days to arrange some introductions. In the meantime, I advise you not to approach any of the homesteads without me being with you."

Matt acknowledged the doctors offer and suggestion. For the remainder of the meal, the conversation consisted of small talk related to upcoming events. Following dinner, Matt excused himself and retreated to his room to resume his review of his notes and the reports. He was becoming obsessed with finding a common thread among the reported encounters.

* * *

After Matt left the room, Dr. Bertram told Allison and Freya about William's concern regarding Dr. Kershaw having gotten a glimpse of an alpha and that he was looking for evidence of their existence. Additionally, William stressed his desire to keep Matt away from the Therian homesteads. "Freya, as the opportunity arises, continue discouraging him from going near the homesteads unless I'm with him. We don't want him stumbling into any of the Therianthropes prematurely." Doc paused a moment, realizing what he had just said to Freya. "I'm sorry," he said apologetically. I was referring to the betas, and …"

"It's alright," she interrupted, "I understand what you meant."

"Dr. Kershaw doesn't appear to be a stupid person, eventually, he'll push for concrete answers." Allison asserted as they stood in the doorway.

"We'll have to keep trying to figure out where he's headed with his investigation and do our best to stay a step ahead. We need to help him along without making him aware of the existence of the Therianthropes. Freya, as you are cleaning his room, see if you can see any of his notes lying about. I'm very curious as to his thoughts and suspicions."

"I'll see what I can find when I clean his room in the morning."

After bidding each other good night, Freya busied herself with clearing the table and cleaning up before calling it a night. This situation was a new experience for her and she was very uncomfortable with being involved in the whole scenario.

Chapter 10

Although he had stayed up late painstakingly reviewing his notes, Matt was up early and ready to get out into the field as soon as he had breakfast and filled his thermos. It was Wednesday, he hoped to get a few cameras and sensors setup by Friday, then he would drive back to Moscow to check on his cabin, making a point to stop by the District Office to visit with Harvey Langston.

Focusing first on the site where the ranger had recently been attacked, Matt set up a couple of motion-activated cameras to record any movement of wildlife in the immediate area. One camera would record images in daylight the other set to record images at night with infrared. Aside from the cameras, he installed a network of sensors to record movement in and out of an established perimeter of the spot where he made castings of the unidentified prints. This would be the focus of his primary research and data collection. At least at this location, he had a known sighting, a documented attack, and tracks of wolves that he was able to identify and document. He recorded the site in his notebook as Site 1A.

While setting up his cameras and sensors Matt kept getting the feeling that there was movement in the woods around him. It sounded much too heavy to be squirrels or rabbits. However, it was distinctive enough to make him a bit nervous knowing that there was tangible evidence of wolves, exceptionally large and aggressive wolves, having been in the immediate area.

After mapping the placement of the cameras and sensors for Site 1A, Matt moved on to the next location. Given the lack of evidence suggesting wolf activity at any of the other locations he had scouted, he planned to establish his secondary monitoring sites, on either side of Site 1A, at some distance to account for territorial range. After setting up and mapping Sites 2A and 2B, he had a couple of cameras that he was able to set up along stream beds he felt would be likely watering holes for wildlife in the area.

By Thursday afternoon, Matt had completed the placement and mapping of the monitoring equipment. On the drive back to the inn, he stopped by Alex and Frankie's lodge.

"Good evening, Dr. Kershaw," Alex called out from the front porch. "It's good to see you again." Alex met Matt halfway up the front steps and shook his hand.

"Thank you. I was passing nearby and I wanted to stop to let you know that I've placed some monitoring equipment along the northern perimeter of the valley. Also, I'll be leaving tomorrow morning to go back home for the weekend."

"Please come inside, if you have time."

"Yes, please come in," Frankie repeated, as she stepped out onto the front porch.

"Thank you, but I need to get back to the inn. I want to pack and clean up a bit before dinner. I just stopped by to see if either of you needed anything from the city while I'm going there."

"That is very kind and considerate of you to think of us. I can't think of anything off hand that I need. What about you Frankie?"

"Nothing that comes to mind."

"Well, if you think of anything, just call me at the inn before I leave in the morning. I should be on the road by eight. I should be returning by Sunday afternoon."

"Take care and have a safe trip," Frankie called out as Matt was backing out and waving good-bye.

* * *

Alex gave Frankie a serious glare, "We need to locate the monitoring equipment and warn William to keep the betas out of those areas for the time being."

"I was hoping he would come in and give us a chance to probe a bit and find out where he had placed them, but I think I know where to look first. It would be helpful to know how many devices he put out. I'll take a run out tomorrow and see if I can spot any of his gear."

"Be careful, we do not want to be spotted on his cameras searching the area behind him."

* * *

"Dinner will be served in just a few minutes. Waiting on the rolls to bake," Freya said to Matt as he passed through the lounge, on his way up to his room.

"OK, I'll be right down. I want to take a shower and change. I'll be quick."

After dropping his gear, Matt took a quick shower and dressed for dinner. Before going downstairs, he gathered up his files and notes putting them into his briefcase. He didn't want to forget anything he intended to take with him and discuss with Harvey tomorrow.

"Ah, just in time," Freya said to Matt as he came down the stairs. She noticed that his hair was still wet from the shower.

"I'm going to miss your cooking the next couple of days," Matt said casually while taking his seat at the table.

"What do you mean by, *miss my cooking*?" Freya responded with a puzzled look.

"I'll be leaving in the morning for a couple of days. I need to go check on my cabin and meet with Harvey to update him on my progress. I hope to be back early Sunday afternoon."

"I'll miss your company. The inn will seem lonely in your absence." Freya remarked with a smile and wink at Matt.

"To tell you the truth I almost hate to leave even for a couple of days. I feel very relaxed and at home here. You make me feel as comfortable as if this were my home away from home. I sincerely appreciate your hospitality."

"Thank you, but it's the way my mother taught me to treat our guest."

"If there's anything you would like for me to pick up for you, while I'm in the city, please make a list for me. I'll be more than happy to gather up whatever you want."

"I do need a few spices if you don't mind. I'll have a list before you leave in the morning."

Finishing his meal Matt sat for a short time talking with Freya. The conversation centered on small talk about childhood experiences and the similarities of their growing up under the influence of Native American teachings and folklore. After some time, Matt excused himself to go up to his room to finish packing before going to bed.

* * *

The next morning Matt was up early and loaded his jeep before taking the time to eat breakfast. *'Man I'm going to miss this for sure,'* He thought to himself. The smell of Freya cooking breakfast and coffee brewing transported him back in time to summer mornings at grandmother's house. After leaving home for college, he rarely had the opportunity to enjoy the early morning wake-up call filled with fond memories.

"Here is my shopping list," Freya said handing Matt a piece of paper. "Oh, Frankie called early this morning and asked if you could pick up a couple of boxes of twelve-gauge double-ought buckshot for her."

"It'll be my pleasure," Matt replied, putting Freya's list in his pocket. As he drove away, he noticed Freya standing on the front porch of the inn watching and waving goodbye to him.

On the road leading out of the valley, Matt kept thinking to himself, how peaceful and unaffected the valley was by the trappings of modern civilization. *'I've not even left the valley and I'm already getting homesick to return. How strange is that?'*

Chapter 11

Shortly after Matt reached the main highway headed south, his cell phone picked up a signal strong enough for him to make a call to Harvey Langston.

"Good morning Forest Service, this is Janice speaking."

"Good morning Janice, this is Matthew Kershaw, I was hoping to talk to Harvey; is he in?"

"Oh, good morning Dr. Kershaw; Yes, Harvey is here. Just a moment, let me transfer you to his office."

"Harvey I have Dr. Kershaw on the phone wanting to speak with you."

"Sure! Sure! Transfer him to this line."

"Good morning Matt, how are things going up there?" Harvey said picking up the incoming call from Matt.

"Great. I'm coming down to Moscow for a couple of days. I was hoping I could stop and visit with you for a few minutes but I didn't want to drive out that direction if you were not going to be available."

"Sure; what time will you be here?"

"I should be at your office around eleven o'clock this morning if you're available."

"Yes, of course. I'll be in my office waiting for you."

"Thanks," Matt said before hanging up the phone.

Matt was eager to talk to Harvey hoping that Harvey could provide additional background information on the people identified in the reports he provided on the encounters with wolves in Misty Hollow.

* * *

"Good morning Janice."

"It's a pleasure to see you again Dr. Kershaw." Janice moved from behind her desk to meet Matt in the middle of the room. "Harvey is expecting you," she said gesturing toward Harvey's office.

"Thank you."

"Matt! I didn't expect you to come down out of the wilderness this soon. Would you care for a cup of coffee? I think Kayla just made a fresh pot."

"Yes, thank you."

While Harvey stepped out to get their coffee, Matt pulled out his notebook and a folder containing the various reports Harvey had given him during his previous visit.

"Here you are," Harvey said, setting the coffee on the table next to Matt. "So, what's so urgent? What is it you need?"

"Quite frankly Harvey, I'm in a bit of a quandary with the nature of the investigation."

"What do you mean?"

Matt got up and closed the outer door to Harvey's office, "Tell me what you know about the wargs?"

Harvey sat back in his chair trying to assess how much Matt knew at this point. "The only time I've heard that term is from old tales my grandfather used to tell us when I was growing up; wargs are just creatures of myth and legend within the valley."

"Do these look like myths and legends," Matt said sternly as he took a couple of castings out of a box and placed them on Harvey's desk in front of him.

Harvey leaned forward to examine the castings, "Where did you get these?"

"Those castings are from tracks left by the animals which attacked Ranger Holmes," Matt replied.

Harvey paused from his examination and looked up at Matt.

"From my preliminary scouting of Misty Hollow I haven't found any evidence that indicates there's a wolf population present *in* the valley. However, I found a few tracks in the area where Ranger Holmes reported the attack. The tracks indicated there were maybe three or four wolves in the immediate area at the time he was attacked. After several days scouting the area, and putting out monitoring devices, I've yet to see or hear a wolf from anywhere within in the valley. Additionally, there doesn't appear to be a predation management issue." After a momentary pause, he continued, "The absence of a dense population of wolves leads me to believe a rabies infected wolf may be responsible for the encounters. However, the reports don't indicate if any of the people identified in the reports tested positive for rabies or any other diseases. Dr. Bertram tells me, there's never been any cases of rabies reported in the valley."

"Well normally, rabies will not begin to manifest itself until about two weeks after someone has been bitten," Harvey interjected. "Besides, as a precaution, people are automatically treated for rabies anytime they've been bitten and the animal's head is not available to confirm if it was indeed rabid," he concluded.

Matt paced in front of Harvey's desk, "Yes, but there's no indication found in any of the other reports you give me, of any viral infections whatsoever. Oddly enough, Ranger Holmes developed some form of infection within forty-eight hours after his attack. By the way, how is Ranger Holmes doing?"

"He is doing better. He is back at home on convalescence leave and hopefully he will be back to work in a week or so."

"Good to hear."

"So Matt, what is it you need from me?" Harvey asks.

"These prints appear to be lupine, but their size is much too large for any of the wolves indigenous to Idaho." Pointing to the mystery print Matt continued. "This animal is a complete unknown at this point, but I believe I caught a glimpse of it a couple of days ago."

Harvey shot a gaze at Matt, "What did you see?"

"I'm not sure exactly. It was dusky and hazy and the animal was too far away to make out any recognizable details. But I'm afraid your initial concerns of a threat to the valley may be warranted."

"What do you mean?"

"Harvey, these animals, whatever they are, don't appear to be coming into the valley to hunt and feed on the livestock; they are coming down into the valley to hunt and kill *people*."

Harvey sat back in his chair again and stared at Matt. "No, that can't be?"

"I'm not a hundred percent sure, but all indications are pointing in that direction. Ranger Holmes happened to be in the wrong place at the wrong time. Wolves don't ordinarily behave like this and I believe these animals may be suffering from some form of the disease, which is causing them to be overly aggressive. The other thing concerning me is; for a lone wolf to become aggressive as a result of a disease is not unusual, but the evidence suggests to me, this pack may be a rogue pack."

"Rogue pack? I've never heard of that."

"Unless I can identify a disease present in the pack, I'm inclined to conclude, the pack has somehow gone rogue and is focused on attacking people. I need to find out if any of the people in these reports developed any viral infections subsequent to their encounter. We may be dealing with one or more wolves infected with a virus other than rabies, such as a strain of distemper or parvovirus, which could be prompting the attacks by a single lone wolf or a small pack. I was hoping to contact the people identified in the reports to conduct follow-up interviews."

Harvey paused briefly, "I tell you what, leave that task to me and I'll have Janice and Kayla run this down for you. No need for you to waste your valuable time doing interviews they can take care of for you. Besides, it might not do for the people in the reports to get inquiries from someone outside the Forest Service office. Leave it with me, and I'll pass along anything we come up with as soon as possible."

There was something about Harvey's response and insistence on conducting the interviews through his office, which struck

Matt a bit odd. Nevertheless, he concluded that Harvey was right, in that, it was work better suited for his office to handle. "Ok, thanks, I appreciate your help on this," Matt acknowledged.

"What else can I help you with?" Harvey offered.

"At the moment, that is it." Matt was careful to pack up all of the cast and notes, not leaving anything behind.

"When are you headed back up to Graymere?"

"Just stopping in to check on my cabin, do some laundry, and pick up a few supplies. I'll be headed back Sunday Morning."

"Well, take care and I hope you have a safe trip back to the valley. I will see you in a couple of weeks or so." Harvey followed Matt out the front door of the building and waved as Matt drove away.

* * *

"Dr. Kershaw, what a surprise. I didn't expect you for another week or two." Sarah said, greeting Matt at the door.

"I'm sorry Sarah, I should have called to let you know I was coming in, but I got distracted and I simply didn't think about calling you."

"Not to worry. The house is in order, and it's been rather quiet around here."

"Thanks. I needed to come to the city to meet with Harvey at the Forest Service and while I was in the area I thought I would spend a day doing my laundry, grab a few things, and pick up some supplies. I'll be leaving out early Sunday morning. I hope I am not screwing up your weekend."

"No, not at all," she assured him. "I've been enjoying the peace and quiet; it has been great to relax and finally get to bury my face in a couple of novels I've wanted to read."

"I need to go into town later to pick up a few things. If you like, you can come along with me and I'll treat you for dinner."

"Cool! Do you have any place in mind?"

"Not particularly," Matt said passively, "You choose the place and it'll be my treat. Just let me get some laundry started and clean up a bit, then I'll be ready to go whenever you are."

Although Matt was in his own home, he felt strangely uncomfortable and restless. The sudden convenience of simple things around him such as lights, the air conditioning, washer and dryer, microwave, television, internet, made him feel as if he was going through culture shock. He tried to busy himself with putting his clothes in the wash, pulling out clothes to pack along with some other things he wanted to take back with him. All the while, he felt a strange longing to hurry back to Graymere.

"I'm ready when you are Dr. Kershaw."

"On my way,"

As Matt was getting into his jeep, he noticed Sarah locking the door behind her. For some reason this captured Matt's attention, reflecting back over the last week, he didn't recall ever encountering any locked doors.

"So, where did you decide we shall dine this evening, my dear Sarah?" Matt asks in a jovial manner.

"There's a new Turkish, or Mediterranean place on this side of town. I don't know where else you wanted to go, but I thought that might be a bit different. Besides, I've been wanting to check it out."

"Sounds interesting, just point the way."

Sarah navigated their way to the restaurant, a quaint little place that appeared to be family owned with a pleasing atmosphere. The hostess greeted them and ushered them to a table. As Matt and Sarah took their seats, the hostess recited the daily special and suggested a wine.

"Yes, wine sounds good," Matt said, looking up at Sarah for confirmation that she wanted wine. Sarah nodded before turning her attention to the menu.

After ordering their dinner, Sarah quarried Matt with anticipation, "So, Dr. Kershaw, have you found your cryptid yet?"

Matt smiled at Sarah's excitement. "Not yet. But…" Matt leaned over the table toward Sarah, "I think that I might be on to something a bit unusual," he whispered.

Sarah leaned in and whispered, "Well! Go on! Don't stop there and just leave me hanging."

Matt held up his hand, "Ok, calm down, it's nothing conclusive. I just came across some tracks, unlike anything I've ever seen before. They were all around the site where a forest ranger was recently attacked. What he described doesn't fit the description of any animal, which I'm familiar with in this region."

"Wow! Maybe you're onto a cryptid; you think?"

"There's not enough tangible evidence to say for sure," Matt replied before he sat back to resume their conversation in a normal tone of voice.

"Well, I hope you are able to find your cryptid."

By the time they finished their meal, Matt noticed it was too late to go shopping. Their conversation had gone on longer than he had realized, so they headed back to the house for the evening.

After putting his clothes into the dryer, Matt decided to call it a night and get up early the next morning to get all of his errands done and pack for his return trip to Graymere.

"I'm going to turn in, Sarah. I'll see you in the morning."

"OK, and thanks again for dinner."

"My pleasure, I appreciate you taking care of the place while I'm in the field."

"Would it bother you if I watch a movie? I'll keep the sound down."

"Not at all, Good night Sarah."

"Good night Dr. Kershaw."

Chapter 12

The next morning Matt was up early. He prepared breakfast before heading to town. Sarah was just getting up when he was about to walk out the front door.

"I should be back by mid-afternoon," Matt told Sarah. "Do you want anything from town while I'm going that way?"

"No, I'm good," Sarah responded sitting down at the breakfast nook with a cup of coffee."

"I made breakfast. It's in the covered plate in the oven to stay warm."

"Thanks," Sarah acknowledged still wiping the sleep out of her eyes.

By noon, Matt had completed his shopping list and stopped for lunch at a local deli. While eating lunch, he pulled out the list Freya had given him. He would work on gathering those items after finishing lunch.

Matt's first stop was Buck's Outfitters, to pick up the shotgun shells for Frankie. He decided to pick up some cartridges for his rifle and revolver he planned to take back with him to Graymere. He usually carried them in the wilderness, but he didn't initially think he would need it on this outing, but *'better safe than sorry,'* he thought to himself.

Next, Matt stopped at the natural food store, where he frequently shopped for his groceries. They would have the spices

Freya requested. Among the extensive array of spices were many Matt never heard of before. In addition to the spices Freya listed, he decided to buy a selection of gourmet coffees. He also purchased a couple larger bags of the everyday blends the clerk recommended as very popular. On his way out of the store, he noticed a small family owned jewelry store, a couple of shops down from the grocery, and decided to stop in just to browse around.

* * *

"May I help you find anything, in particular, today?" The clerk behind the counter said to Matt.

"No thanks," he responded without looking up from the display case. "I'm just browsing for a possible thank you gift for someone. Not really sure what I'm looking for just yet."

"Is the gift for a male or female?"

"Female."

"Age?"

"I guess around mid-thirties."

"Does she favor earrings, rings, bracelets, or necklaces?"

"Well, I can't say. Come to think of it, I don't think I've seen her wear either of those items," Matt answered, lifting his gaze from the display case to acknowledge the clerk.

"Does she favor modern or traditional styles?"

"Traditional I think."

"How about a charm necklace or locket?"

Matt paused, "Yes that might be an option. I think she might like a locket."

The clerk showed Matt a variety of items, but he didn't see anything he could picture Freya wearing. After some discussion of the various items on display, the clerk was a bit stumped to come up with a suitable choice for Matt. Then it appeared as if an idea had come to her, "give me a minute, I may have just the thing you are looking for." A couple of minutes later she came back with a tray of estate jewelry. After setting the tray down on the counter, she selected a locket that was eighteen karat gold, beautifully carved with detailed design work around the outer portion, with a wolf prominently pictured on the front in raised relief, accented by intricate engraving. Opening up the locket there were two pictures that appeared to be very old still affixed on the inside frames. On the back was an inscription which appeared to be a short poem. The chain attached to the locket was also eighteen karat gold and of a unique pattern well matched to the design of the locket. Matt could picture this around Freya's neck. He felt an overwhelming impulse to purchase the locket for her.

"I'll take it," Matt said without taking his eyes off the locket.

"The owner is asking three-hundred dollars for the locket." The clerk offered, as a starting position in negotiating a final price.

Not taking his eyes off the locket, Matt didn't reply to the clerk's asking price. "Can you gift wrap it for me?" he asked, handing the clerk his credit card.

"Certainly. If you give me a few minutes, I'll have the Jeweler polish it and I'll wrap if for you."

"Thank you."

* * *

By the time Matt arrived back at the cabin, Sarah had just finished mowing the lawn and was putting the mower away. "Were you able to get all of your shopping done?" She asked.

"Yes, I did. The yard looks nice," he commented with a cheerful smile.

"Thanks, I like working outside and I love the smell of freshly mowed grass." Sarah closed her eyes and inhaled deeply.

"I brought a few things to cook for dinner if you weren't planning to go out this evening."

"No, no plans."

"OK, let me get my gear packed and loaded for an early morning departure, and then I'll start dinner."

"You don't have to do that on my account, I'm pretty self-sufficient."

"I don't mind; I promise no microwave dinner either." He said smiling.

Sarah smiled and went about putting away the mower and closing the shed. She was walking into the cabin when she bumped into Matt carrying out an armload of things to pack into his jeep. "Do you need a hand?"

"No, I got it."

"Well then, I'm going to shower and change before dinner," she told Matt.

* * *

Matt was in the kitchen chopping veggies when Sarah emerged from her room at the end of the hall. "Just chill for a bit, I'll have dinner ready in a few minutes. There's some white wine chilling in the wine cooler if you would like to pour up a couple of glasses."

"Can I help you with anything?" She offered as she walked toward the wine cooler.

"I got it. Just relax, I'm almost done."

Sarah sat at the breakfast bar sipping her wine watching Matt busy in the kitchen preparing dinner.

"I hope you like pasta." He said rhetorically. "An old girlfriend's mother, who was born and raised in Italy, taught me this recipe."

"Mmm, I love pasta. This is a first. I can't say I've ever seen a man actually cooking a meal before, other than scrambling some eggs and burning toast." Sarah jested.

Matt laughed, "Well, there are a few of us guys, who learned to cook and take care of ourselves. When you're single, you go through a transition from fast food, to TV dinners, and then eventually you get tired of eating pot pies and microwave dinners. Sooner or later you begin to learn to cook or starve."

After Matt had everything on the stove and waiting for the pasta to cook, he sat down at the table with Sarah. "Sarah, do you have any specific plans this summer, other than house-sitting for me?" He asked in a serious tone of voice.

She appeared puzzled, "I'm not sure what you mean. I had planned to go swimming with my friends and catch a movie or two; that kind of thing."

86

"While you are here house-sitting, do you have any specific plans to occupy your time aside for occasionally mowing the lawn or cleaning the house?" he mused.

"No, just chilling I guess. Reading some books. Why do you ask?"

"If you are interested, I would like you to do some research for me. I'll pay you for whatever time you spend doing it, in addition to what I'm paying you to house-sit."

"I guess so; sure. I can always use the extra money. I'm a starving college student. What do you want me to research?"

Turning to look at Sarah directly, Matt had a serious demeanor in his facial expression. "Can you keep secrets and not mention to *ANYONE* the information I share with you, or the data and information you gather from the research?"

"Yes, I'm good at keeping secrets. I don't even share my thoughts with my friends, not even Carol. I never got into the girly gossip, drama bit."

Matt walked over and pulled out a folder from his pack and opened it up in front of Sarah. "You see the sketch of the animal paw print?"

"Yes, what is it?" She asked studying the sketch from various angles.

"I'm not sure. I've never seen anything like it before. This is what I want you to research. Scan the internet and see if you can come up with *anything*, which closely resembles this print pattern." He hesitated to observe her reaction and wait for her response.

Sarah seemed to be studying the print intently. "Do you have anything with a bit more detail? What about the scale?" She asked, not lifting her gaze from the sketch.

"Hang a sec," Matt said. He went to his room and returned with a box he placed on the floor next to the table.

"What's that?"

Matt opened the box and pulled out the castings of the prints he made at the site of the ranger's attack. Sarah almost dropped her wine glass when she saw the castings. "This is incredible! Did you make these from the area where you're working?"

"Yes," Matt replied.

Sarah put the casting up next to her bare foot to compare the size. The casting appeared to be canine based on the front pad shape and arrangement. However, the toes extended a bit farther than a normal dog or wolf paw and there appeared to be a distinctive heel pattern. The overall length from the tip of the toes to heal was a bit longer than the length of her foot and somewhat wider.

"This is huge! What kind of animal would make this track? Is this what you were talking about over dinner last evening?"

Matt watched for a moment as Sarah marveled over the cast impressions before continuing his instructions. "I provided some pictures and notes in the file, detailing the ground conditions where I made the casts you're examining. I want you to take measurements, and do an analysis of the estimated size and weight of the animal that made these prints. In addition, I want you to research every source you can think find, to identify any prints similar to these. From the pad shape and pattern, it's almost certainly canine, but I want you to expand your search to include feline or possibly bear. See if you can narrow it down to a known species if possible."

"I can do that. Is that all?"

"Be cautious not to show the imprints or discuss this material with anyone. I can't stress strongly enough, the need to keep this information to ourselves. Also, there are six reports in the file folder that I want you to familiarize yourself with. Then, conduct a thorough internet research on any statistics you can find regarding wolf encounters with humans in the Pacific Northwest. Stratify the encounters as to either sightings or physical encounters. In particular, I am interested to find out how many of the encounters involved a physical attack. Note what the circumstances were in relationship to the attacks, and if any of the victims of any physical attacks, reported illnesses subsequent to the attack. If so, what were the nature of the illness and any details you can obtain?"

"Wow, sounds like I just got drafted as a research assistant," Sarah said with a confirming smile.

"Well, yes in a manner of speaking," Matt acknowledged. "Depending on the quality of your research, I'll see that you get course credit for an independent study block. Fair enough?"

"Ok, I can do this. It sounds very interesting."

"You have the rest of the evening to ask me questions related to the materials I gave you," Matt instructed. "After tomorrow morning I'll be somewhat incommunicado while I'm in the valley. I can't get cell phone coverage in the valley, but there's a land line at the inn where I'm staying and I'll try to call you every few days."

Matt left Sarah to review the contents of the folder and the castings while he finished cooking dinner. She appeared to be engrossed in the information contained in the file. In addition to photographs and field notes, Matt had provided some background information on wolf species and any known mutations. Time would tell if Sarah would turn out to be a good research assistant. Nevertheless, she was the only person he knew who was capable of doing the research, and whom he trusted to keep the information secret.

During dinner, Sarah divided her attention between eating and going over the contents of the file. Occasionally, she would pause to ask questions, jot down notes, and then resume eating and study the file. When it appeared that Sarah was finished eating Matt started clearing the table and loading the dishes in the dishwasher.

"Oh, I'm sorry," Sarah said. She suddenly realized she had virtually ignored Matt throughout dinner with the exception of the occasional question. "The dinner was very nice, I enjoyed it very much, but this stuff is so fascinating I got lost in reading it."

"No problem," Matt encouraged. "I wanted you to have time to review it before I leave tomorrow morning."

"Dr. Kershaw, from what I see here, and what you have asked me to research, you obviously think you are on to something unusual. May I ask what it might be?" Sarah inquired reverently.

"To be honest I'm not sure what, if anything. At this point, there seems to be evidence of an unknown animal existing in Misty Hollow which doesn't fit the description or habitual characteristics of any animal currently known to exist in the Pacific Northwest. It may turn out it's a known species of animal that's exhibiting unusual behavior due to habitat stress, or it could be a new species of animal previously unidentified or documented. It's hard to say at this point what it is."

"So, would you consider this to be a study of a cryptid?"

Matt smiled, "yes, I guess it would be at that."

"I won't let you down, Dr. Kershaw. I've always wanted to be involved in some sort of research like this. Thanks for letting me do this."

"I left a prepaid visa card in the folder for you to use to purchase office supplies, such as ink and paper for the printer, or anything you might need to purchase over the internet such as a subscription to databases and such. Here's a bit of cash as an advance for your time to do the research and I'll catch up with you when I come back down in two or three weeks."

Matt left Sarah to continue studying the file. He was confident in her work ethic, which she demonstrated in her academics, and he knew she would do a thorough job.

"I'll going to turn in now; I have an early wake-up call." He said, as he waved good night and walked toward his room.

"Good night Dr. Kershaw," Sarah responded.

Chapter 13

When the alarm clock went off at 5:30 a.m. Matt was already awake. He tried to be quiet while getting dressed so not to wake Sarah. He didn't bother to cook breakfast, preferring to grab something on the road. He had already packed the jeep and by 6:00 a.m., he was ready to leave. Depending on the traffic and barring any delays, he hoped to get back to Graymere by noon; early enough to unpack his gear and plan out his week. He could have left later that day, but for some reason, he was eager to get back to Graymere. In his mind, he wanted to believe he was eager to continue his research, but the reality was, he felt a very strange attraction to Graymere he couldn't explain. From the time he left Graymere Friday morning, he had an overwhelming sense of longing to return, making him restless and uncomfortable in his own home which persisted throughout the weekend.

After turning off the main highway onto the road leading to Graymere, Matt began to feel more relaxed the further he drove. This was a bit confusing to him, given he usually felt just the opposite when leaving home and going into the field. It was as if he was arriving home after being away, rather than the other way around. Arriving in Graymere and pulling up next to the Wolf's Lair, he began to feel warm and relaxed.

"Matthew, it's good to see you back," Freya called from the front porch, in a formal welcoming tone, as Matt got out of his jeep.

Matt waved to Freya with a huge smile. "It's good to be back, all of this driving wears me out."

"Would you like for me to help you unload some of those things?" Freya offered.

"No thanks, I can manage."

The last boxes Matt unloaded were the spices and coffees he had purchased for Freya. "Where should I put these?"

"Just put them on the counter," Freya said holding the kitchen door open.

Matt went back out to his jeep to get the other box without saying anything. When he returned Freya was busy unpacking the first box. "What's all of this?" she asked. She appeared to be as excited as a kid opening presents on Christmas morning.

"Well, I got the things you asked for, but I got carried away and picked up a few other items I thought you might like and probably didn't have easy access to. I also asked the clerk at the store to help me pick out a few gourmet coffees for you to try."

"Oh my goodness," Freya said aloud to herself while digging through the boxes. "How much do I owe you for all of this?"

"Nothing, it's my gift to you."

"No Matthew!" Freya responded, examining the selection of spices and coffees. "This is too much. I must pay you for these things."

"I won't have it. You have been very kind and it's the least I can do for you. It's my way of showing my gratitude for your hospitality since I arrived here."

"Oh, Matthew I don't know how to thank you, this is wonderful," Freya said picking up the various packages to smell the different coffee blends.

"You're welcome, and it's truly my pleasure. Now, if you'll excuse me, I'll go unpack and do a bit of work before dinnertime.

"Certainly; Dinner will be at seven as usual. I'll put on some fresh coffee and I'll bring a cup up to you when it's finished brewing."

"That would be nice, thank you."

* * *

Freya knocked on Matt's door. "I brought you coffee and a sandwich," she announced.

"Thank you," he said taking the tray from her.

"I brewed some of the new coffee you brought. It smells wonderful don't you think?"

Matt took a whiff of the coffee, "Umm, I love the smell of freshly brewed coffee."

"It'll just be the two of us for dinner this evening," Freya said stepping out of the room and pulling the door closed.

"Freya," Matt called out before she had closed the door, "could you do me a big favor?"

"Sure, what is it?"

"Could you call Frankie to let her know that I brought her the shotgun shells she asked for and that I'll be out that direction in the morning and drop them off to her?"

"Certainly."

"Ok, thanks again for the coffee."

* * *

That evening Matt and Freya engaged in small talk during dinner. Freya was curious about the city and the university where Matt taught. Matt inquired about the local community and its people. The conversation went back and forth for some time before they cleared the table and put the dishes away.

"Oh, I forgot to tell you, I called Frankie to pass along your message. She said they would be up early and you could stop by anytime you are in the area."

"Thanks, I appreciate you doing that for me."

"My pleasure."

Matt helped Freya clear the table and put away the dishes. Afterward, they went into the lobby near the fireplace to enjoy an after dinner cup of tea.

"How much longer do you think you will be staying to complete your work?" Freya asked.

"Maybe a week or two to finish my investigation, then maybe two or three weeks surveying the wilderness area surrounding the valley."

"I'm going to miss your company when you leave," she said sincerely.

Matt sipped his tea, "Likewise." He took another sip then suddenly sat his cup down. "Oh, I almost forgot. I have something for you I found in the city yesterday. I'll be right back." He excused himself to go up to his room to retrieve the locket he bought for Freya. He eagerly returned a moment later, "I must apologize ahead of time because this may seem a bit inappropriate."

"What is it?" She asked with reservation.

"I debated with myself whether to get this for you…" he hesitated.

"Matthew, what are you talking about?" She asked, growing anxious.

He held the small box in his hand, "Well, I saw this in an estate collection and when I picked it up, it made me think of you. Trust me, this isn't the sort of thing I would normally do, but when I saw it, I had a strange compulsion to get it for you. I beg your forgiveness before I show it to you." Matt was blushing with embarrassment, anticipating Freya would think he was being brash with the gift he was about to give her.

"What on earth are you talking about?" Freya huffed with frustration in her voice.

Matt held out his hand with the small gift-wrapped box and handed it to Freya.

"Matthew!" She said taking the small package and sitting back in her seat, hesitating before opening the package.

"Well, open it," he urged.

Freya looked up at Matt, observing the look of sincerity in his face. She was a bit reserved in accepting a gift from someone she barely knew, even more so after he had gifted her with the spices and coffees earlier. She paused briefly to judge the motives behind his generosity. "Matthew, I can't accept this. You are very generous, but I don't know you well enough to accept such a gift...."

"Open it first," Matthew interrupted, "I assure you, I don't have any ulterior motives. This is simply one of those odd situations where you see something which reminds you of someone and you are compelled to get it for them. Please..." he encouraged.

Freya tore away the gift-wrap to reveal a small velvet bag containing a piece of jewelry. However, she was not prepared for what she saw when she opened it and removed the locket. "OH MY GOD!" she gasped. Her face demonstrated absolute shock, bordering on fear. She clasped her hand over her mouth, speechless.

Freya's response startled Matt, for a moment, he thought she was having a heart attack. "What's the matter? Are you alright?"

Freya started shaking and huge tears started to flow from her eyes as she examined the locket. When she opened the locket and saw the pictures inside, her hand went to her mouth again and she started bawling uncontrollably. "MATTHEW!" She stammered to say something, but couldn't stop crying to catch her breath to talk.

Matt tried to apologize, "I'm sorry Freya. I didn't mean to upset you. But when I saw that locket, it made me think of you and I was compelled to get it. I'm sorry to upset you, please," Matt tried to console her, watching her grip the locket in her fist and holding it tight against her chest.

Freya gestured with her hand for Matt to stop apologizing while she tried to catch her breath to speak.

Matt brought a tissue box from one of the nearby tables and handed it to Freya. Handing her some water, he tried to apologize again. "Please, I'm sorry. I didn't mean to upset you. I'll take it back, please don't cry; please don't be mad or upset, please," he pleaded.

Finally, she was able to regain some composure and dry her face. "I'm sorry Matthew..."

"No, no, no..." Matt interjected. "It's my fault; I shouldn't have given myself permission to be so forward..."

"Please Matthew, let me finish," She said, putting her hand on his. "It's not you… Where did you find this locket?" she asked.

"I was browsing a jewelry store trying to find a small gift for you to express my appreciation for your hospitality. On a whim, the clerk showed me a selection of estate jewelry. In the collection was this locket. For some reason when I picked it up, your face instantly came to my mind and I felt compelled to get it for you."

"I'm sorry for my outburst. But, *this very locket* belonged to my grandmother. The pictures inside are of my grandfather and my mother." She held up the locket for Matt to see the pictures. "The locket was lost, along with a few other personal items, after a group of workers came through here years ago, when I was just a little girl. My grandmother cried for days after the locket went missing. The poem on the back was composed by my grandfather, especially for my grandmother." Freya explained as she showed Matt the engraving on the back.

"Wow!" Now it was Matt's turn to be speechless.

"So, you see, it wasn't that you gave me such a nice or inappropriate gift; which by the way, is highly inappropriate, for which you are forgiven." Freya managed to muster a smile accompanied by a slight chuckle between the tears. "My outburst was from the sheer shock at the miracle this locket found its way back home and was placed in my hand. I can't believe it!"

Matt sat there with a blank look on his face. He was as shocked as Freya from the outcome of a series of coincidental events.

"Matthew, no words can describe how happy I am, to hold this locket in my hands again. I never, in a million years, would have imagined seeing it again. Of all my possessions left to me by my grandmother and mother, this item is the dearest thing to me in this world. My grandmother used to hold me in her lap and read me the poem and tell me the story of my grandfather writing it for her." Her eyes began to fill with tears again as she explained the story behind the locket.

"Well, I'm happy that you're happy, I guess," Matt stumbled trying to collect his composure.

Freya chuckled at Matt's response. She got up from her chair and went to him and gave him a long embrace that seemed to last forever. Matt was at a loss for how to respond without seeming to take advantage of Freya's emotional state. After a momentary pause, he returned her embrace with a gentle hug and a pat on the back. When she released him from the embrace, she smiled at Matt's innocent attempt to return her embrace. "Matthew, you are a true gentleman."

Matt just nodded in humble acknowledgment.

"I'm sorry, and I beg of you not to think me rude, but I need to go to my room and be alone if you don't mind," Freya said apologetically, holding the locket tightly to her chest.

"Not at all, I understand."

"Then I'll bid you good night and I thank you from the bottom of my heart. Your thoughtfulness brought this cherished heirloom back home to me." She gave Matt another hug and surprised him with a small kiss on his cheek.

"Good night," Matt replied, still somewhat taken aback by the surprising outcome from the turn of events associated with his seemingly innocent gift.

"Good night Matthew," Freya said walking up the stairs to her room.

* * *

Freya lay in bed clutching the locket, *'how very strange that the locket would find its way home in such an unlikely chain of coincidences,'* she thought to herself. *'Is there some meaning to the turn of events that this man would have come across the locket and associate the locket with me, AND to be compelled to bring it to me without any notion of its special meaning or family history?'*

Chapter 14

Matt again awoke to the smell of the coffee brewing. He was eager to check his cameras and monitoring devices, anxious to see if any of them had recorded any wolf activity over the weekend. Just as he finished loading his gear into his jeep, Freya announced breakfast was on the table. He sat down to enjoy Freya's cooking and fresh coffee before heading out to the field.

"I see you are getting an early start today."

"Yes, I've got a lot of ground to cover today,"

After he finished eating Matt sat for a few moments talking with Freya. He noticed she was wearing the locket he had given her, but didn't make mention of it. He didn't want to make her feel uncomfortable or obligated in any way. Looking at his watch, he noticed they'd been chatting longer than he realized. "Oh me, I need to get on the road. Thank you for a wonderful meal as usual."

"You're welcome, as usual," she replied with a wink.

* * *

When Matt pulled up to the Lodge, Alex and Frankie were in the yard mending a section of fence. He was excited to see Frankie, although he had only been away for a couple of days.

"Good morning Dr. Kershaw," Alex shouted from across the yard.

Without saying anything, Frankie put her hand up to her brow to shade the morning sun from her eyes to gaze across the yard toward Matt.

"Good morning," Matt shouted back, waving to both of them. "I brought Frankie her ammunition she asked for." He walked to the back of the jeep and opened the back to get the case of shotgun shells.

Frankie walked over to jeep. "Oh, thank you very much. How much do I owe you for this," She asked.

"You don't owe me anything, with my compliments to you and Alex for your generous help and hospitality." Matt handed Frankie the case of shells. "It's a bit heavy," he warned, as she felt the weight of the case.

"Thank you very much." She took the box and tucked it under her arm, letting it rest on her hip. "What are your plans for today?" She asked.

"I need to go check my cameras and monitors to see if they recorded any activity over the weekend."

"Would you mind if I tagged along?"

"Not at all," Matt said with a shy smile. "But, I don't want to take you away from your work. Besides, you may find it a bit boring."

"Still, I'd like to come along with you, if you don't mind. Give me a few minutes to change and get my pack."

"She seems to be very interested in your work," Alex commented, watching Frankie rush up the steps and into the lodge, skipping every other step. "We don't get much company around here and she doesn't have any friends to spend time with. I'm sorry if she's getting in your way."

"Not at all, I welcome her company," Matt responded without hesitation. "I don't usually have anyone with me when I'm in the field. Occasionally, I'll take students involved in a field study out to the field, but then, that's more of an outdoor classroom setting. Besides, later this week I plan to trek up into the wilderness, north of the valley. Having Frankie as a guide would be appreciated."

"I'm sure she would enjoy that very much. She's in her element when she's backpacking in the mountains."

"Ok, I'm ready," Frankie announced, bouncing down the stairs, backpack and shotgun in hand.

"Be careful," Alex said with a more serious tone directed at Frankie.

* * *

Arriving at site 1A, Matt got his gear out and plugged into the monitoring devices to download the stored data. While getting the gear set up he observed Frankie loading her shotgun and diligently standing guard. It suddenly occurred to Matt, Frankie might be tagging along with him more as a bodyguard rather than from her personal interest in his work.

Watching Matt take a camera down from a tree mount, Frankie asked, "What's that?"

"A camera. I'm reviewing the frame sequence to see if it recorded any movement of wildlife through this area over the weekend."

"What do you mean by frame sequence?"

"I set the camera to take pictures if the sensor detected any movement in front of the camera. It records standard images during daylight and can pick up infrared images at night." Matt explained as he was reviewing the screen.

"Did you get anything?" She asked as she walked over and started looking over his shoulder.

"Yes," he said casually while scanning through the frames. He pointed to the screen as he advanced the frames, "Here you see a mule deer. Whoa! Did you see that!" Matt anxiously paused and backed up a couple of frames. "Something spooked her," he said to Frankie, slowly advancing the frames to observe the deer bolt out of the view of the camera. "What was that?"

"What did you see?" Frankie asked.

"I'm not sure; it was just on the edge of the field of view for the camera. It didn't capture a complete picture. Whatever it was, it was big and fast. You can make out part of a body in one or two frames." Matt looked over his shoulder in the general direction of where the animal would have crossed through the area. He didn't see any tracks in the underbrush.

"What does that mean?" Still looking over Matt's shoulder, Frankie strained to make out any detail in the single image. "I can't tell what it is."

"Once the camera is activated by a motion sensor it begins to snap an image every second until the sensor no longer detects movement. The image you are looking at was captured a couple of seconds after the deer bolted and the image is somewhat blurred. This indicates that the animal in that frame was moving quickly."

"So, it must have been something chasing the deer, maybe a dog or wolf?" Frankie suggested.

"Maybe, but I don't think so," Matt countered. "The deer bolted off into this direction, and the second animal was moving in that direction." He continued to scan the camera for additional images. Other than an occasional bird, squirrel, or rabbit, he didn't see anything that would suggest wolves were prowling the area. After downloading the images to his laptop, he reset the camera and began to download data from the other instruments.

"What's that gadget?" Frankie asked inquisitively.

"This is an instrument we use in our field research at the university. It's a simple remote monitoring device that scans the area for signals from tracking collars plotting and recording the movement of any wolves wearing monitoring collars, while it's within the range of the monitor."

"Have you tagged any wolves in this area before?"

"No, the closest area we've tagged any wolves is about a hundred miles north of here. However, a wolf tagged elsewhere may migrate through this area. They have been known to migrate hundreds of miles."

After collecting the data and resetting the instruments, they loaded up and moved on to the next site. Matt again noticed Frankie being very vigilant in her scanning of the forest around where they stopped, always on alert.

Matt removed a camera from its mount and began scanning the frames when he heard Frankie whispering his name. "Matt!" She called out in a loud whisper. "Pssst! Matt!" She repeated.

Looking up he could she had the shotgun to her shoulder in a ready position, looking out past where he was working. He looked around to see if he could identify what she was looking at but saw nothing. "Yes Frankie, what's it?" He acknowledged as he resumed his work.

"Matt, come here, back to the jeep, NOW!" She said in an excited low voice.

Matt anxiously looked around him, "What is it?"

"Just drop what you are doing and come here now, PLEASE!" She insisted, in a more agitated tone of voice.

Matt got up and started making his way to the jeep. As he moved, he kept turning his head in the direction that Frankie was pointing her shotgun, but couldn't see anything moving nor could he hear anything.

"Get in and start the engine," Frankie instructed.

Matt did as she instructed, deciding to trust Frankie's instincts and she was not just being melodramatic. Matt was about to start the engine when Frankie bolted to the jeep, jumped in and closed the door just as four huge, strange looking wolves charged from the timber, seemingly out of nowhere.

"Let's get out of here!" she yelled.

"I need to take some pictures before they run off," Matt responded somewhat calmly. "This is what I came here for, to locate and document any wolf activity in the valley." He continued as he attempted to retrieve his pack from behind his seat to get his camera.

"No! There's no time!" Frankie insisted as she grabbed his arm. "They're not going to run away; we are. Now go!"

"These are very unusual wolves and I need to get some pictures," Matt insisted.

"Matt, these wargs are not coming out to pose for your camera. Now, please! Let's get out of here!"

Matt was a bit confused at Frankie's level of anxiety. After all, they were inside the vehicle and the wolves could not harm them, so he thought. Then looking up, he noticed that the wolves exhibited a very unusual posture and were moving to surround the vehicle. "This is very odd," he said out loud to himself.

Matt's attention immediately focused on the wolves' trying to make mental notes of their unusual features and appearance. Looking at the animals in front of him, he recalled the description that Ranger Holmes had related to him from his encounter. They were, indeed, much larger than a gray wolf and the one feature that stood out to Matt was the strange evil appearance in the wolves' facial expression. Familiar with the facial expressions exhibited by gray wolves, this was like nothing he had ever experienced before.

"Please, Matthew we have to get out of here! NOW!" Frankie screamed at him.

Matt decided to do as Frankie asked and put the jeep in gear and started to drive away.

"Faster," she urged, "FASTER!"

Matt sped off and after driving a couple of miles down the road, Matt suddenly pulled to a stop. "OK, what's going on?" He said to sternly.

Frankie did not respond preferring to stare out the window. Matt surmised that she was either too scared to answer or she was deliberately ignoring his inquiry.

Matt's frustration finally bellowed out, "First of all; locating, observing, and studying *any* wolf activity is why I'm here. I can't run the other way when I get a chance to observe a pack in the open. It's rare that you ever get to see a wolf in the wild. They are very elusive and wary of humans." He waited for some response from Frankie, but she remained quiet occasionally glancing up as he was talking.

Matt put the jeep in gear and drove further down the road. After driving a few miles, they came to an opening in the trees offering a few of an open meadow. Matt pulled over and switched off the engine. Getting out of the jeep with his backpack, he poured a cup of coffee in an effort to calm down and collect his thoughts. There was something about the whole situation that was making him very uneasy. It's unusual for wolves to take aggressive action when the pack had an opportunity to avoid contact completely. Even stranger was the pack's attempt to surround the vehicle, contrary to normal wolf behavior. A few moments later, Frankie got out and sat on the hood with her back leaning against the windshield, and her arms folded across her chest.

"Would you like some coffee? Matt offered.

Frankie glanced at him and nodded, clearly still shaken up by the encounter.

"What can you tell me about these wargs? I assume those were wargs; the ones Alex and Peter mentioned." Matt handed the coffee to Frankie. He assumed she knew what he was talking about, and he was hoping to force a response.

Frankie's gentle nod of her head and facial expression confirmed his suspicion that she knew more than what she had previously told him, but still she remained silent to his inquiry.

"When I asked you last week about any wolf activity in the valley, you told me there wasn't any. But, you carry a shotgun everywhere we go and you are constantly on alert to some perceived threat. Your actions alone contradict what you've told me." Matt paused to gauge Frankie's response. "The tracks we found last week, the sighting on the road, and the encounter today all suggest there's a definite presence of wolves, or wargs if you prefer, here in Misty Hollow. There *is* a pack prowling the valley; isn't there?"

Frankie stared into the distance and did not answer.

"The evidence suggests we are not dealing with any ordinary pack of wolves foraging for food. I believe we may be dealing with a rogue pack or maybe a new species altogether."

Frankie turned to Matt as if she wanted to say something, but stopped short of making any comment. After a brief pause, Frankie finally spoke up. "The wolves we just encountered are *wargs*; at least that's what we call them. Until recently, none of us, except a few of the elders, have ever seen one. We hear them howl from the ridge above, and on occasion, we will see a track, but no one has seen a warg in many years. However, recently there's been reported sightings, which have many of the elders in the valley on edge. I think that is why they wanted you to investigate. Harvey trusts you and the elders don't want other outsiders involved. So, everything we have told you is true relative to a history of any *wolf* presence in the valley. As far back as any of us can remember, there hasn't been any serious *wolf* problem."

Matt pressed for more answers, "What about the strange track we saw last week at the location where the ranger was attacked?"

"I don't know anything about that. That was the first time I've ever seen a print like that."

"And what about the animal, we vaguely got a glimpse of last week, when it crossed the road in front of us and scared the shit out of you?"

"I think that was an alpha…," She paused to collect her thoughts and choose her words. "None of us have ever seen one, but the old timers told us about them. They say, they are even larger than the rogue wargs and have the intelligence of a man. We grew up believing such tales were a kind of boogieman story. It might be the animal that made the strange print you found."

"Well, sooner or later I'll figure it out. And, I'm not leaving this valley until I do," Matt said, in a scolding tone of voice. Visibly angry, he threw his pack into the back of the jeep, got in, and started up the engine. As soon as Frankie got in and closed the door, he put the jeep in gear and drove away. They both sat in silence as Matt drove Frankie back to the lodge.

* * *

"Thank you for your help today," Matt said curtly, as they pulled up in front of the lodge. Without saying anything, Frankie got out of the jeep, collected her pack and shotgun, then walked up the steps to the lodge. Matt didn't take the time to say anything to Alex before backing out and driving away.

Alex heard the jeep pull up to the lodge. However, by the time he emerged onto the front porch, Frankie was storming up the steps and he saw Matt speeding away without her. "What happened?" Alex asked, realizing that something was amiss.

"We were jumped by a warg pack earlier." She answered angrily, brushing past Alex.

Alex pressed for an explanation, "AND?"

"He knows there's a rogue warg pack roaming the valley and he's pissed that I won't tell him everything I know about them. Although he didn't say so, I believe he's aware of the existence of the Alpha Prime."

"Has he seen an Alpha Prime?"

"No; but he's convinced that we know something about them and we're not telling him." Frankie marched over to the kitchen to make herself a cup of tea. "He's not stupid; he knows what he's looking for and can interpret the signs better than we can."

"Why did you let him leave to go out on his own?" Alex huffed as he followed Frankie into the lodge.

Frankie turned abruptly to face Alex. "I DIDN'T LET HIM DO ANYTHING," she barked. "He thinks I know more than what I've told him. Now he doesn't trust me and suspicious as to why I am tagging along with him. So, he ditched me and went off on his own."

"Where did the wargs jump you?"

"On the road near the big rock below Shady Bluff," she huffed.

"I'll call William and update him on your sighting and have him send out the Betas to keep an eye on Dr. Kershaw. Did he say where he was going next?"

"No, but I believe he'll be headed down to an area on the other side of the low water bridge on the upper fork of Beaver Creek," Frankie said before she disappeared into her room, slamming the door behind her.

* * *

Matt completed the scans and reset the equipment at the third monitoring site without incident. He was a bit edgy working alone and found himself wishing Frankie were there standing guard with her trusty shotgun. He was eager to go back to site 1B where they encountered the wargs but decided to wait until tomorrow before going back to retrieve his equipment. He

106

wanted to allow the wargs time to move out away from that area before he returned there alone. *'Tomorrow I should be able to study the tracks to determine the size of the wargs and from what direction they were traveling to and from,'* he thought to himself.

After packing up his gear, Matt headed back into Graymere to catch up on his field journal and type out his notes. Today's events shed new light on his investigation. Although his encounter was brief, it helped explain what was behind the reported encounters. However, he was very disappointed the people of Misty Hollow, and even his old friend Harvey were obviously withholding pertinent information related to the wargs and their presence in the area.

*   *   *

"This is Freya," she said answering the phone.

"Are you alone where you can talk freely?" Freya recognized the voice on the line as William Barret.

"Yes," she answered, feeling a bit apprehensive as to why William would be calling her.

"When Dr. Kershaw arrives back at the inn this afternoon, I need you to try and find out what he knows, or thinks he knows, regarding the Alpha Prime and the wargs. Don't mention the Alpha Prime directly and don't confirm anything, just ask open questions about his progress and listen."

"I understand," she responded, "anything else?"

"Yes. Dr. Bertram and Allison will dine with you and Dr. Kershaw this evening if that is all right with you?"

"That's fine," she answered hesitantly, unsure what was going on. "Dr. Bertram and Allison have dinner with me on a regular basis and they are always welcome."

"Good, Dr. Bertram will fill you in tomorrow after Dr. Kershaw goes out to the field. Have a good evening Freya." William said before hanging up the phone.

Chapter 15

Once back at the Wolf's Lair, Matt went straight up to his room to shower and change before going downstairs, to the dining room, to update the entries in his field journal and type out some notes on his laptop.

"You're back early today," Freya said when she stepped through the kitchen door and noticed Matt working at a table near the window.

"Yes, I surveyed my monitoring stations and now I need to update my journal."

"Are you making any progress?"

"Yes and no," Matt said, pausing from writing and looking up at Freya with a half-hearted smile.

"Well, OK," she responded, nodding her head in confused affirmation. "I guess that's a positive thing?" She said in jest, hoping to prompt Matt for further explanation.

"Yes, I guess so."

Freya carried a carafe of coffee over to top off Matt's coffee cup. "Dr. Bertram and Allison will be joining us for dinner this evening."

"Thanks," He acknowledged by lifting his cup in a toasting gesture before taking a sip.

"Is there anything I can get for you before I start preparing dinner?"

"Yes, if you don't mind I need to use the phone to call my research assistant. My cell phone doesn't get reception here."

Freya gestured toward the reception counter, "Sure, help yourself. You'll find it behind the counter. If it won't disturb you, I will finish cleaning up here before starting dinner."

"No problem, Thanks."

While Matt was calling Sarah, Freya busied herself with wiping down the tables in the dining area and filling shakers in an effort to be inconspicuous while trying to ease drop on Matt's phone conversation.

"Sarah?" Matt prompted when Sarah answered the phone.

"*Yes,*" she answered, "*Dr. Kershaw?*"

"Yes, it's me. Just calling to see if you found out anything about the animal paw impressions I left with you."

"*Well, I've been able to confirm it's almost certainly canine. However, I haven't been able to obtain an exact match in any of the databases I've accessed in either North America or Europe. Nevertheless, I'm still searching for references in Eastern Europe and Asia. So far, it appears to be a completely unknown species.*"

"Great, keep searching. We need to be definitive either way. I have another task for you."

"*Let me get my pad and pen..., Ok, shoot.*"

"I need you to search for any existing research or publications regarding rogue wolves. and or rogue wolf packs."

"*You mean like a 'lone wolf' phenomenon?*"

"Yes, anything along those lines." Matt paused searching for a way to explain the objective of the search. "Lone wolf' would suggest a single wolf ostracized from a pack, forced to search for a new pack to join, or otherwise left to survive on its own. I'm specifically looking for any references to packs of wolves going rogue and exhibiting rogue behavior as a pack characteristic. Look for anything that mentions packs being aggressive and killing, for the sake of killing, rather than for food. A point of reference may be something similar to the rogue elephant phenomenon which occurred in Kenya when they relocated young elephants into new areas without their parents."

"*Ok, I got you.*" Sarah acknowledged. "*What else?*"

"That's it for now. I'll be in touch in a couple of days to follow up with you."

"Ok, if I need to reach you can I call the number you're calling me from?"

"Yes. If I'm not here, just leave a message with Ms. Freya and I'll call you back. Have a good evening."

"Alright, I'll give you a shout if I find anything," Sarah said before hanging up the phone.

Matt went back to the table and resumed his work. Freya having heard bits and pieces of the phone conversation, worked her way back to the kitchen to prepare dinner. After finishing the updates to his notes, Matt took his coffee out to the front porch of the inn to relax and enjoy the fresh air. He could detect a slight bit of coolness in the breeze and the cloud pattern suggested there might be rain in the forecast. Looking up the street, Matt saw Dr. Bertram emerge onto his front porch, take a deep breath and stretch. When Matt noticed Dr. Bertram looking back in his direction he waved to him. Dr. Bertram waved back and began walking toward the inn to visit with Matt.

"Good afternoon Dr. Kershaw," the doctor said, as he approached the front porch of the Wolf's Lair.

"And to you Dr. Bertram," Matt said, getting up from his chair to greet the doctor.

"I'm out for my afternoon stroll if you'd care to accompany me," Dr. Bertram offered.

"Thank you, I think I will."

"So, how's your investigation coming along?"

"Well, this stage of the study is always a bit slow. You have to conduct a broad survey of the area to try to identify indicators of a wolf activity, to begin with. Then focus your research on the areas where you believe you will find activity."

"Have you found signs of any wolves in the valley, so far?"

"Yes, as a matter of fact, we came across a small pack this morning."

"We… I assume you were out with either Alex or Frankie?"

"Frankie was with me. I was checking some of my equipment at a monitoring site when a pack came upon us."

"A frightening experience I would imagine."

"Well not so much for me, but they scared the crap out of Frankie," Matt smiled and chuckled. "I'm used to seeing wolves in the wild, and as a general rule, they don't frighten me. I have a tremendous respect for the danger they pose if they are threatened or cornered. I try to keep a safe distance when I observe them." Matt paused and his expression denoted confusion, "However, there was something very unusual about the wolves we saw this morning."

"How so?"

"Beyond their enormous physical size and unusual general features. They gave me the willies."

Dr. Bertram's eyebrows peaked. "How many did you see? Were you able to observe them or take pictures?" he asked with heightened interest.

"We saw four of them before we left the area. Frankie was freaking out and I had to drive away before I could get her to calm down. We left in such a hurry I left some of my equipment laying on the ground. I'll have to go back tomorrow morning to finish resetting my monitors and collect my gear."

"How fortunate you got to see some wolves. And it sounds like you got to see them at a fairly close range."

"Yes indeed," Matt replied with a puzzled expression. "Unfortunately, to close for comfort in this case."

"I take it from your expression, this was not a normal situation." Dr. Bertram asked trying to appear interested in Matt's work, but not overly focused on extracting details.

Matt pondered the doctor's observation for a moment before answering. "Actually, the situation was extremely unusual. For the wolves to *approach* us at all, was totally unexpected. Normally, wolves will avoid human contact. Even in the wilderness, you have to spot them from a long way off to observe them. Once they catch wind of your scent or see you, they will relocate to another area, even abandoning their dens and moving their young in the process. This morning, the wolves had to have known we were in the area, long before we were aware of their presence. They made no attempt to avoid us. Instead, they

111

deliberately advanced on our location, maneuvered to surround us, then took an aggressive posture in preparation to attack us."

Dr. Bertram remained silent, allowing Matt to collect his thoughts and continue.

"Doc, has there always been an active wolf population in the valley?" In spite of what Matt had been told so far, he asked the question, assuming an affirmative answer, hoping to prompt Dr. Bertram into elaborating and sharing new insights.

"Well, I'm not sure I can say ALWAYS since we've only been back in Misty Hollow for the better part of five or six years. I grew up in the valley, but I left here when I went off to college. Except for the occasional visit, I lived and worked outside the valley most of my life."

"Ok, during the time you lived here, has there been an active wolf population?"

"Of the time that I lived in the valley, there has only been an occasional sighting of a wolf here and there. I don't recall ever hearing any mention of a pack. Oh, you hear of a farmer or homesteader killing a lone wolf on a rare occasion, when they suspect one may be threatening or killing their livestock."

"How often do you hear of a wolf being sighted or killed?" Matt began to inquire with a keen interest in the doctor's knowledge of the valley.

"Oh," the doctor paused, "maybe once a year or sometimes it might be two or more years before anyone mentions seeing a wolf."

"Have you noticed any increase in reported sightings over the last year or so?"

"Not that I can say for sure. Typically, a sighting or killing of a lone wolf is rare. Any news of a sighting or killing of a wolf would circulate rapidly through the valley. To be honest, until the incident with the forest ranger, I haven't heard of any sightings in more than two years."

"It's interesting that you made a reference to a 'lone wolf.' Do most of the sightings typically involve a single, lone wolf? Are you aware of any reports of a roaming pack?"

"As far as I'm aware, the sightings have always involved a single wolf."

"That's interesting," Matt said rhetorically as they continued to walk.

"What are you thinking? Do you think we have a wolf problem we should be concerned with?" Dr. Bertram asked, probing for insights to what information and evidence Matt had collected so far.

"I'm not really sure at this point in my investigation. I have determined a pack is active in the valley, at least in one area along the northern boundary. I believe we are dealing with a small pack of rogue wolves, maybe half dozen or so. From the evidence I have been able to gather so far, it appears these wolves are coming down from the wilderness area to hunt and attack people."

In his discussion with Dr. Bertram, Matt was cautious not to refer to wolves in his investigation as *wargs*. For one, he was not sure if the animals he saw were not wolves. Further, he didn't have enough information regarding the supposed *wargs*, to discuss them, if, in fact, the animals he saw were an unknown species.

Matt and Dr. Bertram's strolled led them to the water mill. Dr. Bertram gave Matt a short guided tour around the mill, explaining that the mill powers the town's electric generator and introduced him to Sam the caretaker.

"We are in need of some rain Dr. Bertram," Sam said.

"Yes, the valley could use some for sure."

"There's barely enough flow in the creek to keep the mill operating. If we don't get some rain soon, people will have to start cranking up their generators." Sam informed the doctor with a hint of selfish concern regarding the continued operation of the mill.

"I think we may be in for some wet weather over the next couple of days."

"I hope so," Sam said as he resumed his maintenance and cleaning of the mill.

113

Matt and Dr. Bertram began their return stroll back toward the inn. "Sam is a bit single minded with regards to that mill. His entire life revolves around the care and maintenance of that mill," Doctor Bertram commented.

"I don't see many people out and about the village. Where is everyone?" Matt asked Dr. Bertram.

"Most of the population of the valley live among the various homesteads. Very few people live here in Graymere itself. You have met most of them already. The others are older and focused on pursuing various arts and crafts they take to festivals a couple of times a year. A few put their crafts on sale at the mercantile thinking a flood of tourist will someday come through and buy their wares." Dr. Bertram chuckled at the prospects of tourist coming into the valley.

"I've not seen any children since I came here."

"Oh, we have plenty of children out among the homesteads. During the summer, they are all busy helping on the family farms and such. During the school terms, a bus makes the rounds to pick them up and bring them here to attend the one-room schoolhouse which also serves as the town hall." Dr. Bertram said, pointing to the town hall in front of the traffic circle.

Nearing the inn Matt looked at his watch realizing it was getting close to dinnertime. "I should be going in to put my things away and get ready for dinner."

"It's quite alright; they won't start without us," Dr. Bertram replied with a sly wink. "But I should be getting along as well, or Allison will have me by the ears."

"Thanks for the stroll and conversation," Matt said, waving to Dr. Bertram.

"Any time you need a sounding board, just knock on my door. I welcome the opportunity for a stroll accompanied by intellectual conversation."

Matt gathered up his journal and computer and took them up to his room. He barely had enough time to clean up and change clothes before Freya announced that it was time for dinner. Dr. Bertram and Allison arrived just as Matt was coming down the stairs.

"Good evening Mrs. Bertram." Matt greeted Allison.

"Good evening, Dr. Kershaw. I trust you are doing well and your investigation is progressing?"

"Yes, on both accounts, thank you."

"Howard tells me that you got to see some wolves today, how, exciting." Allison inquired as they were walking toward the dinner table.

"You saw wolves today?" Freya asked excitedly before Matt could answer.

"Yes, a small pack of four. Nothing overly exciting, but it does confirm the presence of a pack in the valley. I found tracks last week in the area where the ranger was attacked and today's sighting was in that same general area."

Sitting down for dinner, the conversation continued around Matt's findings since he had arrived in Graymere. He decided to answer their questions but was careful not to speculate or elaborate on the details. He shared with them a couple of highlights, such as the sighting on the road that spooked Frankie and the incident that morning which also upset her. Following dinner, they moved to the lounge area, near the fireplace, to have after dinner tea.

"Dr. Kershaw, now that you've determined there are wolves roaming the valley, what do you do next?" Allison asked.

"In general, I'll try to gather as much data as I can in order to determine the size of the pack, its range, and boundary, and if I'm lucky, I'll be able to tranquilize one and put a tracking collar on it. The other thing I need to determine is whether the pack poses an immediate threat to the community."

"What do you mean by the threat to the community?" asked Freya.

"Well, if the pack is operating at the farthest reaches of their boundary, then their presence would constitute an occasional patrolling of their boundary. In that case, they would not pose any real or lasting threat, only the occasional nuisance. However, if the pack is being pushed into the valley by habitat pressure and they intend to claim the valley as their primary hunting territory, then their presence will become a problem for the residents of the valley."

"Do you think they will start attacking the residents?" asked Allison.

"Generally, that is not a problem. Typically, wolves do not initiate aggressive attacks against humans, only their prey."

"But, if I heard you correctly before, when you were talking about the attack on the ranger and reports of previous encounters with humans, you indicated that Harvey was concerned that the wolves were being aggressive and attacking humans." Dr. Bertram interjected.

"In most cases, in which wolves have been known to attack humans, the animals were infected with rabies or some other disease. I will start testing for the presence of rabies if I can tranquilize any wolves. While fitting them with collars, I'll also take blood samples to test for any type of disease present in the pack that would indicate the potential for any overly aggressive behavior."

"Sounds like you still have your work cut out for you." Dr. Bertram commented.

"Yes," Matt responded. "And I'm afraid that work comes early in the morning and I must beg to be excused so that I can go to my room to catch some shut-eye."

"By all means," Dr. Bertram responded. "Allison and I must be getting back home as well."

After exchanging parting farewells, Matt retired to his room to get some sleep. He wanted to get to site 1B to finish resetting his monitoring devices and collect the gear he had left behind before it began to rain.

Chapter 16

Matt hurriedly ate breakfast, loaded his jeep and headed out to monitoring site 1B before the rain settled in. This morning, he decided to take along his rifle and his revolver, which he carried in a shoulder holster. With the encounter yesterday, that makes twice within three weeks, wolves in that general area appeared and demonstrated aggressive behavior. In both instances, it seemed as though the wolves had stalked humans before attacking. This type of behavior was both unusual and highly unpredictable and Matt was not about to take any chances until he had a better understanding of why these wolves seem to be behaving so uncharacteristically.

"Good morning Freya." Dr. Bertram greeted as he walked into the inn. "Am I too late for breakfast?"

"Good morning Doc." She said looking up from where she was sitting at the table. "You're just in time; I was about to start clearing the table. Please have a seat and help yourself; I'll pour you some coffee."

"Thank you, I was looking forward to having breakfast with you this morning."

"You are always welcome at my table, you know that," she said politely with a warm smile.

"I saw Dr. Kershaw pulling out. Did he give a hint as to where he might be working today?"

"He mentioned he was going back to the location where they saw the wargs yesterday morning. He was going to finish up there and collect the gear he had left behind. I saw him carry a rifle out with him this morning."

"May I use your phone for a moment?" Doc asked as he got up from the table and walked over to the counter.

"Alex, this is Doc Bertram. Just calling to let you know that Dr. Kershaw is headed back to the area where he and Frankie encountered the wargs yesterday morning."

"Ok, I'll call William and let him know. One of us will catch up to him and keep an eye on him."

"Alright, talk to you later," Dr. Bertram said, the hung up the phone and went back to the table to eat his breakfast.

"Is someone going to be out there with Dr. Kershaw?"

"Yes, Alex or Frankie will follow him out and William has asked a couple of betas to keep an eye on him from a distance."

Freya sat staring at her plate, picking at her food, and occasionally sipping from her coffee cup.

"Were you able to find out anything from him when he returned yesterday?" Doc asked.

"He was not very forthcoming with information when I asked him about his work. However, I overheard a bit of a telephone call he made to his research assistant. And, when he went for a walk with you, he left his journal on the table and I was able to look through it."

"What does he know about the Alpha Prime and the wargs?"

"From the notes in his journal and what I overheard, I believe he has some idea that the alpha prime may be out there and he is looking for them. He thinks he is investigating a possible new species of wolf. He is focusing on the warg pack as an *anomaly*. He refers to them as a possible *rogue pack* and I overheard him tell his research assistant on the phone, to search for information regarding any known instances of wolf packs going *rogue*."

"Interesting," Dr. Bertram acknowledged. "Did his notes mention anything about seeing the Alpha Prime?"

"No, but in his journal, he had sketches of the alpha's footprint. He also had notes from an interview with the ranger, who was involved in the attack a couple of weeks ago, which included a description of the alpha. From what I could gather from his conversation on the phone, I think she is researching to identify the alpha's footprint."

"I'll talk to William and let him know what you found out. In the meantime, continue trying to find out all you can on Dr. Kershaw's investigation. Thank you for a wonderful breakfast." Dr. Bertram said. "I'll check in with you later today or tomorrow."

* * *

After Matt stopped the jeep, he shut off the engine, and sat for a few moments, scanning the forest along the side of the road for any signs of movement before getting out. He began to feel a bit apprehensive about working alone after yesterday's encounter. He had just stepped around the front of his jeep, making his way toward where he had left his equipment laying on the ground when he heard a vehicle approaching. He paused to wait for the vehicle to pass. As the vehicle got closer, he could see it was Alex and Frankie.

Alex pulled up next to Matt's Jeep. "Good morning Dr. Kershaw. Looks like you are getting an early start this morning." Alex noticed Matt carrying his revolver in a shoulder holster.

"Yes, I'm afraid it's going to start raining any moment and I wanted to collect my gear before it got soaking wet. Moisture and electronics don't play well together," Matt joked.

"Would you like some help? We are on our way to the Sobel farm to purchase fresh meat. We can give you a hand if you like."

Without waiting for a response from either Matt or Alex, Frankie got out of the truck taking her shotgun with her. "I'll stay here with him while you go ahead to the Sobels." She said to Alex. "You can pick me up on your way back or I can hitch a ride back to the lodge with Matt."

Matt didn't object, and truth be known, he was a bit relieved they came along. "I'll give her a ride back to the lodge from here, I won't be long. Once I finish here I'm headed back to the inn to wait out the rain."

"As you like. I'll catch up with you guys later on then." Alex said before he drove away.

Matt turned to Frankie with a lighthearted smile, "I'm glad you decided to stay and keep an eye on me."

Sounding a bit snarky, Frankie asked, "Were you expecting trouble?" She gestured with her head and eyes to Matt's revolver.

Matt patted his revolver and winked at Frankie. "Just a precaution."

Stepping across the ditch, Matt entered the wooded area where he had left his equipment. He quickly took down his camera mount and collected the other devices, then loaded everything into the jeep. Frankie was not making any pretense about standing guard with her shotgun. As Matt was carrying the last load of gear to the jeep, he noticed a track in the soft sandy soil in the ditch. Pausing to examine the track, he noticed that it was the same print pattern of the mystery animal he took imprints just a few days ago. Before leaving the area, he took out his camera and snapped pictures of the prints.

"Why did you take down all of your monitoring equipment from this location? This is where you saw the wargs yesterday."

"Yes, but once they realized an area they have been bedding down has been compromised, they generally move. After it stops raining I'll search the area for fresh paw prints and I'll set out cameras."

"What about the other gadgets?"

"They are intended to pick up and track the movement of any wolf that had previously been tagged with a tracking collar. The monitors didn't detect any tracking collars among the pack working this area. It's fair to assume none of them wore tracking collars and it's a waste of time and effort to continue putting them out."

On their drive back to the lodge, a soft steady rain began falling. Passing near site 1A, where the attack on Ranger Holmes occurred, Matt noticed something in the road in front of them. When they got closer, he slowed and was able to make out three wargs standing across the road facing the vehicle.

"If I didn't know better, I'd say they were deliberately trying to block the road. How strange." Matt said aloud to himself.

He coasted to a stop about fifty yards from the wargs. Matt reached for his camera behind his seat.

Frankie was clutching her shotgun while trying to remain calm. "What are you doing?" she asked with tension in her voice.

"I'm going to take some pictures." Matt tried to snap a couple of shots through the windshield, but with the rain and windshield wipers swishing back and forth, he couldn't get a clear picture.

"Just drive through them, they'll move," Frankie suggested nervously.

Noticing that the wargs showed no sign of running away or advancing, he decided to get out of the jeep to try and get a clearer picture. Thinking the wargs were far enough away not to be an immediate threat, he opened the door of the jeep and stepped out and from behind his open jeep door, he began snapping pictures of the wargs in front of him.

"No Matthew, get back inside!"

Intently focused on taking pictures of the wargs in front of him, Matt didn't notice the others off the road to his left, stalking closer. Suddenly, he was startled as Frankie stepped out of the Jeep, held her hands up to her mouth, and let out a very loud howl, identical to a wolf alert and location howl. The wargs in front of them stopped, hunkered down, and began snarling. Matt could clearly see the hair on the wargs bristling as they bared their teeth.

"Matthew, get back into the jeep," Frankie shouted as she swung her shotgun over the hood of the jeep shooting a warg to his left, just as it leaped across the ditch toward Matt. She pumped another round into the chamber and shot a second warg following behind the other she just killed.

Matt was shocked at Frankie's sudden response and disoriented, as to what was happening. He'd been so focused on taking pictures of the wargs in front of him, he was unaware of what was going on around him. Before he could collect his wits and get back into the jeep, the three wargs in front of them began to close in. Frankie fired a shot over their heads hoping to scare them off, but they kept advancing. Suddenly, something large and heavy hit Matt hard from behind. The force of the impact slammed him up against the open door of the jeep, knocking the wind out of him. Matt immediately felt a sharp searing pain in his shoulder near the base of his neck.

"Matt!" Frankie screamed at the sight of an alpha sinking his fangs into Matt's neck and upper shoulder. She tried to swing her gun around, over the hood of the jeep to shoot the alpha, but couldn't get a clear shot. Then, out the corner of her eye, she saw the wargs charging from the front of the jeep. She turned and fired rapidly at all three, killing one and wounding the other two, which quickly turned and ran away. Meanwhile, the Alpha Prime was viciously trying to maul Matt, clawing at his head and chest, but the alpha couldn't get a good attack angle to go for the throat. Frankie was horrified as blood splatter flew everywhere.

Matt had fallen to the floorboard of the jeep, between the steering wheel and doorframe, partially shielding him from the alpha's attack. Attempting to fight back, Matt managed to pull his revolver and got off at least one shot wounding the alpha prime. Suddenly, something slammed into the alpha prime from behind, knocking it up against the open door of the jeep almost tearing the door off the hinges. Victor, a therian beta, who had heard Frankie's call, arrived just in time to pull the alpha off Matt. Immediately, Victor and the alpha took the fight to the side of the road.

Matt had, by now, slid out of the jeep and was lying in the mud, under the side of the jeep and the car door. He had blood and rain in his eyes, but could make out what appeared to be a man boldly fighting a wolf-like creature in a vicious animal brawl. By now, Frankie had reloaded and had moved around to the front of the jeep to get a better shot at the alpha. Taking a bead on the alpha prime, she nervously waited for an opportunity to shoot.

After a few tense moments of fighting, Victor and the alpha separated, squaring off, facing one another. Victor spread his arms and shoulders wide and bellowed out a very loud howl that sent a chill through Matt. Finally getting a clear shot, Frankie fired at the alpha prime, striking it in the shoulder and upper arm. The alpha turned and ran off into the forest.

"Matt!" Frankie screamed as she ran to where he was lying in a pool of blood on the muddy road. Matt was dazed and slipping into shock with lacerations to his head, face, arms, chest and a deep bite at the base of his neck.

"He's losing a lot of blood; we need to get him to Dr. Bertram fast," Victor said as he picked Matt up out of the road.

"I'll put him in the back and you drive. Does he have a first aid kit?" Victor asked.

Matt could hear them talking and pointed toward the pack in the back of the jeep. Although he was semi-conscious and had blood in his eye he could make out the figure of a man who appeared extremely hairy and had strange features. Matt assumed he was going into shock and was not seeing or thinking clearly.

After getting Matt loaded into the jeep, Frankie drove as fast as she could on the narrow road to Graymere. "How's he doing?" Frankie asked while trying to concentrate on the road.

"He is in bad shape, but I think he'll be alright once doc sews him up. I don't see any arteries ruptured; I used the bandages to slow the bleeding around the deeper wounds. But, he will have some serious scars to talk about."

"We're almost there."

Frankie started blowing the horn as soon as they pulled up in front of the clinic. Hearing the horn, Dr. Bertram came running out to see what was going on, followed closely by Allison.

"Oh my God," Dr. Bertram said aloud when he saw the damaged door and blood all over the jeep. Running to the vehicle, he saw Victor and Frankie pulling Matt out of the jeep, all three of them covered with blood and mud.

"My dear God!" Allison gasped, putting her hands up to her face in shock at the site horrific sight. "What happened?" She asked while holding the door open.

"We were attacked by a warg pack and Matthew was mauled by an alpha prime," Frankie answered on the verge of tears and trembling.

After they situated Matt on the examination table, Dr. Bertram ordered them out of the room as he and Allison began cutting away Matt's clothes.

By now, Freya came running into the clinic. She had heard the horn blowing when Frankie pulled into the village and stepped out onto her front porch just in time to see her and Victor carrying Matthew into the clinic. Even from that distance, she could see how bloodied they were. She was horrified at the sight of Victor and Frankie carrying Matt's limp and bloodied body into the clinic.

"How bad is he hurt? What happened?" Freya asked frantically while trying to make her way into the examination room.

Victor held her back, attempting to console her, "He'll be alright; Doc and Ms. Allison are looking after him."

"What happened" Freya repeated.

"I tried to tell him not to get out of the jeep," Frankie started to ramble, trembling and with tears streaming down her face.

"Victor, can you take everyone out of here. Please!" Dr. Bertram scolded. "And send someone for Keira, I need her right away!"

Just as Victor lead Frankie and Freya to the front porch, Peter came running across from his shop. "Peter, can you go get Keira? Quickly please, the doc needs her."

"Sure," Peter replied before turned on his heels and ran toward the apothecary shop.

Victor and Frankie were explaining to Freya what had happened when Peter returned with Keira. Victor ushered her inside without explanation.

"Peter can you stay with Freya and Frankie while I call William to let him know what has happened."

"Sure, thing." Peter was confused not knowing himself what had happened.

* * *

"Dr. Kershaw, this is Doc Bertram, can you hear me?"

Matt looked back at Dr. Bertram with glassy eyes and gently nodded his head in acknowledgment.

"You've been in an accident, but you'll be alright. We just need to clean and treat your wounds. You've lost a little blood, but nothing to worry about, you are in good hands."

Allison monitored Matt's vital signs and reported them to Doc.

Doc instructed Allison, "Start him on oxygen and IV with a unit of plasma; he's lost a fair amount of blood."

Doc tried to swab away the oozing blood as he poked and prodded Matt's wounds. "Dr. Kershaw, I'll be giving you a shot for pain and a mild sedative to help you relax while we clean your wounds and sew you up."

"Keira, I believe Dr. Kershaw has been infected with the virus. I need you and your mother to prepare a strong herbal mixture to counteract the effects of the virus."

"Do you think he was infected?"

"He has multiple bites and lacerations, his hair and clothes were soaked with drool; it's in his wounds, his eyes and face. He is most definitely infected." Dr. Bertram paused and looked into Keira's eyes, "he was mauled by an alpha prime."

"An alpha prime! Are you sure?"

"Yes, Victor pulled the alpha off of him."

"We haven't ever treated someone infected by an alpha prime before. I'm not actually sure what to expect; do you?" Keira said to Dr. Bertram.

"I'm not sure either. But, if we can't control the initial stage of the viral infection and keep his temperature under control, it will more than likely kill him. Particularly, with the amount of blood he's lost, he will be very weak."

Matt drifted off under the sedative while Dr. Bertram and Allison worked to clean his wounds and sew him up. Afterward, while Allison was dressing the wounds, Dr. Bertram stepped out onto the front porch to get some fresh air. Waiting for him there were Freya, Frankie, Peter, and Victor.

"Ok, we patched him up. There was no life-threatening wounds to worry about. However, he's lost a lot of blood and it took more than eighty stitches to sew him up. However, with the number and nature of the wounds, we have to guard against infection. Our immediate concern is his ability to handle the initial stage of the LTV infection."

"How bad is that?" Freya asked showing a great deal of concern.

"To be honest, we really don't know." Dr. Bertram said with a sigh of apprehension.

"What do you mean you don't know; others have gone through this before… yes?"

"Yes, but not after being bitten by an alpha prime. We'll know more in twenty-four to thirty-six hours. We'll keep him here tonight and you can check on him in the morning. In the meantime, I suggest everyone go home and get some rest."

"I called William and informed him of what happened," Victor told Dr. Bertram.

"Good, you should come inside and let me look you over and tell me what happened," he said to Victor. "Frankie, did you sustain any injuries?"

"No Doc," she replied. "None of them got that close to me; just scared the crap out of me." She was still trembling from fear and the adrenaline rush of the incident.

"Well then. All of you go on home and I'll call you when he wakes up. Peter would you take Dr. Kershaw's gear from his vehicle up to his room and then take his vehicle and clean it the best you can."

"Certainly Doc, I'll do it right away."

* * *

"Frankie, I'll give you a ride home if you like." Freya offered.

"If you don't mind I would like to go have a cup of tea and wash some of this blood off."

"Yes, for sure," Freya replied. "Come on over to the inn and I'll fix you up." Freya wrapped her arm around Frankie as they walked toward the inn. "First, I think I have some clothes you can change into; we are about the same size I think. You can shower and change out of those bloody things while I brew a fresh pot of tea."

Chapter 17

"I'll have to burn these," Frankie said when she entered the dining area where Freya was setting out the tea cups and pot of freshly brewed tea.

Freya pulled a trash bag from under the counter and held it open for Frankie to put the bloody clothes in. "I'll take care of it for you."

"Thank you."

"Have a seat, I'll be right back."

Freya took the bag with Frankie's bloody clothes to the back porch. When she returned, she handed Frankie a warm hand cloth for Frankie to wipe her hands then proceeded to serve the tea.

"Frankie, are you alright?" Freya asked.

"Yes, just scared the holy crap out of me that's all. Oh shit, I should have called Alex; he will be worried sick that I'm not at the lodge." She said getting up from the table to go find a telephone.

Freya reached out and touched Frankie's forearm, "It's ok, he knows what happened and you're alright. He came by while you were in the shower and he is over at the clinic checking on Dr. Kershaw." Freya gently tugged Frankie's wrist and pulled her back to the table. "He'll be back here after he checks in with Doc."

"How did he know? Who called him?"

"He said he drove back to the area where he let you out with Matthew. When you were not there, he thought you were on your way back to the lodge. Driving farther down the road, he came across the warg carcasses, blood everywhere, and spent shotgun casings all over the road. He realized that something bad must have happened. He drove by the lodge looking for you. When you were not there, he naturally assumed one or both of you were injured and must have driven to the clinic."

"They are getting bolder and more aggressive," Frankie said to Freya with fearful anxiety in her voice.

"Who?"

"The alphas and the rogues; they were hunting us," Frankie whispered. "The rogues deliberately set up a roadblock with intent to ambush us."

Freya sat back trying to judge if Frankie was talking nonsense or if what she was saying was an accurate observation.

* * *

Matt was still groggy from the sedative, but could vaguely make out voices in the next room.

"They were lucky," Dr. Bertram said to Alex.

"Dr. Kershaw doesn't look so lucky to me," Alex said, looking through the door at Matt.

"Well, it could have been a lot worse. Fortunately, Frankie and Victor were not injured."

"I went over to the inn and Freya had given Frankie some clothes and she was taking a shower."

"After you get her home and she has a chance to calm down, find out all the details of what happened. William is concerned with the presence of the wargs in the valley. He is beginning to think we may be dealing with a rogue pack and their aggressive behavior is alarming."

"Ok, I'll see what Frankie can tell us. I'll call you tomorrow Doc."

Dr. Bertram bid him farewell and stood on the porch as he watched Alex walk down the street to the inn.

Allison came out to the front porch with Dr. Bertram. "I think Dr. Kershaw is coming around. Should I give him another sedative?"

"No," Dr. Bertram replied. "I want to examine him further and check his responses while he's awake. Then we can sedate him before the pain starts to take hold again. We need to take his vitals every half hour. I'm concerned that the viral vector from the alpha will cause the transgenesis to be much more widespread throughout his whole body. If it's as extensive as I believe it might be, we will have to be very aggressive in trying to keep his temperature down and guard against dehydration. My biggest concern is his organs shutting down."

* * *

"Dr. Kershaw, can you hear me? Dr. Kershaw, this is Dr. Bertram, can you understand me?"

"Yes," Matt answered in slurred speech.

"How do you feel?"

"Feels like someone kicked the shit out of me. What happened? Where am I?"

"You are at my clinic in Graymere. You were in an accident. Do you remember what happened?"

"I was taking some pictures and I think a big warg attacked me." Suddenly, Matt's eyes searched the room frantically, "Where's Frankie?"

"Frankie is fine, she brought you here."

Matt tried to move but felt a great deal of pain from several areas of his body. "Holy Moses!" He moaned. "I must have been hit really hard." he grimaced as the pain seemed to wake him up a bit more.

"You're going to be sore and stiff for a few days," Dr. Bertram told him with a reassuring smile. "You suffered bites and lacerations to your head, neck and shoulder, your left arm, and your chest. You are lucky to be alive."

Matt laid back and tried to be still. "May I have some water? I'm dying of thirst."

"Sure, but sip a little at a time."

Dr. Bertram instructed as Allison held a cup up and placed a straw to Matt's lips.

"You lost some blood and I am giving you a unit of plasma, I'll give you something for pain and a sedative to help you rest. I'm concerned about a possible infection so we will be monitoring you closely throughout the night. Otherwise, try and get some rest."

"Ok," Matt replied as he closed his eyes and slowly drifted off to sleep.

"Go ahead and give him a morphine drip into his IV. I think we can take him off the oxygen for now." Dr. Bertram instructed Allison. "I'll check with Mrs. Moonjoy and Keira to see where they are at with the LTV treatment."

When Alex entered the inn, Frankie and Freya were sitting at a table having tea. Alex rushed over to Frankie and gave her a huge hug. "Are you alright little sister? How are you feeling?" Alex asked.

"I'm fine. I feel much better after I showered and got all the blood washed off, but I can still smell the blood." She said before she started to tear up again.

"Are you ready to go home and rest?"

"Yes, I'm ready."

Frankie gave Freya a hug. "Freya, thank you so much for everything."

"It was nothing. I'm just glad you're alright."

Alex gave Freya a hug and a kiss on the cheek. "Thanks for looking after Frankie."

"Frankie, your shotgun and pack are behind the counter."

"Thanks."

Freya stood by the window watching Alex and Frankie drive away. She couldn't wait for them to get out of site before she ran down the street to the clinic, to check on Matt. Allison looked out the window and saw Freya coming across from the inn. She met her at the door just as it began to rain heavily.

Recognizing Freya's apparent concern for Matt's condition, Allison gave her an update. "He's doing fine so far. We gave him something for the pain and he's sleeping at the moment."

"I know it's silly of me, but I'm so afraid for him," Freya whimpered then started to cry.

Allison tried to reassure her. "He is strong and he'll be fine, I'm sure."

"He will recover from the bites and cuts, but I'm afraid of what the LTV will do to him. Frankie said it was an alpha prime that attacked him and Victor said the LTV from the alpha would be a stronger strain than what he would have gotten from one of the rogues."

"Mrs. Moonjoy and Keira are working on an herbal treatment and we're monitoring him very closely. The next twenty-four to thirty-six hours will give us an indication of how well he can handle the initial viral infection. Once he clears that hurdle, the transgenesis will simply be a matter of time."

"What about afterward? How will he be physically affected by the virus, given it was an alpha that infected him?"

"I'm not sure we can answer that now. This is something new for all of us. As I said, only time will reveal the level of transmutation he will experience, if any at all." Allison said as she embraced Freya trying to comfort her.

"Can I see him?" Freya asked.

"Doc has him sedated and he will be out all night, but you can go in and see him if you like."

Freya pulled up a chair and sat next to Matt taking hold of his hand. The overall mood was made gloomier by the steady rain and occasional clap of thunder. She could not make herself leave Matt's side, remaining there all night resting her head on the bed next to him, not letting go of his hand.

Chapter 18

"Good morning," Allison said softly as she brought Freya a cup of fresh coffee.

Freya sat up pulling the blanket over her shoulders. "Oh goodness, it's morning," Freya said looking around the room. She took the coffee from Allison. "Thank you." Freya wiped the sleep out of her eyes. "How is he doing?"

"He is doing ok, but he is beginning to develop a fever. Doc has him on a strong antibiotic to help battle any infection from the wounds, however, it appears that the virus is beginning to take hold."

When Freya looked up at Allison, she could see tears forming in Freya's eyes. From the way she was clutching Matt's hand, Allison knew that Freya had developed feelings for Matt, but was fighting hard not to show it. "Why don't you go back to the inn and get some rest. I promise to call you if there's any change in his condition."

"I want to be here when he wakes up," Freya pleaded.

"Doc will let the sedative and morphine wear off and he should be waking up around noon. You can come back then to visit with him before doc sedates him again."

"Why is he sedating him?"

"He has several wounds that are deep wounds and over eighty stitches, Doc is not sure how he will respond to the initial stage of the viral infection and he doesn't want him thrashing around, ripping out the IV, or tearing open stitches when he slips in and out of delirium and hallucinations. He brings him out to be able to examine him and judge his condition, he wants to be able to talk to him and ask questions. Then he will sedate him just enough to keep him calm."

"I'll be back around noon then; can he eat anything, should I bring him breakfast or lunch?"

"Doc wants to keep him on IV and minimize any solid food in his system until the virus peaks. Go on home and I promise to call you when he wakes up."

Freya reluctantly went back to the inn to shower and rest. She didn't get any deep sleep during the night and was barely able to keep her eyes open. Listening to the sound of the rain falling on the roof, it wasn't long before she fell asleep.

* * *

"May I have some water," Matt asked opening his eyes and looking around the room.

"Sure thing," Dr. Bertram answered and motioned for Allison to give Matt a sip of water. "How are you feeling this morning?"

"I feel like I've been run over by a dump truck," Matt answered. He tried to sit up but found it difficult to move his arms or shoulders.

"Do you feel like getting out of bed?"

"Yes, I need to stretch a bit and go to the bathroom. How long have I been out?'

"You were brought in here yesterday morning. Allison will help you get up so you can go to the bathroom. Take it easy because you are still a bit groggy from the sedative and pain medication."

Matt started to get up on his own but found the pain and stiffness overwhelming. "Whoa!" He said, reaching out and grabbing Dr. Bertram's arm with his good arm.

"Allison, let's get him up and have him move around while he can. After he goes to the restroom, we need to get him cleaned up while he's able to get to the shower." Dr. Bertram instructed.

Dr. Bertram and Allison helped Matt out of bed and steadied him as he walked to the bathroom. "I'll pull the door closed;

when you are finished using the toilet, just knock on the door and I'll come help you into the walk-in tub. We need to get you cleaned up a bit." Allison told him.

Allison busied herself with changing out the bed and putting out materials to apply fresh dressings to Matt's wounds. When she heard him knock on the door, she helped him into the walk-in tub and shower unit. After washing the remaining dried blood out of his hair and carefully cleaning around the wounds, Allison dried him thoroughly before helping him into a set of hospital scrubs.

"How do you feel? Are you feeling light headed or weak?" Allison asked him before trying to get him back to his bed.

"I'm good," Matt responded as he struggled to stand up. "Feels like someone beat the crap out of me."

"Fairly close assessment I'd say," Allison replied in jest.

Matt was feeling tired and the pain was starting to resurface by the time Allison finished changing his dressings and reconnecting his IV. After checking his vitals, she noted that Matt's temperature had risen slightly, but his other vitals were still close to normal.

"Knock, Knock," Freya said as she peeked around the door into Matt's room.

Matt seemed to perk up a bit when he saw Freya at the door. "Good morning," He said motioning for her to come in.

"If you need me, just pull this cord and it will ring the bell," Allison told Matt. She finished fluffing the pillow behind his head then left the room to give Matt and Freya a few minutes alone.

Freya stood by Matt's side and squeezed his hand. "I wanted to bring you something to eat, but Doc wouldn't let me."

"Thanks, but I don't feel much like eating anything right now."

"Are you feeling? Any better?"

"I guess, they are keeping me pretty well doped up, so I'm not sure how much different I am today, from yesterday."

"Well, you look better than you did when they brought you in yesterday morning," Freya said as she started to cry.

135

"I'm OK; Nothing to cry about."

"You scared me half to death," she sobbed.

Listening to Freya and judging from her emotions, Matt realized she had developed feelings for him that weren't evident before now. It was also at that moment, he admitted to himself he had developed an emotional attraction to her as well.

"I think it looked worse than it really was," he said, trying to reassure her.

"No, it was bad! That thing almost killed you, and it would have if Victor hadn't been there!" She chided him before she broke down crying. "I'm sorry, I'm being silly." Freya sniffled as she tried to dry her face.

"What do you mean 'that thing', would have killed me; what are you talking about, and who is Victor?" Matt asked pointedly.

"Don't you remember what happened?"

"It's all a bit fuzzy, it happened so fast. I think one of those wolf creatures jumped me from behind slamming me into the door of the jeep. I hit my head on the doorframe and got the wind knocked out of me. I fell half in and half out of the jeep and I was being pinned to the floorboard by some big ass wolf that was trying its best to maul me. I remember thinking that the narrow space between the seat, doorframe, and steering wheel prevented the wolf from getting at me full force. Then something or someone tackled the wolf and knocked it off me. I recall seeing them in a brawl on the side of the road as I slid out of my jeep and fell onto the road before passing out. Next thing I remember is waking up here."

"I should let you get some rest. I'll come back later this afternoon to check on you."

Matt realized that Freya wanted to leave to collect herself and not to upset him. He was feeling tired and the pain was beginning to get worse, so he didn't argue for her to stay. "Ok, maybe they will let me have some of your roast beef and gravy," he said to her while trying to muster a reassuring smile.

Freya squeezed his hand, bent over, and kissed him on the forehead as she brushed the side of his face. "I'll be back in a little while."

Matt squeezed her hand tenderly and winked at her.

* * *

By that afternoon, Matt's temperature was steadily climbing and he appeared flush.

"How are you feeling?" Dr. Bertram asks while reviewing his vital signs.

"I'm beginning to feel like death warmed over. I think I'm coming down with a cold or flu on top of everything else. I have a headache, and I feel nauseous."

"I think we have avoided any infection from the wounds, but I'm afraid you have contracted the Lupine Transgenic Virus."

"What in the hell is that? I've never heard of that virus?"

"Think of it as a mutated strain of canine distemper. I can explain it, but it would take a while. For now, it's just easier to compare the symptoms to the measles or the bad flu. There's no vaccine for it and you are already on antibiotics to ward off infection from your wounds, so we will just have to ride it out."

"How bad is this Lupine Transgenic Virus, compared to distemper," Matt asked in a concerned voice.

"As I mentioned, the symptoms are very similar to the Flu, but it may be a bit more severe. It will probably knock you off your feet for two or three days with vomiting, diarrhea, nausea, chills, sweats, body aches, and fever. We will treat you for dehydration, fever, aches, and pains and keep you as comfortable as possible. Like the flu, it will take a few days after your fever breaks to regain your strength and appetite."

"Wow, a lot to look forward to," Matt joked with Dr. Bertram.

"Just try and rest. If you need to get up ring the bell and one of us will be here to help you; I want to leave the IV in so we can keep you hydrated and administer meds without having to poke you or have you swallowing anything."

Shortly after Dr. Bertram left the room, Freya came to visit Matt. "I'm back, but Doc wouldn't let me give you any roast beef," she said jokingly. She could tell from Matt's appearance; he was not feeling well. Walking over to the side of his bed, she put her hand on his forehead to feel for fever as she stared into his eyes.

"So, has anyone moved in and taken my room yet?" Matt joked with Freya.

"No, not yet, but I'm hoping someone will come along before too long." She replied with a soft laugh. "Peter took all of your gear up to your room and he took care of cleaning out your jeep. He said he was going to have someone look at the door and get an estimate for you to have it repaired."

"Repaired?"

"Yes, between you, the wolf, and Victor, your jeep took a bit of a beating." She smiled and snickered at Matt's surprised look.

"Jesus Pete! No wonder I hurt so much." His failed attempt at humor turned to a grimace. "Please don't make me laugh it hurts."

"Alex and Frankie called to check on you and they wanted to wish you a speedy recovery."

"Send my regards to both of them; would you? And thank Frankie for helping me out of the scrape with the wolves. She tried to warn me, but I was so intent on getting pictures and observing them, I ignored her advice. Tell her I'm sorry for putting her in that predicament."

"I will. I'm sure Frankie understands. That's why she wanted to be there to watch over you." Freya winked at Matt. "Besides, she's the type that enjoys a bit of drama and excitement every now and then."

"I'm sorry I upset you," Matt told Freya. "A stranger comes to town and disrupts everyone's routine."

"Why don't you try to rest? I'll sit here for a while."

Matt reached for Freya's hand, gently squeezing it before closing his eyes and drifting off to sleep.

* * *

The next two days and nights were very tense for Dr. Bertram, Allison, Keira and Freya as Matt was phasing through the initial stages of the LTV infection. Matt ran a high temperature and Dr. Bertram and Allison worked day and night trying to keep it under control. Mrs. Moonjoy' s herbal treatment helped to reduce the most severe effects of the viral infection and Dr. Bertram attributed her holistic medicine for saving Matt's life. Matt slipped between periods of unconsciousness and delirium experiencing nightmares and hallucinations. Freya never left his side during the entire time he battled through this stage of the transgenesis.

By the morning of the third day, Matt's fever broke; a sign that the worst was over. Now it was just a matter of time for Matt to recover his strength and get back on his feet.

* * *

When Matt woke up, Freya's face was the first thing he saw. Still very weak, he managed to squeeze Freya's hand to reassure her he was going to be all right. Realizing Matt had made it through the most critical stage of the viral infection, she started to cry again. However, this time, it was for joy; joy that Matt survived.

"Don't cry," he told her, trying to wipe away her tears. "I'm ok. Maybe they will let me have some of your roast beef and gravy now; you think?"

Freya could not contain herself and she leaned across and embraced him, laying her head on his shoulder. Matt reached around her with his good arm and patted her on her back turning to give her a gentle kiss. After a few moments, Freya recovered her composure and sat back in her chair.

For a few minutes, they sat quietly, not saying anything to one another. It was during this time Matt overheard voices out in the hallway. The conversation caught his attention because he thought he recognized a couple of the voices. For sure, he recognized Dr. Bertram, the second person he never heard before, but the third was unmistakable; it was his old friend Harvey Langston. '*What on earth is Harvey doing here?*' Matt thought to himself as he strained hard to eavesdrop on the conversation going on in the next room.

"What is it?" Freya asked, noticing Matt straining to listen to the voices.

"Shish," he whispered, holding a finger to his lips.

* * *

"So Doc, what's going to happen now?" Harvey asked.

"We're not sure at this point. His fever broke early this morning and it will be a few days before he regains his strength and able to walk and maybe a couple of weeks before he can resume working. After that, we're plowing new ground."

Harvey was becoming frustrated, "Matthew Kershaw is a trusted friend I've known for many years. I arranged for him to come here to conduct the investigation of the *warg* attack on Ranger Holmes, so we could keep this matter contained within the valley."

"I warned you it was going to be difficult to restrict his investigation. Under the circumstances, next to impossible to avoid any contact with the alpha primes." William interjected. "In the past, we haven't had to contend with the alphas; it's normally the rogues that venture down into the valley. Now we're facing a real threat from a pack led by an alpha prime. We're not sure how many are out there, and where they are ranging from. What's more frightening is their apparent level of human-like intelligence. We're just not sure how to deal with this threat."

"We grossly underestimated the inherent danger they pose, for sure," Dr. Bertram argued. "This situation may have been avoided if we had trusted Dr. Kershaw enough to tell him upfront about the alphas and the rogue pack. He would have been better prepared to focus on his investigation while exercising a bit more caution. He was under the impression he was simply studying a lone wolf that wandered out of the wilderness, no wonder he found himself in this situation."

"So, where do we go from here?" Harvey asked of both Dr. Bertram and William.

William spoke first, "We need to let Dr. Kershaw recover his strength. I agree with Doc; it was a mistake not trusting Dr. Kershaw. We should have properly briefed him on the true scope and nature of our problem in Misty Hollow. Therefore, I suggest

Dr. Bertram take the opportunity, over the next couple of days, to explain to Dr. Kershaw, about the wargs and the lupine virus. He needs to know what to expect over the next few months. In the course of those discussions, Dr. Bertram can enlighten Dr. Kershaw on the real situation we're facing here in the valley, and *maybe* we can solicit his help in dealing with it. By the time he is strong enough to get back to work, he should be fully versed on our plight with the wargs and the Lupine Transgenic Virus."

"Matt is very knowledgeable in wildlife biology. Coupled with his experience as a cryptozoologist, he is the ideal candidate to work with Doc in seeking a solution." Harvey explained. "He is convinced of the existence of a cryptid species of wolf. He has devoted a great deal of time searching for this fabled creature. I believe he will comprehend what Doc has to share with him regarding LTV, wargs, and the alpha primes. I assure you, he will be quite eager to renew his efforts to study them in exhaustive detail. However, I'm not so sure he's prepared for the realities of the existence of the Therianthropes. But, if any outsider can embrace it, it would be Matthew Kershaw."

Dr. Bertram shared his insights, "From the notes in his field journal, I believe Dr. Kershaw has already begun to suspect the existence of the alphas, he just hasn't had any tangible proof until now. As for the rest, I am confident that before too long, his intellectual reasoning will lead him to conclude the existence of Therianthropes."

"Ok, I'll leave it all in your hands," Harvey gestured to both Dr. Bertram and William. "I'll stop in for a short visit with Matt before I head back home."

Harvey poked his head into the room and seeing Matt was awake, stepped into the room, "Hey buddy, how are you feeling?" Before Matt could respond, Harvey greeted Freya. "Freya, it's good to see you again."

"Good to see you again as well," Freya replied.

Matt could not contain himself and interrupted the introductions. "Harvey, what's going on here? He scolded.

141

"Glad to see you too," Harvey said jokingly, trying to calm Matt. "I've known Doc for quite some time. When you were injured, Doc gave me a call, so I came up as soon as I could get away."

"What was all of that about out there? We have known each other for twenty years, I trusted you, and now it seems you've conspired behind my back to get me here under false pretenses. Tell me that I'm not laid up in this bed, a damaged chew-toy for some overgrown wolf beast that you *somehow* neglected to warn me about?"

Freya was as shocked as Matt regarding the whole situation. She too felt like an unwilling participant in a scheme she still didn't fully comprehend. She decided to slip out of the room and went to have a seat on the front porch, leaving Matt and Harvey alone to continue their discussion.

"I admit, this disastrous situation is entirely my fault," Harvey said apologetically. "The good people of this valley are my friends and family; they are desperate for help to deal with a very real threat. I was hoping to be able to contain the situation within the valley by having you conduct the investigation. The last thing we need here is for a group of outsiders coming in and getting in the middle of a very delicate situation – one that needs to remain isolated here in this valley."

"I can't believe you would knowingly send me into a dangerous situation; withholding critical information… And I still don't understand what's going on." Matt said, visibly agitated.

"I can appreciate your anger and disappointment, given the situation. But, after Doc explains everything to you, I think you will agree, under the same set of circumstances, and if the roles had been reversed, you would have taken the same approach I did."

"I certainly would not have sent you into the lion's den with your hands tied behind your back and blindfolded." Matt scolded Harvey.

"You're right, and I'm sincerely sorry for deceiving you," Harvey said, trying to defuse the tension between them. "For now, I'll leave you to rest and get your strength back. Doc will explain things better than I can."

"You are lucky that I am as weak as a kitten or I would kick your sorry butt all the way back to the city." Matt threatened with a hint of forgiveness.

"Get well buddy, I'll give you a call in a couple of days and check on you."

* * *

"Your fever has broken and you are on the downhill side of the viral infection. Would you be more comfortable recovering in your room at the inn?" Dr. Bertram asked Matt after examining him.

"Yes, I would! Especially if you tell me I can start eating solid food again."

"You miss Freya's cooking no doubt."

"No offense Doc, but you are a terrible cook," Matt joked as he gestured toward the IV bags and tubes.

"Alright then, we will keep you here tonight and tomorrow we will move you over to the inn to convalesce. I'll tell Freya and she can have your room ready."

Chapter 19

As Dr. Bertram was wheeling Matt over to the inn in a wheelchair, Matt looked up at the sky and took a deep breath of fresh air. It had rained during much of the time he was laid up in the clinic and now everything appeared fresh and clean. "Doc, is it alright if we stop here on the front porch? The fresh air smells nice and the breeze feels good."

"Certainly. I think I would like to enjoy the fresh air myself. Do you mind if I join you?" Doc parked Matt next to a small coffee table.

Gesturing to the chair next to him, "Be my guest," Matt said.

"First, let me see if Freya might have some coffee or tea made if you are up to it?"

"Either would be great, Thanks."

Dr. Bertram returned a few moments later with a carafe of coffee and a couple of cups on a serving tray. As Doc poured the coffee, he told Matt, "I think Freya is cooking roast beef and gravy for dinner."

"Yes, I can smell it out here," he said as he closed his eyes and breathed the aroma of Freya's cooking. "I joked with her about sneaking me in some of her roast beef and gravy, I guess she took it to heart." He laughed with Dr. Bertram.

"She is a good woman. And, excuse me for being direct, but I think she has grown very fond of you."

"I believe you're right, and to tell you the truth I've grown fond of her as well. But, such notions are not sensible given our circumstances."

"How so?"

"We are worlds apart. Graymere village and the inn are her home, all she owns and all she knows. For me, my life is my work at the university, when I'm not in the wilderness. What time I'm not in a classroom, I'm in the lab, or backpacking into the wilderness, searching for an elusive cryptid wolf."

"Well, you never know what life has in store for you. One thing for sure, you do not want to wake up on the back side of fifty and start looking back at a life filled with regrets."

Matt changed the subject by querying Dr. Bertram on his relationship with Harvey Langston. "Doc, how long have you known Harvey?"

"Oh, I've known Harvey's family for many years. A few years ago, quite by chance, I ran into Harvey when he was visiting relatives. During my brief conversation with him, I realized his aunt and uncle were old childhood friends and schoolmates of mine. Through Harvey, I reconnected with my old friends and since then Harvey and I've kept in touch."

"So he has family here?"

"His grandparents passed away years ago before I came back to the Valley. But, he has an extended relative still living in the valley."

Taking the last sip from his coffee, Matt was feeling a bit weak. "I'm feeling a little tired, can you help me get up to my room?"

Freya met Dr. Bertram and Matt at the base of the stairs as the doc wheeled him in. "Take your time getting out of the wheelchair and hold on to the stair rail, I'll steady you from the other side." Dr. Bertram helped him get up and gave him a moment to steady himself. "We'll take it slow, just stop when you need to."

They carefully made their way up to Matt's room where Freya turned down the covers while Dr. Bertram helped Matt settle into his bed. I'll stop by later to check on you, but you

145

should try to drink plenty of liquids, soft foods, and juice. I'll leave some pain pills with Freya. Your wounds are healing, but you will be stiff and sore until you are strong enough to start moving about. Try to start moving your arm, shoulder, and neck as much as you can bare it, in order to stretch and loosen the muscles. Just be careful not to overdo it and tear your stitches loose."

"Ok, Doc," Matt acknowledged, "Thanks for everything, I appreciate everything you and Allison have done for me."

"You're welcome. Now, it's Freya's turn to take care of you for a few days."

Matt turned to Freya and smiled, "I'll try not to be a burden."

"Get some rest and I'll see you later." Dr. Bertram said before he left the room.

* * *

"Hello," Freya answered the phone.

"*Ms. Freya, this is Sarah, Dr. Kershaw's research assistant. I have been trying to reach him for a couple of days now. Is he there?*"

"I'm sorry Sarah; Dr. Kershaw came down ill with a viral infection. He has been bedridden and under a doctor's care for the last few days. He's in bed resting at the moment."

"*Oh dear,*" Sarah reacted. "*How is he doing?*"

"He's doing much better, his fever broke yesterday morning and he should be up and about in a day or two. Shall I have him call you when he wakes up?"

"*Yes please,*" Sarah acknowledge. "*Tell him I called and that I'm sorry he has been sick and I hope he feels better very soon.*"

"I will. Is there any message I should pass along to him?"

"*No, nothing terribly important. I was just checking in with him. Thank you, Ms. Freya.*"

"My Pleasure. Goodbye Sarah," Freya said as she hung up the phone.

* * *

"Are you hungry?" Freya asked as she entered Matt's room carrying a bed tray.

146

"Yes," Matt replied. "I'm hungry enough to eat a horse, but still a bit nauseated."

"Well, I made you some roast beef extra tender, pulled, spread on toast, smothered in brown gravy, mashed potatoes, steamed peas, and carrots. Some juice and cool spring water to wash it down with."

"Freya you should not have gone to all that trouble."

"No trouble," she replied. "By the way, Sarah called for you while you were sleeping."

"What did she say? Did she leave a message?"

"No, she said she was just checking in with you. I told her you would call her in the morning."

"Did you tell her anything about what happened?"

"No, I just told her you've been ill with a viral infection and that you would call her when you got up and about in the morning."

"Thank you."

"I'll put this bell next to your bed. If you need anything, just give it a jingle." Seeing Matt's grimace when she tried to set him up to eat, Freya could tell he was in a great deal of pain. "How about a pain pill; are you hurting very much?"

"No, I'm ok for now. I'll take one after I eat, to dull the pain before I lay down to rest."

"Alright, I'll bring your pain pill when I come back up to take your tray. Is there anything else I can get for you?"

"No thank you. You have done more than enough already. I'm sorry for being a burden on you."

"You are not a burden Matthew, I'm happy to do whatever I can, to make you comfortable and help you get back on your feet as soon as possible."

"Thank you."

"Enjoy your lunch." Freya left the room and pulled the door closed behind her.

A little while later Freya returned to Matt's room with his medications. "Here you are, sir. One is an antibiotic, a pain pill, and the other for inflammation. Would you care for coffee or tea?"

"Only if you will sit and have a cup of tea with me," Matt responded.

"I would love to. I'll be back in a few minutes."

Returning with tea, Freya sat in the chair near Matt's bed. Soon they were deep in conversation about various topics related to their respective lives and unique experiences. They talked for over two hours before Freya noticed Matt's eyes getting heavy.

"I need to take these things downstairs and clean up the kitchen while you rest. I'll check in on you before I turn in."

"Ok," he replied. "The dinner was delicious as always. Thanks again, it was a welcome treat."

"It's my pleasure. Is there anything else I can get for you before I go downstairs?"

"No thank you."

"Rest well then," Freya said as she closed the door behind her.

* * *

After finishing downstairs, Freya went to her room to clean up and change into her nightgown. Before turning in for the night, she wanted to check on Matthew once more. Putting on her housecoat, she went down the hall to his room. Knocking softly, she opened the door, and quietly entered his room. Matt was still sleeping as she felt his forehead for signs of fever. She decided to sit in the chair next to him for a little while, to make sure he was resting well before she went to bed. It wasn't long before she fell asleep.

"NO!" Matt shouted in his sleep. "FRANKIE, LOOK OUT!"

Freya sat straight up in the chair from a dead sleep, startled by Matt's outburst. Realizing Matt was having a nightmare, she sat on the bed next to him to try and calm him.

"Over to your left, SHOOT!" Matt continued to mumble in his sleep. "What the hell is that?"

Freya held his hand and stroked the side of his face gently. "Sheesh," she whispered, trying to relax him and coax him back into restful sleep.

148

Matt clutched her hand tightly, pulling it to his chest causing her to lie next to him. She shifted to try and get comfortable for a few minutes expecting Matt to release her hand when he relaxed. Instead, in his sleep, he pulled her closer to him. Freya decided to lie there until he was in a deep sleep to avoid disturbing him. Before long, Freya had fallen asleep herself, lying next to Matt.

Sometime just after midnight, Matt woke Freya groaning in pain. Realizing she had fallen asleep next to Matt, Freya quietly got up and slipped out of his room. She returned a few minutes later with Matt's medication. "Matthew," she whispered. "Matthew, here take this." She lifted his head to put the pill in his mouth. Putting a straw in his lips, she instructed him to take a sip to wash down the pills. After she was sure he had swallowed the pill, she sat back down in the chair next to his bed and slept there until morning.

Chapter 20

When Freya awoke, Matt was still fast asleep. She got up quietly and went to her room to freshen up and change before going down to put on some coffee and start preparing for breakfast.

* * *

"Are you awake?" Freya whispered.

Matt moaned softly as he rubbed his eyes.

"I brought you coffee."

"Umm, I can smell it. Thanks."

Freya sat the coffee on the night table next to his bed and proceeded to help Matt sit up and propped him up with some pillows so he could sip his coffee.

"I'm preparing breakfast; would you prefer to have breakfast in bed or would you like to come downstairs?"

"Umm, I would rather come down to eat. I need to get out of this bed."

"Do you need me to help you get up?"

"If you could help me get to the edge of the bed, I think I can manage from there."

With some difficulty and a great deal of pain, Freya gingerly helped Matt maneuver until he was sitting on the edge of the bed.

"Can I put out any clothes for you?" She offered.

"I think I can manage, but I'll ring the bell if I need help."

"OK, I'll have breakfast ready in about thirty minutes." Freya left the room and closed the door behind her.

Matt could barely muster enough strength to get up and move around. Dr. Bertram was right; he was stiff and extremely sore. Finding it extremely difficult to bend over or reach, he did manage to get his clothes out from the closet and drawers. However, he couldn't manage to change by himself. Reluctantly, he rang the bell to summon Freya for help.

"Yes!" Freya said, entering the room after a brief knock. "Are you alright?"

"Yes…, well, …actually no," he admitted. "But out of curiosity, how did you hear this dinky bell all the way downstairs?"

"I guess I have good hearing, and I was listening for it. There's not much background noise this time of the morning, so it makes the sound more noticeable I guess." Freya struggled to explain her exceptional hearing without disclosing any details. "What can I help you with?"

"I'm sorry," Matt said, blushing in embarrassment. "I'm having difficulty getting my shirt off. I need to shave, but I can't turn my head or reach up with the razor. I can't maneuver the razor without cutting my own throat," He explained with a bit of humor.

"That's OK, I can help you," Freya said reassuringly.

"This is embarrassing. I feel bad having to ask you for help with this."

"Matthew, relax; I don't mind. If it helps, just think of me as your sister."

"I don't have a sister." He responded with a smile acknowledging Freya's attempt to put him at ease.

Freya first helped Matt remove his scrub top. Then she got him to the bathroom sink and started prepping him for a shave. "I'll try not to cut your throat," she joked. Freya took her time to shave him, trying to avoid cutting any stitches around the multiple lacerations on the right side of his face. After she finished shaving him, Freya gave Matt an upper body sponge bath trying to avoid getting his bandages wet. Then she managed to get his shirt on with his left arm still in a sling tucked under the shirt. With a bit of awkwardness, she managed to help Matt get his pants changed, buttoned and zipped. Socks and shoes served to break the tension of the ordeal before heading down for breakfast.

"Forgive me for being presumptuous, but I would guess you have done this before," Matt said inquisitively.

"Once or twice," she responded casually, without further explanation.

Making their way slowly down the stairs, they were met by Dr. Bertram standing at the bottom of the staircase. "I see your strength is coming back. How is the pain?"

"I'm as stiff as a board. I can deal with the pain if I get out of the bed and start moving around. I need to get my muscles working again. I think a large part of it may be these bandages.

"Can we get some of them off?" Matt asked.

"After breakfast, we'll go over to the clinic and see what we can do. I'm sure some can be removed and others replaced with something a bit more flexible."

"If you guys want to pour yourselves coffee, I'll finish getting breakfast ready," Freya said before she disappeared into the kitchen.

"Alex and Frankie called several times to check on you. They asked me to extend their regards and wishes for your speedy recovery."

"I must get by there to thank Frankie personally. And Victor. Who is he anyway? I didn't meet him before and the attack happened so fast, I didn't really get to say anything to him. I only recall fuzzy images. Of course, I was half out of it and I had blood, rain, and mud in my eyes. It could have been Santa Claus loading me in his sleigh and I would not have recognized him."

"Victor is one of the residents of the valley. He and his family manage a herd of sheep near where the wargs attacked you and Frankie. He was probably out trying to round up strays when he came upon you and Frankie fending off the warg pack."

"I must meet him and thank him personally."

"I'll arrange for us to go by their farm after you've had a couple of days to recover more of your strength."

* * *

After finishing breakfast, Dr. Bertram took Matt to the clinic to redress his wounds. "Ah, you are healing nicely. Actually, some of your wounds are almost healed over. Remarkable," Dr. Bertram marveled. His facial expressions indicated a puzzling curiosity. "I can remove some of these stitches and in a few more days I should be able to remove the others from the deeper wounds."

"It feels good to get some air on those areas."

After Allison finished cleaning up around the wounds, she applied antibiotic ointment and fresh bandages on the remaining stitched wounds. "These bandages will not be as bulky and binding as the previous ones. You should be able to move more freely," Allison said.

"I want you to keep this arm in the sling and avoid overstretching the shoulder for several days. It will be weeks before you can do any lifting." Pointing to Matt's shoulder and neck, "You suffered a couple of very deep wounds here and here where the alpha sank his fangs into you and tore these muscles." Dr. Bertram demonstrated with his hand how the jaws clamped down across the area where the neck and shoulder meets. "You are lucky; one fang missed your jugular vein by less than an inch and another narrowly missed your spinal column. Fortunately, he only got hold of the meaty portion and damaged the muscle tissue around these areas in the process of trying to rip your head off."

"Why is it, I don't feel so lucky?" Matt joked.

"I suspect, when you fell to the floorboard of the jeep, you hit your head a couple of times going down, which accounts for the bruised areas on your head and other shoulder. The wounds on the side of your head, face and chest are from the alpha's claws as he tried to drag you out from the vehicle. Your left arm was mauled when you apparently put your arm up to shield your face and neck." As Dr. Bertram turned to wash his hands, he opened up to Matt a bit, "you're lucky because you are the only person I know, who suffered an attack from an alpha prime and lived to tell the tale." Turning back to Matt, he continued. "If Victor had

153

not pulled the alpha off of you, it would have certainly killed you."

Matt sat stunned for a moment. "What do you mean by *alpha*? And you said that as if the wolf had the intent to kill me personally."

"Not you so much personally, but it seems the alpha prime was intent on killing you none the less."

"And what do you mean by *alpha prime*?"

"The alpha primes are wargs. And they run packs of rogue wargs. As of lately, they seem hell bent on attacking humans in the valley."

"Wait, you said 'warg'. Alex used that term when describing the wolves, north of the valley." Matt said.

"*Wargs* or *vargs* are from old Norse mythology, referring to monstrous wolves that possessed human-like qualities such as intelligence. In Norse mythology, the wargs were large enough to ride and were capable of some level of communication with humans."

"I assume you refer to these animals as *wargs* instead of *wolves* for a reason?" Matt asked.

"Yes, they are larger than the typical gray wolf with the alphas being almost twice as large. They exhibit varying degrees of human intelligence and cognitive skill. They are far more aggressive by nature than a gray wolf. We believe wargs are genetically differentiated from other known wolves in many ways."

Again, Matt was stunned. "You knew this all along and you never thought to share this information with me, knowing that I would be out there, roaming around, trying to find them."

"Let's go back to the inn where we can sit comfortably and I'll do my best to explain everything, including, why we sought your help to study these wargs."

As Dr. Bertram wheeled Matt back to the inn, Matt was speechless from the revelations Dr. Bertram shared with him. When they entered the main hall, Freya was on the phone. "Just a minute, Dr. Kershaw just came back in; I'll get him for you."

Freya motioned for Matt to come to the phone, "it's Sarah your research assistant," she said handing the phone to Matt.

"Sarah," he answered.

"Dr. Kershaw! Thank goodness, you're all right, I was so worried. Ms. Freya said you were very ill from some virus you contracted."

"Yes, but I'm alright. I was just laid up for a few days."

"What virus was it; do they know?"

"Oh, something along the line of a bad flu bug. Not to worry, though, I'm out of bed and moving around again. What have you got for me?"

"I've done exhaustive research of all secondary sources such as the internet and available databases. As far as I've been able to determine, there's no known animal with a paw pattern like this one. I've not queried any primary sources like universities or zoologists, to obtain a first-hand analysis. You told me not to say anything to anyone, so I held back from proceeding with the primary sources until I talked to you."

"You did exactly as I asked you to do. That's great. Write up your findings with references and send it to my personal email. What else do you have?"

"From the measurements of the impression and your notes related to the soil conditions. I have calculated that the animal must be around two-hundred and twenty-five pounds maybe even two-hundred and fifty pounds. Cross referencing the print to forensic data charts, the size and pattern of the print suggest that the animal was comfortable walking on its hind legs and would be around seven feet tall."

"Include that in your analysis as well. Were you able to dig up any information about rogue wolf packs?"

"I've been researching that. As of yet, the only thing I can find relates to 'lone wolf' behavior and characteristics. But, I'm still working on it."

"You're doing well," he encouraged her. "How is everything around the house? You need anything from me?"

"No, all good here. Just take care of yourself."

"I will," Matt replied. "I'll call you in a couple of days."

"OK, bye Dr. Kershaw."

After hanging up the phone, Doc wheeled him over to the lounge. "Sorry Doc. That was my research assistant updating me on some research she is conducting for me."

"Quite all right, I understand," Dr. Bertram replied.

"Doc, I hope you will understand and appreciate my frankness, but I need some straight answers. I have questions about what's happening here in Misty Hollow and the real reason I was asked to come here."

"Don't hesitate to ask me whatever you like, you will not offend me or upset me. On the contrary, it's you who should be upset. It is because we weren't honest and straightforward with you before now, that led to your current condition."

"The other morning, before Harvey left, I overheard a portion of a conversation between you Harvey and another gentleman. Afterward, Harvey admitted he asked me to come here under false pretenses and said you would explain the real reasons why I'm in Misty Hollow. I'm all ears."

"Before I get into details, I need to clarify that your assignment to conduct an investigation into the attack on Ranger Holmes is legitimately the primary purpose for your presence here."

"However...," Matt interjected.

"However, the reason *you* were asked to do the investigation is where the deception lies. The truth of the matter is, we have been harboring a secret here in Misty Hollow and the natural isolation of the valley from the rest of civilization has helped us maintain that secret. Subsequent to Ranger Holmes's attack, an investigation was necessary, concluding that the attack on Ranger Holmes was a random act of a lone wolf. The report would state that locals killed the wolf and eliminated the problem. Harvey felt that your knowledge, reputation and your position at the university would legitimize such a report. We expected you to come here, do your investigation, and find no evidence suggesting any long-term threat by encroaching wolves. We would show you a dead wolf that a local killed, you would write your report, and case closed. What we did not anticipate was, the increased presence of the wargs and their aggressiveness leading up to your encounter with them."

"Ok, but why *me* and what is this secret that almost got me killed?" Matt insisted.

"Harvey suggested that *you* conduct the investigation because he trusted you and once you finished the investigation and the report was filed, all eyes would be off Misty Hollow. Additionally, he expected you to find enough evidence to encourage your search for a cryptid in the valley and surrounding wilderness. Certain you would eventually discover the existence of the wargs and alphas, we hoped we could enlist your help to find solutions to our unique problem and circumstances. Harvey convinced us that your ethical standards and discretion made you a unique candidate to aid us. It was our hope that your genuine interest in discovering a new species of wolves make it easier for us persuaded you to help us.

Matt was growing impatient for Doc to get to the punch line. "And, this secret is?"

"Before I get into that, it might be helpful for you to know a little about me. After medical school, I practiced medicine as a trauma surgeon before I returned to medical school and specialized in pathology. Subsequently, I did field work for the CDC, out of Atlanta, for several years, researching DNA and RNA virus. Like you, I have been on a quest, fueled by a personal interest in a specific area of science; researching retroviruses and in particular, transgenic disease vectors."

"I suppose this comparative analysis of our resumes has something to do with why two brainiacs like us are doing in a valley, situated in the middle of the wilderness area, a hundred miles from nowhere." Matt was now getting agitated.

"Yes, and I beg your patience as I take this one step at a time." Dr. Bertram got up to get a carafe of coffee and poured another coffee for the both of them before he resumed his explanation.

"Thanks," Matt said as Dr. Bertram filled his coffee cup. "Please go on. I'm all ears."

"How familiar are you with '*transgenesis?*'"

157

"I know that it's a process of introducing an exogenous gene into a living organism so that the host organism will take on, and exhibit a new physical property, that can then be passed on to its offspring. Something along the lines of genetic engineering," Matt replied.

"Precisely, and the exogenous gene can be introduced through a variety of methods, but the method of interest to both you and I, involves the use of viral vectors. Specifically, a *retrovirus*," Dr. Bertram stressed to begin focusing the discussion.

"I follow you so far; molecular biology 101."

"Let's say a mutated retrovirus infected a host, invading its cells and merging with the host genome. However, the host was already infected with a different virus and when the retrovirus merged with the host genome, that the retrovirus then mutated."

"I follow so far," Matt said.

"Subsequently, this new host passed the retrovirus onto its offspring, which by now is hardwired into the F1 offspring complete genome. What if, the F1 offspring were able to infect another host, a cross-species infection, spreading the retrovirus to a new recipient within a different species?"

"I suppose it would merge with that new species genome and mutate again," Matt replied.

"Let's take it one step further. The cross-species recipient has now acquired a DNA virus, which theoretically carries with it, elements of the genome of the original host. Under certain conditions, the new host could experience a mutation of its DNA structure, augmented with the genome of the original host. Hence, the naturally mutated DNA virus has acted as a vector to introduce the original host's genome into the genome of the newly infected recipient of the virus."

"Wait, are you suggesting that a disease could act as a catalyst that would result in a naturally occurring transgenic mutation across species?"

"Certainly. There has been researching of the human genome which concludes that as much as five to eight percent of our genome is made of retrovirus DNA. Another research report indicates that as much as three to five percent of the human genome is comprised of DNA from other species, specifically canine."

"Yes, but are you suggesting that transgenesis results in cross-species physical mutations?"

"Yes," Dr. Bertram answered. "Hasn't this been done already in the lab through various experiments in genetic engineering? Take, for instance, the mice that have had its genome modified, resulting in transgenic mice, which express a green fluorescent protein that glows under a certain lamp color. Another work involves human-animal hybrid experimentation."

"Ok, but what's all of this leading to?"

"One last element," the doc interjected. "It is relatively common for a host to be infected with more than one virus at the same time and the two viruses mutate, resulting in a new virus strain. And, retroviruses are notorious for frequent mutation into new strains when they transfer from one host to another."

"Yes," Matt responded impatiently.

"Well, this is the fundamental problem we are dealing with here in Misty Hollow." Dr. Bertram revealed.

"Now you totally lost me."

"In a nutshell, here it is," Dr. Bertram began. "At some point, generations ago, the wolves in the region north of the valley acquired a mutated retrovirus. From what I've been able to determine, I believe the virus is a mutated strain of distemper. However, I don't have the equipment to break it down and confirm my hypothesis. History of the valley tells of French trappers who originally came into the valley after being bitten and mauled by wolves. Then sometime after they arrived, one of them started exhibiting varying degrees of lupine transmutation. Eventually, the descendants passed the virus to subsequent generations until many of the residents of the valley carry it in their bodies. As you are probably aware, once a host acquires a retrovirus, the virus will be with them the rest of their life and passed to their offspring. Subsequently, those with the acquired viral infection experienced DNA transgenic mutation, possibly resulting in varying degrees of phenotype mutations."

"You said many of the residents are infected, but I see people who don't have any signs of infection or transmutation," Matt observed.

"Four out of five people infected, exhibit no observable phenotype mutations, but one in five, do develop beneficial or detrimental mutations. For generations, it has been referred to as *'The Curse of Weyekins Himi-n-pelu'* because people didn't understand what was happening to them or the source."

"Weykins Himi-n-pelu," that's Nez Perce is it not?"

"Yes, over the years the original language and translation have been garbled somewhat, but loosely translated it is supposed to mean *'Spirits of the wolf people.'*

"What type of mutations are you talking about?"

"Of the one in five who develop lupine transgenic mutations, many exhibits such mutations as enhanced hearing, enhanced night vision, minor enhancements in strength and agility. These are among the more beneficial mutations. Conversely, some exhibited increased hair growth, deformity of fingernails and toenails. The more prominent mutations occur among hosts who *inherit* the virus. The Lupine Transgenic Virus or LTV, as we call it, can and does affect the germ cells and therefore the virus is inheritable. Being present in the stem cells, the transmutation spreads throughout the entire body of the embryo host inheriting the LTV. Therefore, the phenotype mutation becomes more dominate from the infant stage onward. Of those who inherit the LTV, some may never develop a physical mutation while others may exhibit major physical mutations."

Matt suddenly lost all color in his face. "Wait a minute! Is this the infection I acquired from the warg that mauled me?"

"Quite simply, yes," Dr. Bertram replied.

"Are you telling me that I'm going to grow fangs, chase rabbits, and be able to leap tall buildings in a single bound?" Matt said, followed by nervous laughter, at the prospects of morphing into a werewolf.

"To be quite honest, we don't know what to expect in your case."

Matt's attitude quickly shifted to deep anxiety, "What do you mean, you don't know what to expect?"

"Unfortunately, the LTV goes through an evolution of sorts, each time it's transmitted from one host to another. When it infects a new host, the virus carries genome from the original host to the new host. Until recently, the effects of the LTV have been limited to descendants of the valley residents who have inherited the LTV from their forefathers."

"I hear what you're saying and theoretically, I suppose this is all quite possible. But, the reality of it is a bit difficult to accept."

"Give me a moment," Dr. Bertram excused himself and disappeared into the kitchen.

Matt poured himself another cup of coffee while waiting to see what the doctor had in store for him. A couple of minutes later Dr. Bertram returned with Freya.

"Freya would you mind calling Keira and asking her to come over and join us for a few minutes. When you are finished would you come join us as well?"

Freya nodded as she picked up the phone to call Keira.

"What's this about, Doc?"

"Show and tell," he replied.

After Freya hung up the phone, she walked over and sat near Matt and Dr. Bertram. A few minutes later Keira came in to join them.

"Freya, could you please pull your hair back behind your ears for a moment please?"

Freya turned so that Matt could clearly see her ears as she pulled her hair back, revealing a pair of slightly pointed ears lightly covered with fuzz resembling puppy ears.

Matt could not believe what he was seeing. Freya's ears were not unattractive. Matt thought to himself how they actually looked cute. It wasn't her appearance that shocked him, but the evidence that validated what Dr. Bertram had been trying to explain to him.

"I inherited the LTV from my parents, who inherited it from their parents, as did many of the other residents," Freya explained

161

to Matt. "In addition to my physical mutation, I also have very acute hearing and highly developed sense of smell."

"Both Alex and Frankie inherited the LTV, but neither exhibit any obvious physical mutations. Alex has no known mutations while Frankie has enhanced the sense of smell and hearing." Dr. Bertram offered as additional examples.

Matt sat speechlessly.

"I believe you've met Keira?" Dr. Bertram asked Matt.

"Yes, during dinner the first night I was here," Matt said while still in a daze.

"Keira, would you please remove your veil, if you don't mind?"

"My pleasure." Keira lifted her veil and pulled off her head cover.

Matt was shocked beyond words. He tried his best not to stare, but he was unable to stop studying her appearance. Keira had a short pixie-cut black hair, her face, neck, and any area he could see exposed, was covered with a coat of fine black hair, not real heavy, just dense enough to be abnormal. Her ears were similar to Freya's, only slightly more pronounced. When she smiled, her fang teeth showed to be elongated. The most striking aspect of Keira's appearance was her eyes. The pupils and irises resembled the shape and translucent color of a wolf or lupine eyes. In spite of, or maybe because of her obvious mutations, Keira appeared to be hauntingly attractive.

"It's perfectly alright Dr. Kershaw. I understand your reaction for which I was prepared. Dr. Bertram asked me to come over to demonstrate the possible variations which often result from the inherited LTV. Now, you can see for yourself and understand what's happening to us." Keira said before removing her gloves to reveal hands covered with hair and fingernails developed more like canine claws.

Matt just sat dumbfounded, not knowing what to say.

Freya motioned toward the kitchen, "If you have no further need of me, I need to return to the kitchen to prepare lunch."

"I have work to do as well if you don't mind," Keira said.

"By all means, please return to whatever you were doing. I appreciate your assistance." Dr. Bertram said to them.

As Keira turned to walk away, Matt called out to her. "Keira! Doc told me that if it were not for your and your mother's potions, I might not have made it through the worst part of the viral infection. I want to thank you." Matt told her.

"I'm glad that I was able to help you and to see you up and about again," Keira replied before she left the inn.

"Do you feel like a short walk to stretch our legs and get some fresh air?"

"Yes, I would."

Dr. Bertram wheeled Matt out the front door in the wheelchair. Once on the porch, Matt asked him to stop. "Doc, I would like to try and walk and stretch my legs, if you don't mind lending me your arm to lean on."

"Not at all," Doc replied.

Dr. Bertram helped Matt out of the wheelchair and gingerly led him down the steps to the street. Doc held Matt's arm as they slowly walked down the street. Dr. Bertram remained silent as they walked, allowing Matt time to mentally digest and process all he had seen and heard.

After they had walked a short distance, Matt broke the silence. "So, this is the secret you are trying to keep from the outside world," Matt stated rhetorically. "Doc, although I comprehend the theory and science behind what you explained, it's hard for me to wrap my head around the reality of it. I've always believed nature could produce dramatic mutations, which I've spent much of my adult life searching to prove. Now the evidence is standing in front of me, the truth and facts are a bit hard for me to mentally process. I literally can't believe what I'm seeing."

"Why is it so hard to grasp. As a biologist, you are certainly aware of Darwin's work. Even he alluded to the possibility of transgenic mutation as a possible explanation for evolutionary change. Maybe shocking you with the 'show and tell' was not the best thing to do, but you wanted answers and we have wasted too much time already. We had hoped you would become acquainted

163

with these revelations gradually as you pursued your investigation. However, the attack by the alpha and warg pack necessitated the need to lay it out all at once. Besides, you need to be prepared for what may be in store for you in the coming weeks or months."

Matt stopped and turned to face Dr. Bertram, "What do you mean by that?"

"You were bitten by an Alpha Prime. Although we are not sure of the exact transgenic genome contained in the LTV you acquired from the alpha, it's almost certain to be an advanced strain. And it's painfully obvious that you acquired the LTV from him."

"I not sure I understand what you are getting at, but it doesn't sound good."

"Well, to some extent, I'm not actually sure myself. Based on the little data and information we've been able to accumulate; I came up with a hypothesis regarding the evolution of the Lupine Transgenic Virus or LTV."

"I'm all ears," Matt said to Dr. Bertram.

"We believe the virus we refer to as LTV first emerged as a mutated virus among a pack of wolves in the wilderness area north of the valley. A French fur trapper then acquired the virus after an attack by wolves carrying the LTV. Subsequently, the virus was inherited by his progeny and passed down through generations and spread among the residents of the valley as the families intermarried."

"Ok, we have already established all of that." Matt was becoming a bit impatient with Dr. Bertram's explanation.

"Bear with me," Dr. Bertram continued. "Eventually, the wolves from the north ventured into the valley which killed and fed on a valley resident who carried the inherited LTV. The wolf, having killed the human, would have gotten the blood and tissue into its system. Subsequently, the LTV from the human triggered a transgenesis of the human genome back to the wolf. I believe that wolf may have carried the original strain of LTV, which then experienced a major human transgenic mutation within its own genome. In turn, it would have been passed it to its offspring."

164

"Again Doc, I'm not sure I understand." Matt sounded confused.

"The animal that bit you was an Alpha Prime, a generational transmute who carries human DNA in its genome. Think about it," Dr. Bertram said as he started walking again. "By now you understand the basic concept of how the mutated LTV was passed to humans, yes?"

"Yes."

"Then the next evolution of the LTV is when it's inherited by the human offspring of those who *acquired* the LTV originally. You follow me?"

"Yes."

"We now call the generational LTV infected humans who exhibit phenotype mutations Therianthropes. In the scenario, I just explained a multi-gen Therian was killed by a multi-gen wolf with LTV, which in turn resulted in transgenic mutation transferring human genome to the wolf facilitating a whole new strain of the LTV."

"Given what I know about canine distemper and what happened to me, I would think that the newly infected wolf would die."

"Most young canines with the distemper do die from the virus when they contract the base strain you're familiar with. However, keep in mind, we are dealing with, what I believe is, an entirely different virus, one we know relatively little about. Under the scenario I just described, the wolf acquiring the Therianthrope strain of the virus, more than likely, had the base LTV hardwired into his own DNA."

Matt thought for a few moments. "I suppose, under the hypothesis you outlined, the wolf would, through transgenesis, experience a transmutation incorporating elements of the human genome."

"Yes, and take it a step further, after what you have observed with Freya and Keira, which resulted from the generational evolution of the LTV in humans, what do you think would result from the wolf who acquired the Therianthrope LTV and then passed it on to its offspring?"

165

Matt thought a moment, "The wargs?"

"Think of the Alpha Prime and the wargs as you would think of our community. Some of the generational offspring may exhibit little or no observable phenotype mutations while others do. The wolves who now exhibit observable human genome transmutations we refer to as Rogues. Some are able to walk upright, grow to impressive size, with highly developed cognitive skills, evolved fingers and toes."

"The alphas," Matt responded.

"Yes, but in most cases, even those who don't exhibit observable human transmutations still may develop other beneficial mutations."

"Such as intelligence and cognitive skills," Matt responded.

"We are not sure if the wargs were originally a different species of wolf, but it is undeniable that they have, through transgenesis, evolved into a new and very dangerous mutant species." Doc said as he touched Matt's arm to gain his undivided attention, "Now consider this; a warg, an Alpha Prime, encounters a human and infects that human with the warg alpha prime strain of LTV."

Matt went white and weak. Dr. Bertram helped him over to a nearby bench to sit down.

"Holy Mother of Jesus! I think I'm going to be sick."

"Just relax, you'll be alright. Just try to breathe normally." Dr. Bertram said trying to calm Matt.

"I'm so screwed," Matt said looking up into Dr. Bertram's eyes.

Chapter 21

"**W**here's Matthew?" Freya asked Dr. Bertram when he came into the kitchen.

"I helped him up to his room to rest for a bit before lunch. He's not feeling very well at the moment."

Freya had a concerned look on her face as she asked, "What's wrong, is he alright?"

"Physically yes; unfortunately, he had questions, of which he was not mentally prepared for the answers. I think he is suffering more from mental shock than from any of his wounds or effects of the virus."

"Maybe I should go check on him," Freya said as she started to remove her apron.

"No, leave him be for now. His views of science and reality have been suddenly shattered. He has to digest everything he's learned this morning, regarding the LTV infection and its effects."

"What do you think he is going to do?"

"I believe he will become obsessed with unraveling *The Curse*. He came here on a quest to find a cryptid wolf species and he found far more than he expected. He will not be able to rest until he can study it, classify it, map it, label it, document it, and wrap it up with a silk bow."

"Lunch will be ready in about an hour if you would like to tell the others."

"Sure thing. If you need me, just call over to the clinic."

* * *

Matt had taken a pain pill then dozed off soon after he lay down on his bed. He woke up to the smell of Freya's cooking and he thought to himself how pleasant it was in light of all he had experienced the last few days. Looking at his watch, he noticed it was time for lunch. *'Don't want to disappoint Freya; she's a stickler for being on time for her meals.'* He said to himself as he chuckled aloud. As he slowly made his way downstairs, he heard voices in the conversation.

"I think with Dr. Kershaw's knowledge and expertise, we will be able to get a handle on the situation," Matt overhead Dr. Bertram saying to the others.

Freya came through the kitchen door with dishes in her hands and stopped briefly when she saw Matt stepping off the stairs and struggle to make his way slowly toward the dining area. "Matthew, you're just in time for lunch." After setting the dishes down on the table, she went to help him the rest of the way to the table.

Entering the dining area, Matt recognized Dr. Bertram, Keira, and there was a third person he didn't know. This third person appeared to be a Therianthrope from his distinctive lupine transgenic mutations. Matt tried to act casual, not wanting to stare or react to the person's appearance.

"Dr. Kershaw," greeted Dr. Bertram. "I believe you have met everyone except William." He said, gesturing toward the Therianthrope seated at the head of the table.

William got up from his chair and approached Matt. "Dr. Kershaw, it's a pleasure to finally meet you in person, I'm William Barret" the man introduced himself with a deep, raspy voice.

Extending his left hand to shake hands with William, Matt noticed William was approximately four to six inches taller than he was, and his entire body was covered with fine fur. His head and face had distinctive lupine features, a mildly elongated jawline, piercing, translucent, yellow canine eyes, accented with by a heavy brow. His ears were almost fully canine. While shaking hands, Matt noticed William's fingers and palms had a

168

hint of raspy padding, similar to a canine's paw. Nevertheless, for all the obvious canine features, William still had the distinctive stature and appearance of a distinguished human.

"It's my honor and pleasure to meet you, sir," Matt responded. He got a distinct impression, William was someone of importance within the community.

"Please have a seat," William said, gesturing for Matt to sit to his left across from Dr. Bertram, who was seated to his right.

"Dr. Bertram tells me he has filled you in on the background to our evolving situation."

"Yes indeed," Matt responded.

"What are your thoughts or questions at this point?" William posed to Matt.

"I'm bit overwhelmed, to be honest. I'm still trying to come to grips with everything that has happened over the last few days."

"Well, first I feel that I owe you an apology," William began. "I assigned my betas to keep a watchful eye on you, and I asked Frankie and Alex to stay close to avoid any close encounters. However, it seems we failed to protect you properly and our negligence resulted in your injuries and subsequent infection by the Alpha Prime."

"Thank you, but the fault is all mine," Matt admitted. "In spite of Frankie's best effort to warn me, I ignored her advice, putting us both into the situation resulting in the encounter with the alpha and his rogues. If it were not for Victor and Frankie, I fear I would be dead instead of nursing a few wounds, a wounded pride, and having lunch with you." Matt responded humbly.

William gave Matt an approving look, nodding his head recognizing Matt's humbleness in accepting blame instead of directing it toward others. "The truth of the matter is, the fault is mine because I was reluctant to make you fully aware of the situation, upon your arrival in Graymere. However, based on what you know now, I hope you can appreciate our dilemma in not sharing all of this information with an outsider, we didn't know. It was our hope and belief, you would be able to complete your investigation and file your report without incident. And, in your pursuit of the cryptids, we expected you to eventually discover the wargs on your own. At that point, we planned to fill in the details and solicit your help in finding a solution to our *curse*."

Matt scanned the table to make eye contact with everyone present before he told them, "It's a bit ironic; I came here with the hopes of discovering a new species of wolf; one that I imagined would have the features and characteristics exhibited by the alpha prime. But I guess, in as much as I was looking for it, and hoping to find it, nothing could have prepared me for the reality of actually finding what I spent years searching for."

"Ironic indeed," William acknowledged as he lifted his cup in a toast to Matt, before taking a sip.

Abruptly the front door opened and Allison entered. "My apologies for being late," she said humbly.

William stood up to greet Allison, followed by Matt and Dr. Bertram. "Ah, Mrs. Bertram, I'm pleased you could join us," William said with a slight bow.

Allison bowed in a slight curtsy to William.

"If I may interrupt," Freya said as she sat the last dish on the table. "Lunch is served."

"Thank you, Freya. It looks and smells delicious," William said, then nodded to the others as he took his seat.

Matt observed Freya and Keira served William before offering to serve either he or Dr. Bertram. It appeared to him lunch was taking on a bit more formal atmosphere than it had at previous meals. After serving William and Dr. Bertram, the women served themselves, all sitting at the opposite end of the table across from one another.

"You mentioned 'your intent' to solicit my help in finding a solution to the *curse*? What do you mean by that?" Matt asked William.

"I believe Dr. Bertram has made reference to our local curse, '*The Curse of Weyekins Himi-n-pelu.*

"Yes, he did."

William began to tell the story of the curse. "For many generations, our transgenic condition was blamed on a curse,

170

which was thought to have been brought into the valley by a pair of French fur trappers. Being of Native American decent yourself, you are probably aware that Native Americans don't actually have a word for 'curse or cursed.' Native American spiritual traditions don't generally have a concept of hell or the devil in the same way Christians view it. However, some do harbor superstitions of evil spirits and bad omens which arise from acts that offend mother earth or any of the many animal spirits. Such is the case with our 'curse', which is a poorly translated reference to the spirit of the wolf killed by the trappers, after being bitten and mauled.

As the story has been told for almost two hundred years, the trappers arrived in the valley gravely ill suffering from an infection thought to have been caused by bites they received from wolves, north of Misty Hollow."

"Yes, Freya told me a little of the history of the valley as it related to the French trappers."

"As Freya may have told you, those men were accepted and integrated into the local tribes and took wives, thus settling in as part of the community. However, some months after their arrival, they started to exhibit a physical transformation, taking on features resembling those of a wolf. At first, it was nothing significant, just enough to notice the change. As the physical transformation became more dominant and pronounced in their children, the people of the tribe began believing the white men were haunted, or cursed, by the wolf they killed. Ultimately, the men and their families were shunned by the tribes who believed that the spirit of the dead wolf came back to haunt them by invading their bodies and of their children and their children's children. Eventually, they were forced, in part, to set up their own settlement which eventually became the village of Graymere."

"I recall much of this from the history Freya shared with me."

"In the years and generations that followed, the descendants of the Frenchmen exhibited varying degrees of physical mutations, as one might expect. The villagers ultimately shunned those who exhibited any outward manifestation of lupine mutation. However, after decades of marriage and admixing

171

among the descendants of the Frenchmen's families, the LTV became more integrated into the DNA of the valley residents. After two centuries, virtually everyone in the valley now carries the LTV in his or her genome. It wasn't until Dr. Bertram returned to the valley some five or six years ago and started putting the pieces of the puzzle in place, that we realized the scope and nature of '*the curse*' as a product of a virus. Since then, Dr. Bertram has been working tirelessly to study the virus and develop a cure."

"What about people like me who have acquired the LTV virus and live outside the valley? Why do we not see the transmutation surface outside the valley?"

"Dr. Bertram," William redirected the questions to him.

Dr. Bertram picked up the queue and began to explain. "Since the initial infection emerged with the two trappers, there have been only a handful of encounters with the wargs from north of the valley, where we believe LTV originated. In recent years, there have been relatively few outsiders who have ventured into the valley, and none of them, that I'm aware of, were attacked by wargs or exposed to the LTV. The last instance of a warg attack in the valley involved an incident back in the 1930s when the CCC camps were set up with workers building firebreaks, roads, and such. Aside from that incident, only within the last couple of years, have wargs from the north begun to venture down into the valley. Therefore, the transmission of the LTV has been limited to the residents of the valley through generational transgenesis."

"*The key word is until 'recently*,' William interjected. "Now that we understand how the LTV can perpetually mutate into new strains as the virus passes back and forth across species, we desperately need to find a means to stop the spread and affect a cure."

Matt looked at Dr. Bertram and asked, "Why not contact the CDC? I'm sure you still have some contacts there or at least some inroads to involve the right people."

Dr. Bertram and William looked at each other very seriously before Dr. Bertram replied to Matt's query. "The last thing we want is for ANY government agency to get involved in investigating the source and nature of the LTV. Can you imagine what the government would do with such a virus once they saw the potential of manipulation and exploitation?"

Matt looked at both Dr. Bertram and William puzzled, "I'm not sure I understand what you are getting at."

"Dr. Kershaw, take a look at me," William said as he stood up. "Do you have any idea of my strength or capabilities? Hell, they are already trying to create human-animal hybrids. What do you think the government would do if they had a virus that would allow them to breed an army of soldiers like me?"

Dr. Bertram spoke up before Matt could answer, "We have three primary objectives; first, we want to isolate the LTV and prevent any further evolution; second, stop the spread of any strain of the virus; and third, to eradicate all strains of the virus."

"In the meantime," William began, "we have a threat facing the valley residents that you are all too familiar with. We must neutralize this threat as we work to achieve the three objectives Dr. Bertram just outlined. We need your help to study the wargs in order to deal with that threat and give Dr. Bertram time to develop a vaccine to eradicate '*the curse*.'"

Matt was overwhelmed at the daunting tasks laid before him. He had been so engrossed in the conversation he hardly touched his food. Now, he was not sure he had an appetite at all. Sitting back in his chair, Matt contemplated the scope of what they were asking of him. His perspective influenced by what might potentially happen to him as the LTV transgenesis started to invade and modify his own genome.

William interrupted Matt's silent moment, "I'll leave you and Dr. Bertram to discuss any further thoughts or questions you might have. For now, I must beg your pardon as I must leave to attend to some other matters back at my homestead." William took Matt's hand and shook it firmly which he felt in his wounded shoulder, grimacing slightly from the pain.

Matt could feel the strength in William's grip as they shook hands while looking each other in the eye. "I'm pleased to have met you and talked with you in person," Matt said to William.

"The pleasure is all mine," William reiterated, "It's you, you and Dr. Bertram, that we are all putting our hopes into, to help lead us out of this terrible situation." With that, William bid his farewell and left the inn.

Following William's departure, Matt felt the need to be alone. "Dr. Bertram, if you will forgive me I want to go lay down for a short while. I feel that I may have overexerted myself this morning and I need some rest." Matt said in an effort to excuse himself.

"By all means, please go and rest. I understand and I'm at your disposal if you have any further questions or if you would just like to talk."

"Thanks, Doc." After extending his apologies to Allison, and Ms. Keira, Freya helped Matt up to his room to lie down.

Chapter 22

It was late afternoon when Freya knocked lightly on Matt's door. "Are you awake?"

"Uhh…, yes," Matt muttered opening his eyes. "Come in."

Freya entered his room carrying a tray she sat on the table. "I thought maybe you would enjoy a cup of tea, I find it refreshes and relaxes me in the afternoon," she told Matt.

"That's thoughtful of you." With some difficulty and help from Freya, Matt slowly inched his way out of bed and sat at the small table next to the window. "Please have a seat and join me."

"I don't want to disturb you."

"No, please I welcome your company. Please have a seat," he insisted, still grimacing from pain.

Freya poured two cups of tea and sat at the table across from Matt. "I'm sorry," Freya said.

"For what?"

"For all of this," she struggled to find the right words to say. "It's not fair that they involved you without telling you everything up front." Tears began to form and roll down Freya's cheek.

Matt reached across the table and squeezed her hand. "It's ok, everything will be alright. None of this is your fault. Believe me when I tell you, if I *had known* everything that I know now I wouldn't have chosen any different path. Besides, if none of this had happened, I would never have met you and fell in love with your roast beef and gravy." He said as a veiled attempt to express his feelings for her while trying to cheer her up.

Freya sat there for a few moments before asking Matt, "What are you going to do?"

"About what?" He replied.

"About anything and everything," she uttered. "About your infection, dealing with the wargs, helping Doc find a cure for LTV, about your job, your future, EVERYTHING!" she rattled off as she broke down in tears.

Matt started to ask her why she was so upset, only to realize how stupid the question would sound before he uttered the words. He knew she was scared in general and for him in particular. In truth, he was scared too, except he dared not show it. Instead, he said nothing.

"Would you care to take a walk with me?" He asked Freya.

"Yes, that would be nice. Do you think you are up to it?"

"Let's finish our tea and go for a stroll."

* * *

Outside, the mist had started to form in the valley. As they walked along the street, Freya pointed out the various buildings, told Matt who lived there, and some history of the village. When they arrived at the mercantile, they wandered in to look around.

"Good afternoon Simon," Freya said when they stepped through the door. "You remember Dr. Kershaw don't you?"

"Yes indeed," Simon replied from behind the counter. "I'm glad to see you again Dr. Kershaw." Simon came from behind the counter to shake Matt's hand. Grasping Matt's hand with both of his, Simon shook violently overjoyed to see Matt up and about. Matt grimaced as the violent shaking caused pain to resonate throughout his injured upper body. "Oh, I'm sorry. I heard you had been injured, I trust you are recovering."

"I'm assured by Dr. Bertram, I'll make a full recovery and be back to work before I know it."

"Welcome to my humble little mercantile, please take your time and look around. If you need anything just let me know."

Freya pointed out a shawl one of the local women knitted. There were three or four on display and each showed exceptional artistry and detail in the design. "Mrs. Howard makes these. Since Mr. Howard died a few years ago, she occupies her time knitting. The income from her crafts keeps her in yarn and needles." Freya said with a smile.

In another area of the shop, Matt saw a homemade quilt hanging on display. The artwork sewn into the quilt was a wolf standing on a rock outcropping silhouetted by a red full moon. It was, possibly, the most beautiful thing he had ever seen.

Freya observed Matt staring at the quilt. "This quilt was hand made by Keira's mother, Mrs. Moonjoy. She is our local folklorist. The rock the wolf is perched on is a prominent landmark on the north side of the valley, '*Lupine Rock.*" The quilt is titled *Blood Moon Rising*, and the scene is intended to depict the Blood Moon Prophecy."

"Blood Moon Prophecy?"

"Yes, you would have to get Mrs. Moonjoy to explain it to you, but it has something to do the legend associated with the men who first came into the valley. Supposedly, the wolf they killed in the wilderness was the alpha's mate and her death resulted in the death of their young pups, which were not yet weaned. The alpha tracked the men to this valley and would stand on the rock and howl to them, cursing them with the spirit of his dead mate and their dead pups. The 'Blood Moon Prophecy' associated with this curse suggests that one day the wolves would become strong and intelligent like a man. And, the wolves will rise up to wipe out all the descendants of the two men and anyone who helped them.

Are you familiar with the blood moon phenomenon and related prophecies? I understand there are many such prophecies, which signal the coming of evil and dark times culminating in the end of time apocalypse. This curse is just our local version of the *Blood Moon Prophesy.*"

"I would like to meet Mrs. Moonjoy," Matt said. He was mesmerized and haunted by the scene on the quilt and could not stop staring at it. Simon, what's the price of the quilt on the wall?"

"Mrs. Moonjoy is asking $400 for it."

"Can you take it down and wrap it up for me? I'll be back later to pick it up."

"Certainly, Dr. Kershaw, my pleasure."

"Thank you, Simon."

Freya said nothing. She found it curious how Matt became fixated with the scene depicted on the quilt.

"Do you mind if we walk down to Dr. Bertram's clinic?" Matt asked Freya.

"Not at all; are you feeling OK? Are you hurting?" She asked with concern in her voice.

"I'm fine, I just want to ask Doc something and see if he will let me take a look at his lab."

Freya walked closely to Matt trying to support him as he struggled to walk. Approaching Dr. Bertram's clinic they saw the doctor sitting on his front porch.

"Good afternoon Doc," Matt called out while trying to raise his arm to wave.

"Glad to see you out and about. Are you feeling better?"

"Yes, somewhat; I feel a little stronger, but still very stiff and sore."

"Freya, we don't often see you out and about. How did the Dr. Kershaw coax you out of your den?"

Freya responded with a coy smile. "Someone had to prop him up and keep him from falling on his butt."

"Dr. Bertram I was hoping you would give me a brief tour of whatever lab facilities you have available in your clinic." Matt requested.

"Sure, come on in." Dr. Bertram opened the door and ushered them inside. "Allison, we have company!" Doc called down the hall.

Allison met them in the hallway, "Dr. Kershaw, I'm glad to see you moving about."

"Right this way," Doc said leading Matt into the small lab.

Dr. Bertram walked Matt through the lab and highlighted the few instruments he had set up as well as his wish list for things he needed. Meanwhile, Freya and Allison went into the library and sat down to chat.

* * *

"Freya, how are you holding up?" Allison asked.

"I'm not sure what you mean?" Freya responded trying to hide her emotional distress.

"You forget that I'm a woman too, I saw how you reacted to Dr. Kershaw's attack and how you have been sitting up day and night watching over him. I would bet you slept very little last night, most likely sitting in a chair somewhere near him."

Freya leaned forward with her elbows on her knees, covering her face with her hands, "I'm so frightened," she whimpered as she started to cry. "I try not to show it, I try to distance myself from him, but I am finding it harder and harder to do." She looked up at Allison, wiping her face. "I know, I'm being silly, I've only known him for a few days."

Allison smiled at Freya while holding her hand. "Time is not a good measurement for formulating a relationship. Have you said anything to him about your feelings?"

"No, not directly," Freya replied. "I'm confused if its love, infatuation, or am I just genuinely concerned for him as a friend and guest in my inn. Oh, I don't know what I'm feeling."

Allison tried to choke back a chuckle. "Freya, just let it go wherever it takes you. Don't try to force it one way or the other. Be patient. Right now, Dr. Kershaw is suffering physically, as well as mentally. He is trying to cope with all that has happened to him and the prospects of how his body is going to react to the LTV transgenesis. He is just as, or even more, confused than you are. Not to mention very frightened at the prospects for his future."

"What do you mean?"

"Doc has noticed Dr. Kershaw developing an emotional attachment to you, just as I've observed in you. It appears that you two will eventually grow closer. So, just be patient, when it happens it happens."

"Thank you, Allison," Freya said as she hugged her. "I should wash my face before they see me like this."

Allison smiled at her and led her to the bathroom so she could freshen up and dry her face.

* * *

"Thanks for the tour Doc," Matt said as he and Dr. Bertram walked toward the front door.

"Where did the ladies go," Dr. Bertram said, loud enough for Freya and Allison to hear him.

"We're in here Doc," Allison replied.

"I believe Dr. Kershaw is ready to go back to the inn if Freya is ready?"

"Yes Doc, I'm ready. I need to get back and whip up something for dinner. Would you and Allison care to have dinner at the inn this evening?"

"Thank you for the invitation, but I think we are going to settle in early this evening," Doc replied.

"Yes, it's been a hectic day," Allison said apologetically.

"As you wish," Freya acknowledged "Good evening to you both."

"Good evening," Matt said.

Dr. Bertram and Allison followed them to the front porch and waved as they walked away toward the inn. Without saying anything, they looked at each other as if reading each other's minds regarding the evolving relationship between Matt and Freya.

* * *

Stepping through the front door of the inn, Freya asked Matt, "How is your shoulder feeling? You need a pain pill?"

"I'm feeling the pain. I think the pain meds are wearing off, but I'm good for now. I will take another pill before I go to bed."

"Are you hungry? I'm starving," she said rubbing her tummy.

"Yes, I am. I didn't eat much of my lunch today."

"Hope you don't mind leftovers."

Matt could not hold back a big smile, "Not at all."

Following Freya into the kitchen, Matt leaned against the counter while she pulled food dishes out from the cooler. "No need to cook on my account. I would love a roast beef sandwich if it's all the same to you."

"Ok, one roast beef sandwich coming up."

Matt stood silently watching Freya busy herself with making sandwiches. He didn't realize he was staring at her until she paused and looked up at him. "What?" She asked, wondering why he was watching her so intently.

"Nothing," he replied.

Freya resumed making the sandwiches, occasionally looking over her shoulder catching Matt staring at her. "Here you go," she said, holding up the plates with the sandwiches on them. "Where would you like to eat?"

"How about by the fireplace," he suggested.

"Fine, lead the way."

Sitting on the hearth, Freya and Matt occasionally exchanged glances, saying little as they ate. After they finished eating, Freya stacked the plates and carried them to the kitchen.

Matt got up slowly, feeling the pain and stiffness returning to his wounded body. "Let me help you with that."

"No problem, I'm just going to take them to the sink. Just sit and relax, I fear you have overdone it for one day."

Matt sat down in the wheelchair waiting for Freya to return.

Returning to the lounge area Freya sat down on the hearth across from Matt.

"Maybe you can get some sleep tonight," he suggested to Freya.

She smiled, unsure if he was aware of her sitting up with him during the night.

"I need to go up and take a shower, I've not been able to take a proper shower or bath since I was injured. Doc would not let me shower earlier because of all the bandages."

"I see he removed some of your bandages and many of your stitches; can you take a shower now?"

181

"Yes, I still have a couple of bandages covering the deep wounds. He gave me some patches to go over those to keep them from getting wet. The problem is, I can't put the patch on or move my arm and shoulder enough to wash very well."

"I can help you. I can put your patches over the areas you would like."

"No, you have done enough already. I can wait."

"Don't be silly. You should know by now I don't mind doing anything for you. Besides, I feel partly responsible for you being in this situation anyway."

"Now who is being silly. You had nothing to do with the attack; it was entirely my fault for not listening to Frankie in the first place."

They both laughed aloud.

"Come on let me help you upstairs and get you into the shower."

As Matt was getting up and walking slowly toward the staircase, Freya turned down the lights in the lobby, lounge, and dining area before helping Matt make his way up the stairs and to his room. Once he was in his room, he sat in the chair while Freya removed his shoes and socks, then she carefully removed his shirt trying not to hurt him in the process.

"Where are the patches Doc gave you?"

"Over there on the highboy."

Freya carefully removed the bandages and applied the patches to cover the areas containing the stitches. "When you get finished showering I'll remove them and put fresh bandages back on you."

"Thank you."

Freya went into the shower and started running the water. "How do you like it, cold, warm, or hot?"

"I like it warm to hot."

After adjusting the water temperature, she helped Matt get to the shower, she removed the sling from his injured arm and around his shoulder noticing him grimace as the weight of the injured arm and shoulder took hold. He obviously was still experiencing significant pain and couldn't move the arm and shoulder. Finally, she helped him undo his belt buckle and unsnap his pants.

"Can you get it from here?" She asked, observing him grimace from pain.

"I think so," he replied.

"I'll be just outside if you need me."

"OK."

After Freya left the bathroom, Matt struggled to get his trousers off and then his boxers. Finally, he was going to be able to take his long awaited and badly needed shower. However, after getting into the shower he was finding it difficult to squeeze the shampoo into his hand or lift his good arm high enough to wash his hair. At one point, he lost his balance causing him to fall against the shower wall taking the force of the fall on his badly injured shoulder.

Freya heard the bump and Matt cry out in pain and called to him through the bathroom door, "Matthew, are you all right?"

"Yes, I just slipped, I'm good."

A few moments later Matt was surprised when Freya opened the shower door and stepped naked into the shower with him.

"Here, let me help you," Freya said casually as if this was a normal thing between them.

Matt didn't know what to say. On one hand, it was a bit awkward, on the other hand, he was happy she was there to help him.

Freya took the shampoo and washed his hair and then hers. Then, she continued to wash Matthew being gentle around his shoulders and arm. Matt stood so the hot water could spray on his shoulder giving him some relief and loosening the tight muscles. While he stood letting the shower spray his back and neck Freya washed her own body. When she finished washing Matthew's back, lower body, and legs she stood up to rinse them both off. When they came face to face, all barriers broke down and they kissed each other passionately.

Regaining their composure, Freya turned off the shower, stepped out and wrapped herself in a towel. After putting down a floor towel so Matt wouldn't slip, he stepped out and she dried him. Without saying anything or displaying any awkwardness, she helped Matt put on his clean boxers and sweat pants.

"How do you feel," she asked.

"Much better, thank you," he replied. When he turned to face her, their eyes met before he kissed her again.

Freya led Matthew to the bedroom and turned the covers down for him. "Here, take your pain pill." Directing him to sit in the chair, she removed the shower patches, dried the wound areas thoroughly before reapplying fresh bandages. Being very careful, she helped him put on a t-shirt before helping him to bed.

Freya returned to the bathroom to gather up her clothes before going to her room. Matt watched in silence, not knowing what to say, as Freya walked toward the door.

"I'll be back to check on you after a while," she said then pulled his door closed behind her.

Matt lay there thinking if he had made a mistake by kissing Freya. Maybe she was just being kind in helping him shower; after all, she did seem to be somewhat casual and didn't appear to try to get amorous with him. However, that didn't seem logical, since she did kiss him back. Matt was going crazy trying to figure out the situation and evaluating his feelings for Freya, as well as, trying to assess her feelings for him.

A short time later Freya returned dressed in silk pajamas wearing a housecoat over them. "Are you comfortable?" she asked. "Can I get anything for you before I turn in?"

"Can you stay a minute," Matt asked motioning for her to sit on the bed next to him.

Without saying anything, Freya sat down next to Matt looking him in the eyes. She was trying not to encourage the situation, but her eyes gave away her true emotions.

"Freya can I be open and honest with you?" Matt asked her in a gentle voice.

"Yes, you can tell me anything." She sat with her hands folded in her lap looking back into his eyes.

"I'm frightened and I don't know which way to turn," He told her.

"Frightened of what?" She asked surprised.

184

"Over the last few days, my world has been turned upside down. Through the ordeal of the attack, LTV infection, and the events today, so much as happened, so quickly, I'm having a hard time processing everything. I've always been good at assessing a situation and then quickly finding a solution. Now… I feel helpless as a lamb surrounded by a pack of wolves. No pun intended." Matt smiled. "However, every time I felt myself being thrown off balance thoughts of you would bring me back to center. I don't know how I would have handled this if you were not here with me. I guess I'm afraid to trust my feelings. I'm not sure if I'm developing a sincere emotional attachment to you or if you are an emotional crutch."

Freya didn't say anything, she just stared at her hands and started to tear up before looking back into Matt's eyes.

Matt reached over and grasped Freya's hand. "I am forty years old and I haven't had one single solid long-term relationship in my adult life. My work always seemed to take precedence and I never devoted quality time to foster any meaningful relationship."

"I can't believe you never had a relationship with a woman. Even dorky guys like you get lucky every now and then." She tried to joke as she wiped tears from her eyes.

"Oh I've had a girlfriend or two over the years, but I never found anyone who captured my heart long enough to make that special someone apart of my thoughts and plans for the future. That is until now." He said squeezing Freya's hand.

Freya looked him in the eyes again not knowing what to say.

"I'm afraid," he continued, "because I don't know what the future holds for me; for us. I can't see my life going anywhere without you being a part of it, but with all that has happened and will happen, for the first time in my life I don't know what to do."

"Oh, Matthew." Freya laid her head on his good shoulder with her arm around him and began to cry. "I'm also afraid," she sobbed. "I've tried to remain distant, knowing that one day soon, you would leave and I would be alone again. But each day, everything about you kept drawing me closer to you. Then, when

185

I saw you covered in mud and blood, my life seemed to shatter right in front of me."

"Would you do something for me?"

"Yes, anything," she replied as she lifted her face from his shoulder and wiped her eyes as she looked Matthew in the eyes.

"Can you turn down the lamps and lay next to me for a while."

Freya looked into his eyes and paused for a moment, then without saying anything, she did as he asked. She turned back the covers and lay next to Matt, curling up with her head on his good arm and her back to him while pulling the covers over them.

Chapter 23

Rising early the next morning, Freya slipped out of bed and went down to brew coffee. For the first time in many years, she felt content. She recalled the advice Allison gave her, to be patient, and she decided to let things take their course and to be happy whichever way the wind blew. Freya realized from their talk last night, Matt was just as unsure about the future as she was and somehow that seemed to open the door for many possibilities. It was becoming apparent, the events of Misty Hollow would decide their fate, separately or together. '*Live in the moment,*' she said to herself, '*live in the moment.*'

When Freya returned to Matt's room with coffee, she was surprised to see him in the bathroom trying to lather his face to shave. "Well, you look much stronger this morning. I take it your arm and shoulder is feeling better?"

"Surprisingly yes," he said moving his good arm, demonstrating some improved mobility, while still experiencing significant pain. "I guess the hot shower loosened up my muscles quite a bit. Unfortunately, not enough so that I can manage to shave."

Freya sat a cup of coffee on the counter next to the sink, then took the shaving cream and razor away from Matt. "Here, let me do it before you cut your throat and then Doc will blame me for it."

Matt leaned over slightly and kissed Freya on the cheek. "Good morning."

187

"Good morning," she replied as she started dabbing shaving cream on his face, careful to dodge the wounds on the side of his face and neck.

"Ok, you're done," she announced. She gently cleaned the residual shaving cream with a warm face cloth. "I'm going to my room to change, then I'll be back to help you get dressed before I go down to get breakfast started."

* * *

Matt made his way downstairs to the dining area, feeling much stronger than the day before. He was still extremely stiff and sore, although he could tell his mobility had improved somewhat. He was sitting, sipping his coffee when Dr. Bertram came through the front door.

"Good morning Doc," Matt said with a strong and lively tone.

"Good morning, Matt."

While walking toward Matt, Dr. Bertram observed that Matt was holding his coffee cup in his right hand and able to lift it to sip his coffee with minimal signs of pain or stiffness. "You are looking much stronger and nimbler this morning."

"Yes, I feel one-thousand percent better. The pain and stiffness in my shoulder are not as bad as yesterday and I feel much stronger as well."

Dr. Bertram stepped closer and examined his arm. "Have a seat for a moment please," Doc instructed, directing Matt to a chair next to the window.

"Do you mind if I remove your shirt?"

"Sure." Matt proceeded to unbutton his shirt then slowly worked it off with a little help from Dr. Bertram.

Dr. Bertram noticed how Matt, although still in considerable pain, managed to remove his shirt. When Doc removed the bandages, he noted that all but the deeper wounds had nearly healed over. The wounds from which he had removed the stitches from the day before, appeared to be forming scar tissue as if the wounds were weeks old rather than days. "I'll leave these bandages off and after breakfast, I'll redress your wounds."

188

Freya came through the kitchen door as Matt was putting his shirt back on with Dr. Bertram standing next to him. "Is everything alright?"

"Everything is fine," Dr. Bertram replied. "Actually, Matt is healing much faster than I expected. It's remarkable."

"What do you mean by remarkable," Matt asked.

"What I mean is; you have healed about five times faster than anyone else with the same level of physical injuries. Under normal circumstances, I wouldn't even expect to see this level of cellular regeneration among any of the Therians."

"How is that possible?" Matt asked.

"It seems you are starting to exhibit one of the positive elements of the LTV mutation. And that in itself is remarkable."

Matt rubbed his face, demonstrating confused frustration, "I thought you said it would be months before any of the mutations began to materialize?"

"Correct. Under normal circumstances, that would be the case. However, your LTV infection is from an Alpha Prime, carrying an advanced mutated strain of LTV, which we haven't experienced before. Now, the virus is mutating and developing a completely new strain. This is the cycle of LTV evolution we must stop as soon as possible."

Freya resumed setting out breakfast while Matt paced around the room nervously. Dr. Bertram sat down at the table and allowed Matt time to think through what was going on inside his head.

Interrupting Matt's contemplation, Dr. Bertram asked, "Matthew, do you mind if I speak frankly with you?"

Matt paused and looked up at Dr. Bertram to listen to what he had to say.

"You need to stop looking and thinking as a victim and start attacking the situation as a problem and working to solve the problem by thinking as a scientist. I don't have all the answers, that's why we need your help. Knowledge of viruses is my strength and knowledge of cryptids and wildlife biology is yours."

189

Matt sat down next to Dr. Bertram, "Doc, I hear what you are saying; nevertheless, I'm out of my comfort zone here. My life, my career, my world has been turned upside down and my head is spinning like the girl in the movie '*The Exorcist.*"

"Listen to me," Dr. Bertram put his hand on Matt's shoulder. You need to pick yourself up and refocus your thoughts toward investigating and solving a complex problem. Step back and look at the situation objectively, stratify the elements to the problem and start tackling them methodically. You are a scientist, start thinking and acting like one. You can get through this; we can all get through this together."

"You're right I suppose; I just need some time to get my head on straight."

Freya interrupted, "Ok, breakfast is served, dig in."

Dr. Bertram noticed that Freya seemed to be a bit fresher and joyful than usual, "you seem happy this morning."

Freya smiled and continued serving breakfast, "I'm just happy that Matthew is feeling better."

* * *

Matt sat on the examination table as Dr. Bertram removed a few more stitches from his arm and shoulder. "I'm pleased that you are healing so quickly, but you're going to have a collection of sexy scars to tell stories about."

"I think it will take more than a few sexy scars for a dorky guy like me," Matt replied.

"Dorky?"

"Yeah, that's what Freya calls me," he said followed by a half-hearted laugh.

"She is a good woman, I'm sure she was just joking with you."

"Yes, she is and she enjoys pulling my leg when she gets the opportunity," Matt acknowledged.

"Alright, you're all done. But, don't over exert that arm or shoulder for a few more days. There is a tremendous amount of deep tissue damage."

"Doc, can we take another look at your lab before I go?

"Certainly," Dr. Bertram replied as he led Matt back to the lab.

"Do you have a pad and pencil I can use?"

Matt began taking notes on what equipment and supplies the doctor had in the lab. "Doc, is there anyone in the valley who has any lab experience?"

"Well, besides myself and Allison, there's a young man from the valley who is a trained lab tech. He lives and works at a hospital outside the valley, otherwise, the answer is no."

"Is there a building in the village not being used we could possibly convert into a wet lab?"

"The only building in the village which is not being actively used is the constable's office."

"You mean the jailhouse?"

"Yes."

"Can we go take a look at it?"

"Sure, let me tell Allison we're going out for a stroll."

The jailhouse appeared abandoned for some time evidenced by the thick layer of dust throughout the interior. Matt stood in the middle of the main room and scanned in all directions looking at each corner, nook, and cranny as if he was visualizing the placement of lab benches and equipment. On one side of the main room, a door opened into a hallway leading to a bathroom, small bedroom, and a kitchenette. He checked the condition of the bathroom, and kitchen, which was complete with a cooler, stove, and sinks. Another door on the opposite side of the main room opened into a narrow hallway that ran along the front of two jail cells.

"This is perfect. Who do we see about getting permission to use this building and to do some remodeling?"

"It's done," Dr. Bertram said abruptly, "I'll call William and he will provide whatever resources we need."

"Doc, am I good to travel?"

"What do mean?"

"If I drive to the city, will I spaz out and cause a wreck, or turn into a beast and kill my neighbor's goat, suck the blood from her cat or anything like that?"

Dr. Bertram laughed aloud, "No, I don't think you will morph into a werewolf if that's what you are asking. But, I would feel better, if you are planning on driving back to the city, for someone to ride along with you."

"I need to go check on my jeep and see if it's in any condition to drive."

"Actually, Peter just brought it back from the shop yesterday."

"From the shop?"

"Yes, it was badly banged up during the attack. The driver's side door and front corner panel had to be repaired."

"Doc, I don't know how to thank all of you for your kindness and hospitality."

"You can thank us, the whole village, the whole valley, by helping us deal with the wargs and find a cure for the LTV."

Matt nodded in acknowledgment, "Doc, I need to go to the city and pick up some stuff from the university. Also, I need to see Harvey and see if he can arrange for the acquisition of some lab equipment we'll need. Make a list of any medical supplies you need and I'll bring them back with me." After taking one last look around Matt and Dr. Bertram started walking back toward the inn.

"Ok, I'll have Allison do an inventory and make you a list. When do you want to go?"

"I would like to leave tomorrow morning if possible if I can talk Freya into riding shotgun." Matt paused to think briefly, "This is early June; July, the first week in August," he said aloud to himself. We have roughly two months before I have to be back in the classroom." He said.

"What are you thinking," Dr. Bertram asked.

"I should be gone two maybe three days. When I get back, I should be prepared to sit with you and William to map out a plan to tackle the objectives you laid out. Doc, you do know this is going to take months if not a year?"

"Matthew, I've been working for fifteen years just to identify the basic viral nature of LTV. I suspect it will take us much longer than even you expect. Nevertheless, we have to start now rather than later. Is there anything I need to do for you here while you are gone?"

"One thing we need is to get someone working right away on creating a census of the valley residents, complete with family trees, as far back as you can map them. I'll bring back a computer so we can start building a database. We will need to model the various strains of the LTV and other factors."

When they arrived back at the inn, Matt noticed his jeep parked at the side of the building. He walked over to check it out. Opening the door, he could not detect any evidence of damage and the interior was spotless. "Wow, looks better than it has in quite some time." The keys were in the ignition, so he reached in and started the jeep.

"Doc, if you will take care of those things we discussed, I'll visit with Freya and get ready to leave tomorrow."

"I'll see you later this evening to give you my supply list and update you on the other items."

* * *

Upon entering the inn, Matt saw Freya sitting in the lounge area sipping a hot cup of tea.

"You're back," she said looking up at Matt. "Are you alright?"

"I'm fine. Still very stiff and sore, but moving around helps me loosen up." Matt made his way over to sit near Freya.

"Would you like some tea or coffee?" She asked.

"Whatever you're having would be fine."

"I saw you and Doc walk down to the jailhouse. Are you thinking to arrest someone?" Freya said smiling.

Matt laughed, "No, we are going to convert the jailhouse into a lab. I need to go to the city, pick up some stuff from the university, and gather some supplies for Doc. I also need to go visit Harvey while I'm in town."

"How long will you be gone?"

193

"Well, maybe two or three days, but it depends on..." Matt sipped his tea without looking up at Freya.

"Depends on what?" She insisted.

"Doc says I'm ok to drive, except he doesn't want me driving alone on a long road trip. He says I have to get someone to ride along with me in case I start morphing into a werewolf."

"WHAT! NO!" He never said anything about that!" Freya jumped up in a panic.

Matt started laughing uncontrollably.

"You jerk." She smacked him on the shoulder realizing Matt was playing a mean joke on her. "I hope that really hurt." She said regaining her composure.

"But seriously, Doc wants me to have someone go with me. He is still not sure of what symptoms I might experience and would feel better if someone was with me. And to be honest, I'm still too sore and stiff in the neck and shoulders to drive, especially that far."

"Who are you going to get to go with you?" Freya said curiously.

"I was hoping Frankie might like to spend a few days in the city with me." Again, Matt sipped his tea without looking at Freya.

"Well…" Freya stammered, "I guess she would go with you." Freya had a dejected look on her face as if you had taken a toy away from a child. Then when she looked up, she noticed Matt snickering. "You Jerk!"

Matt smiled then winked at Freya. "I was hoping you would ride along with me."

Freya thought for a moment, "I don't know. There's no one here to watch after the inn."

"Watch after what? I'm your only guest and I'll be on a road trip with you. Are you expecting a tour bus of visitors in the next two days?"

"No, of course not," she replied.

"Then it's settled, you will be my escort and driver. You might want to pack for at least three days or maybe five. You should make up a shopping list of stuff you need or want while we are in the city. I'm not sure when we'll get to go back before the fall semester starts."

Freya got up, went to Matt, embraced him, and kissed him passionately before she skipped off to make her preparations for the road trip.

Matt called after Freya before she left the room, "May I use the phone? I need to call Sarah and Harvey."

"Help yourself," she replied.

Matt called Sarah to let her know that he was driving down the next day. She was anxious to fill him in on her research and findings, but Matt encouraged her to wait until he arrived there and they could sit down and review it in detail. Matt told Sarah he was bringing a guest so she would be prepared when they arrived. After talking to Sarah, Matt called Harvey to let him know he would be coming to the city and wanted to visit with him. He told Harvey he didn't want to talk on the phone and maybe it would be better if they could talk outside his office somewhere. Harvey agreed and suggested Matt come to the office and from there they would make an excuse to go conduct a site visit to one of the nearby facilities.

The last order of business before he left was to recover his gear from the monitoring sites. He decided to call Alex to arrange for him to collect his equipment at the various sites.

"Alex, this is Matthew Kershaw," he said when Alex answered the phone.

"*Matt, it's great to hear your voice. I take it you are up and about already.*"

"Yes, doc says I'm healing well and will be fully recovered in no time."

"*Great; Frankie and I have called Doc every day to check on you.*"

"Doc relayed your messages and very thoughtful of you two to call."

"*We are very pleased you're recovering. You gave us quite a scare.*"

"Thanks again. Listen, the reason I've called is, to ask you for a favor."

195

"*Sure, anything. What can I do for you?*" Alex replied.

"I was hoping you would be willing to go out and recover my equipment from the field. Frankie knows where the equipment is located and what to look for. I'm going to be out of the valley for a few days and I would like to have my gear picked up from out of the field."

"*We would be pleased to take care of that for you. Frankie and I'll get Victor to go along with us tomorrow and gather it up if that's soon enough.*"

"Tomorrow would be great. And Alex, don't take any chances, I don't want anyone to get hurt or killed, it's not that important."

"*No problem. But if you prefer, we can just drop it off at the inn for you so you don't have to worry about lifting it.*"

"Thanks, I truly appreciate your help. I'll talk to you in a few days." After hanging up, Matt sat down to make out his own list of items he needed from the city.

Later that afternoon Dr. Bertram came to the inn to give Matt the list of medical supplies he needed. "Tell Freya we will look after the inn while she is gone and not to worry about anything."

"Thanks, Doc."

Chapter 24

Matt and Freya woke early. Peter came over to help Matt load the jeep. Soon, Matt and Freya were ready to leave.

Stepping off the front porch of the inn, Freya stopped and turned to look back at the inn gazing at the sign over the front porch. "I don't think I've ever spent a night way from the inn, my entire life," she said aloud to herself.

Matt had stopped and overheard her comment. "It will be here when you get back. We'll only be away for three or four days," he said to reassure her. When she turned around, Matt noticed she was grasping the locket he had given her.

"I think it's going to rain," Freya commented, looking at the sky before they got into the jeep.

Driving along the road out of Graymere to the main highway, Freya tried to avoid bumps and potholes, nevertheless, the ride was very painful for Matt. He silently wondered if he would be able to stand the ride all the way to the city.

In spite of the pain, Matt couldn't help but notice an air of excitement in Freya's demeanor. Matt thought to himself, '*if this is the first time she's ever spent a night away from the inn. She's really in for a treat.*' The idea made him smile.

"What are you smiling about?" Freya asked.

"Nothing," he replied. "I have to warn you beforehand; I don't talk much while I'm traveling. I tend to zone out."

"Ok, no problem," she replied. "How far is it to your place?"

"It's about three to four hours depending on how many times we stop. We should arrive at my cabin around noon. I told Sarah you were coming with me, so she will have the place ready for us."

"Sarah, your research assistant?" Freya asked confused.

"Yes, she is the grad student who house sits for me during the summer when I'm away doing field research. This summer she is doing some research for me in addition to house sitting."

"Do you live far from town?"

"Not too far, you can drive to the city from my cabin in about twenty minutes."

Matt and Freya chitchatted until they got out of the valley and onto the main highway. Freya stopped at Jack's Trading Post to fuel up and to get snacks for the road.

"Freya," Jack said as he came out from behind the counter to give her a hug. "Long time no see."

"Good to see you as well, Jack. Looks like Mrs. Wilson has been feeding you well," Freya joked as she patted him on his tummy.

"Dr. Kershaw, how are you my friend," Jack greeted him shaking his hand.

"Doing well Jack," Matt replied trying not to show pain.

"So where are the both of you off to today?" Jack inquired.

Freya spoke up before Matt said anything. "Just going into town to pick up a few things."

"You guys have a safe trip," Jack said as Matt paid for the fuel and snacks.

"Thanks, Jack," Matt said as they left the store.

Back on the highway, there was not much traffic and it was beginning to rain. Matt had taken a pain pill after stopping at Jack's Trading Post and it was not long before his eyes were getting heavy and he dozed off.

* * *

Matt woke up when Freya pulled over to take a break and give Matt time to wake up so he could navigate the rest of the way to his cabin.

"We ready to go," he asked as Freya came out of the store and got into the jeep.

"Yes, I believe so," she replied.

Pulling out the thermos to pour a cup of coffee, Matt took a sip, "umm that feels good on a damp day like today," he said then offered the cup to Freya.

"How far are we from your cabin," She asked, handing the cup back to Matt.

"Maybe a half hour." Settling back in his seat, Matt gave Freya directions to his cabin. He was happy that Freya seemed to be relaxed and he hoped she would enjoy the trip. The last few minutes passed quickly for Freya as she was taking in the sights of the world outside the valley.

"Here we are," Matt announced when they pulled off the road and onto the narrow drive up to his cabin.

Coming around a gentle bend in the drive, the trees opened up to reveal a quaint cabin situated on the edge of a small field. Off to one side was a large pond with about a dozen ducks paddling along the shoreline.

To Freya, it looked lovely and peaceful. "Oh Matthew, it's beautiful."

As Freya pulled into the carport and parked, Sarah came out to greet them. She immediately thought it odd that Matt would be riding and someone else driving his Jeep. "Welcome home Dr. Kershaw. And, you must be Ms. Freya. I'm Sarah," she said while giving Freya a girlie hug. "Dr. Kershaw has told me nothing about you, so we have a lot to talk about." Sarah started rambling as she led Freya into the house without noticing that Matt was having difficulty getting out of the jeep and moving slowly.

Freya looked over her shoulder at Matt curiously, as Sarah whisked her into the Cabin. Matt just shrugged his head and eyes at Freya.

"I mowed the yard before it rained; I wanted it to look nice when you got here." Sarah continued to ramble. "Come on in, I made lunch. I didn't know what time you guys would be here, but I guess I timed it about right."

199

Matt followed them into the cabin getting slapped by the screen door when Sarah let it fly, not realizing Matt was lagging behind and not able to catch the door before it slapped him on the shoulder. Freya again looked at him as if asking if Sarah was a bit off or what. Matt simply chuckled to himself.

"Dr. Kershaw, I know you just drove four hours or so and you may want to chill, but after lunch, I would like to show you the stuff I researched and the reports I've prepared for you. I hope you don't mind, my friends and I are going out for dinner and a movie this evening."

Matt smiled at Sarah, "how much coffee have you had today?"

"Why?" She asked.

Matt just smiled and shook his head in response.

Seeing Matt's response Sarah just shrugged her shoulders and continued her hyperactive chatter. "I'm sorry. I guess I'm just glad to have company."

"Don't you go out and relax with your friends?" Matt asked as he struggled to carry one of the small bags down the hall.

"No, they've had their noses buried in their textbooks for a summer class and I've been immersed in the research assignment you gave me. I haven't gone out since you left last week. By the way, how are you feeling?" Sarah finally asked when Matt came back into the room.

"I'm doing fine. Just a few lacerations and a bit of infection, but I'm recovering alright."

Noticing Matt pointing to the injuries on his arm while talking, Sarah became speechless, after she finally slowed down long enough to notice the wounds on Matt's face, neck, and arms. "Oh my God!" She grabbed his arm to examine the wounds more closely, causing Matt to grimace. Tracing the wounds up his arm, she discovered the deep wound at the base of his neck. Reaching up, she pulled down his collar to reveal the wound extending down the back of his shoulder. Stepping back, she put her hands to her face, "Oh, my God, what happened to you?" She said, stunned at the extent of Matt's wounds.

Freya spoke up before Matt could respond, "He was attacked and mauled by a wolf. It almost killed him." She said emotionally.

Sarah stepped back again and sat hard on a chair, staring at Matt. "Dr. Kershaw I had no idea. When did this happen?" Sarah was in a state of mild shock.

"Tuesday morning."

"And I assume you were in the hospital all week and that is why I couldn't reach you?" She got up to examine the wounds again. "They look to be almost healed," she said when she studied the wounds again.

"A lady in the village practices homeopathic medicine and she applied some of her magic salves to them. Even the doctor was amazed at how fast my wounds have healed." Matt explained glancing at Freya.

"That's not all of them," Sarah observed as she traced some of the wounds beyond his sleeve and collar.

Matt looked at Freya, then he unbuttoned his shirt to reveal multiple claw marks across his chest shoulders, and upper arms. When he turned his back to her, she could see the full extent of the deep wound where the 'wolf' sank his fangs just above the collarbone, at the base of his neck diagonally across his upper shoulder to a point near his spine.

Sarah had to sit down again. "I can't believe it. Oh, my God," she repeated. "Dr. Kershaw I'm so sorry."

"Why are you sorry," Matt replied while buttoning his shirt back up, "you didn't do anything."

Freya poured Sarah a glass of water and handed it to her. "Are you alright?"

"Yes ma'am," Sarah replied, taking a sip of water.

Freya gave her a friendly smile, "Just Freya if you please."

Trying to change the subject, Matt asked, "So what did you fix for lunch?"

"Peanut butter and jelly sandwiches," Sarah said without flinching still stunned at the extent of Matt's wounds.

"What!" Matt responded.

"Just kidding. I made lasagna. It should be done about now." She said getting up to check the oven. "Yes, I believe it's ready." She pulled the dish out of the oven and sat it on top of the stove. "It needs to set for a few minutes. You guys can freshen up, while I set the table."

Matt led Freya down the hall and showed her around the cabin.

"This is my bedroom." He hesitated a moment, stepping back into the hall. "There is the spare room, whichever you prefer." Matt tried to be casual in his suggestion. After the tour, Freya brought in their bags, which she placed in Matt's room while Matt was washing his hands and face. When he came out of the bathroom, he saw Freya unpacking.

"You're welcome to put your things in these drawers, they're empty," Matt told her, pointing to one side of his dresser.

Freya pulled out her toiletry bag and winked at Matt as she brushed past him, stepping into the bathroom to freshen up.

Back in the kitchen, Sarah was setting the table when she looked up to see Matt entering the kitchen. "She's beautiful," Sarah whispered.

Matt smiled and slightly shook his head at the girlish nature of her comment.

"No really, she is," Sarah continued, "are you two, like....?"

Matt chuckled without giving Sarah an answer. "What do you want to drink?" He asked.

"Sweet ice tea for me please."

Freya turned the corner just in time to hear Sarah's reply. "Iced tea?" Freya asked.

"Yes, I think you'll like it," Matt replied.

Sarah furrowed her eyebrows at Freya's question but didn't say anything.

Sitting at the table, Freya casually looked around the room and started noticing various gadgets and conveniences she had never seen, other than pictures in a magazine. The room seemed so bright compared to the inn. The cabin had more windows augmented by bright electric lights making the room appear filled with sunlight.

Sarah sat the lasagna dish in the middle of the table, "lunch is served, and I hope you like it?"

"Umm it smells delicious," Freya said, closing her eyes and breathing the aroma gently.

Sarah served Freya first, then Matt, before sitting down to eat. She lifted her glass to toast, "to good friends and good health."

Matt lifted his glass and Freya followed along. 'Clink, clink, clink' the glasses all touched before they drank to the toast.

"This is an experience I'm not used to," Freya commented.

"What's that, Ms. Freya?" Sarah asked.

"Someone else cooking and serving me meals as the guest, instead of the other way around."

Sarah just looked at her curiously without making a comment.

Matt noticed Sarah's confused expression. "Freya owns and operates an inn single-handedly. It's also the local meeting place and the only restaurant within a hundred miles. So, Freya's day is oriented around taking care of and serving others, from the time she gets up until she goes to bed at night."

"Oh my dear woman, have you never heard of women's lib?" Sarah asked with a tone of indignation.

Matt burst out laughing and almost choked on his food.

"What?" Sarah barked, "Why are you laughing?"

Freya couldn't help but start laughing, prompted by Matt's laughter and then compounded by Sarah's response.

"Girl, we are going to have to talk before you leave here. This is the 21st century, not the middle ages." Sarah said sternly.

Sarah's comment renewed Matt's laughter. "I'm sorry, but that was so random," He finally mutter.

"I'm serious; I'm going to hook you up by the time you leave here." She said to Freya. "And I better not find out you have been taking advantage of this woman," Sarah said pointing her dinner knife at Matt.

Matt had to put his napkin over his mouth for fear of spitting his food out; he was laughing so hard. He tried to hold it in, but Sarah's final comment put him over the top.

Freya did her best to refrain from laughing and sought to encourage Sarah, "What's a girl to do; I'm surrounded by male chauvinist pigs. This is my life, day in and day out." She said while trying to keep a straight face.

"Uh uh," Sarah wagged her knife, "we are going to change all that," she affirmed before she resumed eating.

Freya looked at Matt still trying to hold back her laughter.

"Dr. Kershaw you laugh now, but I'm telling you, I'm going to make a new woman out of Ms. Freya." Sarah scolded.

"Excuse me," Matt said before he got up from the table and went back to his room to laugh uncontrollably.

Freya was trying hard to hold back her laughter as she casually ate her lunch. Satisfied she had exacted revenge on Matt for the jokes he played on her, his comments about morphing into a werewolf, and Frankie spending a few days with him in the city.

When Matt returned he was doing well to compose himself when Freya spoke up, "Are you alright? I was about to come check on you, I was afraid you were in there morphing."

Matt lost it again and had to excuse himself for the second time.

Sarah looked at Freya with a confused expression on her face.

"Sorry, it's an inside joke," she told Sarah.

"Oh,"

While Matt was out of the room, Freya enlightened Sarah. "My life is not that bad. I own my own inn, and I do, more or less, what I want to do, when I want to do it. I enjoy the peace and quiet of the small village."

"Oh, cool. Maybe I should come check it out sometime."

"You should," Freya suggested.

Matt was finally able to return to the table and finish his meal. "Sarah, in all sincerity, your lasagna is excellent. Thank you."

"Yes, it's delicious," Freya told her.

"Thank you, my grandmother taught me how to make it."

After they finished clearing the table, Sarah pulled out her files and went through them briefly with Matt. She highlighted a couple of reports she had found and handed him the research paper she had written as he requested.

Freya found Sarah to be delightful; she was twenty-seven or twenty-eight years old; at around five-feet-four inches tall with a petite, athletic body. She appeared to be of mixed race with African American and Native American heritage with beautiful smooth light chocolate skin tone. She wore her hair cut in a pixie hairstyle.

"If you don't mind Dr. Kershaw, I'm going to go shower and get ready to meet my friends. After you have had time to review some of the material this evening I can go through it in more detail with you tomorrow if that is alright."

"Sarah, go have fun with your buddies, I need to rest and this can wait until tomorrow. I'll be here for two or three days before we head back to Graymere. There will be plenty of time to go over this stuff in detail. So, go have fun and relax."

While Sarah was showering and getting ready for her evening out, Matt took Freya by the hand and led her on a stroll around his cabin. Matt stopped first in the carport to scoop up a cup of animal food before leading Freya down to the pond to feed the ducks. Freya watched Matt treating the ducks to their favorite food. She noticed how relaxed he appeared standing among them gingerly feeding and talking to them. She took some of the food, coaxed one of the ducks up close, and fed it from her hand.

"He likes you. He will not do that for me," Matt told Freya.

"He's cute. Does he have a name?"

"I call him a duck."

"You Jerk," she said with a smile as she tossed a morsel of the duck food at him.

"Look," he whispered pointing across the pond at a fawn near the far edge of the pond. "Do you see it?"

Freya looked up and watched the fawn make its way down to the edge of the pond to take a drink and graze along the shore.

Matt took Freya to the back yard where he had a swing situated in a gazebo. "Have a seat and I'll be right back. Matt returned with two glasses of ice tea. Handing one of the glasses to Freya, he sat down next to her and gently rocked the swing.

"Good night guys, have a good evening," Sarah called out from the corner of the house to Matt and Freya.

"Be careful, no drinking and driving!" Matt called back to her.

"I won't," Sarah replied, disappearing around the corner.

Shortly after Sarah left, it started to sprinkle rain. Sitting in the covered swing, protect from the gentle rain, Matt and Freya continued to relax and watch the deer across the pond. Suddenly, the bottom fell out of the sky and they were getting wet from the blowing rain.

Matt jumped up and took Freya's hand, "Quickly, let's get inside!" They ran across the yard, through the torrent of rain, to the carport.

Freya started laughing as she stood dripping from head to toe, attempting to shake off some of the water.

Matt kicked off his shoes and quickly stripped down to his boxer. "Stay here, I'll be right back," he instructed, then ran into the house through the wet room connected to the garage. He emerged a few seconds later with towels and noticed Freya was already shivering. "Here, take those wet things off before you catch a cold."

Freya looked at Matt and then scanned the open carport without saying anything.

Matt smiled at her. "It's ok, there isn't anyone around. My nearest neighbor lives a half mile away," Matt reassured her. Matt picked up his wet clothes and told Freya "I'll go get the water running in the shower. Just drop your wet clothes into the washer on your way in." He then went back into the house dropping his closes into the washing machine, indicating to Freya which one it was before disappearing into the cabin.

Chapter 25

When Freya had showered and dressed, she found Matt at the table in the breakfast nook reading through the material Sarah left with him. She leaned back against the island in the middle of the kitchen while she finished towel drying her hair, watching Matt studying the reports.

Looking up from what he was reading, Matt asked Freya, "Do you feel better?"

"Yes, very much so, do you want to shower now?"

"I showered in the other bathroom. I have a blow dryer if you want to use it to dry your hair?"

"A what?" Freya asked looking puzzled.

"A blow dryer," he repeated. "Come and I'll show you." Matt led Freya back to the bathroom and pulled a blow dryer from under the sink, plugged it in, and started blowing her hair with it. After giving her a minute to get the idea, Matt handed her the dryer and returned to the kitchen.

When Freya rejoined him some time later, her hair had a soft silky glow to it. "That was amazing," she said.

Matt smiled. "You look beautiful," he said, looking her in the eyes. "You should have put on your casual clothes, so you can get comfortable and relax."

"What do you mean casual clothes, this is all I wear," she replied.

"Girl, Sarah is right, you need to get out more," he winked at Freya. He got up and led her back to his bedroom where he picked through his closet and dresser drawers until he found a pair of exercise pants and a jersey T-shirt. "Here, put these on, you'll be more comfortable." He left her to change and returned to the kitchen to resume reading the reports.

"How's this?" Freya asked.

Matt looked up and stared at her for a minute without saying anything. She looked like a completely different woman. The transformation was simple but amazing."

"What's wrong?" Freya asked as she started checking herself to make sure she didn't have something on backward or inside-out.

"Nothing at all." He got up and went to Freya, and cupped her face in his hands. "You look beautiful."

For a moment, they stood there staring into each other's eyes before Freya reached her arms around Matt and embraced him with her head against his chest. Matt thought he heard her crying softly. Pulling back from her, he looked into her face and saw tears rolling down her cheeks. "Why are you crying?"

"Nothing," she replied.

"No nothing, something; what is it?" he insisted compassionately.

Looking up, into Matt's eyes, "No man has ever told me that I was beautiful."

Matt pulled her close and held her for a long while until she stopped crying. Then he led her across the open room to the couch, sat down in a reclining position, and pulled Freya down in front of him so she lay back on his chest. He wrapped his arms around her and just held her as they listened to the rain outside.

"Matt, can I ask you something personal?"

"Sure; what?"

"Have you been married before?"

Matt chuckled then answered, "No, what makes you ask that?"

"I don't know, you said the other night that you had not had any solid relationships, but you didn't say you ever had a wife. You are so thoughtful, caring and considerate. It's almost as if someone had trained you at some point." She turned her head to look up at Matt's face with a smile.

Matt chuckled again and shook his head, "No, no hubby training."

"So why haven't you gotten married before now; if you don't mind me asking?"

"I guess I never stopped chasing my mythical wolf-man long enough to devote any quality time toward developing a meaningful, long-term relationship. Most women are looking for someone to smother them with attention and make her the center of his universe. I could never slow down long enough to devote that much energy to a relationship." Matt paused and then redirected the question back to Freya, "What about you?"

"What about me?"

"Have you ever been married?"

"No, I had a couple of relationships over the last few years, but none ever lasted very long, for one reason or another. Truth to be known, it probably had more to do with the fact, I've been on my own for so long, it's hard for me to be subservient to someone else. The culture of the Valley is such that, the man takes the dominant role, and I could never get used to that."

Matt gave her a firm hug of reassurance.

"What's that," Freya asked pointing to the huge flat screen television.

Matt painfully started trying to get up from under Freya. "What kind of movie do you like?"

"What do you mean by type of movie?"

"Do you like western, drama, mystery, science fiction, spy thriller, chic-flick, a love story?"

"I like to read stuff like Sherlock Holmes, Agatha Christie novels, Moby Dick, and stuff like that if that's what you mean."

Matt dug through his collection of old classic movies until he found the 1956 version of Moby Dick featuring Gregory Peck. "Have you ever seen this one?" He held up the CD for Freya to see.

She didn't know what he was talking about so she just shook her head. "No, I don't think so."

209

Matt put the CD into the disk player and went to the kitchen to pop some popcorn while the movie was loading.

"What are you doing?" Freya asked looking over the back of the couch.

"Popping popcorn; be finished in a minute."

Just as the movie title and credits had finished, he returned to the couch and resumed his position behind Freya to enjoy popcorn and movie with her.

These were all new experiences for Freya, but she refrained from saying anything. Instead, she just sat back, relaxed and enjoyed the feeling of snuggling with Matthew. She had never felt so comfortable around anyone else as she did with Matthew. She thought to herself, '*here I am thirty-six years old and aside from the affections from my mother and grandmother, I've never felt the sincere, tender, loving touch from anyone else in my life. Maybe I'm dreaming; if so, I hope I don't wake up anytime soon.*'

As the movie was ending, Freya looked up at Matt and commented, "We will have to get some of this to take back with us to Graymere?

"What?"

"Popcorn; only I don't have a microwave to cook it or a screen to show movies like this."

"Are you hungry, I can warm the lasagna Sarah made if you like?"

"I'm not real hungry, but if you're hungry we can eat if you like."

Matt went to the kitchen to heat the lasagna in the microwave and he put some garlic bread in the toaster. Freya was watching him from over the back of the couch and marveling at the convenience of gadgets that ran on electricity.

While the food was heating up, Matt set the plates and silverware on the table. "Would you care for some wine with dinner?

Freya normally only drank wine on special occasions. However, this constituted a special occasion in her books. "Sure; why not," she replied.

"I have a Chianti I think you'll like." Matt pulled a bottle off the rack, opened it to let it breathe before setting it on the table with the wine glasses. By then the food was ready, "Dinner is served."

Freya had been watching Matt from over the top of the couch and marveled at how quickly he prepared a hot meal. It was so strange for her not to be in the kitchen cooking and serving the meal.

Matt lifted his wine glass in a toast. "To the future, may all your days be filled with joy and happiness." Tipping the wine glasses Matt and Freya sipped their wine while staring into each other's eyes.

As they ate, Matt outlined his plans for the next day. "Tomorrow I need to go to the university to gather some books and reference materials. If you like, I'll have Sarah take you out to see the town and do some shopping while you're in the city. Then tomorrow evening I'll take you out for dinner."

"I didn't bring anything to wear appropriate to be running around the city."

Matt laughed, "You don't worry about that, Sarah will take care of you in that department, trust me."

Freya just shrugged her shoulders in agreement to Matt's suggestion.

"Cool, and Tuesday, I need to run up to see Harvey. You are welcome to come along. But, if you and Sarah can spend that day gathering some supplies for Dr. Bertram and doing some shopping for popcorn and other items to take back with us, we can probably leave here Wednesday morning, heading back to Graymere. Otherwise, we will spend Wednesday gathering the supplies and we can leave Thursday morning. What do you think?"

Freya was surprised that Matt asked her opinion and gave her choices for what she wanted to do if anything at all. It was nice to be included in the decision process, not just being told what to do. "What if I don't want to go back?" She asked without giving a hint if she was serious or joking, throwing an apparent curve ball at Matt.

211

Matt paused a moment trying to assess the motive and sincerity of Freya's question. He wiped his face with his napkin, took a sip of wine, and sat back in his chair turning his body toward Freya. "If you decide that you would rather stay here instead of returning to Graymere, and it would truly make you happy, you are welcome to do so for as long as you like. For my part, when I finish my work in Graymere and return here for the fall semester, I would like nothing better than to have you here waiting for me, and knowing that you are safe. If you decide to return to Graymere, and that's what makes you happy, then I'll be there with you. The two most important things to me right now are your safety and happiness." After finishing his remarks, Matt returned to eating.

Freya was speechless; she was totally unprepared for such a deep emotional response to an impromptu question. As she digested Matt's response, she felt a flood of emotion welling up inside her. "Excuse me," she said then got up and ran to the bedroom to cry. Just as Matt's life and future had been disrupted by recent events, she now found her life equally altered and confused. She was unprepared for someone to step into her life, who genuinely cared for her and valued her opinion, with total disregard to any imperfections or shortcomings she may have. She was totally unprepared for Matthew Kershaw to enter her life, in the same way, Matthew Kershaw was unprepared for Freya and the *Curse of Misty Hollow* to enter his.

Matt decided to give Freya a few moments to herself. He busied himself with clearing the table and putting the dishes away. Leaving the porch light on for Sarah, he turned out the lights in the front rooms, then went to check on Freya.

Entering the bedroom, he found Freya face down on the bed with her face buried in a pillow still crying. He went to her and rubbed her back. "Why is it, I'm always making you cry?"

Freya rolled over and looked up at Matt, "Because you make me so happy," she sniffled.

Matt handed her a tissue, "If I make you happy, why do I always make you cry?"

212

"Matthew, I'm thirty-six years old, and except for my mother and grandmother, NO ONE in my entire life has ever shown more than casual concern for me, physically, emotionally, or intellectually, NO ONE, except for you. It's just you, the person that you are, the things you say, the things you do. Everything seems to come from your heart, not from some selfish motive."

"I love you too," Matt said pulling Freya to him in a firm embrace.

"Damn you, Matthew, you're doing it again."

Matt leaned back to look into Freya's face, "Do you love me?"

"Yes damn you, yes!"

"Then everything from this point forward in our lives is secondary to that. Whatever comes our way we will face it together and trust that our love for each other will guide us through any obstacle or danger we have to face. From now on it's you and me."

Matt got up, closed the bedroom door, turned down the covers on the bed, turned out the lights, and got into bed next to Freya and pulled her close to him.

The silence and passion of the moment were broken when Matt asked Freya, "by the way, what's your religious affiliation?"

"What?" Freya responded, surprised at such a random question at that moment.

"Well, do you have a religious preference?" He repeated.

"Not really, my grandmother claimed to be catholic and she taught me from the bible. We don't even have a church in Graymere. What prompted such a question anyway?"

"Nothing, I was just wondering what minister I would need to perform the ceremony."

"What ceremony; are you planning on conducting an exorcism to chase away the wolf spirits?"

"No silly, the wedding ceremony."

Freya rolled over trying to see Matthew's face in the dark. "What wedding ceremony? What on earth are you talking about?" At the very moment she asked the question, she grasped

213

what Matt was saying or proposing. "Are you asking me to marry you?"

Matt sat up in bed, reached over and turned on the lamp next to the bed, then took Freya's hand as he asked, "Freya Fasset, will you marry me?"

Freya sat straight up in the bed, looking at Matt as if he was crazy, "Matthew we've only known each other for two weeks."

"Is that a no?"

"No, I mean, no it's not a no. Oh, Matthew, you have my head spinning."

"Look, my grandmother once told me that time is not a good measure of true happiness or a test of love."

Freya found Matt's anecdote from his grandmother interesting, in that Allison had said the same thing to her only a couple of days earlier. "Matthew, are you sure of this?"

"Freya, I think after forty years, I can trust my heart when I've found true love and happiness. Yes, I'm sure."

Freya wrapped her arms around him, "Then Yes, Yes, and Yes! I think I'm going to cry again."

Matt reached over and turned the light out, "Ok, if you must cry, get it over with." He said. Then, with a soft chuckle, he pulled Freya next to him and kissed her passionately.

Chapter 26

Matt was up early reviewing the reports and analysis Sarah had prepared. Sitting in the quiet of the early morning, he poured through Sarah's research until the dawn started breaking on the horizon. Quietly, he made breakfast of eggs, blueberry bagel, turkey bacon, cream cheese, grape jam, orange juice, and coffee, from which he prepared a breakfast-in-bed tray he took into Freya.

Matt sat on the bed next to Freya and started rubbing her back, "good morning," he whispered.

"Umm," Freya responded. "Something smells yummy."

Rolling over and sitting up in the bed, Freya rubbed her eyes as Matt positioned the tray in her lap and gave her a kiss.

"Umm," She repeated. "I'm not sure if you're trying to spoil me, bribe me, trick me, or what?" she said smiling.

"All of the above."

"My life in Graymere will never be the same, you realize that don't you?"

"Welcome to my world, life here will not be the same for me after Graymere."

They both laughed and smiled at each other.

Freya noticed Matt repeatedly rubbing his ears. "What's wrong with your ears?"

"I've been having this ringing in my ears, it keeps getting louder."

"When did it start?"

"Yesterday morning; it comes and goes, but it just started getting louder to the point that it's becoming very annoying."

"You say it comes and goes?"

"Yeah, just happens every now and then; just enough to aggravate me."

"Let Doc take a look at it when we get back."

While Freya finished her breakfast in bed, Matt shaved and got ready to go to the university. "Don't be in a hurry to get up. Relax and enjoy your morning," he told Freya as he was getting dressed. "I'm going to sit with Sarah for a few minutes to review her research; afterward, I'll leave to go to the university."

"Ok," Freya replied.

When Matt entered the kitchen, Sarah was sitting at the table with her coffee sorting the various documents waiting for Matt.

Before she could say anything, Matt sat down across from her, "Sarah, can you do me a huge, huge favor?"

"Sure Dr. Kershaw; what is it?"

"Freya didn't bring many clothes with her because we didn't expect to stay long or be going out. But our plans have changed slightly. Would you be a darling and take her shopping today while I'm at the office?"

"Sure, you know girls like to shop." She winked with a happy smile.

"What do we need to shop for?"

"Well, some casual clothes, maybe a couple pairs of shoes. I want to take her out to eat this evening so maybe something appropriate for dinner out. Maybe some around-the-house type casual clothes would be nice as well. Oh, by the way, there are no Victoria Secret shops and such up around Graymere, so make sure she has a chance to shop for girlie things while she is in the city."

"Dr. Kershaw," Sarah said teasingly. "I got you covered. How much do you want us to spend?"

"Whatever. Just try to encourage her to shop while she is in the city. She is a bit shy and never splurges on herself. This is my treat to her. For your assistance in performing this task, you can pick out a couple pairs of jeans or slacks for yourself.

"I'll give Freya my credit card before I leave."

"Credit Card? Are you sure you're prepared to turn two women loose, shopping, carte blanche, with your credit card? Man, surviving a wolf attack sure made you a brave soul." She said laughing.

Matt laughed, "Yes, and thanks for doing this for me."

"No problem," Sarah said as they redirected their attention to the research material she had compiled.

"Were you able to find ANY other known or reported tracks like the casting?

"No, nothing anywhere," she replied. "But, as I told you on the phone, the pad shape and configuration is definitely canine." Sarah pointed to a series of animal tracks for comparison. "Note the distinctive pattern of the canine versus any other known animal in North America. Do you want me to show it to Dr. Anderson and ask him if he can help identify it?"

"No, that's not necessary, I know what made the track," Matt said casually while leafing through some of the material.

"You do! What was it?"

Matt paused and glanced at her, "The animal that did this to me," he responded gesturing to his recent wounds.

"Oh my God! You saw it, like up close, face-to-face," she gasped.

"Yes, but let's keep this between us for the time being, NOTHING to anyone, understand, NO ONE."

"Roger, you can count on me. This is getting interesting, but kind of freaky in a way."

"How much wet-lab time have you had at the university?"

"Quite a lot I suppose." She paused to calculate in her head, "I've had at least six courses with wet labs and then I was the lab tutor for the biochem lab. Why do you ask?"

"Nothing at the moment, but I may need your lab skills at some point." Matt thought for a couple of seconds, "Your degree is in molecular biology, right?"

217

"Actually, my undergraduate degree is in microbiology and master's degree in molecular biology."

"Ok..."

"Good morning," Freya said walking up to the table where Matt and Sarah were working.

"Good morning Ms. Freya," Sarah said with a fresh happy smile.

Freya smiled back at Sarah, "you can call me Freya, drop the Ms. and ma'am, a bit; you make me feel old. Think of me more like your older sister."

"I can do that," Sarah acknowledged. "Well, I need to go get ready if we are going shopping. It won't take me but a few minutes. I don't spend a lot of time prepping like the girlie girls do." She said jotting off to her room.

After Sarah was down the hall, Freya looked at Matt, "is she always this high strung?"

"Yes, I'm afraid so." Matt stood up to kiss Freya.

"Umm, good morning," Freya said in a low voice.

"I'm about to leave, but Sarah will take you out this morning and afternoon shopping for clothes and whatever. Here is my credit card to use to shop with."

"No Matthew I can't do that; I can't spend your money."

"Freya, if you are going to be Mrs. Kershaw you will have to get used to the fact that it's not my money, but *our* money. Besides, for all these years I've had no one or nothing to spend my money on. It would make me happy for you to relax and splurge a bit while you're in the city."

Freya embraced Matthew again and kissed him before accepting the credit card. "What should I buy? To be honest, I rarely shop, when I need a new dress or slacks I shop at Simon's mercantile and buy what he has on the rack or order from a catalog."

"Well, today Sarah will teach you the joys of shopping in the city." He said, laughed and then he kissed Freya.

Sarah came back into the room. "I'm ready," she announced.

"Sarah, you have my number. Sometime around noon when you guys are ready to eat lunch, give me a call and I'll meet you in the mall at the Chinese buffet."

Matt kissed Freya, "Have a good time."

Freya waved goodbye as Matt walked out the door.

"You two are in love up to your eyeballs," Sarah told Freya teasingly.

Freya blushed, "why do you say that?"

"Girl, I'm a girl and I have eyes. I've *never* seen Dr. Kershaw give any woman a second look in the four years I've known him."

* * *

The university was not the usual hustle and bustle Matt was accustomed to seeing. The summer sessions were not as hectic as the fall and spring semesters. Matt didn't see anyone in the hall on the way to his office. Once there, he started selecting various books and manuals he thought would be helpful in setting up a lab and training lab techs. He was scanning the bookshelf with his back to the door when James knocked on the open door to get his attention. The sound resonated loudly in Matt's ears creating a sharp echoing pain. He turned to see who was knocking and grabbed his ears in pain.

"Sorry buddy," James apologized. "I didn't realize I knocked that loud."

"No, not a problem, I've just had this nagging pain in my ears the last two or three days." Trying to dismiss the subject, Matt stepped over to shake hands with James, "How has your summer been going so far," he asked.

"Same old, same old, you know how summer sessions are, fast and furious. What are you doing back here; I thought you would be in the field chasing your cryptid."

"Yes, I'm still conducting the investigation, but I needed some reference materials. I have Sarah doing some secondary research for me and I was pulling a few things to help her." Matt put his hands on his ears again appearing to put pressure on them in an attempt to relieve the pain.

Concerned, James asked, "What's up with your ears hurting?"

"Ever since I was attacked I've had this ringing that gets louder and louder and certain sounds will send a sharp pain resonating in my ears." Matt had just opened his big mouth without thinking and he realized he was disclosing more information than he wanted to.

"Wait! What attack?"

Matt was careful to make up a story to explain, without going into too many details. "Last week I was attacked and mauled by a huge wolf."

"My God! It's obvious you survived; how bad was it? Have you been tested or treated for rabies?"

"Over eighty stitches," Matt replied pointing out the wounds. "The doctor at the local clinic tested me for rabies and found that I didn't have rabies, but instead I had contracted some form of the virus. I spent three days in the local clinic recovering before they released me."

"Shit fire, Matthew!" Astonished by the array of wounds Matt suffered. Examining Matt's injuries, James commented, "If you didn't contract rabies, maybe it was Parvovirus or distemper. If I recall correctly, there are only a handful of canine related strains of parvo, and maybe three or four known to infect humans. To the best of my knowledge, you don't contract parvo through bite wounds. Distemper maybe. Distemper is very closely related to measles in humans you know."

"Yes, I had the doc isolate some of the blood and tissue samples. From the symptoms, he thought I had the flu bug. The doctor sent off samples to be tested and confirmed it." Matt was trying to give James an explanation that he hoped would get him off the subject. Matt had already opened his mouth and said too much. He was trying to do damage control and avoid divulging any more information than what he had already shared with James.

"So, have they posted the class schedules yet?"

"No, they will wait until the last minute to post them. You know how they are."

"Yeah," Matt sighed. "Well, I should be back in town a week or so before classes begin. I'm certainly not cheerfully anticipating the freshman advisor ritual."

"I know what you mean." James stood up. "Hey look, I have to go teach a class. If you need anything just give me a call. And I'm glad you're ok after your ordeal."

"Thanks, I'll see you in a few weeks," Matt called out to James as he headed down the hall.

Matt had gathered all the materials he thought they might need. Before he left the office, he wanted to do one last thing that he had on his mind for the last two days. He sat down at his computer and Googled '*Dr. Howard Bertram.*' There were several hits on the search, but one, in particular, caught his attention. A news article, from an AP post, summarized the firing of Dr. Bertram from the CDC after he went public with insider information, disclosing the existence of obscure government programs to exploit the use of retroviruses to facilitate transgenic mutations within human test subjects. The article highlighted Dr. Bertram's stellar career before the CDC fired him. Dr. Bertram claimed that the government intended to create super troopers through cross-species transgenic mutation with targeted animal genomes. The article quoted government officials who denied any such programs existed. Not surprising, everything was made hush-hush after the CDC gave Dr. Bertram the boot.

Matt's cell phone rang; the caller ID showed it was Sarah. "*Dr. Kershaw, this is Sarah.*"

"Yes, Sarah, what's up?"

"*We are at the mall and it's getting close to noon. You said to give you a call when we were ready for lunch.*"

"Ok, I'll leave here in a couple of minutes," looking at his watch, "I'll meet you in front of the Chinese buffet in about thirty minutes. Ok?"

"*Cool, see you then.*"

Matt erased the history from his search engine before shutting down his computer. He piled the books and manuals he selected into a tote box and strapped it to a trolley he used to wheel it out to his jeep.

221

Chapter 27

After scanning the lobby in the mall for several minutes, Matt hadn't spotted Freya or Sarah. '*They should be here, where are they?*' He thought to himself.

"Matthew," Freya called out as she tapped him on the shoulder.

He turned around and was astonished at this beautiful creature of a woman standing in front of him. He hardly recognized her, "Oh my goodness you're gorgeous!"

Freya blushed as she gave Matt a hug and kiss, "thank you," she whispered.

It was not that Freya had glammed up, but it was the fresh look of a bit more modern Freya which stood out. He couldn't help but notice a radiant glow of happiness on her face.

"What about me," Sarah asked as she spun around modeling her new jeans.

Matt smiled at Sarah, "You are as lovely and stylish as ever my dear." He took some of the bags they had and ushered them into the restaurant.

Freya followed Matt's lead as he introduced her to the concept of a Chinese buffet without embarrassing her in front of Sarah. Freya seemed to be in a constant state of culture shock from the moment she arrived at Matt's cabin. She was aware of the world outside the valley on a limited basis from her trips to the town nearest Graymere. To experience firsthand all that a larger city had to offer was at times almost overwhelming.

Sitting down to enjoy their lunch, Sarah went on and on about what shops they had been to and the bargains they found. The shopping adventure was as exciting for Sarah as it was for Freya.

"What's on your agenda after lunch?" Matt inquired.

Sarah spoke up, "I'm going to take Freya to Macy's to shop for lady stuff, then a manicure and to pick out the perfect perfume for her. After that, we can hop over to Bath and Body Works."

Freya looked up at Sarah and then at Matt as she started smiling at the thought of Sarah as a tour guide with a full agenda.

"Well, while we're here, I need to take Freya down to one of the shops to pick out something before you guys resume your shopping rampage," Matt said as he reached over and squeezed Freya's hand.

"Ok, I'm ready when you guys are," Sarah announced.

Matt and Freya looked at each other and smiled at Sarah's endless flow of energy. "Are you ready?" Matt asked Freya.

"Yes, I'm stuffed," she replied. "I need to get up and move around."

After paying the tab, Matt led them to the other end of the mall stopping at Harry Ritchie's jewelry store.

"Oh my God!" Sarah gasped, then she charged poor Freya giving her a hug while jumping up and down.

Freya was not quite sure why Sarah was suddenly all excited. Freya didn't show any emotion when they entered the jewelry store. She didn't have any idea what Matt was shopping for.

"Aren't you excited," Sarah said as she was holding onto Freya's arm with a death grip.

"Excited about what?"

"He asked you, didn't he? I know he asked you; he did, didn't he?"

Freya had a puzzled look on her face, "Asked me what?"

"He asked you to marry him, didn't he?" Sarah said with so much excitement Freya was afraid she was about to pee on herself.

Freya just blushed and didn't say anything.

"What can I help you with today," the clerk asked.

223

Matt pulled Freya close to him and while looking Freya in the eyes, he told the clerk, "We would like to look at an engagement and wedding ring set please."

Freya felt her knees go weak. Most people in Misty Hollow didn't indulge in wedding rings. In fact, Allison is the only *married* woman she knew who actually wore a wedding ring.

"Well, we have a fine collection of engagement rings and wedding sets," the clerk said, leading them to the showcase.

Matt and Freya spent the better part of an hour looking at different styles and combinations of rings before they settled on a set Freya liked. Once Freya slipped the engagement ring onto her finger, she dared not take it off. Matt paid for the rings and they no sooner stepped out of the jewelry store when Freya broke down and started crying as she kissed Matt and embraced him. Even Sarah started to cry.

"Honey, you are going to have to get this crying bit under control. You can't be doing this, every time I say or do something." Matt said in jest.

Freya slapped him on the arm.

Matt pulled a handkerchief from his pocket, "I anticipated this emotional episode."

Freya smacked him again as she smiled at him before embracing him tightly.

"Ok ladies, I'm going to take all of this stuff with me back to the cabin. Take your time and enjoy your day. I need to do some work at the cabin and finish reading Sarah's report."

Freya was overwhelmed with the chain of new experiences and the flood of emotions she was going through.

"What time should we be back at the cabin?" Sarah asked.

"I would like to take Freya to dinner this evening so plan on being back in time for her to get ready."

"Ok, we'll be there in like three hours, say around five'ish," Sarah suggested.

"That would be good."

Freya embraced Matt once more before he left for the cabin and she and Sarah continued their odyssey.

* * *

Back at the cabin, Matt carried all of the packages into the living room for Freya and Sarah to sort out when they got home. Then he sat down to continue reviewing the materials Sarah had prepared and to start formulating a game plan to accomplish the goals and objectives outlined by William during their lunch meeting. The article he read about Dr. Bertram bothered Matt, recalling Doc's comments cautioning not to let the government get involved with anything going on in the valley. He decided to table those thoughts, for now, to focus on the material in front of him.

* * *

Freya and Sarah arrived just after five, talking and laughing when they entered the cabin. They didn't slow down as they proceeded to pile all of the bags into the living room, rummaging through all of their packages and pulling out various garments as if they had not seen them before. In the short time Matt had known Freya, he never saw her so carefree and happy.

After allowing them their fun time, Matt interrupted them to announce, "Freya my dear, I made dinner reservations for 7:00pm." This led to a protracted fashion show between the two girls to decide what Freya should wear to dinner.

"Where are you taking her," Sarah asked in an apparent effort to finalize which outfit would be best for that setting.

Matt chuckled while watching the two of them derive so much fun from picking out something to wear to dinner. While the two women were going through their girlie ritual, Matt excused himself to go shower and get ready for dinner.

Matt was coming out of the shower when Freya came into the bedroom. Seeing Matt still struggling to raise his arms or turn his body, she helped him finish drying off. "Matthew, why are you doing all of this," she asked, reaching up to put her arms around his neck and kiss him.

"Doing what?" he asked sincerely.

"All of this; the trip, the shopping, the rings, everything?"

"Above all else, everything I do for you is because I want us to be able to enjoy life, enjoy being with you, and you to enjoy being with me. As to why am I doing it now, that's not such a short answer. But we can discuss it over dinner."

Freya kissed him before she kicked him out of the bathroom so that she could get ready.

* * *

"WOW!" Sarah said aloud when Freya entered the living room glammed up for dinner. She got up and circled around Freya, checking her out, "You look ravishing. Definitely not the same Freya I saw getting out of the jeep yesterday. Girl, you're stunning."

Matt came around the corner and when he saw Freya his jaw dropped; her simple beauty astounded him. It was a simple outfit for a casual dinner out. Nevertheless, the contrast from the Freya he first saw hustling and bustling around the inn, compared to the Freya he was looking at now, were worlds apart.

"You are the most beautiful creature I've ever seen in my life," Matt said without taking his eyes off Freya.

Freya blushed from all the attention focused on her. "Shall we go?" She asked, hoping to redirect that attention away from her.

"Certainly," Matt replied.

Sarah gave Freya a cat-call whistle as she and Matt walked out the door.

* * *

Matt selected an upscale Mexican restaurant to take Freya for dinner. It was not too posh, but a quaint little place with an authentic atmosphere, candlelit tables, and a mariachi moving about the restaurant playing Spanish love songs.

After placing their order, Freya reminded Matt that he had not finished answering her question, "Matthew, why are you treating me to all of this?"

"As I told you, I love you more than you can possibly imagine. I've seen you, who you are, without pretense, and I fell in love with that person. The other side of the coin is a bit selfish on my part."

"In what way are you being selfish? You haven't asked anything from me."

"I am being selfish because I feel like I've wasted forty years of my life without someone to spoil or share life with. While you think I'm being generous, the truth is, I'm enjoying a new array of experiences myself by spoiling you. Besides, who knows when we may have this chance again anytime soon? I want to enjoy my time with you while we have the chance."

Looking a bit confused, "I'm not sure I understand what you are trying to say."

"Look, in a couple of days, we have to return to Graymere. The focus of our lives will shift dramatically toward events and priorities which are not of our own choosing. The gravity of what we must do there is much larger than you or me, and who knows how long it will take to see it through to the end. While we are here, for today and tomorrow, and the next, the things we choose to do together and allowing me to give you a moment of carefree joy and happiness are events and priorities of our choosing. This little window of time is our time."

"I love you Matthew; every day and every moment of each day I realize it more and more."

After a few moments of silence, Matt and Freya shifted their discussion to various topics mostly related to what things they needed to purchase to take back with them to Graymere. After finishing their meal, they sat and talked for a while before deciding it was time to return home and get some rest in anticipation of a busy day tomorrow.

Chapter 28

Freya was awakened in the middle of the night by Matt violently thrashing around and yelling in his sleep, scaring her half to death.

"SHOOT FRANKIE, SHOOT BEFORE IT GETS ANY CLOSER! ALEX WATCH OUT BEHIND YOU!" Matt was drenched in sweat; his forehead was on fire.

Freya called out, "SARAH, COME HERE, SARAH PLEASE I NEED YOU QUICK!"

Sarah came running into the bedroom rubbing her eyes, "What's wrong, what's happening," she asked in a panic.

"Turn on the light for me please, and bring me a damp washcloth" Freya instructed.

Sarah did as Freya instructed, "What's happening?" Returning with a damp washcloth she saw the state Matt was in and asked Freya, "Should I call an ambulance?"

"NO, just relax. I need you to do something for me."

"What do you want me to do?"

"Take Dr. Kershaw's cell phone and call the number I'm going to call out to you."

"Ok," Sarah acknowledged as she took Matt's phone from the nightstand.

"VICTOR, NO! DON" T GO IN THERE, THEY'RE WAITING FOR US IN THERE." Matt yelled out.

Sarah was visibly shaken watching Matt thrash around and obviously hallucinating. "What's happening?" she asked.

"Sarah Focus!" Freya snapped, trying to get her to calm down, "Call this number, put the phone on speaker, and hold it where I can talk." Freya called out Dr. Bertram's phone number to Sarah.

Sarah nervously dialed the number and waited for someone to answer, "*Hello is this Dr. Bertram?*" Sarah said when she heard someone answer the phone.

"Sarah put the phone on speaker and bring it over near me," Freya instructed.

Sarah nervously fidgeted with the phone putting it in speakerphone mode as she sat on the bed next to Freya.

"Doc?" Freya spoke into the phone while trying to hold Matthew.

"*This is Allison. Freya, is that you?*"

"Yes Allison, I need to talk to Doc, it's an emergency!"

"*Ok, he's getting up now. What's wrong Freya?*"

"It's Matthew, I think he's having a relapse of the virus, he's running a very high fever, sweating profusely, and hallucinating."

Freya could hear Allison in the background telling Dr. Bertram what was happening.

"*Freya, this is Doc Bertram, tell me what's going on.*"

"Matthew woke me up a few minutes ago screaming. Then I noticed he was sweating profusely. He feels like he's on fire. He's hallucinating and screaming out to Frankie, Alex, and Victor."

"*If you have a thermometer check his temperature; if it's over 104 degrees we need to try and bring it down.*"

Sarah ran from the room and returned with a digital thermometer. "Here it is."

"Do you know how to use it?" Freya asked.

"Yes."

"Ok take his temperature while I try and hold him still," she instructed.

Sarah did as Freya instructed, "it reads 104.6 degrees."

"CRAP!" Freya said aloud to herself. "Ok Doc, his temperature is 104.6, what do we do?"

"Ok, first of all, don't panic. Temperature is his body's normal reaction to fight off the virus as it tries to spread within his body. However, we don't want his temperature to get to high. You need to get him into a bathtub half full of cold water."

"Ok Doc," Freya responded. "But Doc, he's a big guy and he's flopping around."

"If his temperature gets above 105 degrees he could go into seizures if it goes above 106 degrees he could go into a coma and suffer brain damage. We need to monitor his temperature and keep it down below 104 degrees. You have to get him in the tub with cold water."

"Sarah, go start running the water in the tub and come back and help me get him up."

"What do we do after we get him in the tub, doc?"

"Once you get him in the tub, start putting ice in the tub, a little at a time. Don't dump a lot in at once or you will send him into shock. All you want to do is to try and keep his temperature below 104 degrees."

Freya started to cry from anxiety and fear.

"Freya, you can do this, just calm down, it'll be alright. His body's natural mechanisms should prevent his temperature from going over 105. This is just a precaution since I'm not sure to what extent the LTV has invaded his body."

Freya tried to collect herself before Sarah came back into the bedroom.

"Ok, water is running," Sarah said to Freya.

"Help me get his clothes off and then get him up."

They struggled to get Matt's t-shirt and exercise pants off before dragging him to the edge of the bed. Once they got him to the edge, they sat him up where they each got under a shoulder, on either side, then lifted him up, before dragging him to the bathtub. With some difficulty, they laid him on the floor next to the tub and then stepping with one foot in and one foot out of the tub clumsily lifted Matt over into the tub.

"Can you go get the phone and bring it in here with us?" Freya asked Sarah.

"Ok, Doc we have him in the tub."

"Give it a few minutes and check his temperature. If it is still above 104 degrees, start putting ice in the tub a little at a time. While you do that keep his upper body submerged as much as possible; put rolled up towels under his head to keep him from going under, but the cold water will soak the towels and help cool his head from behind. Then just keep dipping a washcloth in the cold water and wetting the top of his head."

"Is that Sarah who's with you there?" Doc Bertram asked in an informal introduction over the phone.

"Yes, sir," Sarah answered

"Sarah, this is Dr. Bertram, as you put ice into the tub, can you check Dr. Kershaw's Temp every half hour and tell me the readings? As soon as you think he can swallow anything, give him a dose of Tylenol."

"Yes sir," Sarah replied.

Slowly Matt's temperature started to drop. As his temperature receded, he stopped thrashing around along with his hallucinations. It was after daybreak when his temperature dropped below 103.

"Doc his temp is at 102.6," Sarah said to Dr. Bertram over the phone.

"Ok, good job girls, I think he is out of the woods. Do your best to get him out of the ice bath and back into bed. Call me back when you get him situated."

Freya pulled the plug from the drain, allowing the water to drain out. Then she and Sarah struggled to dry Matt off while trying to figure out how they were going to get him out of the tub. In the process, Matt started to come around but was weak and nauseous to sit up on his own. Now that he wasn't as limp as a dishrag and dead weight, Freya and Sarah were able to get him out of the tub with a little help from Matt. Still half dragging him they managed to get him back to the bedroom where he started to shiver with the chills.

"Sarah, look in the dresser and see if you can find dry boxers," Freya told her as she finished drying him off.

"Found them," Sarah announced as she retrieved a pair and handed them to Freya.

"You have to help me, Sarah," Freya said as she pulled off Matt's wet boxers and they laid him back on the bed with his legs hanging off.

Sarah was trying to close her eyes and look away to avoid looking at Matt naked. Freya found it a bit humorous, "Have you never seen a naked man before?" She asked Sarah as she maneuvered Matt's dry boxers and exercise pants over his feet.

"Yeah, but not Dr. Kershaw; it's like looking at my dad naked," Sarah replied.

Freya laughed as she managed, with a little help from Matt to get his pants on. "Sarah, help me sit him up and get his t-shirt on."

It was during this process when Sarah realized the full extent of the wounds Matt's body had suffered from both the war injury and the alpha attack. She paused to measure with her hand the bite wound that extended over his shoulder from front to back and using the tip of her finger to gauge the size of the punctures from the fang teeth. Freya noticed Sarah focusing on the wounds allowing her a moment to satisfy her curiosity.

"Get his other arm into the sleeve," Freya said, prompting Sarah to refocus.

"Sorry," Sarah replied. "The wolf that did this must have been huge," Sarah commented to Freya.

"Bigger than him," Freya said implying that the 'wolf' was bigger than Matt.

"My God," Sarah said astonished as they laid Matt back down on the bed and lifted his legs up onto the bed.

Pulling the covers up over Matt's chest, Freya said to Sarah, "Ok, we need to call Dr. Bertram back."

Plugging the phone into the charger next to the bed, Sarah dialed the number. "Dr. Bertram? This is Sarah."

"How is he doing?"

"Hang a sec." Sarah handed the phone over to Freya.

While Freya was updating Dr. Bertram, Sarah retrieved the thermometer from the bathroom and took a current temperature reading, "101.2," she read out the temperature to Freya.

232

"His temp is 101.2," Freya repeated to Dr. Bertram. "Doc he has the chills and is shivering, I covered him, but he's still shivering."

"Ok, some temperature is normal as his body is dealing with the LTV. Just keep an eye on his temperature and treat him as you would someone with the flu. Check the thermostat and set the house temperature to around 74 degrees."

"I'll go check it," Sarah said. "Then I'll put on some coffee. If you need me just shout," Sarah said as she left the room.

"Is he still passed out?"

"Yes, he came to a little when we were getting him out of the tub, now he is sleeping again," Freya replied.

Sarah returned a few minutes later. "Here you go," she said handing Freya a cup of coffee. "You look exhausted."

"So do you," Freya replied. She reached out and squeezed Sarah's hand, "thank you, I would never have made it through this without you."

"Freya, is Sarah there?"

"I'm here Dr. Bertram," Sarah answered.

"Sarah, can you get me the name and phone number of the nearest pharmacy, preferably one that is open twenty-four-seven. I'll call in a prescription I need you to go pick up. Can you do that?"

"Yes sir," Sarah replied. "Anything else?"

"Yes; can you give a shot with a hypodermic syringe?"

"I've done it on lab animals before," Sarah answered.

"Close enough; after you pick up the prescription, I'll tell the pharmacist to provide you with a couple of syringes. One of the prescriptions will be for B12 you will need to inject into a muscle. I'm sure you can handle that easily. Call me back when you have the information."

"Ok, will do," she replied.

Sarah went to the computer in the living room to search the contact information for the nearest pharmacy. A few minutes later Sarah returned with the information and called Dr. Bertram.

"Give me about twenty minutes and you should be able to pick up the prescription from the pharmacy." Dr. Bertram advised Sarah.

Freya got up and took a credit card from Matt's wallet, "Here you can use this to pay for the prescriptions," Freya instructed Sarah. "Pick up some fruit juice with vitamin C; he will need to drink a lot of liquids to keep from getting dehydrated."

"I'll pick up some Gatorade, it helps put replenish some of the electrolytes. I should be back within the hour. If you need me, my number should be programmed into Dr. Kershaw's phone." Sarah showed her how to look up her phone number on Matt's phone before she left.

After Sarah left, Freya climbed back into bed with Matt, sitting up with her back to the headboard where she could be close to him. Checking his temperature again, the thermometer indicated that he was hovering around the 101-degree mark. She was exhausted and within a few minutes, she dozed off and napped until the sound of the front door opening and closing woke her.

Freya got up and went to the kitchen where Sarah was unpacking the things from the pharmacy. "Thank you so much for going to pick this stuff up."

"Not a problem," Sarah replied as she closed the fridge door and put the empty bags into the trash. Turning toward Freya and leaning back against the counter Sarah asked, "What happened last night? What's happening to Dr. Kershaw?"

Freya tried to explain without too much detail, "When Matthew was bitten and mauled by the '*wolf*', he was infected with a virus. Normally, the virus will typically run its course within three or four days with symptoms very similar to a severe case of the flu. Matthew recovered within two days after the initial onset of the viral infection."

"So what's with the episode last night?"

"Once a person acquires the virus it stays with them the rest of their life. According to Doc, in Matthew's case the virus resurfaced somewhere in his body and his immune system is trying to fight it off resulting in symptoms similar to the flu bug."

"This shit isn't contagious, is it? I don't need any of that crap."

Freya smiled at Sarah, "No, only if he bites you or you get some of his blood into you through an open cut or transfusion."

"I need to call Dr. Bertram and let him know I have the stuff he ordered for Dr. Kershaw," Sarah said as she started walking back to the bedroom.

"Dr. Bertram; this is Sarah. I have the meds you ordered for Dr. Kershaw. What do you want us to do now?"

"Ok, you know how to draw the medicine from the vial into the syringe, yes?"

"Yes sir," Sarah replied.

"Draw up the B12 in the dosage written on the prescription into one of the syringes, and inject it into the muscle of Dr. Kershaw's upper arm."

"Ok, got it," she acknowledged. "How often do I need to give him a shot of B12?"

"Only the one, the other meds are for nausea and fever. He should get over this in a day or two. Just keep an eye on his temperature and give him plenty of liquids. Don't hesitate to call me if you need me."

"Thanks, Doc," Freya said as she hung up the phone.

"Freya, why don't you take a nap, I'll be in the living room watching a movie if you need me," Sarah suggested.

"I think I will," she agreed.

Chapter 29

Sarah had fallen asleep on the couch while watching a movie. Around noon, a knock on the front door woke her. She got up to answer the door thinking to herself, '*who in the world could this be?*'

Opening the door, she was greeting by a tall middle-aged man, "You must be Sarah; I'm Harvey Langston."

"How do you know my name," Sarah asked curtly.

"I'm sorry; I'm a friend of Dr. Kershaw, Freya and Dr. Howard Bertram. Doc called me and told me that Matt was ill and asked if I stop in to see if you guys were doing ok and see if you needed anything."

"Just a minute please," Sarah said as she looked at Harvey cautiously. Sarah went back to the bedroom, "Freya, there's a man at the door who says his name is Harvey Langston and he says that Dr. Bertram sent him to check on Dr. Kershaw."

"It's alright; he's a friend of Matthew's," Freya replied. Freya got up to go with Sarah to greet Harvey.

"Harvey, it's nice to see you again," Freya greeted him and welcomed him inside. "I apologize for our appearance; we've been up most of the night with Matthew."

"Yes, Doc Bertram called me and asked me to come by and check on you, to see if you needed anything."

"I know that Matthew wanted very much to talk to you about something. He was planning to come to your office today, to meet with you, but I don't think he's in any condition to do so today." Freya told Harvey while offering him a seat.

"Yes, Matt and I talked briefly the other day and made plans to meet. When Doc phoned me, I thought I could kill two birds with one stone, so to speak. I would come check on you guys and if he was awake and feeling up to it, we could visit and save him a trip."

"May I offer you something to drink Mr. Langston?" Sarah asked.

"No thank you," he replied to Sarah's offer. "Is Matt awake?" He asked Freya.

"He was stirring a few moments ago. Let me go check on him and see if he is awake. He has been very much out of it, all night and through the morning." Freya got up and went back to the bedroom.

* * *

Entering the bedroom, she saw Matthew trying to sit up in the bed, but was still too weak. "What happened?" he asked Freya when she sat next to him.

"You had a relapse of the LTV infection last night," she told him. "How do you feel?"

"I feel as weak as a newborn lamb but otherwise ok. What time is it?"

"It's a little after 1:00pm. Harvey is here. He stopped by to check on you and asked if you felt like visiting."

"Harvey? Why is he here?"

"Doc called him and told him about your relapse last night and suggested he come by to check on us and see if we were OK."

"Doc called him? What happened?"

"You spiked a fever last night near 105 degrees and you were having hallucinations. Sarah and I had to give you an ice bath to bring your temperature down. This morning she gave you a shot of B12 and now you are awake. That's the five second summary of our night of terror."

237

"Is that all? I thought something serious happened," Matt said with a slight smile in a failed attempt to joke with Freya.

"You jerk," She said as she smacked him on the arm. "You scared the crap out of both of us last night. Do you feel like talking to Harvey?"

"Yes, tell him to give me a minute and I'll be out to visit with him."

"Ok. I'll be back in a minute to help you."

* * *

"Matthew is awake and he wants to talk with you. He is getting up and changing, he'll be out in a few minutes."

"Thank you Freya," Harvey replied.

"If you'll excuse me, I need to make something for lunch, Matthew hasn't eaten all day."

"No problem, I apologize for showing up without calling ahead. But, when Doc called me, he had a sense of urgency in his voice. So, I just dropped what I was doing and rushed down here."

"You're welcome to have a seat here at the table and we can talk while I prepare lunch." Freya offered while gesturing toward the table in the breakfast nook.

Sarah went into the kitchen to help Freya organize lunch.

"Do you have any soup in the pantry," Freya asked Sarah. "Matthew needs something soft with a broth."

"How about *Wolf Brand* chili?" Sarah joked holding up a can of chili.

Freya looked at her with a raised eyebrow and smiled.

"How about chicken noodle soup?" Sarah suggested holding up a can for Freya to approve.

"That's good," Freya acknowledged. "What do you suggest for the rest of us? I'm not sure what you have in the pantry or refrigerator to cook with."

"I tell you what; you go help Dr. Kershaw and I'll take care of lunch," Sarah told Freya gently nudging Freya out of the kitchen.

Freya smiled, "you're a peach." Then she kissed Sarah on her forehead.

Sarah gestured for Freya to leave the kitchen, "Get out of here."

"I'll go check on Matthew," Freya said to Harvey.

A few minutes later, Matt and Freya emerged from the hallway. "Matthew, glad to see you buddy; how are you feeling? According to Doc you had a rough night."

"That's what Freya was telling me," Matt replied. "But I think Freya and Sarah had it rougher than I did." Matt tried to make light of the situation as Freya helped him sit down at the table with Harvey.

"Well, it's good to see you are able to get out of the bed. You were flat on your back the last time I saw you. Let's not make this a habit." Harvey joked with Matt.

"I'll try not to."

"I know you were planning to come to the office today, but as I told Freya after Doc called me, I decided to run down here to check on you. And if you were feeling up to it, we could visit here instead."

"Thanks, Harvey, that was thoughtful of you."

Freya and Sarah busied themselves in the kitchen with Sarah teaching Freya the art of stir-fry chicken with veggies while Matt and Harvey talked.

"Saturday you mentioned that you wanted to talk to me about acquiring some equipment. What is it you need?"

"I need to set up a lab in Graymere, and I need a DNA analyzer."

When Sarah heard the reference to a DNA analyzer, she paused and turned her attention to Matt and Harvey, almost slicing her finger.

"Man, when you need, you need big," Harvey said leaning back in his chair.

Freya leaned next to Sarah and whispered, *"What's a DNA Analyzer?"*

Sarah whispered back to Freya, *"it's a very expensive piece of lab equipment, depending on what model and features most cost around $600 to $700 thousand dollars and up.*

"Don't you have access to the DRMO and GAO bone yards?" Matt asked.

"Yes, but I doubt they have an analyzer laying around; even if they did it would be one of the old antiquated units.

"I'm interested in one of the smaller desktop units. For what we need it for, it doesn't have to be the top of the line with bells and whistles. If I email you some specs can you check to see if anything might be lying around."

"Sure, I'll scan the disposal listings. So, what's the purpose of the lab you want to set up?"

"We are going to have to map the genome of the valley residents in an effort to isolate and stratify the various strains of the virus. We will have to do the same thing to the warg population to see what, if any, genetic correlation exist between the human strains and lupine strains."

Harvey leaned closer to Matt, *"is it safe to discuss this here?"* He whispered gesturing toward Sarah with his eyes.

Matt replied in a soft voice just above a whisper, "yes, I trust her and she is already handling some research for me, and I may need her help in setting up and running the lab in Graymere. She is one of the very few people I know, who I *can* trust."

Freya casually observed Sarah eavesdropping on Matt and Harvey's conversation and gave her a bump with her hip to focus on preparing lunch and not listening in on their discussion.

"If we are going to try and eradicate the virus or if Doc has any hopes of developing a vaccine we must isolate the base strain and map the mutations."

"You do know you're talking about a project that will take months if not years, don't you?"

"Yes, and it's funny; I made the same comment to Doc a couple of days ago when we were discussing setting up the lab."

Now it was Freya lending an ear to the conversation when she overheard them mention a project taking months or years. Sarah noticed Freya eavesdropping and gave her a bump with her hip. They both started snickering at each other.

"Why set up a lab in Graymere; why not just send your samples out for testing?"

"For the most part, the virus is isolated in the valley, and as Doc says, it's better that it remains isolated there. If we send samples to third-party labs, we lose any control over who has access or knowledge of the virus and its potential effects. How do you think the scenario would play out if some unethical genius got hold of a sample of an Alpha Prime strain?"

"I understand what you are saying," Harvey nodded in agreement. "Email me an inventory of equipment and supplies you will need. Even if I'm not able to put my hand on a DNA analyzer, I know I can get you some excellent microscopes, computers, GC, Mass Spec, Gas Chromatography, as well as glassware, burners, and such."

"Don't make a big deal of it. We need to try to fly below the radar on this. Maybe you can say you are acquiring the equipment for an outreach program to help Graymere put together a technical training program or something like that."

"Ok guys; lunch is ready," Freya announced. "Sarah has prepared a lovely dish that Matthew will not be able to enjoy, but the rest of us will," Freya said teasingly as Sarah served the stir-fry to the table and Freya placed a bowl of chicken noodle soup in front of Matthew.

During lunch, the conversation shifted to more of Matt and Harvey reminiscing about their bygone days as college roommates. They exchanged stories of pranks they pulled on professors and graduate assistants when they were underclassmen.

After everyone finished eating, Freya started clearing the table while Sarah refreshed the drink glasses.

"Matt, when are you planning to head back to Graymere?" Harvey asked.

"If I feel well enough, tomorrow I need to round up some supplies from the city. Doc gave me a shopping list of medical supplies he needs for the clinic."

"Do you have a site picked out for the lab or are you going to do that when you get back?" Harvey asked.

"Doc and I decided to use the old constable's office."

"You mean the old jailhouse?" Harvey chuckled.

"Yes," Matt replied smiling. "Actually, it has the basic infrastructure we need to work with. Doc is coordinating with William to arrange the resources to start cleaning it up and doing some renovations before we can begin setting up the lab."

"If I can't put my hands on a DNA analyzer, what are you going to do? It sounds like you are pretty much dead in the water without it."

"I researched some options yesterday while I was at the office. I found a couple of places where we might be able to put our hands on a used analyzer at a fraction of the cost of a new one."

"Even a cheaper used one is not cheap," Harvey replied.

"Yeah, I saw a couple of units that would serve our purpose for around $75 to $80 thousand dollars. But as you say, that is still a lot of money, money we don't have."

Harvey got up from the table, "Well buddy, I should be heading back to the office."

Matt tried to stand and walk Harvey to the door. "Thanks for driving down."

"Sit down, you don't have to get up for me," Harvey said as he put his hand on Matt's shoulder to encourage him to relax. "Freya and Sarah, I thank you for the lovely lunch, it was delicious, and I'm not just saying that to tease Matthew."

"You're welcome," Freya and Sarah said in unison.

Freya walked Harvey to the door, "I expect to see you back in Graymere soon. When you come up, you are welcome to stay at the inn, we would be glad to have you stay with us."

"Thank you, I'll keep that in mind."

After Harvey left, Matt tried to get up and make his way back to the bed. He was still very weak and could barely stand by himself. "Man, this virus really zaps your strength."

Freya helped him walk back to the bedroom.

A few minutes later Sarah came down the hall and knocked on the bedroom door, "can I come in?"

"Yes, come on in," Freya answered.

"I brought you some juice and Gatorade to keep next to you for when you get thirsty."

"Thank you," Matt said. "Freya told me how much you helped her last night. I appreciate you and how you stepped up and handled the challenge."

"You didn't tell him everything did you?" She asked Freya, blushing referring to her helping Freya take Matt's clothes off, bathing him in ice practically naked, and then having to remove his wet boxers and put dry clothes on him.

Freya laughed and after a moment's hesitation she said, "no, not *everything*."

"What are you talking about?" Matt asked.

Sarah replied, "Nothing, just an inside thing between us girls."

Chapter 30

When Freya came into the kitchen, she saw Matt sitting at the table focused on an array of papers and reports. "You're up early," Freya said leaning over and giving him a warm embrace and kiss.

"Umm; I can get used to that," he replied, kissing her in return.

Freya picked up Matt's cup to refresh his coffee and to pour a cup for herself. "How are you feeling this morning?" she asked sitting down at the table.

"Much better; I feel a little stronger, still a bit of fever, but I don't have nausea."

"How about we make each other a promise?" she asked smiling.

Matt hesitated for a moment '*making promises?*' he thought to himself.

Before he could reply Freya told him, "I promise to stop crying all the time if you stop scaring the crap out of me all the time."

"I'll do my best," he replied before getting up to kiss her.

"Good morning everyone," Sarah said entering the kitchen.

"Good morning," replied Freya. "I hope you got some sleep last night."

"Good morning," Matt said.

"Yes, I slept like a baby," Sarah replied. Pouring herself a cup of coffee, she walked over to sit at the table with Matt and Freya. "What's on the agenda today, Dr. Kershaw?"

"Here's what I'd like to do. Freya and I'll go to the city to gather the medical supplies for Doc and do whatever shopping we need for stuff to take back with us. We may not be back this way before August."

"What about me," Sarah asked.

"I need you to start compiling an inventory of supplies, materials, and equipment we'll need to set up a molecular bio lab."

"I'm not sure I know what all is needed to set up a lab, I've never done that before."

"You've worked in several labs, haven't you? Just close your eyes and look around the labs you've worked in and start writing down everything you see, such as Bunsen burners, glassware, microscopes, slides, centrifuge, and so on." Matt pulled out a big thick catalog from a stack of books he brought from his office. "Scan through this, it should help you organize and compile your list."

Taking the catalog from Matt, Sarah told him, "Ok, I got you."

"You might do an online search and see if you can find a startup inventory list already compiled by a lab. Don't concern yourself with being one hundred percent accurate or complete at this point. When I get back, we can go over it and then you can put the initial list into a spreadsheet and shoot it over to Harvey. He will let us know what he can provide us with from his sources," Matt instructed. "If we can get everything wrapped up today, Freya and I will leave early in the morning for Graymere."

* * *

By midafternoon, Matt and Freya were on their way back to the cabin having completed their shopping, including the acquisition of popcorn.

On the drive back home Matt asked, "Freya, you remember the other night I asked you about your religious preferences? You mentioned that there was no church in Graymere."

"Yes."

"So, if there isn't a church or preacher in Graymere or Misty Hollow what do the people do when they want to get married?"

"Well, there aren't that many people living in the valley so it's not often that people get married. Besides, getting married isn't as big of a festivity in Graymere as it is outside the valley," She replied.

"Yes, but don't people in the valley get married?"

"Yeah, I guess so."

"So who performs the wedding ceremony?"

"We don't perform a formal ceremony like you guys do outside the valley."

Matt tried to understand what Freya said and he was not quite sure he understood how or if the residents of Graymere actually got married. "Freya, what would you think if I asked you to marry me right away?"

Freya thought a few seconds, "You asked me to marry you and I said yes. For us, it's not a matter of '*when*' since we don't do a ceremonial ritual. Traditionally, the marriage bond is sealed between the man and woman when they agree to accept one another as husband and wife and the marriage are consummated."

"So, if I understand what you are saying, we *are*, in your eyes, *a married couple* according to traditions of Misty Hollow."

"Yes," Freya replied. "I understand what you are asking; you are thinking we are not married since we haven't performed a ceremony in front of a minister as you guys do in the world outside Graymere. For me, I am satisfied we're married in heart and spirit, but if it makes you more comfortable I don't have any objections to participating in a traditional '*wedding ceremony*' which you may be more accustomed to."

Matt thought a minute, "If you are satisfied that we are married under your traditions then I can live with that. I'll just have to take care of getting all the legal junk done for insurance, pension, property, and such. I'll talk to Doc about it and sort it out, Mrs. Kershaw."

Freya reached across the seat and gave Matt a kiss, "I love you, Matthew."

* * *

"I've created a spreadsheet and I'm almost finished inputting the inventory," Sarah told Matt. "Here's a copy of what I have so far if you want to look over it."

Matt took the list, "thanks."

"While you two are talking shop, I'm going to start packing," Freya interrupted before going back to the bedroom.

"I was able to find several online sources that provided planning guides and articles on different aspects of setting up a molecular lab. I printed off a couple of the articles that deal with setting up a PCR lab and issues related to PCR contamination issues."

"Good job." Matt praised Sarah for her initiative and diligent efforts. "I'll have to get with Dr. Bertram when I get back to determine the extent of pathology testing we are going to have to perform and the level of containment."

"Dr. Kershaw, may I ask how your investigation went from a 'simple study of wolves'" – Sarah held up her hands gesturing quotation marks with her fingers, "to setting up a molecular lab for the purpose of studying a mutated virus and genome mapping. This is somewhat of a radical shift in scope if you ask me." Before Matt could answer Sarah interjected, "Don't get me wrong, whatever you're working on, I'm down for it. I'm just getting some vibes that whatever it is, it's something which should be hush, hush and I just want to know what I'm getting into."

"You're a smart cookie. I suppose that is why I chose to bring you on board with helping me do research. Above all, I trust you, and you're right. The scope of the research has broadened and it needs to remain hush, hush. At this point, I don't want to go into details with you; and I'll explain why. First, I'm not sure of the true scope and nature of what we are working on. Secondly, until

I get a better understanding of what we are dealing with, I don't want to involve you in something over *our* heads. Initially, we will do some fact finding to determine if further research is feasible. I don't want to commit to any more than that at this time. My involvement is a product of me blindly stumbling into a situation resulting in an accident which nearly got me killed. I don't want you to be put into the same situation."

"Ok Dr. Kershaw, just remember I got your back and I'm here when you need me."

"Thanks," Matt said as he put down the papers he was reviewing. "By the way, I wanted to give you this before I forgot. I didn't want to leave out in the morning without paying you and giving you more money to work with." Matt dug into his pack, pulled out his checkbook, and started writing Sarah a check. "I don't know when I'll be back so I'm giving you money for house-sitting and some for the time you put in so far on the research you've been working on. Keep track of your time and I'll settle up with you when I get back. I put $300 on this pre-paid card for expenses," Matt explained as he handed her the check.

Sarah looked at the check and saw that the amount was much more than she expected. "Thank you; I appreciate the extra work and *cash*. I was worried about being able to earn some money for the fall, this is a big help."

Matt finished reviewing the list that Sarah had prepared. "This list is good to start; at least it gets Harvey something to work with. When you send Harvey the email, attach the link to this web page." Matt instructed. He handed Sarah a hardcopy of a spec sheet for a DNA analyzer with the website information. Here is Harvey's business card, it has his email and telephone numbers on it. I wrote his personal cell phone number on the back in case you have to call him outside the office."

* * *

Freya came back into the kitchen where Matt and Sarah were working. "I'm packed and ready for tomorrow," Freya said.

"Ahh, Freya my dear; one last order of business before we relax for the evening," Matt said as he got up and ran down the

248

hall, "be right back." Returning to the room with the boxes containing the wedding bands, Matt told Freya, "While we have Sarah as a witness, I would like to publicly declare my vows to you as your husband."

Matt took the rings out of the boxes and handing his ring to Freya. Sarah was standing with her eyes wide open and her hands to her mouth in girlish excitement. Freya looked over at Sarah and gave her a wink as she fidgeted nervously.

"Ms. Freya Fasset, I Matthew Allen Kershaw, do solemnly take you to be my wife, to have and to hold, in sickness or in health, for richer or poorer, until death does us part," Matt recited before he slipped the wedding band onto Freya's finger.

Freya nervously tried to compose herself and focus on saying her vows, "Matthew Kershaw, I Freya Fasset, do solemnly take you to be my husband, to be the one and only love of my life, in sickness or health, rich or poor, until death does us part," Freya recited as she slipped the ring onto Matthew's finger.

"OH MY GOD! You're married; I think," Sarah said jumping up and down as Matt and Freya embraced and kissed each other. "I think I'm going to cry," she told Freya. Then she gave Freya a huge hug. "Congrats! Dr. Kershaw, can I tell anyone about this or do I have to keep it to myself?" She asked barely able to contain her excitement.

"Unless Freya objects I don't care who you tell," He said proudly.

Freya gave Sarah an approving smile as she embraced Matthew. "I'm so happy you are in my life," she whispered to Matt.

Sarah hastily called her friend Carol to be the first one to spread the news that Dr. Kershaw got married. "Carol! You're not going to believe this," Sarah shouted excitedly into her cell phone.

Chapter 31

Matt finished loading the jeep just before sunrise, "I filled the thermos if you want to top off your mug before we shove off," Matt told Freya.

"You guys take care and good luck to your future," Sarah said as she gave Freya a hug. "Watch after him," she whispered to Freya.

"I will," Freya replied.

"Sarah, I will give you a call when we get back to the inn," Matt told her before getting into the jeep.

Sarah waved as they drove away. She could not help feel a little anxiety over them going back to Graymere with whatever it was that attacked Matt. She was not privy to any details, but from what she saw of Matt's wounds and he had her researching, Sarah had a bad feeling about what was lurking in the woods around Graymere. She began to recall some of her experiences, when she was a lab tech in the Army, working at the *research center* with Dr. Hobart. All of what she saw and heard so far was eerie reminders of the human-animal hybrid experiments she witnessed while working for Dr. Hobart.

The selfish side of her had gotten used to being around them for the last few days. She was surely going to miss Freya's company and she hoped it would not be too long before she saw her again.

* * *

Matt and Freya hadn't traveled far when Matt asked Freya, "Do you mind if we take a detour on our way back to Graymere?"

"What kind of detour, where to?"

"I want you to meet my family before we go back. They live about fifty miles north of here. I didn't go see them before I left for Graymere this summer, thinking I would not be there more than two or three weeks. Now it appears we may not be back this way for some time. And, I want you to meet them and for them to know you. My mom and I never met my father's family and I have no connection to them. I don't what that to be the case with you and my family."

Freya reached over to hold Matthew's hand, "I would love to meet them," she replied.

Matt picked up his cell phone and dialed the number to his grandmother's house through the car's hands-free phone so Freya could hear the conversation. "Hello, Grandmother," Matt said.

"*Matthew?*" his grandmother replied.

"Yes, Grandmother, it's Matthew. How are you doing?"

"*I'm doing well; where are you, Matthew? When are you coming home?*"

"Grandmother, is mother there?"

"*Yes, she is next door helping Charlie in the garden. When are you coming home?*" his grandmother repeated.

"I'm on my way home now. I should be there in about an hour. Grandmother, I'm bringing someone with me I want you to meet."

"*You know your friends are always welcome here, bring them along.*"

"No Grandmother, this is not one of my buddies from the university, this is a young lady who is very special to me."

"*Oh Matthew, my dear boy, I'll tell your mother and Uncle Charlie. What's this young ladies name?*"

"Her name is Freya Kershaw, Grandmother."

"*Yes Matthew, I would be deeply disappointed if you didn't bring this young woman to see your grandmother.*"

"Ok, Grandmother we will be there within an hour."

251

"*Alright Matthew,*" Grandmother replied as she hung up the phone.

The time seemed to fly by as Freya pumped Matt for information about his family, how she should act, what to say, how to address them, and so forth. She started getting nervous, as they got closer to his grandmother's house.

"What if they don't like me?" she asked Matt, almost in a panic.

"Relax; they will love you as I love you, especially Uncle Charlie. He is my grandmother's brother, but he is the closest thing to a father or grandfather I've ever known."

"What does he do?"

"Nothing much anymore, he used to work at the tribal cultural center. Did I ever tell you he is a medicine, man?"

"No," Freya replied inquisitively.

"He is also one of the tribal elders. At the cultural center, he organized educational programs to teach the tribal youth about our ancestral ways and put on programs for tourist. At one time he was being invited as a guest lecturer at universities in Idaho, Washington, Oregon, and as far away as New Mexico."

Before Freya realized it, they were pulling into the city of Plummer where his family lived.

* * *

Before they could get out of the Jeep, Matt's grandmother, great uncle, and mother burst out of the front door of the house and descended upon them with great anticipation and excitement. Matt's mother and grandmother went straight to Freya giving her hugs and kisses while Uncle Charlie came to Matthew giving him a big bear hug, from which Matt could not help but grimace in pain.

"Congratulations son," Uncle Charlie said to him before hugging him again. Matt again grimaced. "It's good to see you home." Noticing Matt's expression of pain, Uncle Charlie stepped back slightly and looked at Matt. That's when he noticed the scratches on his face and neck, then the ones on his arm. "What happened? Are you alright?" he asked in a low voice.

"It's nothing, just a few scratches. I got too close to a wild critter."

"Oh, my dear girl you are so lovely." Grandmother made Freya lean down so she could hug her and kiss her.

"Welcome to our home, your home. I'm Nina Kershaw, Matthew's mother, this is Nizhoni, Matthew's grandmother, and the handsome one with Matthew is his Great Uncle Charlie."

Matt stood next to Freya, "Mother, Grandmother, Uncle Charlie, I would like you to meet Freya, your new daughter, my wife.

Matt's mother hugged him tightly before she hugged both of them together. Matthew's grandmother broke up the group hug to get Matt to lean down and give her, a big hug, and kiss.

"My dear boy, welcome home," she said before taking them both by the hand and leading them into the house.

The women all congregated in the kitchen chatting away getting to know one another. Matt's mother and grandmother were curious about how and where Matt and Freya met and why he had not mentioned he was involved in a serious relationship or engaged for that matter.

Matthew and Freya tag teamed the story of how they met while Matt was staying at her inn, conducting an investigation in the area around the village of Graymere. They each told their side of how they fell in love in such a short period. The women wanted to hear more about the romantic side of the courtship, ignoring Matt and Uncle Charlie who eventually went out onto the porch to sit and talk.

After getting caught up discussing his work at the university and classes Matt was slated to teach in the fall, their conversation turned more toward the work that Matt was doing in Graymere. Matt noticed Uncle Charlie raising an eyebrow when he first mentioned Graymere, but Uncle didn't say anything. At first, Matt downplayed the investigation as mundane and nothing

253

worth discussing. Eventually, Matt's desire to pick Uncle Charlie's brain about the legends got the better of him.

"Uncle, do you remember when I was a boy you would tell me stories of skinwalkers and such?"

"Yes, you would listen to them over and over."

"Ever since I was old enough to think about what I wanted to do with my life, I pursued an education and career which would allow me to research these legends and seek to find real life connections to animals that could explain those legends."

"Matthew, these are legends and myths handed down through generations to help us in making a connection to nature. They teach us to honor the earth, sun, moon, and stars, and to embrace our fellow creatures as our brothers and sisters. They were not intended to be taken literal."

"What if these legends had some basis in fact rather than just pure myth?" Matt was hoping Uncle Charlie would give him more of a shaman's insight beyond the basic story line.

"Are you asking if I believe the skin-walkers are real?"

"I guess that is what I'm getting at. Have you ever heard of a curse known as *Curse of the Wolf Spirit*? A curse associated with the valley of Misty Hollow."

Uncle Charlie sat straight up in his chair and with a deadly serious expression, he asked Matt, "From whom did you hear of this?"

"Misty Hollow is where I'm conducting the investigation of a wolf attack on a forest ranger. However, I was told by a long time resident of the valley that the Native Americans who originally inhabited the valley spoke of the curse."

Uncle Charlie seemed to lose his color and said nothing.

Matt continued, "I think I may have found a real life connection with a new species of wolf which might be the animal of legend."

"What makes you think such a creature exists?" Uncle Charlie asked anxiously, almost dreading the answer.

Matt stood up and unbuttoned his shirt, "because it did this to me," he said while turning around to allow Uncle Charlie a chance to see the full extent of his wounds he received from the Alpha Prime.

Uncle Charlie jumped back in his chair as if he had seen a ghost.

"What is it, Uncle Charlie?" Matt asked as he buttoned his shirt.

Uncle Charlie sat motionless for a few moments unable to speak or afraid to speak.

"Please don't say anything to Mother or Grandmother, I don't want them to be upset or worried," Matt asked Uncle Charlie.

Charlie went to the front door and poked his head inside and called to his sister, "Niz, Matthew and I are going over to visit Old Joe."

Nizhoni looked up and waved without interrupting the conversation going on among the women.

"Why are you taking me to see Old Joe? Isn't he a bit loony?"

"Just come with me and listen, he knows things you should hear."

Old Joe was sitting under a shade tree near the front corner of his house when Charlie and Matthew arrived. "Hello, Joe," Uncle Charlie called out and raised his hand to wave.

"Charlie, what brings you to see Old Joe today? I see you have a young boy with you all grown up into a man."

"You recognize young Matthew?"

"Yes, it has been a long time, but Joe remembers Matthew."

Matt went to shake hands with Joe; but when Joe took Matt's hand to shake, he abruptly jerked his hand back as if he had been shocked. "Why you bring this boy to Joe?" He said to Charlie with fear on his face.

"Joe I need you to look at something and tell me what you see." Uncle Charlie told Matt to show Joe the wounds he received from the 'wolf' attack.

Matt unbuttoned his shirt and pulled it off so that Joe could see the wounds. Matt was turning around and Joe stood up to examine the wounds reaching out as if he wanted to touch them, but never allowing his hand to make contact with Matt's skin. "He has the curse of his Great Grandfather, the curse of the wolf spirit." Joe suddenly stepped back away from Matt.

"Joe, have you ever seen marks like this before?" Charlie asked, already knowing the answer.

"The boy's great-grandfather, your father received the same wounds from a wolf possessed by an evil spirit that made it walk like a man. The locals of the valley say to be bitten by the evil spirit would result in a curse to the person and their children for twenty generations."

"Can you tell Matthew the story of how you know this?" Charlie prompted as he and Matt sat down near Joe.

"During the depression, when times were hard, many men from the Rez took work with the CCC. Several of us went up into a valley many miles away from here, to help cut fire trails and clear some access roads for the Forest Service. One day some of us, along with your great grandfather, were in the forest cutting trees. Suddenly, a huge wolf appeared in front of us. The creature stood on its hind legs, as a bear would, and then slowly started walking toward us. We were too scared to move. We knew that if we ran, the creature would run us down. Therefore, we stood our ground thinking it would back away. We were not so lucky. The creature charged toward us and just as it leaped at me, your great grandfather jumped in between us, intercepting the wolf's charge. The wolf was big and strong, but your great grandfather fought with it until me and another man hit it with large sticks of wood wounding it before it ran back into the forest. Unfortunately, your grandfather suffered many severe wounds and was bleeding badly. We managed to get him out of the forest and to a local doctor who cleaned and bandaged his wounds. His wounds were similar to yours with the same size claw pattern." Joe mimicked the wolf's claw with his hand to demonstrate the size, spread of the claw marks and bite wounds.

"What happened after that," Matthew pressed Joe for information about the attack.

"After the doctor treated him, your great grandfather was sick in his bunk for many days suffering from a high fever, dysentery, and out of his mind for much of that time. After a few days, his fever broke. When he was strong enough, we left the valley and came back home. We never went back."

"Why do you say our family has this curse?" Matt asked Joe.

"The Doctor who treated your great grandfather said that once someone was bitten by a wolf possessed by an evil wolf spirit, he would become stricken by the evil spirit himself. The local people of the valley said anyone bitten by the creature would turn into a wolf, a skin-walker. It was said, this spirit of the wolf would be passed down through the victim's family for twenty generations."

"What happened after you came back home?"

"Nothing much, when we told our friends here what had happened to us, they didn't believe us. They thought we were lying or crazy and eventually we stopped mentioning anything about the incident. A short time after that, your great grandfather married your great grandmother and had two children Charlie and Nizhoni. After the war broke out, several of us joined the army to fight in the war, your great grandfather was killed somewhere in the pacific during the war, I never saw him again."

"Thank you, Joe," Charlie said.

"Thank you," Matt repeated.

As they were walking away Old Joe cautioned Matt, "Beware young Matthew, your great grandfather suffered from the evil spirit and fell ill many times after we came back home. After each episode, he would begin to change little by little into a wolf man. I do not recall much of this as we went different paths during the war. But take care to watch for the signs."

"Thank you again, Joe," Matt said waving good-bye.

* * *

When Matt and Uncle Charlie arrived back at Grandmother's house, the women were putting lunch on the table. "Just in time for your lunch," Matt's mother announced as they came in through the front door.

When Freya saw Matt, she could sense something was wrong. Freya went up to him and kissed him, whispering in his ear, "What's wrong Matthew? You look like you've seen a ghost."

"Nothing, it's just hot outside and I stayed in the sun too long," he replied, trying to make an excuse to hide his shock of learning the story about his great grandfather. "I'll just go wash my face with some cool water and I'll be ok."

As everyone sat down to eat Lunch, Freya asked an open question, "Did Matthew get into much trouble when he was a kid?" The question started a chaotic round of tales and laughter about Matt's youth and the mischief he would get into. Uncle Charlie received blame for instigating many of Matt's mischievous endeavors.

Grandmother inquired of Matt and Freya, "how long will you get to stay with us?"

"We have to leave very soon Grandmother; my investigation is not finished. We had to go back to the Moscow for materials and supplies and we wanted to come by and visit before we had to return to Graymere. Besides, Freya owns and operates and inn with no one there to take care of it while she is away."

Everyone expressed their disappointment that Matt and Freya could not spend more time with them. Matt's mother begged Freya to come back and spend time with them, even if Matthew was not able to come with her.

"I promise to come back and visit you. Now that we have met, I understand why Matthew has such a warm spot in his heart for this place. I feel like I have a family again," Freya said and she started to cry.

Grandmother embraced Freya. "My dear girl, this is your home and you *are* a member of this family. You are our daughter, as Matthew is our son."

"We need to get on the road so we can get through the mountains before dark," Matt urged Freya.

After many tears and extended goodbyes, Matt and Freya were back on the road headed back to Graymere.

258

* * *

"Thank you," Freya told Matthew.

"For What?"

"For taking me to meet your family. I don't know what it is about you and your family, but it's so easy to fall in love with you guys. Maybe it's been so long since I've had any family around me to laugh with, to cry with, to share happy times as well as sad, or just share life's experiences. You don't realize how important it is to have family around you until you don't have anyone. Today, your family gave me a feeling of wholeness I haven't felt in a long time. Thank you." Freya said as she leaned over and kissed Matthew.

Chapter 32

The sun had already dipped below the ridge and the shadow of darkness was beginning to settle over the valley when Matt and Freya pulled up to the inn. "I'll pull over to Doc's and drop off his supplies."

"I'd like to go with you, I have something I would like to share with Allison," Freya told Matt with a twinkle in her eye. Matt smiled at her and embraced her before they went out the front door of the inn.

Matt backed the jeep up to the front of the clinic and opened the back hatch to unload the oxygen bottles and other supplies while Freya went in to visit with Allison.

"Matthew, glad to see you back, how was the trip?" Dr. Bertram asked as he started helping Matt carry in supplies.

"Other than the little episode the other night you mean?" Matt asked rhetorically. Then they heard a loud squealing noise coming from the living room. "Oh, and that," Matt added.

"Doc, come see!" Allison called out.

"What on earth," Dr. Bertram said as he put down the box he was carrying and went to the living room to see what was happening.

"Look!" Allison said holding up Freya's ring hand showing off her engagement ring and wedding band.

With a surprised look on his face, Doc turned and looked at Matt then grabbed Matt's ring hand and held it up for both he and Allison to see. "Well, I'll be," Dr. Bertram said.

Allison hugged Freya and then Matt. "Congratulations to both of you."

Dr. Bertram shook Matt's hand and gave Freya a huge bear hug. "Congratulations my dear, I wish you all the happiness in the world."

Freya kissed Dr. Bertram on the cheek, "Thanks, Doc," she said with tears of joy rolling down her cheek.

"Well, this deserves a toast," Doc said. He left the room and returned with four glasses of wine. "To Mr. and Mrs. Matthew Kershaw, may all of your days be filled with joy and happiness. Salute!"

After a few moments of congratulatory well-wishing, Doc turned to Matt, "We need to finish unloading the supplies," he said gesturing to Matt with his eyes, urging him back outside.

After Dr. Bertram and Matt left the room, Freya had to start telling Allison about her trip, shopping with Sarah, and meeting Matthew's family, with whom she fell in love with.

* * *

Matt got the feeling Dr. Bertram wanted to tell him something. When they got outside, Matt asked, "What's wrong Doc?"

"There was another attack by an alpha and warg pack this morning."

Matt sat the package down and gave Dr. Bertram his undivided attention. "What happened, when, where, was anyone hurt?" Matt rattled off.

"As far as I know, no one was hurt, but an alpha and a pack of about six rogues raided the Samuels's homestead just after sunrise this morning. The pack killed all of the livestock and attempted to get into the house when Alistair shot through the front door and killed a rogue and wounded the alpha before the pack ran off."

"You said they killed all their livestock. Were the wargs feeding?"

"I'm not sure, but from the sketchy report I got from William, it appears that the pack raided the homestead with the intent to kill everything… and *everybody*."

"I need to go out there first thing in the morning before the area is disturbed."

"I'll make sure the Samuels are expecting you and I'll ask Victor to ride along with you and show you the way."

"Also, I've formulated a preliminary plan toward accomplishing the objectives you and William outlined. See if we can meet tomorrow after I've had a chance to visit the Samuels's homestead."

"Ok, I'll have Victor meet us for breakfast in the morning. I'll let you know when and where we can get together with William after you get throughout at the Samuels place."

"I also have some preliminary thoughts on the lab which I would like to discuss with you. We can discuss that over breakfast in the morning."

"Ok, let's get this stuff inside so you and Freya can get back to the inn and you can get some rest. I think it's going to be busy the next few days."

* * *

"Well, Mrs. Kershaw, which room are you going to designate as the bridal suite?" Matt jokingly asked Freya.

She paused for a moment not having considered that dilemma before he asked, "for now, we can sleep in your room? I'll clean up the master bedroom and we can settle in there."

"I thought you were sleeping in the master bedroom?"

"No, I've been sleeping in the same room I have since I was a child. After mother died, I was so depressed, being left on my own. I never bothered to occupy her room because it kept reminding me of her."

"And now?"

"And *now* I have you. From the moment you first stepped foot into this inn, you have brightened up the place just by your presence. Now that I have a family again and I'm no longer alone, the inn seems to be alive again."

Matt embraced Freya, "Freya, words can't describe how much I love you. I think I fell in love with you the moment I stepped through the front door and looked up to see you behind the counter."

"For a time I thought you had developed an interest in Frankie," Freya said teasingly still standing with her arms wrapped around Matt's waist.

Matt laughed softly, "Well, I do like Frankie... a lot ---"

"What!" Freya interrupted by jerking on Matt's waist.

"Well, she is attractive, she likes the outdoors, knows how to handle a shotgun...."

Freya interrupted Matt with another quick jerk to his waist. "What?"

"Let me finish. I like Frankie, but she has always appeared to me like a cousin you hang out with to go hunting, fishing, skinny dipping, hiking, and such."

"Don't you think she's pretty?" Freya asked winking at Matt.

"Oh Yes, she is a very attractive woman, but she's just not my type... romantically speaking," Matt added before kissing Freya.

"You know some men in the valley have more than one wife," Freya teased.

"Oh Yeah; really?"

"No, not really. You jerk. And, I had better not catch you skinny dipping with your new found cousin either." She said before she took his hand and led him upstairs.

"I have to get up early in the morning. Doc and Victor will be here for breakfast and then I'll be going with Victor out to the Samuels's homestead at first light."

"Why are you going out to the Samuels?" Freya asked, stopping on the stairway.

"Doc says that an alpha and a pack of rogues raided the Samuels's homestead this morning.

"Oh God! Was anyone hurt?"

"Doc said none of the Samuels were hurt, but the alpha and the rogues slaughtered all of the Samuels's livestock. I'm going out there with Victor in the morning to see what I can discover from the scene that would help me understand the alpha and Rogues better."

"Do be careful Matthew," she said as she resumed climbing the stairs up to Matt's room.

Chapter 33

"Good morning," Victor said to Freya as he walked into the kitchen where she was preparing breakfast.

"Oh good heavens Victor, you scared me. I didn't hear you come in."

"I'm sorry; I thought I made enough noise to wake the dead. I think you were deep in thought and not paying attention."

"Maybe so."

"I hear congratulations are in order," Victor said leaning down to give her a hug.

"Thank you."

"If you don't mind me saying so, you look radiant. You have a smile and a shine on your face I haven't seen in quite some time."

"I'm very happy Victor, Matthew is a good man and I feel like I'm breathing fresh air."

"I'm happy for you, I truly am. You're a good woman and you deserve to be happy."

"Thank you, and can I beg a favor of you?"

"Certainly, what is it?"

"Keep an eye on him and keep him safe."

"I'll do my best little sister," he replied as he kissed her on the forehead.

"There's fresh hot coffee out on the counter. I'll have breakfast on the table in a few minutes. Matthew should be down any minute."

* * *

Matt was pouring coffee when Victor came out of the kitchen.

"Good morning Dr. Kershaw, I'm Victor. I don't think we've been formally introduced."

"Good morning," Matt replied as he shook hands then handed Victor the cup of coffee he had just poured. "It's a pleasure to meet you. I understand I have you to thank for saving my life. I appreciate you pulling that alpha off my ass and saving me from the jaws of death."

Victor noted Matt showed no signs of shock or surprise at his Therian physical characteristics. "Not a problem. I'm sure, if it were the other way around, you would have done the same for me. By the way, I'd like to offer my congratulations. Doc shared the good news when he called me last night. I hope you don't mind."

"Not at all, I'm sure the news will make its circuit around the valley sooner rather than later," Matt said with a smile. "And please call me Matt or Matthew, only my students call me Dr. Kershaw," he told Victor.

"If you prefer, Matt it shall be."

"Victor, what do you know about yesterday's attack on the Samuels homestead?"

Before Victor could answer, Dr. Bertram walked through the front door. "Good morning gentlemen."

"Good morning Doc," they each replied.

Freya stepped through the kitchen door carrying a platter of eggs, bacon, and biscuits "Good morning Doc."

"Good morning young lady," he said.

"I was just asking Victor if he had any new information regarding the incident at the Samuels's homestead yesterday."

Victor glanced toward Doc, "Nothing new from what William shared with you, yesterday afternoon. We're hoping, Matt can shed some light on the situation when we go out there this morning."

"Has anything like this ever happened before?" Matt inquired.

"We were discussing that yesterday, and no one recalls ever hearing of an attack by wargs like what happened at the Samuels's place. Over the last hundred plus years, there has only been a handful of instances in which alone warg has ever ventured into the valley and attacked a human. This is truly a bizarre situation." Victor replied.

Puzzled by the situation, Matt commented, "Bizarre indeed, I've never heard of a wolf pack raiding an established human homestead or settlement."

"You should get out there first thing, I think we're in for a thunder storm by mid-morning," Doc suggested.

"Doc, I have Sarah working on compiling an inventory of equipment, supplies and materials we will need to set up a molecular lab. Obviously, we would not be operating a full-blown wet lab. I suggest we focus on the requirements necessary to conduct the essential test and analysis related to isolating the LTV and mapping the strains among the valley residents. We need your input on materials and equipment priorities for the pathology side of our research."

"As you mentioned the other day, a DNA analyzer will be essential. Sending samples out to a third party lab will pose too much risk," Dr. Bertram reiterated. "We'll need centrifuges, a desktop electron microscope, and possibly a GC, Mass Spec, etc. We can discuss this in more detail later."

"We sent Harvey the specs on a desktop analyzer and he is going to check the government bone yards to see if he can find a surplus unit for us. Otherwise, I found a couple of units through used equipment dealers for less than $100,000 dollars, but it might as well be $1 million dollars. I'm sure Harvey can get some of the basic stuff like microscopes, centrifuge, and other core equipment through the DRMO program. I brought you a copy of the preliminary list Sarah prepared for you to go through. I think containment may be an issue we'll need to solve before we start getting very far with any remodeling of the jailhouse."

"I've had a crew cleaning it up and maybe this afternoon we can go check it out and I can share some ideas with you."

"What about meeting with William after Victor and I get through at the Samuels's place?

Victor spoke up, "I'll call him from the Samuels when we are ready to head back here. He will meet us at the town hall building."

"Ok, sounds like a plan," Matt said as he took the last sip from his coffee. "Victor, I'm ready to roll when you are."

"I'm ready."

Matt kissed Freya, "we'll be back before long, maybe by 10:00 or 11:00."

"Be careful, please," Freya pleaded in a soft voice.

When Matt and Victor arrived at the Samuel's homestead, Mr. Samuels was working to board up the holes in the door where he had blown a hole through it with his shotgun. Matt grabbed a field pack from the back of his jeep as Mr. Samuels came out to greet them.

"Good morning Victor," Mr. Samuels said as they shook hands.

Victor stepped to one side and turned toward Matt, "Alistair, this is Dr. Matthew Kershaw. Matt, this is Alistair Samuels."

"Pleased to meet you, Mr. Samuels," Matt said shaking hands.

"Pleasure is mine, Dr. Kershaw. Please call me Alistair."

"Only if you call me Matt."

"Fair enough," Alistair nodded. "William called me and asked me not to touch anything until you got here. I'm sorry, but we had already moved the animal carcasses yesterday before William called."

"That's fine, we will work with what we have," Matt reassured him. "What did you do with the carcasses?"

"We piled them up at the other end of the field; we were preparing to burn them. They will start stinking in this summer heat after a day, fortunately, it's a bit cloudy and the rain may keep the smell down a bit."

268

"Can you walk us through what happened in as much detail as can recall?" Matt requested.

Alistair walked to a point just in front of his house and began describing the situation, "It wasn't long after sunrise when my boys and I were about to go out and feed the livestock when we heard the animals making a fuss. I thought it might be a lone wolf or a coyote after my chickens. When I looked out the window to see what was happening, I saw the alpha standing over there just beyond the fence in front of us. On each side of the alpha were two wargs which appeared to be standing guard. In the middle area here, I saw three wargs chasing down my livestock and butchering them."

"You use the term *butchering*; can you elaborate on what makes you use that particular term?"

"The wargs were just going animal to animal, attacking them indiscriminately. Once they got a grip on an animal, they viciously ripped out its throat before targeting the next victim."

"And from what you were able to see, it didn't appear they were feeding?"

"No, not that I could say for sure. Even when they ripped out the animals' throats, I saw them spit out the flesh they had in their mouth before going on to the next one. After all of the livestock had been slaughtered, they would tear out a mouthful of flesh and eat it as they passed by one of the slain animals, but as far as I saw, none stopped to actually feed on any of the slain animals."

"Did they drag off any of the animals to possibly feed on later?"

"No, we accounted for all of our livestock. Every one of them had been brutally slaughtered; not a single one left alive."

"Curious," Matt muttered aloud to himself.

"After they finished with the livestock, they started moving toward the house. By then, I had my shotgun loaded and I was waiting for them. The alpha appeared to be giving them instructions. The alpha stood about here and would look at one of the wargs and in a kind of half growl and bark, he appeared to be giving instructions. Then the warg would react to whatever command the alpha appeared to have given him."

Matt looked around the area where Alistair indicated the alpha was standing and he found prints consistent with the ones he made castings of at the site where Ranger Holmes was attacked. However, this track was somewhat smaller than the casting he had made.

Alistair continued, "The pack then began making their way toward the front of the house while two remained on guard on either side of the alpha." Alistair walked up onto the front porch and pointed toward the windows along the front of the house. He described where the wargs took a position at the windows and two at the front door. "The two wargs at the front door were clawing at the door taking turns at trying to ram it open with their bodies. I timed it when one rammed the door and I shot through the door at it. I believe I killed one and wounded the other. That's when the alpha walked up onto the porch. I saw him through the glass when he reared and stretched back his shoulders, bearing his chest as he let out a chilling howl. I shot through the glass and hit him in the shoulder, knocking him back down the porch steps. He barked and howled then he and the others ran away."

Matt opened his pack and pulled out a sample collection kit. He went about methodically taking samples of the blood where Alistair said he shot the rogue and alpha. "Can you take us to the animals the wargs killed?"

"Sure, give me just a minute," Alistair replied. He went into the house and came back a moment later with his shotgun. "Ok, this way." He led Matt and Victor to the pile of carcasses next to a brush pile at the far end of a field.

"Does it appear any of the carcasses have been disturbed since you piled them here yesterday?"

"No," Alistair replied.

"Where is the warg carcass?"

Alistair went to the other side of the pile to point out the warg but, to his astonishment, it wasn't there, "we put it *here*. I remember seeing it every time we threw another of our livestock onto the pile, now it's gone. I don't understand," he said.

Matt examined the wounds on the animals and found almost without exception; the only lethal wound was a bite to the neck where the wargs had ripped out their throats. On a few of the animals, it appeared there were bite marks in locations which suggested the wargs ran the animal down, and then went straight for the throat. While working his way around the pile he noticed, in the general area where the warg's carcass had been left, he found alpha tracks.

"Ok, I'm done here," Matt said. "Do you mind if I spend a few minutes to take some measurements and pictures before we leave?"

"Take your time," Alistair replied. "Can we burn these now?" he asked pointing to the pile of animal carcasses.

"Certainly, we're done with them; thanks," Matt told Alistair.

Back at the Samuels's house, Matt made various measurements, made a casting of the alpha's track, and took pictures. Before he finished packing up his gear, it started to rain. Matt loaded everything into the Jeep before he went into the house to let the Samuels know that they were leaving. Victor took the opportunity to call William and let him know he and Matt were on their way back to Graymere.

"Thank you, Alistair. I'm truly sorry this happened to you and your family," Matt said sincerely.

"Just track these creatures down and kill them before they do this to one of our neighbors or worse," Alistair said with a vengeance in his voice.

* * *

After leaving the Samuels homestead, Matt stared at the road ahead. "What will happen to the Samuels now all of their stock has been wiped out?" he asked Victor.

"When something like this happens, the valley residents pool their resources to help one another to overcome hardships. In this case, the neighbors will each contribute something from their own livestock to help the Samuels rebuild their farm."

On the drive back to Graymere, Matt was strangely quiet. "Matt, what are you thinking?" Victor asked.

"I'm thinking we have a serious problem," Matt replied.

"What do you mean?"

"These animals are using cognitive skills to stalk, ambush, and raid. It appears they are not killing primarily for food or self-defense. The one element confusing me the most is the instances in which the alphas are carrying off their dead and wounded."

"What does that mean?"

"I'm not sure, but I know there's more than one alpha, possibly more than two. Given their level of cognitive skills, the thought sends a chill up my spine. I fear there might be a hierarchical structure among the warg packs. If so, there could even be a supreme alpha controlling and directing two or more alpha packs. Does any of this sound familiar to you?" Matt questioned Victor.

"No, we haven't encountered any wargs for many years and the presence of an alpha prime is exceptionally rare. So rare in fact, many residents regard wargs and alpha primes, more or less as boogiemen. As far as I'm aware we have always assumed that the alpha primes were anomalies among the wargs that occurred very rarely."

"Rarely, until recently," Matt offered and observation.

"Correct. During the last few months, we have seen an increasing level of warg presence in the valley. It started with an occasional sighting, followed by a couple of close encounters. However, recently we've had at least three cases of locals having encounters with wargs. Two escaped unharmed by being able to get behind closed doors."

"And the other?" Matt asked.

"Dead, you are the only person we know who has ever been attacked and survived a physical attack from an alpha prime," Victor said.

"I know of at least one other," Matt replied.

"Who's that?"

"My great grandfather," Matt answered, glancing intently at Victor.

"Are you sure? Did he experience transgenesis or showed any signs of mutation?"

"He did, and before any serious physical mutations emerged he was killed in the war."

"Then you're a Dormer. I'll be damned," Victor said in total surprise.

"A Dormer?" Matt queried.

"A Dormer, a person who inherits the LTV, but the lupine transmutation lies dormant, in most cases all of your life. In situations where both parents are carriers of the LTV, only one in five of their children will show physical signs of transgenic mutation. Four out of five are Dormers. For some reason, it seems that male decedents are more likely to exhibit physical mutations than the females. Therianthropes are ones who exhibit varying degrees of the lupine transgenic mutation."

After a few moments of quiet contemplation, Victor pressed Matt for clarification. "You say your great grandfather acquired the LTV through contact with an alpha, he did not inherit the LTV correct?"

"Yes, that's correct."

"Was this your great grandfather through your father's side or your mother's side of the family?"

"My mother, through my grandmother," Matt replied.

Are you sure your great grandfather was actually bitten by an alpha?"

"Yes," Matt confirmed with confidence.

"Oh shit," Victor said aloud to himself. "Is Doc aware that you were a Dormer before you were attacked the other day?"

"No, I just found out about it yesterday. Doc and I haven't had time to talk much since I got back from the city."

"You need to let him know as soon as we get back to Graymere," Victor told Matt sternly.

"Why, what's the deal?"

"You are an Alpha Prime LTV Dormer, with a secondary Alpha Prime LTV infection. Have you had a second episode of the fever yet?" Victor asked anxiously.

"Yes," Matt replied.

"The first thing we have to do when we get back to Graymere is to talk with Doc; THE VERY FIRST THING, do you understand?"

Chapter 34

Matt pulled up and parked next to the inn. "I'll let Freya know that we are back and I'll meet you at the town hall," Matt said to Victor.

"Ok, see you there."

Matt went into the inn looking for Freya. "Freya; honey, I'm home," he sang out, mimicking a cliché from an old TV show.

"I'm in here," She called from a room down the hall past the staircase.

Matt found her in the master bedroom at the end of the hall, wearing a cleaning apron and rubber gloves. "We're back from the Samuels, but I need to run across the street to the town hall to meet with Doc and William for a few minutes."

"I'll take a break from this and get lunch prepared," She told him.

Matt gave her a kiss on the forehead before he left for the meeting.

* * *

Dr. Bertram was walking up to the town hall building at the same time Matt was crossing the street. "Doc, wait up," Matt called out.

Dr. Bertram stopped and turned around to wait for Matt. "Was it bad?" Dr. Bertram asked.

275

"Bad enough, I'll go over the details in a few minutes, but first I need to talk to you about something. I was going to mention it last night, but I kept getting distracted."

"What's it?"

"Victor said I should tell you as soon as we got back to town."

"Tell me what?"

"Yesterday, Freya and I made a detour to visit my family before coming back to Graymere. A chance conversation with my Uncle Charlie led to another conversation with an old friend of my great grandfather. As it turns out, my great grandfather had been in Misty Hollow back in the 1930s and as fate would have it, he was attacked and bitten by an alpha prime."

"Are you sure of this? This is not an old tale or the ramblings of a senile old man; you're one hundred percent positive he was telling you the truth?"

"Yes," Matt confirmed. "It was my great grandfather on my mother and grandmother's side of the family."

Dr. Bertram paused for a couple of seconds before he sat down on the steps of the town hall in deep thought over Matt's revelation.

"Victor said something about me being a Dormer, and if so, I'd be an alpha prime LTV dormer, with a secondary alpha prime infection. From my limited knowledge of transgenics coupled with what you told me about the effects of LTV, I would guess this is not a good thing."

"No, it's not. I'm not sure how bad because we haven't plowed this ground before. Nevertheless, I expect it's going to be a bumpy ride for you over the next few weeks. We'll discuss this later; we need to get inside, William is waiting."

When Matt and Dr. Bertram entered the town hall, William, Victor, Keira, and Alex were there waiting for them.

"Good morning Gentlemen," William greeted them.

"Good morning," Matt replied.

William pulled Matt away from the group while the others were still exchanging greetings. "It's good to have you back and Doc told me wonderful news about you and Freya. Congratulations."

"Thank you," Matt replied.

"I wish the both of you much happiness."

"Thank you."

While Matt cleaned off the board at the front of the room and wrote down the three objectives in the upper left corner, the others took up seats in a semicircle in front of the chalkboard.

William stood in front of the group. "As some of you may know by now, Dr. Kershaw was asked to come to Graymere this summer to perform an assessment of our warg problem. Unfortunately, Dr. Kershaw didn't have the benefit of knowledge or the history of our kinship with the wargs of the northern wilderness. Although his introduction to our plight was slow in the beginning, he received a crash course, so to speak, giving him a unique perspective on our situation. What you may not know, Dr. Kershaw has unique professional qualifications we hope, when coupled with Dr. Bertram's unique medical background, will lead us toward ridding the valley of our *curse*. I have asked Dr. Bertram and Dr. Kershaw to develop a plan and lead us to the successful accomplishment of the three objectives Dr. Kershaw wrote on the board. However, before they share their plan with us, I would like you to understand something. Both of these men have made sacrifices and commitments to the salvation of Misty Hollow most will never know, and few can comprehend. I have the utmost trust and confidence in their knowledge, skills, and judgment. Therefore, I fully expect our sacrifice and commitment to achieving these objectives to be no less than theirs. To this end, anything they need or ask of us, I would expect each resident of the valley to rise to the occasion and support them without reservation." William stood behind Dr. Bertram and Matt and put his hand on their shoulders. "If either of these men asks anything of you or instruct you to do anything, consider it as if it were coming from me." With that, William took his seat to listen to a

277

preliminary plan that Dr. Bertram and Matt would outline to them.

Addressing the group, Matt outlined an approach to achieving the stated objectives. "Fundamentally we have two independent and diverse population groups, human and lupine, sharing a common core virus, the LTV. At the heart of our plan, is the establishment of a molecular biology and pathology lab here in Graymere. The purpose of the lab will be two-fold. First, facilitate genome mapping of both the human inhabitants and wargs to isolate the genes responsible for supporting and spreading LTV. Second, support gene therapy research led by Dr. Bertram. The goal of this program is to create adenovirus vectors designed to inhibit any further transmission of the LTV strains and to design a DNA integration program aimed at interrupting the generational transgenesis of the LTV to offspring of those who carry the LTV. Initially, I'll be leading the genome mapping efforts among the wargs, as well as, coordinating the efforts to eliminate the LTV from among the warg population. The genome mapping will, in addition to the objectives stated earlier, help us map the extent of the LTV transmission among the warg population and ascertain the diversity of the LTV strains among the wargs."

Victor interrupted, "I understand the program for the human population element, as we have a defined population, but how do you propose we effectively treat the warg population to the extent we're confident the LTV has been eliminated or neutralized?"

"If we're lucky, the gene therapy program, developed for the humans, can be directly applied to the wargs. This depends greatly on the nature and diversity of the LTV strains among the warg population. Ideally, we'll be able to inject the wargs with an adenovirus, which would counter or block the LTV and the wargs would simply breed the virus out of their populations. Alternatively, we could simply exterminate the warg population.

Unfortunately, the wargs north of the valley are posing a serious threat to the valley residents. It appears their population has expanded dramatically and they may be pushing to take over the valley as part of their territory. This may prompt the more drastic approach of extermination."

The group started passing gazes among each other.

Alex spoke up first, "Dr. Kershaw, on the one hand, the extermination of the warg population sounds simple, but in reality, we can't just simply kill every warg or wolf in the wilderness. How do we determine the extent of the extermination program and if we repopulate, will that not provide a fresh population to proliferate the LTV virus?"

"Alex, you are spot on with your assessment and concerns. These, among other concerns, are why we can't just go out into the forest and start killing wargs and wolves willy-nilly. We must take a methodical approach to any extermination program. Any such program would involve tagging, mapping, and treatment."

"What do you mean treatment," William asked.

"As I have already mentioned, hopefully, the same gene therapy program or slightly modified program can be applied directly to the lupine population, wargs and wolves alike. We will treat any wolves brought into the area intended to replace the warg population. Thus, we create a lupine community resistant to any strain of the LTV. Ultimately, through natural attrition, the wargs with LTV will die out and along with them the LTV."

"You mentioned tagging; why tagging?" Alex asked.

"We need to be able to determine the extent of the range of the warg population infected with the LTV. Given the typical boundary dynamics among lupine packs, I'm hoping the LTV infected warg population may be somewhat isolated in much the same way the residents of the valley have been. Therefore, if we can determine the boundary of the wargs territory we can more accurately define the limits to the extermination. Beyond that, we can tranquilize, tag, and test random packs in adjacent areas to the warg territories to determine if the LTV has spread any further in its base strain. By tagging, we can monitor over the coming years to ensure that the LTV does not reemerge."

Keira directed a question to Dr. Bertram, "Doc, why set up a lab here, can we not send out samples for testing? Would this not be more practical?"

"There are three primary problems with sending samples out; first, it is costly, second the time delay in getting results, and third, containment of the virus."

"What do you mean by containment," Keira asked.

"We are trying to eliminate the LTV in all strains. If we send out samples to be tested, there's a risk of contamination and we lose absolute control and access to the virus." Dr. Bertram purposely tried to sidestep the question without directly discussing the possibility of some outside entity exploiting the virus.

William interjected speaking to the group, "we have been lucky over the years. Our isolated location has helped contain the LTV within the valley. Could you imagine what might happen if an unethical lunatic realized the nature of LTV and sought to exploit it for personal or political reasons? We can't risk even the remote possibility that knowledge of the virus goes beyond the valley. And, at any cost, the virus cannot be allowed in the hands of those who are in a position to exploit it. It must be eradicated forever!"

William took his seat nodding for Dr. Bertram and Matthew to continue.

Dr. Bertram addressed the group, "this plan will not result in a quick resolution to the problem. The objectives outlined will require many months if not years to accomplish."

"Dr. Kershaw, you have anything further we need to discuss?" William asked.

"Not at this time," Matt replied.

"It appears we have a viable plan. I understand the first hurdle will be setting up the lab. Are you confident the old jailhouse will be sufficient for your needs?" William asked.

"It's not ideal, but I think we can make it work with some remodeling and modifications," Matt said looking to Dr. Bertram for confirmation.

"Matthew and I'll be going back over our requirements this afternoon and we'll know more at that time."

"Whatever you need, just let us know. I've assigned Victor the responsibility to coordinate any tasking related to dealing with the wargs. Alex will assist in those efforts. Keira will be available to assist you in coordinating the data collection from the valley residents. You can task Peter to arrange any remodeling or construction needs." William dismissed the group but held Matt and Dr. Bertram back after the others had left.

"Where you able to discover anything from your visit to the Samuels's homestead this morning?" William asked Matt.

"Nothing I can say with one-hundred percent confidence," Matt replied.

"Victor told me you voiced some concerns," William prompted.

"Stepping back and looking at the most recent events involving alpha primes and rogues, I'm concerned we may be dealing with a hierarchically structured warg society rather than a couple of warg packs. If so, the problems facing the valley from the wargs is more dangerous than anyone can imagine. If I'm correct, I believe the threat from the wargs will get much worse before we can organize an effective response."

"Please elaborate," William encouraged.

"Just looking at the incidents involving ranger Holmes, the attack in which I was mauled, and now the incident at the Samuels. Each incident demonstrated an overtly aggressive action. Also, each incident appeared to demonstrate a cognitive ability of the alphas to coordinate the actions of the wargs with indications of hierarchical leadership.

The tracks I measured at the sights of each of these incidents suggest there's more than one alpha operating within the same general area. This would further indicate the existence of a supreme alpha managing the activities of what we recognize as the alpha primes. Sharing territory among packs is not characteristic of lupine behavior.

This leads me to my final concern. Wolf packs typically are somewhat consistent in population size, dependent upon the availability of food and water within their established territory. It is rare that wolves would expand their territory unless their population exceeds the available food supply, in which case, you would experience encroachment situations. Under those circumstances, I would expect the wargs to encroach on territories adjacent to them, but north of the valley, not into the valley itself."

"Why do you say that?" William asked.

"Wolves will always take the path of least resistance. I feel safe in assuming the wargs are more powerful and are the apex predator among any animal outside of the valley. Given, their history with conflicts with the valley residents in the past, it would make sense that the wargs would seek to expand their territory by pushing into an adjacent wolf territory rather than deal with the humans in the valley. This suggests to me, that the community of wargs north of the valley may be surrounded by other warg communities to the north, east, and west."

"I would hope you are wrong, but my gut tells me your assessment is accurate. In either case, from here on out, we will operate on the assumption your assessment is correct. Coordinate with Victor whatever actions and precautions we need to implement in order to deal with any possible threat from the wargs." William instructed. "Gentlemen our protection and salvation are in your hands."

Chapter 35

Dr. Bertram, Allison, Keira and Victor joined Matt and Freya for lunch at the inn. The women sat at one end of the table talking about Freya's trip to the city, her shopping experiences and the ordeal she and Sarah went through, the night Matt had a viral relapse.

The men sat at the other end of the table, discussing plans for getting the lab set up. It wasn't long before the conversation at the table focused on the escalating warg threat to the valley.

Matt shook his head and sighed, "From my perspective, this situation has taken on so many competing priorities, it's like trying to corral a barrel of monkeys. We're going to have to task organize and deal with multiple elements simultaneously."

Dr. Bertram spoke up, "Well, I can handle the pathology and DNA mapping, but I'm going to need a lab assistant who has some molecular biology knowledge and who can help train some lab techs."

Overhearing Dr. Bertram's mention of a need for an assistant, Freya interject, "What about Sarah?"

Matt sat back in his seat considering Freya's suggestion. "She would do well technically. She has a B.S. degree in microbiology and a master's degree in molecular biology, not to mention extensive lab experience. She was even the lab tutor for the micro lab."

"Sounds like a prime candidate; do you trust her?" Dr. Bertram asked, looking at Matt and then to Freya.

"I trust her more than anyone I know outside this valley and she understands discretion. She has been doing some work for me from my home, but I've been spoon feeding her just enough information to enable her to do the research I assigned her."

"She would love to do this, you know she would," Freya said encouraging Matt.

"I know she would be here within four hours if I called her and asked her to come. I just don't want her getting unwittingly sucked into a precarious situation like I was. No offense intended."

"Matthew, how in the world can you prepare anyone, from outside the valley, for what they will find here in Misty Hollow? You either trust she can deal with the initial shock and can handle the stress, or not. Beyond that, everything else is in God's hands." Dr. Bertram advised.

Allison interjected, "I understand you trust her from an ethical point of view, but do you trust her judgment? If you trust her judgment, I suggest you bring her here, give her a sneak peek into the world of Therians and wargs. Maybe Freya can show off her cute little ears." Allison winked at Freya. "Then let the young woman make up her own mind.

Victor weighed in on the conversation, "Matt, would you agree the warg threat is such that, at least for the next few weeks, your time will be consumed with organizing a program to deal with the mounting threat?"

"Yes," Matt conceded.

"Then it would stand to reason, you'll not be able to devote any time at all to helping Doc with the lab. That being said, if you trust this young woman, we have no other choice than to bring her here, and let her decide what she wants to do. Graymere has more than sufficient budget to pay her salary and expenses for as long as she wants to remain here working with Doc."

"Freya, you understand my concerns, but you also spent some time with Sarah. What do you think?" Matt asked.

"All I can say; from my observation of her helping me deal with your relapse the other night. She didn't fall apart and she handled the situation as well or better than I did. I think you will find she either knows or suspects more of what's happening here than you realize. I believe she is mature and intelligent enough, if you're honest and upfront with her, she will make a sound decision as to what's best for her. I trust whichever way she decides; you can count on her discretion."

Matt thought for a couple of minutes while everyone else remained silent exchanging looks at one another, waiting for Matt to decide what to do.

"You guys are right. It's not my place to try and be over protective of her to the extent I deny her a choice in this or any other matter." Matt sighed as he got up and went to the phone and called Sarah.

"Sarah?"

"*Yes, is this Dr. Kershaw?*" She asked.

"Yes, it's Dr. Kershaw. Sarah, do you remember the conversation we had Wednesday afternoon when you questioned me about the research we're doing here, and I said you were a smart cookie?"

"*Yes sir,*" Sarah replied.

"After that conversation, are you still interested in coming here, check it out, and see if you would like to work on this research project for the rest of the summer?"

"*OH YES! YES!*" Sarah shouted through the phone without hesitation. Her response was so loud, Matt had to hold the phone away from his head and the others at the table could hear her shouting. "*I was hoping you would call me and ask me to come there.*"

"OK, here is what I need you to do," Matt instructed, "you'll need to get old lady Sawyer down the road to come up and feed the ducks while we're away. Pack enough clothes for at least a couple of weeks. Bring the computer from the cabin and all of the material you've been working on, along with the castings I left with you. Don't leave *anything* behind related to this project. Get a pencil and a notepad and I'll give you directions." Matt gave Sarah the directions to Jack Wilson's Trading Post. "When do you think you can make the trip up here?"

"I can leave tomorrow morning if that's cool with you. I can go now to visit with Mrs. Sawyer and I can have my car packed and ready to go tonight."

"Call Freya before you leave. When you get to Jack's store ask him to call Freya to let her know you are there and then Jack will give you directions the rest of the way to Graymere."

"OK, I can do that."

"Sarah," Matt paused to get her attention. "Jack will be very inquisitive. He probably will ask you about Graymere and what you are coming here for. *Don't* tell him anything, only that you're on your way to Graymere to help Dr. Kershaw with a field study. Got it?"

"Yes, sir."

"You can use the card I gave you for gas, food and whatever you need to get here. You will stay at Freya's inn and other expenses covered on this end. Dr. Bertram will interview you and discuss compensation and job offer when you get here."

"You mean like a real job?" Sarah said excitedly.

Matt laughed, "Yes, like a real job."

"Ok, I'll call Freya in the morning before I leave; anything else?"

"No, I think that's it for now."

"Alright, I'm going now to see old lady Sawyer about taking care of the ducks and I'll stop by the co-op to get more duck food just in case."

"Be careful on the road. We'll see you tomorrow," Matt said as he hung up the phone.

While walking back to the table, Matt told Dr. Bertram, "Freya forgot to mention how hyper Sarah is. You'll need to whip up something to put in her coffee to drop her out of warp speed." He said with a raised eyebrow.

"Sorry, did I forget to mention that in my recommendation?" Freya said then laughed.

"Well, that bit of business being taken care of; I'm supposed to meet Peter over at the old jailhouse to discuss getting a crew in there to clean the place out." Dr. Bertram said aloud.

"Do you mind if Victor and I walk with you?"

"Sure," Dr. Bertram replied.

Allison called out, "Doc, if you don't mind, I'll stay and help Freya for a little while. She'll need to get the inn cleaned up and rooms rearranged before Sarah arrives tomorrow."

Dr. Bertram nodded his head, "I'll see you at home later."

Matt kissed Freya on the forehead before he left the inn.

* * *

As they walked down the street to the jailhouse, Dr. Bertram turned to Matt and asked, "What's on your mind that you didn't want to say in front of the women?"

"Nothing gets past you Doc," Matt smiled. "There's something else I haven't had a chance to discuss with you. Since I recovered from the initial LTV infection, I've had a ringing in my ears that keeps getting louder. At times, I have severe pains when I hear certain sounds or loud noises in general. In addition to that, my muscles continually ache, sometimes accompanied by bad cramps. I've avoided saying anything to Freya because I don't want to alarm her needlessly. Is this a normal part of the side effects of the viral infection?" Matt asked.

"What you're experiencing is typical of a transgenetic mutation. From the symptoms you're describing, I'd say your inner ear is going through a mutation, from which, you'll eventually develop enhanced hearing. Your muscle aches and cramping is a common symptom of transgenic mutation as well. You can expect to gain muscle mass and your strength and agility will show some degree of enhanced physical performance."

"So, is that it? Is the worst of the effects I'll suffer from the LTV?"

"To be honest, it's hard for me to say with any certainty, what you're going to experience. What I can tell you for sure is, you'll experience several more episodes like the one you had the other night. Additionally, you'll start to develop physical signs of lupine mutation, but to what extent, I can't say with any certainty at this point."

"Thanks, Doc," Matt said. "Do you need anything from me at the jailhouse?"

"No, I'm just going to get with Peter to go over the cleanup which needs to be done."

"Victor and I'll go back to the inn to put together a plan to deal with the warg threat."

"Alright, I'll talk to you later then," Dr. Bertram said.

Matt poured a cup of coffee and sat down at his favorite table next to the front window with Victor. "Here's what we need to do. First, we need to establish a rolling patrol along the main road leading into the valley. Their job will be to restrict any transients from venturing into the valley. I'll have Harvey put out a travelers warning, restricting all hikers, campers, and hunters from entering the valley due to possible landslides or washed out roads. There are no designated campsites or hiking trails in the valley. Therefore, we should be able to effectively close off the valley from the outside. We'll need radios with a decent range, with multi channels, so that we can communicate more effectively."

"I'll have Jarvis go to the city and purchase them. How many do you think we will need?"

"I would say at least twenty or so. They need to have car chargers and spare batteries as well," Matt told Victor.

"If you compile a shopping list, I'll send Jarvis to Boise to gather up whatever we need."

"Once we have the valley closed off from outsiders, we'll need to establish response teams on rotating shifts, twenty-four-seven. If a pack is sighted anywhere in the valley, the response team will converge on that location. Intercept the treat and if possible, kill any wargs they encounter. We won't have the lab set up for several weeks, but we will need to make up biosample kits. The teams will need to take and preserve blood, hair, and tissue samples from any wargs they kill or wound."

"I'll get with Doc to find out what he needs for sample kits and any coolers or freezers to preserve the samples," Victor said.

"We need to tag some of the wargs in order to track them back to their dens. I have one tranquilizer gun, but we will need additional darts and tranquilizer. Before we go on the offensive, we need to locate and map the warg dens. I'll have Harvey arrange for additional tranquilizer guns, darts, and tags. We should establish rolling patrols, organized in three to four person teams. One driver, a spotter, and over-watch, and a two-person team to tranquilize and tag the wargs."

"Do you think we will be very successful with the rolling patrols?" Victor asked.

"As many times as we've encountered them over the last two weeks, I expect we will tag two or three, maybe more. But, if the alpha's cognitive skills are close to what I think they might be, they will get wise to our tactics and will soon become gun shy. However, by the time they start figuring things out, we should be prepared to implement one or more ambush or trapping tactics. If we're *really* lucky, we will get at least one warg from more than one pack, which will lead us to the different dens."

"Once we make a move on the warg dens, won't the pack just move to another location?" Victor asked.

"A normal wolf pack would do that for sure. However, I believe the wargs are exhibiting a bit of the human trait creating a tendency to nest and then defend the nest versus fleeing to avoid conflict. This is just an example of why I believe the wargs are unpredictably dangerous."

"How's that? You alluded to that observation this morning," Victor asked.

"Because, if we don't step back and consider the potential and extent of the wargs' cognitive skills, we could easily stumble into a very dangerous situation and make deadly mistakes when we try to approach them. We must look at wargs as a different species with a very different behavior pattern. Forget they might have been wolves at one time or share any behavioral characteristics with wolves. If we don't approach them with a different understanding of their behavior, they will get the drop on us like last week. If it hadn't been for you, that encounter would have been my fatal mistake. Those wargs set us up for an ambush. I was stupid and naive in dealing with the situation and it almost cost me, or us, our lives."

289

Victor sat back and rubbed his chin in thought. "So, we need to develop some protocols on how to deal with certain situations until we learn more about them?"

"Yes, but the thing which scares me most about the wargs is *our* lack of understanding of their motivation for killing. My gut tells me, from what I've seen, there's an agenda behind the warg incursion. They are not killing for food; they are killing with a purpose directed at selected targets. I'm having trouble wrapping my head around this. It just doesn't make sense to me."

"Ok, I'm going to have Alex organize two-person teams to patrol the main road in and out of the valley to stop all non-resident traffic from coming into the valley. I'll have them wear some sort of uniform suggesting official authority for keeping them out. We will get that working by tomorrow. Next, I'll select a group of betas and deltas to begin training right away as response teams. We can set up a training site at Alex and Frankie's lodge. It's a good central location within the valley. I'll have Frankie select six or eight people to train for tranquilizing and tagging teams."

"Why don't you and I meet with Alex and Frankie here tomorrow morning and I'll outline a preliminary training agenda and personnel requirements. By the time we get the equipment we need, we should have the people in place to begin training."

"Sounds good, I'll see you tomorrow morning here say around eight o'clock."

* * *

Matt walked into the master bedroom and saw Freya and Allison scrubbing away. "This looks nice."

"If you like, you can start moving your stuff down here. I'll clean up your room and change the linen so Sarah can have that room when she gets here tomorrow."

"Ok, do you need me to help you with anything here?"

"No, Allison and I are just finishing up. I'll bring my stuff down later." Freya walked over to Matt and wrapped her arms around his waist while looking up and kissing him. "The bathroom has a tub; a big tub," She whispered with a sly wink.

"Humm, we will have to check that out this evening. What do you think?"

"Yes, we want to make sure it functions properly don't we?" She teased.

"Where do you want me to put my clothes?" He asked.

"You can use the wardrobe there, and I'll put my stuff in this one." Freya pointed to the respective armories. "There's a study here," she said leading Matthew across the hall to another room. "You can put your gear and stuff here and use it for your office. You can organize the bookshelves the way you like. My mother said this was where my father liked to sit and read, smoke his pipe and relax. After he died, no one ever came in here. I just came in to clean the dust and cobwebs from time to time."

"This is great; I'll take care of cleaning and organizing it." Matt gave Freya a kiss. "I'll go move my junk out of the room upstairs if you're ready for me to bring it down?"

"Yes, we can sleep in here tonight and test out the tub."

Chapter 36

"Sarah called early this morning and told me she was leaving from your cabin. She said to tell you, she made sure she turned off, locked up, and she paid all the utilities before she packed up the computer. She should be here around ten o'clock this morning." Freya informed Matt.

Matt sat down at the table sipping his morning coffee. "I'm worried about her; I shouldn't have involved her in this mess."

"She's a big girl, and she is making a mature choice. Give her credit that she is going into this with her eyes open and thinking objectively."

"You're right, but I would never forgive myself if anything happened to her."

Freya went over and gave Matt a hug from behind. "She'll be alright."

"Alex, Frankie, and Victor will be here at eight this morning for a short meeting. I need to put together some notes before they get here. Do you need me to do anything before I get focused on my stuff?"

"No, I'm going to finish cleaning the rooms upstairs and then move the rest of my things downstairs. After I get moved, I'll clean my room and get it ready as a guest room as well." Freya smiled then left him to his work and went upstairs to do hers.

Matt and Victor met with Alex and Frankie to outline the task organization of the different groups to deal with the warg threat. Matt outlined how the various teams will have a common core element of training teaching them about warg characteristics and behavior, radio communication skills, navigation, and weapons training. Subsequently, the individual groups will move into specialized training for their assigned tasks. Victor and Matt outlined the basic qualities they should look for in selecting their team members. Matt, Victor, Alex, and Frankie would form the primary cadre of trainers, each teaching their areas of competence and learning from the others. Matt highlighted to the three of them, how each should identify and train someone to take over as the leader of the respective groups. They themselves would be subsequently trained for leadership roles in preparing additional teams to begin hunting the wargs and eliminating the packs.

Victor, Alex, and Frankie all agreed to have their teams formed and ready for training within three days. Before leaving, Alex and Frankie each provided Victor a list of supplies and equipment they needed for their teams. Victor agreed to have Jarvis go to the city, acquire the items on their list, and have it delivered to the lodge before training began.

Not long after Alex, Frankie, and Victor left, Matt sat down to relax and collect his thoughts when he heard the unmistakable sound of Sarah's voice when she came through the front door.

"Dr. Kershaw, I made it!" She was so excited. "Wow, this town is a bit creepy don't you think, I thought I was sucked into the twilight zone when I crossed over the little bridge at the edge of the village."

"I know the feeling, but you will get used to it in no time, I'm sure."

"Where is Freya?" She asked.

"Here I am," Freya said coming down the stairs. "I thought I heard your voice."

Sarah ran to Freya, "I can't believe I'm here. Is this your place? Wow, it's cool. Check out this big fireplace. I bet it's very comfortable to sit next to, on a cold winter day."

"Let me help you get your things up to your room." Freya took some of Sarah's things and looked at Matt with a raised eyebrow as she led Sarah upstairs.

After getting Sarah settled in her room, the two came downstairs where Matt was waiting for Sarah, to introduce her to the unusual diversity among therian residents living in the valley.

"Sarah, have a seat for a minute, I want to try to explain what happening here and a little about the research."

"Ok, I'm ready; shoot."

"Do you recall from your microbiology and molecular biology courses any topics related to transgenesis or transgenic mutation?"

"Yes, I thought the concept was cool and we studied how they made the mouse glow in the dark by modifying its genome by mixing it with the genome of a fish with bioluminescence."

"In the process of trying to understand why the wolves in this area were attacking people, we identified a mutated retrovirus. This virus acts as a vector to cause a transgenesis of wolf genome into an infected human. In some cases, it has resulted in varying degrees of transgenic mutation of the lupine genome. Do you understand the concept I just explained?"

"Yes, if the wolf has the disease and bites a human, the human may or may not experience a phenotype mutation characteristic of the lupine genome. Yes?"

Matt chuckled, "This is easier than I thought it was going to be."

"If you recall, in a transgenic mutation, the mutated genes can be passed on to the offspring."

"Yes, if the germ cell carries the mutated retrovirus."

"This is the situation we are dealing with here. The wolves originally infected the humans; the humans have experienced different levels of phenotype mutations over several generations. At some point they transferred it back to the wolves which are now experiencing transgenic mutations, exhibiting phenotype mutations from the human genome."

"So you guys are setting up a lab to map the genomes, isolate the virus, and design a gene therapy to cure it. Am I right?" Sarah asked.

Matt and Freya looked at each other speechless.

"What's the matter, didn't I get it correct?"

"Yes, you got it correct. But, do you *understand* what you just said?"

Sarah just looked at him confused.

"Freya do you mind demonstrating?"

Freya pulled back her hair to reveal her ears that showed a hint of lupine ear shape with little puppy fuzz around them.

Sarah got up to look at Freya's ears. "Wow, cool. Can I touch them?" She examined them thoroughly. "They're cute. I wish I had ears like that. Are they real?"

Freya had to chuckle at Sarah's innocent fascination in contrast to the expected reaction she and Matt had prepared for. "Yes, they're real."

"Freya, would you mind calling over to the clinic and see if Doc is there?"

"Certainly," she replied.

"Is Freya the only one who has ears like that?" Sarah asked in a low voice so Freya would not hear her.

"No, there are others," Matt told her trying to hold back laughter thinking to himself, '*isn't this going to be a hoot.*'

"Doc is at the clinic," Freya told Matt as she returned from making the phone call. "And yes there are others with ears like this and they can hear as well or better than I can," Freya said to Sarah, not intending to embarrass her, but to demonstrate her exceptional hearing as another beneficial mutation.

"This is going to be so cool," Sarah said, aloud to herself.

Matt and Freya just looked at each other shrugging their shoulders.

"OK, let's take you over to meet Dr. Bertram.

* * *

Dr. Bertram was sitting on his front porch relaxing as Matt, Freya, and Sarah approached the clinic. "Good morning," Dr. Bertram said to them as they came up the porch steps. "And this must be Sarah?"

"Yes, sir." Sarah extended her hand to shake.

"It's truly a pleasure to meet you. You were a trooper the other night when Dr. Kershaw was ill. I was impressed with how calm and clear headed you were during the whole episode." Dr. Bertram opened the door and gestured for them to come into the clinic.

"If you were there, you wouldn't think I was calm at all. He scared the crap out of me," Sarah said. She looked back over her shoulder at Matt with a scolding scowl.

Allison met them in the hallway. "Sarah, this is my wife Allison."

"Sarah, it's a pleasure to meet you. Doc told me what a help you were to Freya the other night."

"Nice to meet you, Mrs. Bertram."

"Allison is an RN with a background working in ERs as a trauma nurse. She and I operate the clinic here in Graymere." He led Sarah into the living room and offered her a seat. Matt sat off to one side and Freya went with Allison to the kitchen to visit.

"Has Dr. Kershaw explained the nature of the research we will be doing here and the situation that has prompted the need to undertake this work?"

"Yes sir, I believe so," Sarah replied. She summarized the conversation she had with Matt just before they came over to meet Dr. Bertram. The extent of her summary clearly demonstrated she had a firm grasp on the basics of molecular biology.

Matt interjected, "She saw Freya's ears and thought they were *cool*."

"Sarah, if you could imagine what would result from a cross-species transgenetic viral infection acquired by a human from a lupine host; describe to me what phenotype mutations we might expect to see."

296

"Well, depending upon the extent of the viral infection spread within the host, how many different type of cells it had invaded, the age of the host when it was originally infected, and so on, the viral vector could result in a variety of phenotype transmutations or none at all. If the viral vector were such, that it affected the germ cells, it could be passed to the offspring and would manifest itself in the offspring, or it could lie dormant for one or more generations before the mutation surfaces."

"Ok, excellent," Dr. Bertram responded. "But, now describe the *physically visible phenotype mutations* you might expect to see in the human, who acquired the transgenetic virus vector?"

"Well, as I said, depending on various factors, you might see something simple like Freya's ears. Maybe some change in hair growth patterns, some minor physical changes. In generational transgenesis, you could expect to see major physical mutations such as hands and feet, face, and muscle mass. Correct?"

"Close enough," Dr. Bertram confirmed while looking at Matt. "Sarah, you didn't get this level of understanding of transgenesis from college courses and college labs. How do you know so much about transgenetic mutations?"

"After I graduated from high school I went to college for a year before I joined the Army. I needed to earn money and to get education benefits so I could finish college without a mountain of debt. At the time, I wanted to go to med school, so I choose lab tech as my specialty when I left the army I was a 68K Level 3."

"Yes, but how did you learn so much about transgenetic mutations?" Dr. Bertram repeated.

"Well, I was the top of my class when I graduated AIT, so the army stationed me at a remote bioresearch facility. When I became a level 3, they assigned me to be lab assistant to Col. Livingston and Dr. Hobart. They were doing research related to genetic engineering. They used retroviruses as vectors to facilitate transgenetic mutations. I started taking online college courses while stationed there and Dr. Hobart would tutor me and teach me as we worked on stuff. After I left the Army, I went back to school and completed my B.S. degree in microbiology. My master's degree is in molecular biology and biochemistry."

Matt interrupted, "Sarah the other day I asked you about your lab experience, and you didn't mention all of this."

"You asked me what college courses and labs I took at the university, you didn't ask me about my work before I studied at the university," she explained.

Matt and Dr. Bertram just looked at each other somewhat surprised at Sarah's resume.

"Dr. Kershaw mentioned that you thought Freya's ears were, 'cool,' would you be surprised if I introduced you to someone who exhibited a bit more advanced phenotype lupine mutation?"

"Really, there's someone here who exhibits the phenotype of lupine genome?" Sarah responded with anticipation. Then suddenly, her demeanor shifted to caution. "You're not talking werewolf type mutation are you?" she asked hesitantly.

"I'll be right back." Dr. Bertram left the room and returned a few minutes later with Keira. "Sarah this is Keira Moonjoy."

"WHOA!" Sarah said astonished. "Oh, I'm so sorry," she quickly apologized. "It's not you I said whoa to, it's the fact that I'm looking at a real transgenetic..." Sarah stumbled over the words. "I'm sorry, I didn't mean to disrespect you, I'm actually intrigued." Sarah tried to compose herself and excuse her initial reaction.

"It's alright, I understand. And, you didn't insult me, it's funny to see peoples' reaction the first time they see a Therian."

"May I?" Sarah asked gesturing for permission to examine Keira's Lupine features. "This is amazing, I worked on some projects related to this, but I never dreamed... It always seemed like such a huge leap from theory to the lab, to reality." Sarah said aloud to herself.

Sarah and Keira immediately started carrying on a conversation about the effects of transgenic mutations. Keira told Sarah about other therians who exhibited varying levels of lupine transmutations. She explained how some exhibited non-visible transmutations such as enhanced smell, hearing, or strength. Sarah and Keira, being about the same age, appeared to form an immediate bond of friendship. Matt and Dr. Bertram walked out to the front porch to talk while Keira and Sarah chatted away.

"I don't know who was more surprised through that exchange, us or Sarah," Matt joked to Dr. Bertram.

"She's a God send and will be invaluable in setting up the lab and training lab techs," Dr. Bertram told Matt.

"She brought all of her work with her and has put together a preliminary inventory of equipment, materials, and supplies for you to review. From here I'll leave it to you guys to establish your working relationship," Matt said smiling.

"I think she will work out just fine. I believe it will be a pleasure to work with her."

By the time Matt and Dr. Bertram went back inside, all four women were sitting together engaged in conversation revolving around Freya's trip to the city and Sarah's perspective of some of the events such as shopping, buying the engagement and wedding rings, and the events of the night Matt fell ill. They were all laughing and enjoying each other's company.

"It's good to see joy, laughter, and life back in Graymere again," Dr. Bertram cheerfully said to Matt.

Chapter 37

Over the next few days, Alex organized, trained, and equipped the teams to patrol the main road leading in and out of the valley. In the days that followed, Graymere seemed to be alive with activity. Dr. Bertram and Allison set up a sample collection, storage, and containment program, while Sarah began recruiting and screening candidates to train as lab techs. Although it could be weeks before the lab would be built and equipped, Dr. Bertram decided that they could begin taking DNA samples from valley residents and documenting as much of their heritage as possible. Keira and Mrs. Moonjoy were invaluable in filling in many of the details of family trees and histories.

Out at the lodge, Victor and Frankie hand-selected members for their respective teams. Along with Matt, they began the rigorous training program Matt had developed for them. Within a couple of weeks, Harvey had supplied the needed tranquilizer guns, darts, and tags to enable Frankie's group to begin tagging operations once they finished training. Victor's group focused on response drills and tracking operations to counter any further warg raids or intrusions.

The raid on the Samuels's homestead puzzled Matt. Victor informed him that some betas had observed wargs watching the activities at the lodge from a distance. Matt was both pleased and distressed at learning the wargs were watching them. On the one hand, he knew they were nearby, making it easier to possibly locate, ambush, tranquilize, and tag them. On the other hand, he was distressed to learn the wargs were actively spying on the activities at the lodge. This was another frightening example of the advanced cognitive skill of the wargs.

After two weeks of training, Matt, Victor, and Frankie agreed they were ready to begin tagging and tracking operations. Matt had a couple of more weeks left to work in the valley before he would have to go back to the city and resume his job as a teaching professor at the university.

"Our objective initially is not to kill all of the wargs, but to tranquilize them and tag as many of them as possible. It's vital that we are able to track them back to their dens. The type of tag we're using goes under the hide so it won't be easily recognized by the wargs as opposed to the old collar type tags."

"What's the main difference?" Frankie asked.

"I'm sure that, if we tag the wargs using the old tracking collars, the alphas will recognize it and banish the tagged warg from the pack or maybe simply kill it. If we insert these tags under the hide, it performs the same function. However, doesn't have the range or battery life the tracking collar does, but they won't know they've been tagged."

"How limited is the range?" Victor asked.

"We'll be able to track them through GPS satellite as well as this handheld monitor. If I'm right, we will find there is more than one group working the valley. If we can tag at least one warg from each group, we will be able to locate the various dens. The more we can tag, the better. If we are lucky we will be able to map the entire warg community. Victor, you should have at least one response team ready to roll if the tagging team calls for backup."

"What about the wargs that have been watching us from the rise, just beyond the pasture?" Victor asked.

"I think they should be the target for our first tagging exercise. Hopefully, we will get one or more tagged and we will start putting them on the defensive and begin pushing them back into the wilderness. Remember, while we have them tranquilized we need to get blood, hair and tissue samples."

A plan was outlined to ambush the wargs watching the activities around the lodge the next morning. Frankie will wait until the betas confirm that the wargs are in their normal location, watching the lodge. Then Frankie's group will circle behind them, staying downwind, and set up an ambush. Victor will wait for word from Frankie that her group is in position, and have good fields of fire. Then, Victor will have the team's supposedly training in the field, turn and form a line facing the wargs and rush the wargs' position. Matt expected the wargs to turn and run away, crossing the path of Frankie's group, who would tranquilize as many as they could. After the wargs were down, the beta group would move in to secure the area and protect the tagging team while they took samples and tagged the wargs before they woke up. If all went according to plan, they hoped to tag two or three wargs.

* * *

Matt entered the new lab and paused for a moment to scan the facilities. "How's the lab coming along?" he asked Dr. Bertram.

"Slowly," Doc replied as he turned to greet Matt. "Allison, Keira, and Mrs. Moonjoy are busy taking DNA samples and collecting data on the valley residents. Sarah is busy training the lab techs. How are things at the lodge?"

"We're going to try tagging a couple of wargs tomorrow morning."

"Are your people ready?"

"I hope so. They are practicing now for tomorrow's tagging operation. We need to start getting some of them tagged. I'll be heading back to the city to begin fall classes in a couple of weeks. I want to be able to supervise a few tagging and sampling operations and test the tracking equipment before I bug out to the city."

"The last few weeks have passed so quickly," Dr. Bertram commented.

"Yes they have, and by the way, how's Sarah working out for you?"

"She is doing a great job training the lab techs. She screened, tested, and selected the group she wanted and passed them to me to approve. Then she went to work setting up training classes for them."

"Is she going to have them ready before we head back to the city?"

"I'm not sure she's going back. I haven't discussed it with her, but I overheard her and Keira talking a couple of days ago. From their conversation, it sounded like she was planning to stay here and continue training the techs and help set up the lab."

"She was accepted into the Ph.D. program with a research fellowship. I'm not sure she wants to forfeit that opportunity," Matt said to Dr. Bertram.

"Maybe you should talk to her about it at dinner this evening. I would hate to lose her at this stage of our preparations, but I understand she has a life outside this valley just as you do."

"I'll talk to her and see what her plans are," Matt replied.

"How have you been doing? Freya mentioned you've had bouts of fever." Dr. Bertram inquired.

"Yes, each time the severity and duration are less than the previous episode. I seem to recover more quickly after each episode as well. I'm still having muscle aches, but the cramping is not as frequent or as severe as it was in the beginning. Overall, I feel stronger and nimbler, my hearing has improved as you said it would, and my sense of smell is starting to intensify. The downside is, my body hair is starting to become thicker and a bit coarser." Matt demonstrated by pinching some of the hair on his arm to visually highlight the observation to Doc.

"Just keep me posted on any changes you experience."

"Ok Doc will do," Matt replied.

"Have you heard anything from Harvey regarding the acquisition of the equipment we requested?"

"Yes, he called this morning; I totally forgot to tell you. He said the U.S. Government was shutting down an animal-bio research facility on Plum Island and moving the operation to a new facility they are building outside Manhattan, Kansas. The equipment at Plum Island was going to be auctioned off and he was trying to get a request in for an interagency appropriation or something like that."

"Plum Island?" Dr. Bertram said with a curious expression on his face.

"That's what he said," Matt confirmed.

"I've spoken with William, and if Harvey doesn't come through for us, we are prepared to use municipal funds to equip the lab." Dr. Bertram told Matt.

"Does the town have that kind of money? The population doesn't seem big enough to support a tax revenue stream."

"I'm not sure if Freya told you, but the residents get a stipend from the government as part of a settlement from decades ago, in exchange for the appropriation of Indian land to designate as national forest lands. The town also receives an annual stipend as well. It's not a huge amount of money relative to the rest of the federal budget. Therefore, it doesn't pop up on the fiscal radar. But, the town and the people have accumulated a tidy sum of cash reserves."

"So that is what's paying for the remodeling, the equipment for the response teams, fuel, and so on?"

"Yes," Dr. Bertram replied casually.

"Well, I should be getting over to the inn, I need to get cleaned up and do a bit of work before Freya serves dinner. You know how she's a stickler for the meal schedule."

* * *

Matt was in the study reviewing his notes trying to characterize the different levels of transgenic mutations and intelligence among the wargs. Freya stepped half way through the doorway. "I hope you don't mind, I invited Doc and Allison to dinner this evening."

"No, problem." Matt motioned for Freya to come closer. As she got near him, he took her arm and pulled her into his lap. "Did I ever tell you how much I love you?"

"No, I don't think you ever have. Is that what you wanted to tell me?" Freya was being coy.

Matt embraced her and held her close for a couple of minutes. "You know we haven't snuggled on the couch and enjoyed popcorn and a movie in quite a while. Maybe we can find a movie on my computer we can watch this evening." He teased.

"Hmmm, that sounds like an interesting prospect, but right now I have to finish dinner."

"You want help?" Matt offered.

"No, almost done and Sarah is in the kitchen getting into the middle of everything," Freya said with a chuckle as she got up and left the room.

* * *

During dinner, the conversation was light and casual, bouncing from topic to topic. Eventually, Dr. Bertram, Matt, and Sarah began discussing the preparations in getting the lab ready to start acquiring and installing equipment. Matt decided it was an opportune time to query Sarah on her plans to go back to the city to begin the Ph.D. program.

"Sarah, are you going to be wrapping up the training program soon?" Matt asked her.

"What do you mean?"

"Classes will begin in about three weeks and we will need to disengage from our work here and get ready to head back to the city in a couple of weeks," Matt explained.

In the middle of the discussion, the phone rang and Freya got up to answer it.

"I'm not sure I want to leave. There's so much to do and I feel my knowledge and skills are truly making a difference here unless Dr. Bertram tells me otherwise." Sarah replied, looking toward Dr. Bertram for confirmation.

"I understand your feelings; I have the very same attachment to Graymere, the people, and the plight of the valley. However, we have commitments back home to consider. You've been accepted into a very limited Ph.D. program and…"

Freya interrupted Matt in the middle of the conversation "Matthew, there's been another raid by the wargs. Victor is on the phone."

Matt got up and went to the phone followed close behind by Dr. Bertram. Victor informed Matt that a raid was in progress at one of the homesteads and he had dispatched two response teams to go there.

"What homestead is it?" Matt asked. He held the phone where Dr. Bertram could hear the conversation.

"The Lancaster Place," Victor told him.

"The Lancaster homestead," Matt repeated, looking at Dr. Bertram to see if he recognized the name and where the homestead was located.

"Doc is here with me; we will be there as fast as we can," Matt told Victor before he hung up the phone.

"I'm coming with you," Sarah said.

"I don't think this is a time and place for you to sight-see," Matt objected.

"I'm coming, either with you or I'll follow you, make up your mind," Sarah said as she got up and started toward her room to gather her jacket and pack.

"Matt, No! You can't let her go out there. Doc, tell him," Freya pleaded.

"Freya, I'm afraid she is going to find her way out there one way or another. I would prefer she was with us, so we can keep an eye on her, instead of her stumbling around in the dark on her own. Besides, I think she is a bit tougher than you think." Matt replied. "Doc, give me a sec and I'll go get my pack and weapon."

"I'll be right back, I'm going to run over to the clinic and grab my medical bag."

Matt went to the study and grabbed his revolver, rifle, and shotgun, along with extra ammunition. Sarah was coming down the stairs as Matt emerged from the study, "Do you know how to use this?" Matt held out the shotgun.

"Yes sir," She replied firmly taking the shotgun and shells from Matt.

Matt gave Freya a walkie-talkie and set it to a particular channel. "Just keep this close and I'll call you and let you know what's going on."

Freya and Allison followed them out the front door. Dr. Bertram returned and gave Allison a kiss before getting into Matt's jeep. Matt kissed Freya and assured her they were just going to investigate the scene before anything was disturbed and they would be fine.

While Matt and Dr. Bertram were saying their goodbyes, Sarah loaded the shotgun and jacked a shell into the chamber. "Are we ready to roll?" Sarah asked, in a very focused and serious tone. Before she got into the jeep, she turned toward Freya and Allison and said with a wink, "don't worry, I'll keep an eye on them."

Chapter 38

Dr. Bertram directed Matt to the Lancaster Homestead. When they got closer, they could hear radio chatter through the walkie-talkie. Mostly acknowledgments from one team member to another, acknowledging a particular area was clear or directing another team member to search an area.

"Sarah, when we get there, we'll sit in the vehicle until we can determine where Victor's people are. Otherwise, we could end up being shot or shooting someone by accident. We are here primarily to investigate the scene of the attack and gather biosamples. When we do get out, the three of us will stay close together, back to back, to be able to watch three-hundred-sixty degrees around us until Victor tells us it's all clear. Do you understand?" Matt instructed.

"Yes sir," Sarah said in a firm military acknowledgment of his instructions.

When they reached the end of the road leading into the Lancaster homestead, Matt picked up the radio and called for Victor, "Victor, this is Matt, do you read me?"

"Yes Matt, I read you. Where are you guys?"

"We are at the end of the road leading into the farmhouse, shall we come on in?"

"Yes, turn off your headlights and drive up to the house with your parking lights on. My people are still searching the area; I think the wargs may still be nearby."

"Ok, I copy. We will – Oh shit!" Matt yelled out when a warg rogue came out of nowhere and rammed the side of the jeep.

Sarah let out a scream, startled by the violent impact.

Before Matt realized what had hit them, another rogue rammed the jeep from the opposite side.

"Matt, what's happening?" Victor called over the radio.

"We are being attacked near the end of the road by at least two wargs!" Matt responded.

"Keep moving toward the house, I have a team headed your direction and will intercept the wargs and pull them off you guys."

"Roger," Matt acknowledged.

"What's happening?" Sarah asked aloud.

"Just stay cool. The response team will meet us near the house." Matt told her just before another warg slammed into the jeep.

Sarah could see muzzle flashes and hear gunfire around them. She was straining her eyes in the dim light around the vehicle, looking in all directions when a rogue slammed into the side of the jeep, near the door next to where she was sitting. Just as she turned to see what had hit the vehicle, she saw someone or something, approach very rapidly from the front of the vehicle and tackle the rogue next to the window where she sat.

Matt kept driving slowly toward the house, which they could see in front of them. Once they pulled up and stopped, a response team surrounded the jeep. From the sound of the gunfire and radio chatter and it appeared the wargs were moving away from the area.

"Well, this was a bit unexpected," Victor said as he opened Matt's door.

"Can we get out now?" Sarah asked from the back seat.

"Yes, but stay near the house for the moment," Victor replied.

"How bad is it?" Matt asked.

"Bad! By the time the response teams arrived, the wargs had breached the front door and killed everyone inside. The rogues were going through the house ransacking the place. A couple rogues were out here slaughtering the few animals the Lancaster's had near the house and barn."

"Can I go in and check the family, maybe someone is alive?" Dr. Bertram asked.

"You can go in Doc, but I assure you, there's no one alive in there. And you may not want to see them in their current condition." Victor cautioned.

"I'm going with Doc," Sarah said.

Victor motioned for one of the team members to accompany them.

"Did anyone see an alpha?" Matt asked Victor.

"Yes; I'm sure at least one was here, but he was careful to stay out of sight. We can search for tracks in the morning."

Sarah came running out of the house, leaned over the porch railing, and threw up her dinner. Matt and Victor casually glanced at Sarah over their shoulders.

"Did you guys kill any of them?" Matt asked Victor.

"Yes, we killed at least three rogues, we're not sure how many we wounded," Victor replied.

"OK, we need to tag them, take samples and leave them lay where they are," Matt instructed.

Unexpectedly, out of nowhere, Matt heard a familiar voice, "Do you guys have any carcasses for us to sample?" Frankie said as she approached Matt and Victor.

"Yes, I want you to get the blood, hair, and tissue samples, then tag the carcasses. But, leave the carcasses lay where they are." Matt instructed Frankie.

"They're dead; why bother tagging them?"

"They've been carrying away their dead. If we tag the dead ones, leaving them lay where they are, maybe the wargs will come back for them. If they do, we can track them to wherever they are taking the carcasses. If my hunch is correct, they are burying them or putting them in some form of graveyard near their dens."

"Joseph will show you where the carcasses are," Victor said to Frankie as he motioned for one of his team members to escort her to the warg carcasses.

310

"Frankie, make sure you note any mutations you can make out when you're taking your samples and tagging each one," Matt instructed.

"We're on it," Frankie replied.

"I need to see what kind of damage they did inside, and then I want to take some pictures of the dead wargs." Matt walked toward the front door of the house. "Victor, as soon as there's enough light, I want you to have your guys track these bastards. Keep your response teams close behind the trackers for backup support. And, warn your people to operate with extreme caution. I want to know, as best you can determine, the route they took coming down, out of the wilderness, into the valley, and what route they took going back."

"Would they not come and go along the same corridor in and out of the wilderness?" Victor asked as they stepped through the front door shining a flashlight around the room.

"If they were normal wolves, we would expect them to follow a familiar path, but I'm betting they used a different route out from the one they followed out of the wilderness." Matt paused to survey the carnage the rogues left inside the house as Victor guided him room to room. "And Victor, instruct your guys to be on their toes and be alert for a possible ambush. I'm not concerned with tracking them back, all the way into the wilderness, to their den. Let the wargs we tag do that for us. What I want now, is to start mapping their approaches so that we can more effectively monitor when and where they will be coming into the valley. If we can determine their routes we can set up our own ambush before they get far enough into the valley to raid again." Matt explained.

By now, Dr. Bertram and Sarah rejoined them. In the dim light, Matt could see the both of them were weak in the stomach from what they saw inside the house.

"Let me guess, the throats have been ripped out," Matt said to Dr. Bertram.

"Yes, and they fed on the bodies," he replied as Sarah ran to rail vomit again.

311

"Do you guys have someone who will come collect the bodies for burial and such?" Matt asked Victor and Dr. Bertram.

"I'll contact William and he will have someone come collect the bodies and do what's necessary," Victor replied.

"I'll fill out the death certificates in the morning," Dr. Bertram added.

"Ok, we will head back to Graymere," Matt told Victor. "I'll see you at the lodge in the morning, and we'll see if the rogues are still watching and decide if we want to proceed with the ambush and tagging plan."

"See you in the morning," Victor acknowledged.

After making a brief stop for Matt to photograph the dead wargs, Matt, Doc, and Sarah loaded up and headed back into Graymere. Matt radioed Freya to let her know that they were on their way back.

Sarah was very quiet during the drive back to Graymere. Matt glanced back at her through the rearview mirror before turning his head back to check on her. Sarah was staring out the window, into the darkness, only briefly glancing at Matt before resuming her gaze out the window.

"Oh thank God," Freya said to Allison when they received the radio call from Matt. The two hugged each other in relief. "Allison, I'm not sure I can handle Matt getting hurt again. I had known him a little more than a week when he was mauled by the alpha, but now I…" Freya could not finish her sentence before she started crying.

"Freya, this is part of our life. People elsewhere, all over the world, are experiencing similar or worse tragedies from war, famine, or some other calamity. We will get through this and you and Matt will have a long and happy life together." Allison tried to comfort and reassure Freya while keeping a brave face herself.

Sarah had been uncharacteristically quiet sitting in the back seat when she suddenly spoke out, "What kind of animal would do such a thing to those people?"

Matt looked at Dr. Bertram, "Have you not explained to her about the wargs?"

"No, I thought you did. We've been so busy with preparations for setting up the lab, training, sampling I never thought to discuss the wargs in any detail with her."

"What's a warg?"

"Quite simply, it's the reverse of the LTV transgenesis you are familiar with, among the valley residents. However, instead of the humans taking on lupine genome transmutations, the wolves have taken on human genome transmutations. It stems from the same original LTV strain, but each time it's transmitted back from wolf-to-human, human-to-wolf, the LTV mutates into a new strain of the virus carrying with it a more complex Lupine-Human genome mix."

"You mean there are real life werewolves out there? Predatory creatures, that have human genome admixed in their DNA?" Sarah asked anxiously.

"Basically, yes. You know the paw imprint you were researching for me. That belongs to one of the third or fourth generation LTV infected wolf – or *warg* as the locals refer to them. They are no longer wolves; they have mutated and evolved into a completely new and much more dangerous species of animal. The more evolved mutants among the wargs, are the alpha primes, which is the animal or beast that made the strange footprint and attacked me."

"I'm lost in the twilight zone! This can't be real," Sarah said aloud to herself.

"The LTV transgenesis cross between the human-wolf we refer to as Therianthropy. It characterizes the collective relationship of LTV cross infection between wolves and humans and then back and forth. The humans carrying the LTV who exhibit lupine transgenic mutations we call therianthropes, or therians. The wolves which exhibit human transgenic mutations are referred to as wargs," Doc explained.

Sarah glanced through the rear-view mirror at Matt, "So, the fever episode you experienced when we were back at the cabin shortly after you were attacked… You've been infected with the LTV haven't you?" Sarah asked.

"Yes," Matt replied.

No one spoke during the last few minutes of the drive back to the inn. When they arrived, Freya and Allison came out to the front porch as Matt parked. Before Freya could run to Matt and embrace him, she was intercepted by Sarah who had jumped out of the vehicle and ran to Freya, embracing her as if she were her mother. Freya comforted Sarah for a moment as Matt and Dr. Bertram unloaded the weapons before they all went into the inn. Allison met Dr. Bertram in the doorway. Uncharacteristically, she clutched him tightly around his neck and began weeping with her face in his chest.

"What's all this," Dr. Bertram said to Allison. He held her face in his hands and wiped the tears from her cheek with his thumbs.

"We were listening to the radio," she replied. "We heard everything."

Matt caught up to Freya and Sarah as they were walking into the inn. Matt put his arm around Freya shoulder and kissed the top of her head.

* * *

Freya and Allison served everyone hot tea in the lounge area in front of the fireplace. "Was it bad?" Freya asked.

"Everyone at the Lancaster homestead is dead. Mr. & Mrs. Lancaster and their two sons are all dead." Doc answered.

"Oh my God," Allison gasped.

Dr. Bertram could see something was troubling Matt, "What is it, Matthew?"

"I'm sorry, what did you ask?" Matt responded.

"I can see you're troubled by something. What is it?" Doc repeated.

Matt hesitated for a moment, "I can't figure out why the wargs are doing this. These raids?" Matt was visibly frustrated.

"They are beast and beasts kill," Dr. Bertram replied.

"No, it isn't that simple. The wargs are exhibiting organization and disciplined control of their actions. The alpha primes have demonstrated cognitive behavior with deliberate planning and control over the rogues. Beasts kill primarily for food, or in defense. These creatures kill for neither reason. It's not unheard of for a lone wolf, bear, mountain lion, or another predator to turn rogue killer, although such cases are very rare. What we are seeing here, appears to be a pack raiding, to kill and destroy, being led by an alpha. The alpha appears to be controlling or directing the raids. This type of scenario is unheard of, anywhere in the world. Why are they raiding in the valley? This is what I need to wrap my head around."

Sarah had been listening and offered an observation, "What's the oldest motivation in the world for wholesale slaughter? Revenge or control."

Both Dr. Bertram and Matt looked at Sarah as if seeking further explanation.

Sarah elaborated, "Look; humans are, by our very nature, animals. We devote a lot of our lives learning to control or suppress our animalistic tendencies. However, the atrocities that humans inflict on each other are unparalleled in the animal kingdom. What's the phrase by Robert Burns, '*Man's inhumanity to man?*' Humans are the only animal on earth that kills for the pleasure of killing, particularly of its own kind. If what you say about the LTV crossing back and forth between lupines and humans is true, our inherent predisposition toward cruelty and blood lust may have compounded the raw animal urge of the predator lupine disposition and spiked it with intelligence. In essence, the LTV has created a predator on steroids which has the capacity to think and reason. Hence, the wargs don't have to have a reason to kill, other than the simple desire to kill. The acquired human intelligence has taken the urge to kill to a new level, beyond self-preservation and into the realm of blood lust – they are killing for the sake of killing. My parish priest would tell you that the raw predator instinct, coupled with intelligence, minus a soul, equals pure evil. What we are witnessing here, is no different from what we see in the news, where warlords in Africa

315

slaughter whole villages. Augmented with the cognitive abilities among the more advanced mutants, the 'alphas,' the wargs are being proactive instead of reactive in targeting the group that poses the greater threat to their self-preservation – HUMAN."

Matt, Doc, Freya, and Allison were speechless. They could only gaze at each other in horror at the prospects of Sarah's assessment of the wargs actions.

Listening to Sarah, Matt recalled, '*Blood Moon Rising*', the scene depicted on the quilt made by Mrs. Moonjoy.

Chapter 39

Matt, Freya, and Sarah sat down to eat breakfast with little more than casual breakfast chatter. Matt assumed Sarah emotionally rattled from her experience at the Lancaster homestead last night. However, He decided to break the ice by asking her about her plans to return to school. "Have you thought any more about going back to the city in time to start your fall classes?" Matt asked Sarah.

Before Sarah could answer, Dr. Bertram joined them in the dining room and overheard Matt's question to Sarah.

"Good morning Doc, you are just in time for breakfast."

"No, No," He said to Freya. "I just finished breakfast; I just wanted to visit with Matt before he left for the lodge. I didn't mean to interrupt your breakfast."

Sarah proceeded to answer Matt's question to her, "I'm not going back. Well, I'll go back to get my stuff from your cabin and get a few more of my things, but other than that I'm staying here to work with Dr. Bertram." Sarah replied.

"I thought after last night's experience you would be ready to go back to the city," Matt said.

"Just the opposite; I'm determined, more than ever, to help rid the valley of this awful disease, before it can be spread outside the valley."

"I hope you don't mind me joining in on your conversation," Dr. Bertram interjected. "But, I curious as to why you are so committed to staying here after what you witnessed last night?"

317

"Well, it's kind of a long story and I'm not sure I should talk about it." She replied as she casually continued eating.

"I hope you forgive me for prying, but here you are at age twenty-six or twenty-seven, with an impressive background and education in molecular biology, accepted to a prestigious Ph.D. program, and you want to put all that on hold to stay here?" Dr. Bertram pressed Sarah for an answer to his original question.

"When I first went to work with Dr. Hobart, he explained the objective of the research project was to create a super-soldier. A human soldier enhanced with sensory traits of a predator species animal. He told me before I arrived at the research facility, they had tried different methods of gene splicing to create a genetically enhanced human. However, all of their attempts resulted in inconsistent and unpredictable outcomes. My arrival at the facility and assignment to the project coincided with a change in the direction of their research. In the second evolution of the research objectives, we started experimenting with using retroviruses as vectors to achieve cross-species transgenesis of the human genome into different predatory animals. The new goal was to create a genetically enhanced predator. The process was much the same way the LTV appears to have done here, naturally. However, what Dr. Hobart attempted to do was to isolate targeted genes which would allow the animals to acquire intelligence and cognitive abilities while retaining their own natural animal genome development. They wanted a species of predatory animal they could communicate specific orders, and for the animal to follow instructions, even under changing conditions. In simple terms, problem-solving skills."

"And," Matt prompted Sarah to continue her explanation.

"Well, at first the results were not so good. Many of the test subjects died from the viral infection. Of those that survived, only a small percentage of the F1 generational transgenics experienced any mutation. Then Dr. Hobart focused on a generational transgenetic transfer of the virus. He found that, although the parent who had *acquired* the viral vector had not fully developed the desired transgenic mutation, their offspring did. The vector, being present in the germ cell, permeated the virus throughout the offspring's DNA structure effectively creating, what appeared to be, a completely new genome. Then, they would expose the F1 transgenic with an additional or secondary viral vector. Then, they would do the same to F2, etc. Each time the subsequent generation demonstrated a more advanced transgenic mutation.

Dr. Hobart found that test subjects developing human intellect and cognitive skills became very aggressive. When they put these test subjects together into a cage together, they would fight, most of the time, to the death. When they put three into a cage, two of them would gang up on the weaker one and kill it, the remaining two would then fight each other to the death. When they put five or more into a cage they would fight until an alpha emerged and would form a rogue pack from among the others, which the handlers couldn't control. In later cases, they had to put the alphas down because they would organize the others to resist and attack the handlers. It became apparent to Dr. Hobart, that once their cognitive abilities developed, the mutants actively resisted any attempt to control them. I overheard Dr. Hobart explaining to Col. Livingston why the mutants were so aggressive and could not be trusted. What I told you last night was in essence what Dr. Hobart tried to explain to Col. Livingston."

"You said they tried to achieve transgenesis of the human genome to predator animals. Did they ever facilitate transgenesis of predator genome to human test subjects?" Dr. Bertram inquired further.

"That was the third evolution in the research objective they were pursuing when I left the Army and came home to finish my degree. I'm not supposed to discuss anything I saw or heard while working with Dr. Hobart. However, I once overheard Col. Livingston telling Dr. Hobart that the program should shift from trying to creating transgenic predator and focus on a fully transgenic human-animal super-soldier. He wanted Dr. Hobart to start with the human genome and fully integrate it with animal DNA, thereby creating a human chimera soldier. Col. Livingston told Dr. Hobart how the government planned to breed an army of these beasts. They wanted to send the beast into battle instead of

319

our own human troops. After what I've seen since I arrived here, I'm horrified at the prospects of what someone like Col. Livingston would do with LTV if he ever got his hands on it. It frightens me more than anything you can imagine. That is why I'm determined to eradicate LTV before it can spread outside the valley."

"Why would they pursue such a program?" Matt asked.

"Any time Dr. Hobart questioned the morality or inherent risk associated with the program, Col. Livingston was fond of saying, 'the ends, justify the means'. Col. Livingston justified the program in that it would save American Soldiers from much of the front line fighting, and that the mutants were expendable. Col. Livingston relished in the prospect of the mutants fighting without fear or conscience, would not retreat, fighting until killed or incapacitated. He referred to the potential army of transmutes as '*cannon fodder*.'"

"I take it that Dr. Hobart was not on board with the revised program objectives?" Dr. Bertram asked Sarah.

"Well, in the beginning, under the original program directives, he was all gung-ho about the whole research thing, until they started witnessing the results. After a few trials, he tried to warn Col. Livingston that mutants which developed cognitive abilities, became overly aggressive and unpredictable – just as you described with the wargs. He warned Col. Livingston, ultimately the mutants could become our greatest threat instead of our greatest asset. Col. Livingston argued with Dr. Hobart, saying his concerns were just like the doomsday fanatics who warned about the development of artificial intelligence."

"But, he continued to work on the project in spite of his concerns." Dr. Bertram prompted Sarah.

"Yes. Well… he was still there when I left, but when I was clearing for separation from the Army I had to go through debriefings on what I could or couldn't talk about once I left the military. When I went through my debriefing with Dr. Hobart, he confided in me, that he was planning to leave the program. He was very concerned with the lack of caution being expressed by the military towards the inherent dangers of developing transmutes with human intelligence, let alone the moral and ethical issues inherent in the new program directives to create a human-animal chimera. He mentioned something about the program going far beyond the limitations established by the Cartagena Protocol on Biosafety." Sarah told them.

"I'm surprised Dr. Hobart confided in you and made you privy to so much of the research which was classified?" Dr. Bertram prompted for an explanation.

"After he found out I wanted to be a geneticist and I had progressed to a level 3 tech far ahead of my peers, he basically took me under his wing to encourage and tutor me as I mentioned before. At first, he would explain things in general terms. Then, the more I learned, he started using specific elements of the research as examples to teach specific concepts. Near the end, just before I left, I think I was the only person he trusted to confide in, to express his personal concerns and discontent of where the research was headed."

"This Dr. Hobart you refer to; by chance, would his name be Dr. Franklin Hobart?" Dr. Bertram inquired?"

"Yes, how did you know that?" Sarah asked a bit surprised.

"The remote facility you worked at with Dr. Hobart; would that have been Plumb Island?"

"Yes, how did you know that?" Sarah asked even more surprised.

Dr. Bertram sat back in his chair and looked as though he had seen a ghost.

"What is it doc?" Matt inquired, assuming Dr. Bertram must have concluded some significant bit of information that disturbed him.

"I'm not certain at the moment," Dr. Bertram replied. "I'll talk to you later after I have a chance to check on a couple of things."

"Did I say something wrong?" Sarah asked confused.

"No, you said precisely the right thing?" Dr. Bertram said cryptically.

"I need to be at the lodge," Matt said. "Was there something you wanted to tell me Doc before I head out?"

"No, nothing that can't wait until later," Dr. Bertram replied.

"Matthew, please be careful out there," Freya pleaded with Matt.

"I will," he replied as he gave her a warm embrace and a gentle kiss before he left.

"Well, Ms. Sarah, are we ready to go to work ourselves?" Dr. Bertram asked.

"Yes, sir."

"Let's take a stroll over to the lab and see how close we are to getting the remodeling completed and ready for installing some computers, equipment, and other hardware."

"How are we looking Peter," Dr. Bertram asked as he and Sarah walked into what was now the new lab building.

"We have all of the walls closed in and we are doing the finish work now," He replied. In a day or two, we will have the cabinets, workbenches, countertops ready to install. After that, we can caulk and seal the building and the individual rooms. We should be ready to test the containment system by the end of next week. By the end of this week, we should have the generator set along with the butane tank which will supply the generator, heating, burners, and kitchen."

"Good, that means within a couple of weeks we should be ready to start setting up the lab equipment and hardware."

"It's amazing; from the outside, it still looks like the old jailhouse situated in a rustic village and inside it's a modern research lab," Sarah observed.

"I'll let you know in a day or two about the lab equipment," Dr. Bertram told Peter, as he and Sarah left to resume their respective tasks.

Chapter 40

Victor, Frankie, and Alex were anxiously waiting for Matt's arrival. When Matt pulled up in front of the lodge, they walked down the front porch steps to meet him as he got out of his jeep.

"Man, they hammered the crap out of your jeep last night," Alex commented after inspecting the large dents in the sides of Matt's jeep.

"Yes, that was something I didn't expect," Matt replied.

"The wargs are back on the rise, watching us as usual; everything is in place and ready to execute," Victor informed Matt as they walked up the steps and entered the lodge.

"Frankie, are your people ready?" Matt asked.

"Yes, they're in position and waiting."

Matt moved over to the map mounted on the wall. "The wargs are located along this rise," Matt said pointing to the map. "Frankie, show me where your teams are positioned?"

"Here and here," she replied pointing to locations on the map.

Matt outlined the plan, "Alright Victor, have your people spread out in a line extending along here facing the wargs then start moving them forward. As the line reaches this point, have the left wing begin swinging in toward the wargs. As your teams proceed, your people should close in, closer to each other. The wargs should feel the pressure of the teams moving towards them and bug out toward Frankie and her people. With any luck at all, we should be able to tag and sample one or two of them. Any questions?"

323

They all simultaneously answered *"no"* as they started gathering up their gear to move out.

"Ok, let's bag some wargs," Matt said.

Once everyone answered the ready check, Victor's teams started moving toward the wargs as instructed. The plan worked better than anticipated and the rogues ran single file away from Victor's teams, directly across the path of Frankie's teams. When the rogues came into sight, they took out the one in the rear of the group. The other two were startled and stopped to investigate. That's when the team fired on them both almost simultaneously taking down all three. After the rogues were down, they waited until the response team arrived before tagging and sampling the rogues. Working quickly to complete the tagging and sampling, they cleared the area, allowing the rogues to awaken in due course without any sign of Frankie's team or indication as to what had happened to them.

Back at the lodge, Matt met with Victor, Alex, and Frankie to discuss their next operations. "Victor, have you heard back from the trackers you sent out to track the wargs that attacked the Lancaster's homestead last night?" Matt asked as he turned on the tracking system and his computer.

"Yes, they reported back just before you arrived this morning." Victor went to the map on the wall and started relating the information reported to him to Matt. "They tracked the rogues from the Lancaster-place, back along this route. The team found a set of alpha tracks at the edge of the Lancaster yard near the barn as you suspected. The tracks all merged and followed the same route away from the Lancaster's place. As the wargs started up the ridge, their tracks faded into the rocky hillside around here. Based on the direction of travel it appears that they exited the valley somewhere up through this saddle on the ridge."

"Let's see if we can pick up any tracking telemetry on the ones Frankie's teams tagged last night and this morning." Matt sat down, turned on the tracking monitor, and pulled up the tracking screen.

"How does this system work," Alex inquired.

"Two ways. The tag we place inside the warg transmits a radio tracking signal on two frequencies. A satellite picks up one signal and records in on a timed interval. That data is accessible through a web portal, in real time. The second signal can be picked up by handheld tracking devices such as this one." Matt held up a device and switched it on to demonstrate. "Or, through the antenna, we erected linked to this larger and more powerful monitor we can monitor the tags in real time. The response teams will be able to station a person here to monitor this screen to detect any of the tagged animals coming into or out of the valley, like an early warning station. Then that person can radio the tagging and response teams and direct them to intercept the wargs. When the tagging and response teams get within range they will be able to pick up the signal on the handheld devices."

"Now it all makes sense," Frankie said aloud to herself.

Matt started pointing to the monitoring screen, "Here are the three targets you tagged this morning. The numbers you see when you mouse over the target blip shows you the individual tag number attached to a particular animal. That is why I had you record the tag number with the samples. You can see them starting to move up toward the wilderness area. The system will record the track and if you pull up a particular tag number you can display a historical path that individual target followed from the time it was tagged to the present."

"Where are the two we tagged last night?" Frankie asked looking at the screen for the target indicators.

"I didn't fire up the tracking system till now so it didn't pick up any signals until now. Since they are not showing, the targets must be out of range of the ground based monitor."

"How do we know where they have gone once they leave the valley?" Victor asked.

"I'll have to access the satellite tracking system from the computer in my office back at the university. The satellite tracking system gives tracking data with GPS coordinates that will allow us to accurately plot their range, normal travel paths, and hopefully show a pack congregation in a stationary location for extended periods of time where the paths intersect we can assume the den will be nearby."

"What's next?" Victor asked.

Matt explained that the overall strategy should be broken down into three phases. The first phase would focus on tagging as many wargs as possible in order for the early warning element of the tracking program to be more effective. The response teams are in place to begin serving as a deterrent to and minimize any warg activity within the valley. The second phase is to transition into offensive operations to hunt down or ambush any wargs coming into the valley. The third phase will be to take the offensive operations into the wargs' territory and mount raids to exterminate them if necessary.

"How many therian betas do you have that can be trained and organized into assault teams?" Matt asked Victor.

"I can put together maybe twelve to eighteen," Victor answered.

"How many of them will come from the response teams?"

"Eight," Victor confirmed.

"Alex, do you have someone trained to take over the security patrols?"

"Yes," Alex replied.

"Ok, here is what I would like to do next," Matt began. "Alex, handover the security patrol responsibility to the person you trained. I want you to take over the training and leadership of the response teams. You'll have to recruit replacements for the betas Victor is going to take from you. You need to integrate the new people with the experienced people in order to facilitate their training as fast as possible. You will have to have teams on standby twenty-four-seven to respond to any incursions, as well as, providing support to Frankie's tagging teams."

"Are there any suggestions for the criteria in selecting the replacements for the betas Victor will take away from the response teams?"

"I suggest you and Victor put your heads together and come up with a recruit list. Victor has a feel for operational needs and you guys know the resident recruitment pool, I don't."

"We got it," Alex replied.

"Frankie, we need you to start organizing your teams into either patrol or hunting parties with an objective of tagging as many of the wargs as possible. Stay on or near the roads to allow the response teams to get to you immediately, once you have a warg down for tagging. Don't get off into the bush where the response teams can't find you to back you up if you get into trouble. Plan to have a tagging team on standby, partnered with a response team, for situations like last night. Remember we need hair blood and tissue samples from all of the wargs we can, including the dead ones. It's critical that the samples be preserved properly and delivered to Doc as soon as practical after sampling."

"I understand and we're on it," Frankie acknowledged.

"Victor, I would like for you to start training the assault teams. Organize them into teams of six. They need to be able to work as independent, six-person teams, as well as in a twelve or eighteen-person group. These teams will focus initially on intercepting wargs coming down into the valley. As we identify any paths the wargs routinely take into and out of the valley, the assault teams will prepare ambushes. Eventually, as we are able to map their territorial range, dens, and social structure in the wilderness areas, we will organize raids of our own. By that time, all three groups should be transitioned into a single force."

"I see where you are going with the overall strategy and we can handle it. I understand you will be leaving in a few days back to the city and the university. What's your plan for monitoring what's going on back here?" Victor asked.

"I'll travel back and forth on the weekends for sure. As I collect satellite telemetry on the tracking tags and able to start mapping the warg movement patterns and territory I'll relay that by phone or when I come back on the weekends." Matt told them.

"I'll pick six people to train on the monitoring equipment. They, in turn, can train everyone else on the handheld equipment as well as how the central unit works." Victor told Matt.

"Good, we should have everything in place and under control before I leave I think."

"No problem." Victor acknowledged.

"Oh, Victor; one last thought, we should establish daylight patrols around the lodge to spot any more onlookers. We should also put out some traps and early warning devices even if they are homemade gadgets. I have a feeling this will become the wargs' next target. Everyone should be on their toes twenty-four-seven." Matt warned. "I'm going back to Graymere to visit with Doc on the lab preparation. If you need me call me on the radio."

"Sure thing," Victor replied.

Chapter 41

Dr. Bertram met Matt in front of the inn as Matt returned from the lodge that afternoon. "Well, how did your tagging operation go this morning?" Dr. Bertram asked Matt.

"Actually, it went better than I expected. Victor and Frankie have done a superb job in training their teams and we were able to tag and take samples of three warg rogues this morning." Matt opened the back of his jeep to retrieve the samples and hand them over to Doc.

"I'm glad you are in a bit earlier than normal, there are a couple of things I was hoping we would have the time to sit and discuss. Let's go put these samples in the containment cooler and grab a cup of tea if you have time." Dr. Bertram suggested.

"I made it a point to get back to Graymere early so you and I could spend some time together going over where we are and anything I need to do for you once I get back to the university," Matt replied. "Let me tell Freya I'm back and then I'll be right over."

* * *

Allison was serving tea for Dr. Bertram and Matt just as Matt stepped into their living room. "Good afternoon Matthew."

"Good afternoon," he replied.

"First things first," Dr. Bertram began. "Prior to you going back to the city and your teaching duties I wanted to visit with

329

you as your doctor. I hope you and Freya have made plans for her to go back with you?"

"We have not discussed it definitively, but that is my expectation. We will be coming back to Graymere on the weekends and holidays."

"Good, and if I need to talk with her I can, but both of you need to know why I'm concerned that she be with you. The episode you had when you were home the last time and the few minor ones since you have been back here are just the beginning of what's to come."

"Wait," Matt interrupted, "I thought the worst was over."

"Sorry, but no. The worst is still yet to come. In terms of the initial reaction to the viral infection, you experienced the worst immediately after you were attacked. Unfortunately, there are other phases of the transgenesis process. Some of the effects may not begin to emerge until weeks or even months after the initial infection. However, in your case, the LTV was already present in your genome, similar to how cancer cells behave. In most people, the cancer cells lie dormant until they are exposed to a carcinogenic agent. The carcinogenic agent acts as a catalyst causing the cancer cells to begin replicating. In your case I'm afraid the secondary LTV infection may have been your catalyst, so to speak."

"But from what you mentioned before, I have a double dose of alpha LTV. You told me you couldn't predict what was going to happen."

"For the most part, that's true. You see, the LTV is only active or resident if both parents carry the LTV otherwise it is dormant, as in your case. If the alpha had not infected you, you probably would have never known you carried the virus or experienced any transgenic mutation. If you hadn't been a dormer with the LTV already present in your genome, chances are, you wouldn't have developed any serious transgenic mutation. However, going off what I know of past infection cases, coupled with the fact that you inherited the LTV, there are some potential effects that you should be prepared for."

"Like what?"

"Well, you mentioned muscle cramps and your bones aching; these are signs that your physiology is changing. It's not like in the movies when the werewolf morphs in a matter of seconds when the full moon rises and morphs back when the moon goes down and the sun comes up. Your body is going through a process of gradual change. Given your age, the changes should occur a bit slower compared to a much younger person, such as an infant, whose cellular growth and regeneration rate is many times that of a mature adult. Over the next few months, you will go through cycles of change, accompanied by periods of intense pain and discomfort, as your body physically changes."

"What kind of changes are we talking about?"

"In a typical mature adult, who acquires the LTV, the virus may affect only a limited aspect of the new host's genome. Typically, this person would experience some minor physiological changes such as increased hair growth, increased sensitivity to hearing, and smell. All of which, you are already experiencing. However, in a person with the inherited LTV, the lupine genome would have been present in their germ cells and thus hardwired into every cell of their body. Therefore, you could, over time, experience a total transformation similar to or even surpassing what you see in Victor or William."

"Doc, this is definitely not something I wanted to hear," Matt said as he stood up and started pacing around the room.

"I can't say for sure you'll experience a transmutation that extreme, I'm just speculating of what *could* happen, given the symptoms you have described. I'm sure you will experience some level of physiological change, I'm just not sure to what extent."

"OK, so now that you have rattled my cage with that tad-bit of information, what other joyous revelations do you have to share with me?" Matt said trying to muster a smile.

"Well, it concerns the lab and acquisition of the equipment, materials, and hardware we are going to need."

"Have you heard anything from Harvey?" Matt inquired.

"No, and I'm growing concerned about getting anything through any agency of the government, even surplus equipment.

We have the money to adequately equip, stock, and maintain the lab and I think we should go ahead and do it ourselves. One, I think it will be faster and two, we will own the lab and not worry about who will be asking questions for a GAO audit of where did this and that go and for what purpose."

"I see what you mean. What do you need from me?"

"You mentioned that you researched some sources for reconditioned or used DNA analyzer. When you go back to the city, Sarah should go with you and sit with you to find a unit that has the specs we need and make contact with that company to arrange a purchase. Also, see if you can locate and do the same for a desktop electron microscope. Once you have the sale pending and invoiced, we will take care of transferring payment and arranging delivery."

"That's doable. What else?"

"I'll send Sarah back with a complete shopping list. She has the catalogs of lab supplies and equipment you provided her. I need you to help her set up a small office, shop, or house, somewhere where we can have materials delivered and temporarily stored there in the city. Sarah will place orders for supplies and equipment and have it drop shipped to that location. We will send someone down to pick up any shipments or you can bring it up on the weekend when you come. Then we should be able to place orders over the phone and have them shipped there. This way no one knows about the lab or start asking questions as to why a molecular bio lab is being set up and operated in the middle of nowhere."

"That isn't a problem. I think I know of a place which would be just right for our needs." Matt told Dr. Bertram.

"The last thing I would like for you to do is, check in on Ranger Holmes when you go back to the city. When you talk to him, play twenty questions and see if he is experiencing any unusual side effects from the LTV. Harvey indicated he was certain that Holmes was not among the twenty percent who experienced any transgenic effects, but I would feel better if you talked to him personally."

"What are you thinking Doc?" Matt inquired.

"Nothing, in particular, I just want to make sure we have the virus contained. No loose ends." Dr. Bertram said, trying to downplay the reason for the follow up with Holmes.

"What about our conversation this morning with Sarah? I noticed your reaction to what she told us."

"I know the Dr. Franklin Hobart she worked with. I thought 'Hobart' sounded familiar, but it didn't click until I heard her describing the research they were conducting. Plum Island is an Animal Disease Center. It was a former military installation, Fort Terry, if I recall correctly. The Department of Agriculture established the Plum Island Animal Disease Center there, PIADC for short. The Department of Homeland Security took over the entire island. They started building a new facility outside Manhattan Kansas, that ran into several delays and repeated shutdowns. It has been the center of a budgetary struggle between the President and Congress for several years. A plan to sell off Plum Island has been on hold since 2012. With what Sarah told us this morning, coupled with the takeover by the Department of Homeland Security, I'm getting a bad feeling that Plum Island may be converted to a research and training area with a single purpose in mind."

Matt sat down even more stunned by this information than what Doc told him about his own potential physical and medical situation. "Doc, I feel like I'm stuck in a nightmare and can't wake up," Matt said sounding stressed. "Do you realize that just two short months ago, I was a happy naïve professor chasing cryptid wolves in the wilderness and harboring a fantasy of one day identifying a new species of wolf? Then one morning I wake up in Graymere, to find out am I in the middle of a war between real life Therianthropes and werewolves. Aside from being attacked by a werewolf and infected by it, I discover I've been a Therian in dormancy since birth. Adding insult to injury, I find out I may morph into a frigging werewolf, over the next few months. To top it all off, we discover our government responsible for genetically engineering a breed of creatures who may have taken up residence next door. I'm with Sarah – I think I must have stepped into the *Twilight Zone*! Pinch me, slap me, kick me

in the balls, anything, just wake me up from this nightmare."
Matt ranted to vent his frustration.

That evening, Matt was exceptionally quiet picking at his food. Freya could tell something was bothering him, but didn't know what to say or if she should say anything at all. Sarah sensed it as well and gave Freya a glance with a twinkle of a smile in a poor attempt to cheer her up.

Concerned, Freya finally asked, "Matthew, are you feeling alright?"

"Yes, I'm fine." Matt looked up from his plate.

"Well, you've barely touched your food and you haven't said a word since you got home."

"I'm sorry," he said trying to muster a smile. "I've just got a lot on my mind I'm trying to sort out."

Freya smiled at him, then reached over gently squeezing his hand as a gentle reminder that she was there for him.

Matt returned her gentle touch and as usual, with a hint of a smile in return. It seemed Freya was able to make him feel better and breathe new life into him with just her touch and caring smile. "You know; the days are counting down for when we'll have to go back to the city for the fall semester." He said softly.

"Yes, I know," she acknowledged. "It's just going to be hard to leave this place."

"We're not leaving per se; we'll be coming back every weekend and our holidays will be here unless we are traveling elsewhere. Sarah can look after the inn while we're back in the city." Matt said to Freya while looking at Sarah for confirmation.

"Yes, I'll be here for quite some time. Hopefully, until we can develop a cure for the LTV." Sarah acknowledged.

"Besides, Doc says I need someone with me over the coming months, due to unpredictable effects of my double dose of LTV. What if I start morphing, and you're not there to dunk me in an ice bath?" Matt asked rhetorically.

"You jerk," Freya replied along with a slap his arm.

"Doc said he could make it a doctor's order if you resisted," Matt told Freya smiling.

Freya got up and went to Matt, sat in his lap and embraced him with her head on his shoulder. "I love you; I won't let anything happen to you if I can help it," Freya said softly in his ear.

"Aww, isn't that sweet, old people doing PDA," Sarah said scrunching up her face.

"Who are you calling old," Freya said as she picked up a crumb from Matt's plate and threw it at Sarah across the table.

They all laughed and smiled at each other.

"Sarah, are you going to try and go see your family when we go back the city?" Matt asked.

"Yes, I should; I need to take some of my stuff from your cabin back to my mom's and a few things I want to pick up from home to bring back here."

"By the way; how is your family doing?" Freya asked.

"Well, there's only my mom and granny now," Sarah said with a bit of sadness in her voice. "My dad was killed in an auto accident during my freshman year in college. My mom is doing all right now. When my dad died, the insurance paid off the house and she works part time. I've tried not to be a burden on her financially and I try to see her when I can."

"Do you not have any brothers or sisters who live near her to help her?" Freya asked as she started clearing the table.

"I'm an only child, but my grandmother, my father's mother, lives near her and mom visits her and tries to take care of granny. They keep each other company and granny keeps mom busy doing stuff for her."

"Make time to go she them before you come back here," Matt told her.

Chapter 42

Freya was packing and getting things in order around the inn before leaving, Sarah was busy dividing her time between training the lab techs and starting to set up the lab, and Matt was busily working with Victor to finalize the strategy, plans, programs, and activities for training and actions against the wargs in the coming months.

Matt spent his last day in the valley going over a few details before he departed for the city. "I'll be monitoring the satellite telemetry on the tracking tags from my computer at home and my office. I'll call the monitoring station here at the lodge if I see any activity moving into the valley. You will have some lead-time in your warning to get your teams into position. How many targets do we have tagged now?" Matt asked.

"We have tagged a total of eight live targets and one additional carcass," Frankie told him.

"OK, I wouldn't use any more tags on carcasses until I tell you otherwise. I'll check the satellite telemetry to see where they are taking the carcasses. If I see a need to continue tracking them, I'll let you know. I'm still puzzled by why they go to the trouble to retrieve their dead?"

"That *is* a bit strange," Victor observed.

Looking at the map on the wall Matt told Victor, "I would like to see a few more wargs tagged before we send patrols into warg territory. I need to get a picture of their size and the social network within their home territorial range before we start wandering in there and find ourselves surrounded and outnumbered. We know from the ones we have tagged and tracked so far that they are coming into the valley from these two entry points. I might suggest that you plan and organize an ambush to tag a few more rogues, and if you are lucky, maybe an alpha."

"Will do," Victor replied.

Matt said his goodbyes as everyone gathered around to wish him well before he departed.

* * *

When Matt walked into the lab, it was abuzz with activity. Sarah directed the techs on where to put various items, how to label them, while another was setting up computers. "Good morning Doc," Matt said.

"Good morning," Dr. Bertram replied. "What do you think?"

"I think you need a DNA analyzer and an electron microscope, and then you'd be in business," Matt said smiling.

"We've been able to acquire most of the items we need from Boise. I've been sending Simon down there on shopping trips to gather up a lot of the non-lab-specific materials and supplies. Once you and Sarah get to the city and place orders for the other equipment and materials, we should be in operation by the end of August."

"Freya and I'll be leaving first thing in the morning and if the good Lord is willing, we shall have your equipment and supplies on their way very soon." Matt walked around the lab checking out the quality of the work the crew had completed.

"Sarah will be leaving tomorrow as well and she has the shopping list with her."

"Ok Doc. We may not be back for a couple of weeks. I'll be busy at the university getting classes started, assigning research projects, and such. Freya will be getting the cabin squared away. If you think of anything else just give me a shout, you have my number."

"Take care. If you have any other symptoms, don't hesitate to call me."

Matt walked into the kitchen and found Freya cleaning and taking inventory. "I'm all packed and ready to leave." She said. We'll need to buy some groceries and supplies to bring back with us."

Matt wrapped his arms around her waist from behind and put his head next to hers. "I'm glad to be getting away from this place for a while."

Freya stopped what she was doing and turn around in Matt's arms so she could look up into his face. "You never mentioned that you were that unhappy here."

Matt smiled, "you misunderstand. I'm glad to get away from the valley so we can spend more quality time together. The situation here consumes all of my energy and I feel like I've neglected you," Matt said to her before leaning down to kiss her.

Freya hugged him tightly around the waist, "Matthew, I'm so happy you're in my life."

Matt and Freya were loaded and on the road back to Moscow early the next morning, followed soon after by Sarah. Once they were out of the valley, Freya noticed a feeling of relaxation the closer they got to the cabin, *'their cabin'* she thought to herself. When they arrived, Freya breathed a sigh of relief, happy to be out of Misty Hollow, at least for a while. The cabin made her feel like a free woman. She never noticed the feeling of confinement before she made the first trip to the city with Matthew. She thought to herself how relaxed she felt, with a different outlook on life in general, like someone released from indentured servitude.

"Wow, I can see the first order of business will be to mow the yard. I'll have to speak with Sarah about why she has not kept up the yard any better than this while I've been away." Matt joked and laughed with Freya.

Sarah arrived not long after Matt and Freya and helped unloaded the vehicles. While Freya and Sarah were unpacking and getting the cabin squared away, Matt went out to mow the yard. Sometime later Freya came out with a glass of ice tea.

"Oh that smells good," Freya said closing her eyes and taking a deep breath of the aroma of freshly cut grass.

"Yeah, I love the smell of freshly cut grass," he replied.

"I'll get out the weed eater and start trimming while you mow," Sarah said as she joined them in the front yard.

"Weed Eater?" Freya asked.

"Yes, I'll show you." Sarah took Freya by the hand, led her to the storage room, and started instructing her on how to start and operate the weed eater. The two of them seemed to be having a good time teaching and learning the simple operation of a weed eater as Matt resumed mowing.

After finishing the yard work, Matt scooped up some duck food and went down to the pond to feed the ducks. Freya joined him and they relaxed and teased each other while tossing food to the ducks. Freya thought to herself, *'how much of the simple enjoyments of life have I missed living in Graymere. What a contrast between the two.'*

"Let's go get a shower and then go into town," Matt suggested to Freya.

She smiled as they walked back to the cabin arm in arm.

* * *

While Freya was finishing getting dressed, Matt assembled his computer; anxious to log into the satellite tracking portal and check on the tagged wargs. In particular, he was very curious about where the wargs were taking their dead rogues.

"What are you working on?" Sarah asked entering the living room area, towel drying her hair.

"I'm checking on the wargs we tagged. I want to see what's going on with them," Matt replied. After entering his access data and codes, he was able to pull up the screen and start searching for his targets. "There they are," Matt said aloud, pointing to an area on the map displayed on his computer screen.

Sarah was looking over Matt's shoulder curious about the tracking system and what information it could provide. "I assume those blips are your targets and the numbers that pop up when you mouse over them are their individual tracking IDs?"

"Yes," Matt confirmed. "Right now I'm looking for four in particular." He zoomed in to gain better separation of the targets and minimize overlap so he could pick out the four tag IDs of the rogue carcasses. "There, one…, two…, three…, and there's the fourth one, all bunched together," Matt mumbled to himself, mousing over a closely bunched cluster of blips on the screen.

Matt copied and pasted the coordinates over to Google Earth and zoomed in on the map. It looked as though the wargs left the carcasses in a small depression not far inside the wilderness area.

"Ok, I'm ready," Freya announced.

Matt turned around when she heard Freya's voice, "Beautiful as ever." Matt stood and kissed Freya. "Sarah, would you like to come with us?"

"Sorry, but I'll beg off, thank you. I'm trying to get hold of a couple of my friends and maybe catch a movie this evening. I'm only going to be here a couple of days and then I'm not sure when I'll be back in town again."

"No Problem," Matt replied. "Enjoy your evening."

Matt's first stop after they left the cabin was at a car dealership. His jeep had seen better days, and it was time to buy a new vehicle. He and Freya made several stops at the various dealerships before deciding on a vehicle they liked; a quad cab, 4x4, pickup. Matt left his old jeep at the dealer for service and repair. He planned to keep it for off road fieldwork. After dinner, Matt and Freya returned to the cabin to relax and snuggle up to enjoy popcorn and a movie.

The next morning Matt was off to the university to start preparing for the fall semester. He hated these few days before the semester began; check the class assignment and schedule, set his office hours, and prepare a syllabus for each class. Then there were the incoming freshman advisor chores that he dreaded.

In between work at the university, Matt managed to lease a small shop on the edge of town, not far from his cabin. The shop was ideal for receiving and storing materials they were going to have dropped shipped. Before Sarah left town she arranged for the purchase of various items on the list she and Dr. Bertram prepared. Matt was excited he was able to find an excellent DNA analyzer, as well as, an electron microscope at bargain prices which Dr. Bertram procured for the Lab.

Time seem to pass quickly and after two weeks, Matt was eager to return to Misty Hollow.

* * *

Freya saw Matt totally absorbed in whatever he was looking at on the computer monitor. She walked over, stood behind him and looked over his shoulder. "What are you looking at?"

"I'm checking out the telemetry of the wargs Frankie and her teams have tagged. I'm looking for patterns in their movement to see if I can identify their den locations." Matt explained.

"How many have they tagged?"

Matt pointed to the screen, indicating the various targets. "Looks to be twelve of them so far." He switched to real-time tracking to show Freya that feature and explain how he used it. That's when he noticed a couple of the targets moving toward the valley. He explained to Freya what was happening while he picked up his cell phone and called the monitoring station at the lodge in Misty Hollow.

"Is that a pack?" Freya asked.

"Yes," Matt answered.

"Hello, who is this?" Matt asked the person on the other end of the line. "Is Victor, Alex, or Frankie nearby?"

The person on the other end told Matt that Victor and Alex were both there in the lodge.

"This is Dr. Kershaw; I need to speak with Victor, right away."

"*Hello Matt,*" Victor answered the phone.

"Victor, there's a pack moving down from the wilderness. I see two target blips moving steadily to a point near the big overhanging rock formation on the ridge. You should be able to pick them up on your monitor in about eight to ten minutes."

"*Ok, we're on it,*" Victor acknowledged.

Matt and Freya continued to watch the target tracks as they moved toward the valley, anxious to see what if anything was happening by watching the blips on the monitor. They followed the targets as they moved down, into the valley, near the perimeter road, then they stopped. Shortly after that, one of the tracking tags stopped transmitting and the other one began moving back out of the valley faster than it came in. Near the top of the ridge, the target stopped for several minutes. Meanwhile, a new tag ID appeared on his screen near the point where the other tag stopped transmitting. About a half hour later, the new target moved off to join the other one up on the ridge, and then together they returned to their territory in the wilderness.

"They must have killed one of the original two targets and were able to tag a new one," Matt explained as he traced the movement of the different tag IDs.

Not long after the targets moved back out of the valley, Matt's phone rang. "Yes Victor, how did it go?" Matt asked anxiously.

"*It went well; we did have one of our people injured in the skirmish, but Doc is sewing him up now. The good news is; we killed three rogues and were able to tag and sample an alpha.*"

"That's good to hear," Matt replied. "Freya and I'll be leaving tomorrow afternoon headed back to the valley. If we don't run into any traffic, we should be back at the inn by around 8:00pm.

"Great, I'll talk to you when you guys get here."

As soon as Matt hung up the phone, he went back to the monitor to track the new target, an alpha. He took out his topographic map of the area and mapped out specific points of interest and jotting down notes related to movement patterns.

* * *

Before Matt left for work the next morning, he outlined their agenda for that day with Freya. "As soon as my last class is over, I'll stop by the storage building and load up the stuff for the lab, then I come back here to pick you up. We'll leave as soon as I can load up our things."

"I'll have everything packed and ready to go by the time you get here," she replied.

Chapter 43

Sarah was waiting on the front porch when Matt and Freya pulled up to the inn. She ran to greet Freya and gave her a big hug. "I've missed you," Sarah said to Freya. "It's been lonely around here without you guys."

"It's good to be home," Freya replied. "I see you haven't burned the place down," Freya joked.

Matt broke up their reunion. "Let's get our stuff unloaded and then I'll pull over to the lab to unload the things I brought from the storage building."

As Matt backed the truck up to the door at the lab, Dr. Bertram arrived and began helping Matt and Sarah unload the lab materials and supplies. Recognizing some of the materials in the boxes, Dr. Bertram told Sarah, "When we get this stuff set up, we can begin prepping the samples we've collected so far."

"I'll check to see if we have all of our standard samples to calibrate the equipment. Also Doc, I'm still working on finalizing some lab procedures you and I need to review before we begin running samples." Sarah informed them.

"We should get the DNA analyzer this coming week. The Tech called me this morning to schedule a time to deliver it, set it up, and do some training on its operation. I told him I would call him back on Monday to schedule a date. I suggest that both of

344

you be there for the training; I just need the day you want me to schedule the delivery." Matt told them.

"Let's schedule it for Wednesday or Thursday," Dr. Bertram told Matt.

"Alright, I'll call him first thing Monday morning and confirm an appointment."

* * *

Matt was up very early and drove out to the lodge before dawn.

Victor was waiting at the foot of the front steps. "I'm glad you were able to get here early. We have been tracking a couple of targets which have been stationary just over the rise, beyond the field in front of us. I have teams moving into position behind them. We plan to attack them straight on from here, when they flee, they'll run directly into the team behind them. Basically, the same plan of attack as we used before."

"Make sure you have a couple of response teams near your teams on the back side, in case they get attacked by wargs from their rear. Always watch your backs, even if you see them in front of you. I'm afraid the wargs you're tracking may be bait to pull you into a trap. The alpha prime may be hanging back, waiting to attack from your rear."

"I'll get response teams into position," Victor said as he radioed Alex and echoed Matt's instructions.

"I'm nervous about this one Victor," Matt warned.

Victor nodded then radioed the ambush team to post rear security at their position. "Are you ready to do this?" Victor asked Matt.

"It's your show, I'm just here as an observer and advisor." Matt gave Victor a wink.

The assault team spread out double arms distance before they moved across the field, toward the rogues, located in the tree line on the far side of the field. The handheld tracking device showed that the rogues were not retreating as expected. Instead, they held their position as Victor and his people approached. Victor instructed everyone to lock and load, ready for contact. When they got to within fifty yards of the rogues' position, four rogues leaped from the brushy cover and charged the assault team. The assault team opened fire on the rogues, but the rogues were leaping back and forth making it difficult to target and shoot them. Two were shot and killed within a few feet of the assault team and the other two were able to engage the betas in a full animal brawl. Two team members pulled one off their teammate while Victor attacked the other, killing it with his bare hands and a knife. While Victor was fighting the second rogue, Matt saw two more charges from the left and right of their position.

"VICTOR, BEHIND YOU!" Matt shouted, shooting the rogue charging directly at Victor from behind.

Another team member shot the rogue coming at him from the opposite side. With all six rogues down, and two assault team members bloodied, the team rallied in a semi-circle in front of Matt and Victor. A minute later, they heard gunfire coming from the general direction of the ambush team's position. Victor called on the radio and ordered the response team to move in and support the ambush team. After a few minutes, the shooting intensified for several minutes before slowly subsiding.

"Victor, we need to get this team back to the lodge and be prepared for an assault on the lodge itself."

Following Matt's suggestion, Victor moved his men back to the lodge and called for everyone around the lodge to arm themselves and take positions. In the meantime, the ambush team and response teams both radioed in. They were attacked from the rear by a large pack of about eight rogues led by an Alpha Prime. They killed four rogues, wounded the others including the alpha. The ambush team had one person dead and two others badly wounded.

Matt and Victor ran back to the lodge to check the tracking monitor. To their surprise, there were no targets showing on the screen.

"You realize they set us up for an ambush don't you?" Matt said to Victor.

"Yes, and if you had not recognized the signs and warned me, it would have been a disaster for us. Thanks." Victor shook

Matt's hand and patted him on the shoulder. "Oh, and thanks for covering my back."

Matt just nodded at Victor.

Victor instructed the person at the monitoring station to call Dr. Bertram to give him a heads up they had four wounded coming his way; two of them seriously wounded.

Matt and Victor jumped into Matt's truck and drove quickly over to the ambush team's location. When they arrived on site, they quickly made sure the area was secure and arranged for the evacuation of the wounded with speed and urgency. Matt took a few minutes to examine the dead wargs and question some of the team members about what happened. Victor instructed the teams to clear the area and assemble back at the lodge, to remain on alert and await the debriefing.

Matt and Victor loaded up and headed back to the lodge to organize security and activities there. After they were on the road, Matt pulled out his map and handed it to Victor.

"Victor, from what I've seen, I'm convinced the wargs are organized into a densely populated community about six miles inside the wilderness area. The telemetry from the targets Frankie and her teams have tagged, show them moving along common corridors of travel, the packs are closely located to one another and move freely among the packs themselves." Matt explained while pointing to areas of interest on the map.

Victor glanced at Matt with a curious expression, "I thought wolves organized in small packs and maintained a territorial domain and didn't tolerate intrusion by other predator groups including other wolves?"

"That's correct, a typical wolf pack travels in a nuclear family unit. In other words, a mated pair and a pack of six to eight of their adult offspring, typically make up a pack. The pack will control a territory in an area from fifty up to a thousand square miles. There have been a few documented incidents where packs have been as large as thirty wolves and controlling territories in excess of two thousand square miles."

"So what are you thinking? what are we looking at here?"

"I think we are facing a densely populated communal pack structure which may contain as many as fifty or more rogues and alphas. I also believe we will find a Maximus Prime somewhere among the packs controlling the entire community."

"You make it sound like we are fighting with a neighboring village."

"Remember what I told you before? We have to stop thinking of them as wolves. They are pseudo-human creatures, that we know little or nothing about. We don't understand their behavior, social structure, genetic makeup, or capabilities. All of which, we are learning the hard way."

"What do we do now?"

"We need to get some eyes on the other side of that ridge and get some idea of the size of the warg community and maybe learn something about their leadership structure. But, before we take that step, I would like to meet with William and Doc to review what we learned so far and get their feedback."

"I'll call William and have him meet us in Graymere later."

Once they were sure security around the lodge was established, Victor instructed the teams to assemble for a debriefing. Afterward, they followed their established routine of cleaning their weapons, checking their gear, and getting some rest.

"Victor, I'm going into Graymere to check on the wounded. I'll see you and William there later."

Hanging up the phone Dr. Bertram called out to Allison, "we have four wounded betas on their way in, and they should be here within ten minutes. Call over to the inn and tell Freya we will need her, Sarah and Keira to come here right away. When they get here, have them change into scrubs; it's going to be a bit messy I think."

Dr. Bertram started laying out his surgical instruments, anesthetics, medications, sutures, and bandages. After Allison got off the phone, Doc instructed her to triage the wounded, then she would assist him in surgery while Keira, Freya, and Sarah

348

cleaned the wounds and prepped the others awaiting treatment. Allison went into the other treatment room and laid out swabs, gauze, antiseptic, and bandages. When Freya, Sarah, and Keira arrived, she handed them scrubs and instructed them to change out of their street clothes. While they were changing, she gave them instructions what they were to do when the wounded arrived.

"We'll triage the wounded, meaning, we will determine who is in the worst condition to the least. That will be the order Doc and I treat them. While I'm assisting Doc in the trauma room, you three will be prepping the others. Remember, first, stop the bleeding, then treat for shock, and then clean the wounds. Don't bother with trying to permanently wrap or bandage any of the wounds. We will rip it all away to treat their injuries once they are on the table. As Doc finishes with one patient, we will rotate out for the next. When we bring the treated patient in here to recover, you three will monitor them as we instruct you and until we're finished will all four."

Freya, Sarah, and Keira appeared shocked by the gravity of the situation. Freya's thought shifted to what might have happened to Matt and was he one of the wounded coming in. She didn't have much time to ponder the possibilities, before they heard Doc call out, "Here they come!"

Dr. Bertram and Allison ran to the front porch and triaged the wounded as they were unloaded. "Let's get this one on the table immediately and start getting him prepped. Keira, apply pressure to this man's wounds to stop bleeding. Apply a tourniquet on his arm if you need to. Freya, you and Sarah take these two and get their wounds cleaned up and apply a compress to the wounds until the bleeding stops."

For the next three hours, the clinic was hectic with activity as Doc and Allison performed surgery and sewed up wounds while Freya, Sarah, and Keira treated and cleaned wounds, shuffled patients, and did post-op monitoring. Two of the wounded were treated and released to go home and two kept overnight at the clinic. Keira volunteered to stay with Allison to change off shifts to monitor them until they were stable.

"You ladies did an outstanding job," Dr. Bertram told Freya, Sarah, and Keira. "I'm sorry I had to call on you and throw you into the middle of this without any warning. We had to have help and I knew we could count on you three. Thanks." Dr. Bertram praised them as he gave each one a hug.

"I'm glad I could help," Freya said.

"I got your back anytime you need me Doc," Sarah told him.

"No problem Doc," Keira said.

"Thanks again ladies."

Freya and Sarah gathered their clothes and headed back over to the inn to shower and change out of the bloody scrubs they were wearing. Matt pulled up to the inn just as they reached the porch steps. Freya ran to him and embraced him tightly.

"Are you guys alright?" Matt asked looking at their blood-soaked scrubs. "What on earth…"

"We were drafted to help in the clinic," Sarah answered.

"I'm going to check on the guys in the clinic while you two go get cleaned up," Matt told them. "I'll be back in just a few minutes."

* * *

"How are they doing Doc?" Matt asked.

"These two are resting. I sent the other two home after stitching them up. These two lost a lot of blood and this one had some serious damage to muscle tissue; missed ripping out an artery by a fraction of a centimeter. He's lucky to be alive."

"We lost one in the field," Matt informed Dr. Bertram. "They should be bringing his body in, for you to examine and fill out a death certificate."

"What happened?"

"They came down in force this morning and set us up for an ambush. I had a feeling something was not right and thank God, I had Victor make adjustments to his plan by putting additional people in place. As it was, we killed ten rogues and wounded several along with an alpha. I suspect there was a second alpha, but he didn't see him."

"My God! So many rogues and alpha running in a joint pack," Dr. Bertram said aloud to himself.

"Doc, they are very clever and tactically cautious," Matt said nervously. "These things are highly intelligent. This was not just a raid. They attacked in force, in a premeditated and coordinated attack. It was as if they had been led by someone with military training."

"Sounds like a dangerous situation."

"That's not the half of it. William is on his way to Graymere, I need to meet with both of you if you can get away for a few minutes."

"Yes, the patients are stable and we can meet at the inn. If Allison needs me, I'll be close. Give me a few minutes to shower and change then I'll be right over."

"Ok Doc," Matt acknowledged.

When Matt arrived at the inn, Freya and Sarah were still showering and changing. He radioed Victor to let him know Doc was available and they could meet at the inn when William was ready. Matt made a fresh pot of coffee and sat down to collect his thoughts and think through the actions that morning.

'*There are too many unanswered questions related to the 'natural evolution' of the wargs being attributed to LTV. There has to be something more going on, but what is it?*' Matt thought to himself. '*The DNA analyzer is critical to finding out what's going on with the transgenesis process among the wargs and the extent of the human genome transformation.*'

"Oh God, it was good to get the smell of blood off me," Sarah said to Freya meeting each other at the bottom of the staircase.

"I know what you mean," Freya replied.

Matt was so deep in thought, staring out the front window, he didn't notice the girls coming into the dining area.

"Matthew, are you alright?" Freya asked.

Matt looked up to see the girls standing there looking at him, "Yes, why?"

"You looked like you were in another world," Freya said to him.

"Close to it," he replied. "William, Victor, and Doc are on their way here. They'll be here any time now."

Freya sat down next to Matt. "Matthew, what happened this morning?"

Sarah took a seat at the table across from Freya. "Those betas looked like they had been through a battle," She said.

"For all practical purposes that's what happened," Matt told them. "When I arrived at the lodge this morning Victor and his teams had been tracking a six-pack from out of the wilderness to a location near the lodge. It looked as though they were getting ready to raid the lodge. Victor put his teams in place to intercept and ambush them. After taking a read on the situation, I suspected the wargs were setting Victor's men up for an ambush of their own, so I advised him to allow for an ambush contingency and put extra people in place."

Dr. Bertram walked in as Matt began telling Freya and Sarah what had happened.

"What happened?" Sarah asked.

"Victor's assault team moved in on the group they had been tracking and engaged them; six rogues were waiting for us…"

"Us! What do you mean *us*?" Freya interrupted.

"… They were waiting and when we got close to them, they charged from the wood line. We shot two before they got in close, two engaged in hand-to-hand fighting. Then two more came at us from the flanks and we killed them. The rogues wounded two of our betas before we managed to kill all six of them. Shortly after that, an alpha and several rogues attacked the ambush team from behind. The response team moved in to back up the ambush team and they managed to kill another four and wound four more as well as the alpha. They had one beta killed and two badly injured."

"Oh My God!" Sarah said putting her hands to her face. "Déjà Vu; this is exactly the scenario that Dr. Hobart warned would come about if the transmutes were let loose. I used to have nightmares about the things he warned Col. Livingston he thought might happen."

They all were quiet for a few seconds before Victor and William interrupted the silence.

They all stood up to greet William and Sarah appeared to go into shock. This was the first time she had seen or met William. His six-foot-four muscular build coupled with his lupine mutation was far more than she had seen since her arrival.

Seeing Sarah's apparent shock at his appearance William paused for a moment before gracefully introducing himself. "You must be Sarah; the genius I've heard so much about. I'm William Barret. Most people around here just call me William." He said to Sarah, extending his hand to shake hers.

Sarah was even more shocked when she heard his deep raspy voice. She quickly managed to collect herself without further embarrassment, replied to William's introduction, "Please forgive me. Yes, I'm Sarah and it's a pleasure to meet you."

William bowed slightly to Sarah as they shook hands and exchanged greetings with everyone else in the room.

"May I get either of you something to eat or drink?" Freya offered.

"Tea would be nice, thank you," William answered.

"Same," Victor answered.

Freya touched Sarah's shoulder as a signal for Sarah to follow her to the kitchen and leave the others to their discussion.

"Victor tells me if it wasn't for your insightful assessment of the situation this morning, we could have been facing a far worse conclusion to the encounter than the decisive outcome achieved."

"Victor had a good plan in place, it was just a matter of allowing for a possible contingency," Matt replied humbly trying not to take any credit away from Victor.

"A contingency, according to Victor, that saved their asses. He also tells me, if it were not for you, he would be laying up in Doc's clinic or worse. Again, thank you."

"No thanks necessary, a team watches each other's back and does what's necessary, as Victor did for me not so long ago."

"Thank you all the same," William said to Matt. "Victor told me the two of you were reviewing the situation this morning and you had some startling insights concerning the wargs."

Freya and Sarah came back in to serve the tea just as Matt was beginning to explain his assessment of the warg situation. "As you are aware, Frankie and her teams have tagged several rogues and at least one alpha. I've been able to monitor those tracking devices via a satellite GPS tracking system. And after observing the movement of the targets, I believe we're dealing with a large communal society of fifty or more rogues and alphas. The tracking telemetry and behavioral characteristics suggest a densely populated society is organized into a collective, led by what I termed as a Maximus Prime."

"I thought wolves didn't congregate in collectives and they certainly could not maintain a pack that large in such a small area."

"This has been our mistake in reasoning up till now. We have to stop thinking of them as wolves and begin studying their behavior as a pseudo-human species, exhibiting a totally unique culture and behavior characteristic, unlike anything anyone has witnessed before."

Matt offered various pieces of evidence and information he had collected. He tried to make a case for his assessment as a biologist and scientist. He stressed the indicators that illustrated the superior intellect demonstrated by the alphas they encountered, as well as, the apparent level of organization, planning and control the wargs have exercised in their raids and ambushes.

"Your assessment is well supported by the facts you have laid out," William said to Matt before he turned to Sarah. "Sarah, you have been listening to Dr. Kershaw's assessment. What do you think?"

William's question to Sarah surprised everyone in the room except Matt and Dr. Bertram. Sarah was a bit shy to answer. She didn't want it to appear as though she was more knowledgeable on the subject of wolves, wargs, or tactical situations than Matt was.

"Go ahead," William encouraged her, "Dr. Kershaw and Dr. Bertram have praised your insight and intellect pertaining to transgenics."

Matt nodded his head encouraging Sarah to speak up and share her views and opinion on the matter.

"I can only speak from a perspective of the genetic potentialities. I don't have the benefit of Dr. Kershaw's experience in dealing with animal behavior or wolves in particular."

"Please share what you know or even what you think," William insisted.

"I think Dr. Kershaw's assessment is spot on. However, I feel he hasn't stressed strongly enough, the inherent dangers posed by the advanced intellect and cognitive skills demonstrated by the alpha primes and God forbid, if an advanced entity, a Maximus Prime, does exist. I have no doubt Dr. Bertram has made you privy to some of the information I shared with him and Dr. Kershaw regarding a previous research project I worked with. Applying what I know of transgenics and what I learned from that project; I believe everything Dr. Kershaw is trying to tell you is an understatement of what you may be facing in the near future."

"Thank you for your honest assessment and candor," William told Sarah. "Dr. Kershaw, Victor mentioned the two of you discussed a reassessment of our strategy in dealing with the wargs. Can you elaborate on this a bit?"

"Initially, we were looking at the warg threat as a relatively small isolated group of mutant wolves, pressured by habitat to move into the valley. It soon became apparent that foraging for food was not the primary purpose for their presence. Subsequently, it began to emerge that their behavior was more than that of a lone wolf, but in this case, a pack of lone wolves seeking to kill for pleasure. The latter is the basis for our current strategy of simply locating and eliminating the wargs."

"But now?" William queried.

"Based on the assessment I've just shared with you, I think we are facing a large, densely populated community of wargs, numbering in excess of fifty rogues and alphas. Their behavior suggests the wargs have an established collective society led by a central hierarchal leader. I believe the wargs are seeking to eliminate a perceived threat to their existence and assert their dominance as the apex predator in the region. They are operating under the same mindset we established in order to eliminate *them*. In essence, we are, in Sarah's words, engaged in a war with a neighboring society. Our overall goal should be to eliminate them before they do the same to us. Our strategy should be two-fold; we must learn all we can about their strength, organization, and leadership. Then plan and execute offensive actions to eliminate them entirely, while maintaining a defensive posture to fend off any attacks from the wargs, such as we witnessed at the Lancaster homestead and at the lodge this morning. Which, I believe is just the beginning of what's to come."

"What do you suggest as our next step?"

"I suggest we send out a small reconnaissance party to get an eyes-on assessment of the wargs den locations, movement and observe behavioral characteristics and interactions. We need to learn all we can in order to formulate tactical operations to take the battle to their back yard. Given the strength of the group that came down to attack us this morning, I suggest Victor increase the number of people on his teams. The details of their training, organization, and equipment I can coordinate with Victor. Additionally, the DNA analysis of the samples we take from the wargs is critical – The nature of the warg transgenic mutation, as well as, their genome should give us greater insight in understanding their origin, evolution, behavior, and ways to deal with them."

"Doc, do you have anything to add?"

"Not at this time."

"Victor?"

"No Sir."

"Thank you, ladies and gentlemen," William said, getting up, preparing to leave. Pausing, he turned to address everyone in the room. "I can't help but believe that it's by divine providence God had brought this particular group of people together to deal with this threat to the people of this valley, if not the world at large."

Chapter 44

The next morning Matt and Victor worked to formulate plans for organizing and training a more formidable fighting force; teams trained to be able to undertake offensive operations against the wargs. Matt suggested that they occupy the Lancaster homestead and use it as their headquarters and training base. Now that the Lancaster family were all dead, the homestead stood abandoned. The house and barn could be easily converted into a headquarters, barracks. If the wargs were watching, it would provide a more defensible location and take the attention away from the lodge, giving Alex and Frankie back their home and privacy.

Matt also discussed with Victor, the basic qualifications for selecting twelve of his best betas. He wanted individuals who were single and exhibited advanced lupine transmutation traits. When he returned next week, he would begin training these twelve to conduct recon patrols into the warg territory.

"Victor, are there any military veterans living in the valley?" Matt asked.

"Not that I'm aware of," Victor replied. "I've heard mention of people in the past having served in the military, but to the best of my knowledge, there are none currently living in the valley."

"I need someone I can trust, who can devote the time to training your people in certain core military skills and combat tactics," Matt said aloud to himself.

"Do you know of anyone who can be trusted to keep our situation confidential, if you know what I mean?" Victor asked.

"Not off the top of my head," Matt replied. "I'll work on that, but in the meantime; make sure your people stay alert. I don't think the wargs will be back in force for several days. We haven't ventured into their territory yet and I think they'll take a few days to lick their wounds before they come at us again. However, we don't know enough about the wargs to predict, with any degree of certainty, what they will do next or when. Therefore, be ready for anything. Have Frankie and her teams continue hunting and tagging for the time being. By next week, we will most likely stop tagging and integrate her teams into your main assault force."

"I'll make sure they are on their toes. I think yesterday morning was a wake-up call to many of them that we are not organizing a safari."

"I'll coordinate with Doc to arrange for him and Allison to conduct some first aid training with your people. I'll see what I can find in the way of basic first aid kits and battle dressings."

"See you in a few days," Victor said to Matt as he left the lodge and headed back to Graymere to pack and get ready to return to the city.

* * *

"Wow, what a difference since the last time I was in here," Matt said aloud as he walked into the lab.

"We've been busy and it's starting to take shape," Sarah responded.

"This is where the DNA analyzer will be installed," Doc told Matt as they shook hands.

"How are your lab procedures coming along?"

"Working on those and I hope to be finished with the first set this week. Even with using boilerplate templates, it still takes a while to tailor them to a specific lab." Sarah sighed with frustration.

"Doc, can I visit with you for a few minutes?" Matt asked as he ushered Dr. Bertram toward a small office cubical.

"What's on your mind?" Doc asked.

"Doc, I didn't go into details yesterday afternoon in the meeting, but I'm getting some bad feelings regarding the wargs."

"In what way?"

"Looking at the data and information in front of me, I'm confused as to how the wargs, the alphas, in particular, could have evolved naturally to the level of communal organization and overall population dynamics. I can understand the natural evolution of the basic LTV transgenesis, but this goes way beyond that. Although, they haven't begun to forge weapons and tools, their ability to implement battle tactics is beyond what many of our soldiers in the military could organize, left to themselves. The other thing bothering me; is where are all of these wargs coming from? Typically, a wolf pack consists of a mated pair and six or eight of their adult offspring. I'm at a loss as to how a central mated pair could have sired a community as large and complex as what I believe is up there."

"Once we have the DNA analyzer we can begin mapping the genome of those we can get samples of and maybe that will tell us something."

"I'm afraid of what's coming, and it's coming faster than we can prepare for it."

Dr. Bertram put his hand on Matt's shoulder and said to him, "I believe God will guide us through this."

"Oh, by the way, you told me to let you know if I was having any other symptoms; I've been having headaches that come and go. Out of the blue, I'll get a pain in my head as if someone hit me with a hammer and it will pulsate for a short time and then fade away." Matt explained pointing to areas in his temples where the pain occurs.

"Do you black out, or get dizzy?"

"No, but the pain is so intense at times my vision is blurred momentarily and I have a hard time focusing on any particular object."

"What about your hearing?" You mentioned before that you had pain in your ears; could this be related to that?"

"The pain in my ears is not as bad as before and I've noticed a significant improvement in my hearing in the higher tonal ranges. I can hear a clock ticking in another room or my watch ticking from across the room that almost drives me nuts."

"What about your muscle aches and pains?"

"About the same. I've gained a bit of weight, but I think that is more from Freya's cooking than anything else." Matt laughed.

"The pain you're experiencing is your body coping with the mutation of your cellular structure. Keep me posted on any changes. And if the pain becomes unbearable, let me know and I'll prescribe a pain medication for you."

"Thanks, Doc. I need to get over to the inn. Freya is waiting for me to get loaded and head back to the city.

"Have a safe trip. Sarah and I'll see you Wednesday or Thursday, just give me a call and let me know when."

Neither Matt nor Freya said much to each other on the drive back to the city. Each was in their thoughts of the coming days and the events they feared would accompany them. Arriving back at the cabin, Matt unloaded their bags and then took some food out to feed the ducks.

Freya put their things away and began looking for Matthew. By chance, saw him through a window, standing by the pond, feeding the ducks. Watching him, she realized the ducks must be a form of therapy for Matthew. She didn't disturb him and went about preparing dinner.

"Dinner is almost ready," Freya said to Matt when he came in from feeding the ducks.

"Ok, I'll go wash up," Matt replied.

Matt sat down at his computer to check the tracking portal before sitting down to eat with Freya. Studying the screen, he noted that there were a couple new target IDs in the data. *'Frankie must have tagged a couple of new ones,'* he thought to himself. Looking at an overlay of historical tracking telemetry Matt was seeing a clearer picture of the movement patterns.

"Dinner is served," Freya announced.

Matt switched the screen to real-time tracking mode and left it up while he sat down to eat dinner with Freya.

"Did you see anything new?" Freya asked, gesturing at the computer.

"Looks like Frankie and her teams tagged a couple more wargs. I haven't had a chance to look at it closely, but I think we are about beyond the tracking stage. We know where they are and their routes in and out of the valley. Soon, we will have to go in and take a look around and with our own eyes."

Freya paused and looked at Matt with a fearful look on her face, but she remained quiet and did not say anything. She was fully aware Matt, more than anyone, knew the risks of venturing into the wargs' territory, he didn't need her reminding him. The expression on her face said everything she needed or wanted to say.

Matt was excited to see Dr. Bertram and Sarah when they arrived to receive the DNA analyzer and train on the unit with the tech who delivered it. Once they had it set up in the lab and operational, they could begin processing the samples already collected. Soon be able to get a picture of the warg genome, and maybe, begin to understand what they were dealing with. Matt agreed to bring the unit up Friday evening and Sarah would be waiting to get it setup as soon as it arrived.

During the week, Matt also completed a final report to Harvey Langston detailing the investigation into Ranger Holmes's encounter with the *wolves* in Misty Hollow. The report concluded that a couple of lone wolves had wandered down out of the wilderness area and had created a bit of a nuisance for the valley residents. Characteristic of lone wolves, they were prone to attack humans who crossed their path. Matt reported that local residents killed the wolves and the situation had been resolved. He arranged for Harvey to meet him in Misty Hollow the coming weekend to review the report and discuss the actual situation with the wargs. He would deliver the '*official report*' at that time and return the tranquilizer guns, tracking devices, and other equipment. Case closed, as far as the Forest Service was concerned.

The last order of business before he and Freya returned to Misty Hollow was to go shopping at the army surplus store. He also purchased a tactical shotgun with extended magazine along with ample supply of shotgun shells. If he was going to teach and lead recon patrols into the warg territory, he wanted to be properly equipped. Judging from the way the wargs dodged the gunfire in the last engagement, he felt a shotgun would give him a better chance to score a hit, rather than a rifle.

Chapter 45

Sarah was waiting at the lab when Matt and Freya arrived in Graymere. They drove straight to the lab to deliver the DNA analyzer along with the other supplies and equipment that had arrived that week.

"I hope to get everything installed and calibrated this weekend. If all goes well, we will start analyzing samples by Monday." Sarah told Matt as they were unloading the truck.

After everything was unloaded, Matt and Freya took a few minutes to look around the lab and marvel at the work accomplished. Matt praised Sarah, "I'm impressed with what you've done with such limited resources."

"It's a bit crude, but Doc and I focused on keeping it simple and pretty much limited to the type of lab work we *need* to do. We tried to avoid getting bogged down in a lot of bells and whistles which would contribute little to the primary objective of our research." Sarah explained.

"Ah, I thought it was about time for you guys to arrive, and I see you have already unloaded everything," Doc said as he entered the Lab.

"Very impressive Doc," Freya said.

"I would like to take credit, but what you see is mainly all due to Sarah's efforts. I gave a few suggestions here and there, but she is the one who made it happen."

"Doc, I forgot to tell you when you were in the city; I got hold of Adam Holmes and talked with him briefly. From our conversation, he didn't mention he was suffering any extended ill effects from the LTV infection. I told him I would keep in touch with him from time to time." Matt told Dr. Bertram.

"Yes, we need to check on him, occasionally, over the next few months. Hopefully, he is in the eighty percent category rather than the unfortunate twenty percent." Dr. Bertram replied.

"Freya and I will leave you guys to play with your new toys and we'll head over to the inn to get our stuff unloaded," Matt said as he and Freya were walking out the door.

"Good night Doc," Freya called to him.

"Don't wait up," Sarah called to them.

* * *

As Freya and Matt lay down to go to sleep that night, Freya turned to Matt. "Matthew, promise me you'll be careful."

Matt pulled her close and squeezed her gently. "I promise."

"I could not bear it if anything happened to you. I know a lot is resting on your shoulders and you feel some sense of duty or obligation to the valley, but you have a duty and obligation to come home to me as well."

Matt could hear Freya sniffle and the quiver in her voice told him she was trying to fight back the tears. "Freya, I love you more than anything in this world. What I'm doing is not just for the valley, but for you and our future. The valley just reaps the benefit of all that I do for you. This is your home, and now it's my home as well. I'll defend it, and you, with my last breath. I won't let anything or anyone destroy our future happiness. Not here, in our own home. I have experienced more than one near death experience. If God wanted to take me, he has had many opportunities. I trust God will make sure we are able to live a full and happy life, not one in fear and darkness."

* * *

Matt ate a hearty breakfast and before he left that morning, he embraced Freya and kissed her. "I will not be back until tomorrow around noon. I am going to conduct some night training with some of Victor's people."

365

"No Matthew," Freya pleaded. "I know what you are going to do and I beg you please…"

"We are just going to conduct some night training, I'll be fine. It's the other guys you need to be concerned about, they are the ones who I'm going to run ragged." Matt told Freya with a wink and a joking smile.

Freya embraced him and held him tightly. Matt gave her a moment then he kissed her again before he grabbed his pack and headed out the door.

Freya knew what Matt was planning, she had overheard him discussing it with Victor, and she had seen the gear he purchased, as well as the new shotgun. Now, all she could do was wait for him to return and pray to God, to keep him safe. As she stood in the doorway, Freya watched Matthew drive away, no longer able to hold back the tears.

"Freya, are you alright? What's wrong?" Sarah said, entering the lobby area where she found Freya crying.

Freya was crying too hard to catch her breath to explain.

"Come here and sit down," Sarah told her as she put her arm around Freya and guided her to the couch. "Let me get you some tissue." Sarah sat next to Freya holding her and letting her cry on her shoulder. After some time, she looked into Freya's face and asked her, "What's wrong; what happen?"

"I'm afraid Matthew is going to take some of the Betas up into the wilderness tonight, to try and find the warg dens. He told me they were just going to do some night training, but I know what they have been planning to do. He has been studying the maps and the tracking thing on the computer."

"Freya, even if they are planning to do what you said; would you truly expect Dr. Kershaw to sit back and send someone else out to do anything like that without training them and leading them? He is not the type of person to send people out unprepared and you forget he has been trained and is experienced such things. He will be fine, I promise."

"I have known in my heart he would be doing such things and it has to be done. I thought I could handle it, but I can't!" Freya mumbled before she started crying again.

366

Sarah allowed her cry and let the stress, that had been building up inside of her, to flow out. "Don't worry; I'll be here with you," Sarah said reassuringly as Freya cried on her shoulder.

Later, Sarah talked Freya into coming to the lab with her to help her get things set up. She thought, by keeping Freya busy, it would help keep her mind off Matt.

* * *

Matt had arranged to meet Victor at the Lancaster homestead first thing that morning. When he pulled up to the house, Victor was on the front porch waiting for him with a hot cup of coffee.

"Good morning," Victor greeted.

"Good morning. Looks like you guys have been busy this week." Matt surveyed the work that had been done, converting the Lancaster homestead into a quasi-headquarters and training base.

"Yes, several people from the valley have been contributing time and resources to get the base setup as quickly as possible."

"Were you able to get the twelve betas I asked for?"

"Yes, they will be here within the hour."

Matt handed Victor a set of camouflage uniform and tactical gear. "See if you can send Simon into Boise and gather up as much of this gear as he can. We need full sets for the twelve betas I will train for conducting recon and special operations. I suggest, the same gear for all of the personnel recruited and trained for tactical operations."

"Ok, I will have everything before you get back next weekend."

"Great, let's go inside so I can lay out what I have planned."

Matt spread out a map he had marked up with the locations and movement patterns of the wargs in their territory. "Based on the movement patterns of the rogues Frankie's people have tagged, the wargs are using three primary routes into and out of the valley. Their patterns of movement don't indicate they have a fear of anyone following them; they used the same routes in and out of the wilderness. I'm going to conduct some training with the betas throughout the day and I'm going to select four of them I'll lead on a recon patrol into the wargs' backyard tonight."

"Only the five of you?" Victor asked.

"Six if you want to come along," Matt replied.

"Try keeping me away," Victor replied with a confident grin.

"Ok, before we get involved in the training I have planned for today, we need to get hold of Frankie and have her bring all of the tranquilizer guns, tags and tracking equipment here. They need to have it cleaned and ready to turn into Harvey when he gets here tomorrow morning. Have someone take down the antenna tower from the lodge and set it up here near the house. We'll be converting it into a radio antenna. I'll give you the specs for a base FM radio unit we'll set up here which can transmit over into the wilderness area from this location."

Matt surveyed the house and surrounding grounds while Victor began issuing instructions and delegating responsibilities to people to follow through on the tasks Matt had given him. After making the various assignments, Matt asked Victor to join him out on the porch.

"I've asked Harvey Langston to meet me in Graymere tomorrow around noon. We'll brief him on the general situation with the wargs and turn in the gear we got from the Forest Service. Don't ask me to explain, but for the time being, I want us to be very guarded in what information we share with Harvey. I'll tell him just enough for him to know we have plans in place to deal with the wargs, but *I do not* want him to know any details about what he are doing here at the Lancaster place. I don't want to elaborate on what we've learned about the wargs, or the extent of the recruitment and training of betas to deal with them."

"Is there anything either William or I should be concerned with here?" Victor asked.

"I'm not sure; I don't want to raise any red flags until I have something to back up my hunches. A lot depends on the results of the DNA analysis Doc and Sarah will be working on. Sarah is setting up the DNA analyzer this weekend and they should start processing samples next week. After I have a chance to look at some of the data from the warg genome analysis, I'll be able to explain myself, until then, I want to keep information close hold for now."

"Fair enough," Victor acknowledged.

* * *

After the handpicked betas arrived at the Lancaster homestead, Matt and Victor called them together for Matt to explain the scope and nature of the assignments he would be training them to perform. He outlined the nature of the training they would receive and stressed they are not to discuss anything they saw or did, with anyone outside their group. Matt highlighted that the information they would be collecting and tasks performed were vital in saving the lives of the people of the valley. After his briefing, he offered them the opportunity change their minds and go back to their previous assignments; everyone chose to remain.

Next, Matt explained that throughout the day, the group would be involved in a variety of training activities. Afterward, he would select four of them to accompany him and Victor that evening on a patrol into the warg territory. The rest of the group would be assigned supporting tasks, such as security or transport.

For Matt, it was critical to get a firsthand view of what was going on inside the warg territory. So critical, they could not afford to wait for weeks to get teams fully trained. Therefore, he would teach the group some basic patrolling techniques and tactical drills sufficient for him to take a small group into the warg territory that night. For this first patrol, he had conducted a satellite photo recon. He identified a vantage point, to observe the wargs, in an area he believed the warg dens were located. He hoped to accomplish two things that night. First, to get a firsthand visual perspective of the warg territory, and second, to gain patrolling experience for select members of the team, who could, in turn, share that experience with others.

Throughout their training during the day, everyone performed well. When the time came to select the four to accompany Victor and himself on the patrol, it was difficult for Matt to choose who actually performed the best. Instead, he made them draw lots.

Everyone took part in the mission brief. He cautioned that the winds in the mountains carry smells in many different directions and he hoped by remaining on ledges above the hollow, their body scents would not drift down into the warg dens. Although he did not expect the wargs would have sentries, he wanted to be prepared if they encountered them.

Concluding the mission briefing, Matt gave the team thirty minutes to eat and get their weapons and gear ready to move out.

"Ok, equipment check," Matt announced. He lined up the teams and instructed them on how to conduct equipment checks as he and Victor demonstrated on each other. "First you check to see if you have everything you are supposed to carry with you, then you physically check each other to ensure that none of your gear is loose and makes noise as you move; you have your partner grab and shake it, and you jump up and down as your partner checks for loose or noisy gear. Next, you do a weapons check to ensure that your weapon is operational; there are no shiny exposed parts on your weapon, nothing is loose like a sling that will rattle and make noise, and you have a sufficient load of ammo." Matt instructed as he and Victor demonstrated on each other.

Finally, the patrol was ready to depart. Matt gave some final instructions and teaching points. "Remember, always assume the wargs are watching our camp and if you move out on a patrol they will be alerted and will follow. I'm assuming the wargs' eyesight is not that good from a visual perspective, but they can detect movement much better than we can. I believe they are color blind, but their night vision is better than mine is. I believe your night vision is better than the wargs. Your sense of smell is on par with theirs. Therefore, you are better equipped to conduct night operations than dormers like me."

They all chuckled at Matt's admission.

They loaded up and the transport team drove them to their drop point at the eastern end of the valley. From there, they made their way up and along the ridge working their way back toward the hollow containing the main warg community. They timed their departure and movement to allow them to reach a point just below the crest of the ridge before it was fully dark. They would wait at that point until it was dark, then they would cross over the crest of the ridge and make their way to their objective. The security team would wait for them at this location and be prepared to support them if the wargs pursued them when they returned.

It was near midnight before they reached the rocky outcropping from which they made their observations. The position of the moon at that time of night was perfect to cast sufficient light over the hollow. From their position, they could survey the terrain and scan the area with binoculars and the night vision devices. Once they became accustomed to the area and the light, they were able to observe movement in the hollow below them. What they saw astonished them. Below them, were scores of wargs moving around in the hollow, clustered in small groups. The groups appeared to be a densely populated colony, as Matt suspected. As briefed before the mission, each of them conducted their own observations and make mental notes of what they observed. They remained there for about two hours before it was time to make their way back to the base.

Following a different route back from the one they took going in. They used the cover of darkness to navigate through the warg territory until they arrived at a predetermined rally point where the security team was waiting. They waited until first light to proceed down the ridge to the designated pickup point.

Once they arrived back at the base, Matt instructed the team to unload and clear their weapons, grab some breakfast, then meet inside the house for a debriefing. Once everyone dispersed to get breakfast, Matt reviewed the whole process with Victor from training the previous day, mission brief, equipment checks, and so forth. Matt told Victor, that in the coming weeks, he would train the twelve ops team personally, while Victor trained along with them and in turn would teach the skills to his regular tactical teams.

While everyone was eating their breakfast, Matt took the opportunity to call Freya and let her know the training exercise was over and he would be coming home soon. He reminded her

Harvey would be arriving around noon and asked if she could have lunch prepared for everyone. Freya was overjoyed at hearing Matt's voice and knowing he was all right.

Matt had all twelve special ops team members sit in on the debriefing; he went through every aspect of the mission from training the day before, through to the point they arrived back at the base. Matt used the process of asking questions and getting feedback from the patrol members, noting down information as they relayed what they saw and heard at the objective. At the end of the debriefing, Matt emphasized with the group, the debrief was not only intended to compare notes on what information or intelligence they gathered during the mission itself, but to discuss what went right and what went wrong. The purpose being, to continually improve their training and preparations. Matt also reminded them the need to keep anything they saw or heard within the special ops group.

After the debriefing, Matt gave the twelve members of the team instructions for training objectives he wanted them to concentrate on over the next few days. They were to conduct physical training, as well as, continued practice of the tactical training he had taught them the day before. He also instructed the four that participated in the patrol to pair up; two from last night's patrol with four others of the team and conduct at least two practice night patrols on the south side of the valley away from warg territory.

"Victor, I need to get back to the inn to shower and change before Harvey arrives. Can you arrange for the tagging equipment to be delivered to the town hall building?"

"No problem. I'll have Frankie take care of that. I'll get showered and changed then meet you in Graymere around noon."

Chapter 46

Freya anxiously awaited Matt's return and met him at the front door of the inn, "Matthew, you look terrible and Pee-yew," Freya said, pinching her nose. "What on earth have you been doing?" Freya said awkwardly, in an attempt to hide her relief, he was home safe and sound.

Matt laughed, "Honey we have been training for almost twenty-four hours straight, we do get sweaty and dirty in the process."

"Oh dear, you go get in the shower while I finish getting lunch prepared."

When Matt finished showering and changing, he came into the dining room to find Harvey had arrived and was having coffee and chatting with Freya. "Harvey, good to see you, old buddy."

"Looks like you're doing much better than the last time I saw you. How have you been doing?" Harvey asked.

"Very well thanks to Ms. Freya; I'm afraid her cooking is adding a few pounds to my girlish figure, though," Matt said laughing.

"Better than those nasty TV dinners you used to feed yourself," Freya said with a sneer, in response to Matt's joking comment.

"I think Freya will be serving lunch shortly and I believe Victor will be joining us as well. In the meantime, if you pull your van over to the town hall building, we can load up the equipment I borrowed from your station."

"Are you sure you are finished with it?" Harvey asked as they got up walked toward the front door.

"Yes, and I have your '*final report*,' ready. We can go over the actual situation during lunch."

Harvey backed his van up to the town hall building where he and Matt loaded all the equipment, checking everything off against Harvey's checklist.

"If you want to pull back up to the inn, I will go get Doc and meet you inside for lunch," Matt told Harvey.

* * *

Matt walked over to the clinic to catch Dr. Bertram before he left to meet them for lunch. As he was walking up the front steps to the clinic, Dr. Bertram was coming out the door.

"Matt, I was on my way over for lunch, I saw Harvey pull in earlier."

"Doc, I wanted to catch you before you got to the inn; I don't have time to explain, but for now, don't mention anything about the warg samples to Harvey or our plans to do a DNA analysis and genome mapping. In fact, downplay the scope of the planned lab work as much as possible to a basic pathology lab, looking for a drug to counter the LTV."

"What's up?" Dr. Bertram asked.

"I can't explain right now; just be as vague and general as you can and don't mention you are ready to start testing this week. If you would, can you stop by the lab before you come over for lunch and tell Sarah to cover up the analyzer? Tell her to be tight-lipped, if Harvey asks her any questions?"

"Sure," Dr. Bertram replied with a very curious expression on his face.

* * *

"Doc will be here in a few minutes. He ran over to the lab to let Sarah know lunch was ready," Matt told Harvey when he walked through the door of the inn.

"Good, lunch is almost ready," Freya said.

374

After retrieving a file from his office, he handed it to Harvey. "Here is my report for the Forest Service, regarding the incident involving Ranger Holmes in Misty Hollow. It basically contains an analysis of the environmental and habitat related conditions that were contributing factors in two separate cases of lone wolfs coming down out of the wilderness into the valley. The analysis concludes the wolf-human encounters were isolated incidents and not an intrusion by a pack from some extreme habitat pressure."

"What about the incident with Ranger Holmes?" Harvey asked.

"That is addressed in the report. The report states that dead wolf he found was one of the lone wolves shot by a local farmer after the wolf killed one of his sheep. The wolves that attacked Ranger Holmes were ranging wolves seeking to muscle in on the first wolf's kill and Ranger Holmes happened to get too close to the scene. The report attributed the other sightings to the occasional foraging by a small pack which occasionally strays beyond its boundary, into the valley. Bottom line; there are no indications wolves are a major problem in Misty Hollow above any historical level of reported sightings or encounters."

The summary of Matt's report was interrupted when Dr. Bertram walked into the inn. "Dr. Bertram, it's good to see you again," Harvey greeted.

"Harvey, a pleasure as always," Doc replied. Doc stepped to the side and introduce Sarah, "I'd like for you to meet Sarah, my lab assistant."

"I think we've already met," Harvey said as he shook hands with Sarah.

"Yes, we have; please to see you again," Sarah responded.

"Well, everyone please take a seat, lunch is served," Freya announced.

"Am I too late for Ms. Freya's cooking," Victor said stepping through the door as everyone was sitting down at the table.

Freya met Victor and greeted him with a friendly hug and a peck on the cheek, then gestured for him to take a seat at the table with the others.

"Harvey, how was your drive up this morning?" Victor asked.

"It was very pleasant. There wasn't any traffic and the weather is beautiful. So, tell me, how is the lab coming along?" Harvey asked aloud.

"It's coming along, slowly, but surely. Hopefully, we will begin taking blood samples in a couple of weeks or so of the valley residents." Dr. Bertram told him.

"I got the message to scrub the search for surplus equipment. Aren't you guys going to need that stuff to operate the lab?" Harvey asked.

"We decided to scale back the scope of the lab for the time being. I think we were being a bit ambitious in our objectives relative to our resources." Dr. Bertram replied. "As it is, I think the lab, as we have it set up now, is a bit of overkill for our needs."

"I would like to take a look at what you've accomplished so far before I leave," Harvey stated.

"By all means; we would love for you to check it out. Sarah has worked very hard at making something out of very little." Dr. Bertram commented.

"Matthew, what is the situation with the wargs? Are they still coming down out of the wilderness making mischief?" Harvey inquired.

"We encountered a couple of incidents which caused some tense moments, but I think we have thinned their ranks and clipped their tail feathers a bit. We believe the important task ahead of us, is finding a cure for LTV." Matt replied, attempting to downplay the warg situation for the moment.

During the remainder of lunch, they engaged in casual chatter regarding their visions for a future when they would eradicate LTV from the valley and the people would be free to live a normal life in and outside the valley. They talked of their dreams of their children and grandchildren being free to go to college and pursue jobs and careers in the cities.

"Well, I need to be getting back home, it's a long drive and I don't like to drive at night anymore," Harvey said to them. "But before I go, I would like to see your lab."

Dr. Bertram and Sarah walked Harvey over to the lab and gave him a quick tour; displaying only the basic lab capabilities.

"What about the DNA analyzer Matt was so eager to get his hands on?" Harvey asked.

"Well, for the moment, it's not as critical to us and besides, if push came to shove, we can get enough parts and components from Home Depot to fabricate a basic analyzer." Dr. Bertram said in jest.

"What you have done with this old building is remarkable. I wish you good luck in getting your research under way very soon. I am looking forward to witnessing your progress."

"Thank you," Dr. Bertram said as he began walking Harvey back to his van, where Matt and Victor were waiting to say their farewells.

"Matt are you and Freya going back to the city tonight?" Harvey asked.

"No, tomorrow the university is closed for the holiday. We will spend the night here and drive back tomorrow."

After concluding their farewells, Harvey drove away, headed back home. As soon as Harvey left Graymere, both Dr. Bertram and Victor turned to Matt and asked almost simultaneously, for Matt to explain why he withheld details of the lab's progress and the situation with the wargs.

As they walked to the front porch of the inn, Matt began to explain, "Last night Victor and I took a small patrol into the warg territory and had a chance to take a peek at where they live. From what we saw, our situation is far more dire than I could have imagined."

"What did you see," Dr. Bertram asked anxiously.

Matt continued, "From a rock outcropping, we used binoculars and night vision equipment to look down into a hollow where the wargs appear to be congregating. We observed two dozen or more rogues and at least six alphas in one huge communal colony. The alphas were intermingling among the rogues and it appeared there was some level of social interaction among the alphas. It truly reminded me of an encampment of a band of rebels or marauders. We also got a glimpse of what I believe to be the Maximus Prime. I can only describe what I saw to be a true cynanthrope." Matt said with a tone of anxiety in his voice.

"Cynanthrope?" Dr. Bertram said stunned.

"Yes, this creature looked more like a human-wolf hybrid as compared to the warg alphas," Matt replied.

"You don't think this is the entire population in one spot do you?" Dr. Bertram asked sounding stressed.

"From all the raids and engagements we have experienced over the last few weeks, along with what we saw last night, we believe this is just one communal cluster. There could be more such clusters deeper in the wilderness; we don't know at this point." Victor replied.

Matt interjected, "I have a gut feeling, what we are dealing with here, can't all be attributed to nature. The size, stature and general appearance of the cynan exhibited more human phenotype mutation than an alpha. It walked upright as its natural posture and its forearms and hind legs were longer in proportion to its body mass.

We haven't stopped to consider what evolutionary step the LTV might take with an alpha that might have acquired a secondary human LTV infection. If so, the Lupine Transgenic Virus would certainly result in an advanced viral mutation and the resulting transgenesis, far more advanced. But, this evolution can't be a result of any cross infection from the attack on me. The timing is far too short to have materialized into a new generation. Something else is going on that appears to be facilitating the natural evolution of the LTV transgenesis."

"What do you mean?" Victor asked curiously.

Dr. Bertram sat down, "I believe what Matt is saying is, we may be dealing with advanced mutant warg which may have their origins from a source other than natural evolution."

Matt continued, "If this is the case, someone with unique knowledge of the LTV and its effects, possibly someone within the valley, has communicated or is collaborating with some entity outside the valley, who is seeking to exploit the Lupine Transgenic Virus."

Victor interrupted. "Hold up, let me see if I got this correct. The wargs are not the result of the natural evolution of the LTV, but are some improved hybrids engineered by someone outside the valley? That's a bit hard to believe. Why would anyone do that? And besides, the wargs have been around for longer than we can remember."

"Think about it for a minute. For over two hundred years, the wargs and Therians have lived next to each other. Other than an occasional intrusion from a rogue, the evolution of the LTV virus has remained somewhat constant for generations. Sometime after the turn of the last century, the first Alpha appeared, supposedly a result of a secondary infection of the LTV resulting in a mutated strain. Then suddenly, within the last two or three years, the warg population appears to have exploded. Within the last few months, the actions of the wargs have taken on an unprecedented level of deliberate and coordinated aggression against the residents of the valley. And suddenly, we are looking at a completely new evolutionary species, the cynanthrope. Now, does that make sense to you?" Matt highlighted to Victor.

"But why?" Victor questioned.

"Like I said before, I think someone is attempting to exploit the LTV and are possibly using Misty Hollow as a test bed. If I'm right, then whoever is behind this, is pitting the wargs against the therians and then sitting back to observe what happens. I believe the cynanthropes are controlling the indigenous wargs and the Alpha Primes are the link, through which the cynans manage and control the wargs. Keep in mind, the alphas are essentially wargs in form, but with an enhanced intellect and cognitive skills. The Maximus Primes or cynans' evolution is too advanced to be attributed to the natural evolution of the LTV. There is too much of an evolutionary leap. They have to be the result of some form of hybridization that bridges the gap between human and wargs."

"And I gather from your efforts to withhold details from Harvey, you suspect he may be somehow involved in collaborating with this 'outside entity', providing them with information," Victor commented.

379

Matt just looked up at Victor and Dr. Bertram without voicing a response.

"We need to run the genome analysis of the wargs ASAP," Dr. Bertram said. "That will tell us a lot about what's going on with the warg evolution. We also need to get a sample from a cynanthrope."

"And we need to get a closer look at what's going on inside the warg territory. We need a reliable estimate of the size of the force we're dealing with before we start engaging them and stirring up the hornets' nest." Matt concluded.

"I will see if I can pick up any new bits of information from Sarah about the research on Plum Island. And Matt, see what you can dig up on Dr. Franklin Hobart; where is he, what is he doing, is he still with DOD, anything at all." Dr. Bertram said.

"Let's keep all of this to ourselves for the time being; there's a lot of speculation here and I would like to get a few more facts under our belts before we start raising alarms and getting people all worked up. I want to know for sure what we are dealing with." Matt cautioned.

"Agreed," Dr. Bertram replied.

"Agreed," Victor acknowledge.

"Freya and I will be leaving in the morning, sometime before noon, heading back to the city. But, I want to caution you guys; we blooded the wargs nose last week and they've been somewhat quiet since then. I believe you can expect continued incursions, so stay alert and keep everyone on their toes." Matt stressed to both Dr. Bertram and Victor.

"We'll be watching for them," Victor replied.

The three of them said their goodbyes for the evening. Matt sat down in his chair on the front porch and looked up and down the street of this sleepy little village. He was growing nervous in his expectations of what may be unfolding in the developing conflict with the wargs. Fighting a war against other human beings is one thing; you have some understanding of how the enemy acts and react. To some extent, you can use that knowledge to control the engagement. However, this was a whole new game altogether; they know nothing of the wargs true intellectual and cognitive development, particularly that of the Maximus Primes.

Wolves in their natural environment establish a dominant leader, the alpha, which exercises some level of communication and control over the pack to coordinate hunting of prey, but the wargs have evolved far beyond that. Except for maybe the rogues, very little of the wargs' behavior is comparable to typical wolf behavior. Therefore, nothing of his understanding of wolf behavior is of any value in predicting how the wargs will act or behave. What truly frightens Matt, above all else, is the poor state of preparedness the valley is in. He was certain the wargs were coming and the valley residents were grossly unprepared to deal with the organized onslaught of evil and carnage he believed was about to be unleashed upon the valley. Matt was vividly reminded of the scene depicted on the quilt handmade by Mrs. Moonjoy entitled '*Blood Moon Rising*,' which was intended to remind anyone who looked upon it, of the prophecy associated with the coming evil and dark times of apocalyptic proportions. "*How apropos,*" he thought to himself.

A Personal Note from D Allen:

*I hope you enjoyed reading Wargs: Curse of Misty Hollow as much as I did writing it, but the tale does not end here. I invite you to read the sequels to the Wargs Trilogy with book 2 **Wargs: Dominion**, and book 3, **Wargs: Outcast**.*

I would appreciate it so much if you will take a few moments of your time to visit the website from where you purchased Wargs: Curse of Misty Hollow and leave a review. I value the feedback I get from my readers and fans which help me continually improve my writing and focus on new books my fans want to read. I have provided links to some of the websites where my books are sold.

Many thanks for your support,

D Allen

Amazon/Kindle:
https://www.amazon.com/Wargs-Curse-Hollow-Allen-Rutherford/dp/1483433021

Apple iBooks:
https://itunes.apple.com/us/book/wargs/id1009476759

Barnes & Noble/Nook:
http://www.barnesandnoble.com/w/wargs-d-allen-rutherford/1122264465

Kobo:
https://store.kobobooks.com/en-us/ebook/wargs-curse-of-misty-hollow

Lulu Publishing Services:
http://www.lulu.com/shop/d-allen-rutherford/wargs-curse-of-misty-hollow/paperback/product-22451975.html

Printed in Great Britain
by Amazon